THIEF OF HEARTS

THIEF OF HEARTS

HEATHER CLARK

BOOK TEAM
Alpha Readers: Mika Stanard and Nadezhda Miloshevska
Developmental Editor: Addison Horner
Line and Copy Editor: Jules Dyrud
Cover Art: Kyannah Durocher
Book Design: Heather Clark
Map: Inkarnate

Paperback ISBN: 979-8-9999372-0-9
Ebook ISBN: 979-8-9999372-1-6

-FOR THE FAINT OF HEART

THE CITY OF RIME
N
W
E
S
COLIN HOWE'S HOUSE
THE HIGH QUARTER
STAR SYNDICATE HEADQUARTERS
BURNED RUIN
MARKET ROW
THE COMMERCE QUARTER
PORT TOWER
WRECKER CAMP
BELL SQUARE
THE BELL TOWER
KATYA'S BATHHOUSE
THE BASTION
FORTUNE'S FAVOR
VERO'S FORGE
HEALER'S HOUSE
JAYE'S STABLE

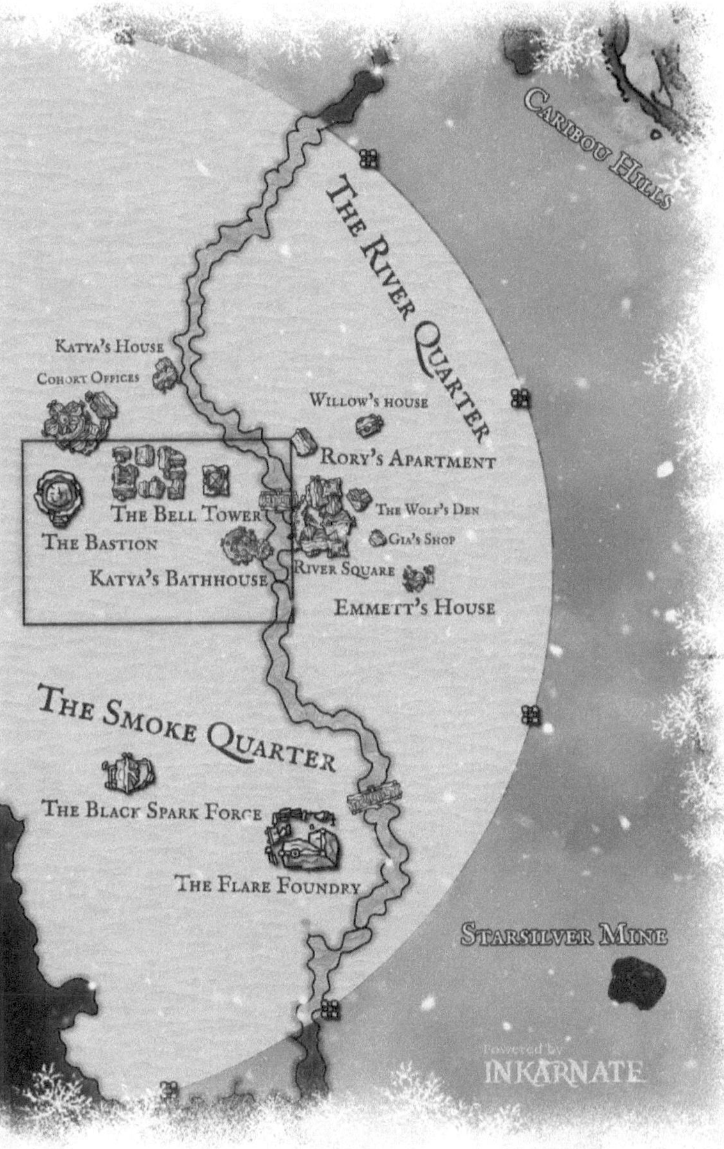

Caribou Hills
The River Quarter
Katya's House
Cohort Offices
Willow's House
Rory's Apartment
The Bell Tower
The Wolf's Den
Gia's Shop
The Bastion
River Square
Katya's Bathhouse
Emmett's House
The Smoke Quarter
The Black Spark Forge
The Flare Foundry
Starsilver Mine
Powered by
INKARNATE

RORY

6 BELLS

Dying of a stolen heart felt almost like falling asleep. But not the comforting collapse into oblivion after a long day's work. Death was the same weightless, unstoppable plunge that usually woke Rory gasping from nightmares where she'd tumbled off the top of the bell tower into the absolute blackness of a Rime night.

This time, the swooping vertigo wouldn't vanish as soon as she came back to reality in her own bed. She was already awake, heart stuttering, sweat trailing down her face. The rough rug under her back and the four walls closing in on her might as well not exist.

The emptiness in Rory's chest had swallowed her whole.

She was freefalling. There was nothing solid she could catch to save herself, even if she could have moved so much as a finger to reach for it. The only things that still existed were the roaring in her ears and the lights bursting in vivid greens and purples and pinks in front of her eyes.

There were worse ways to die. But Rory still wanted to wake up before she hit the ground.

48 Hours Earlier

RORY

6 BELLS

Rory's heartbeat pounded in her ears, nearly drowning out the rasp of a cinderpine match against stone. Before she could steady her shaking hands enough to touch the tiny pink flame to the lantern wick, the icy draft sneaking around the window frames snuffed it out entirely.

She cupped her fingers around the next match she struck, protecting it until the wick ignited and a dull gold glow filled the room.

Rory smashed the layer of ice on her pitcher, dumped the slushy water into the basin beside it, and splashed a handful on her face. The chill instantly shocked her panic-flushed skin. Rory's startled gasp burned her throat and lungs, but her heartbeat began to fade from a frantic gallop to rhythmic thudding. Reaching blindly for the tattered cloth hanging on a nail beside the bowl, she wiped water off her face. Stray drops trickled down her neck, turning nightmare-fueled shudders into chilled shivering.

It had been over two weeks since Old Sue had collapsed on the kitchen floor. Before that, Rory had long since buried the nightmares that had haunted her in the wake of her father's murder. Old Sue's death had been quiet and bloodless, the inevitable conclusion of a lifetime of slow magical poisoning. Nothing at all like bright scarlet against blue-tinged starsilver. There was no reason Rory should be jolting awake every night.

Still, here she was, gripping the chipped edge of her desk, the phantom weight of a bloodstained blade as heavy in her hands as it had been fifteen years ago. The shadows her lantern had pushed into the corners still wavered, taking on almost human forms, whispering in the wind's hissing tones.

Rory wanted nothing more than to crawl back into her tangle of blankets, but sleeping in wouldn't pay her rent. Her landlord insisted she'd owe him for a full month whether she chose to move out in the middle of it or not. Old Sue, not Rory, had signed the lease papers the old drunk had waved in her face, but arguing wouldn't have been wise when his son was a lieutenant of the Coin Syndicate. Rory couldn't afford to risk losing their business. She'd earned more money delivering invitations for one of the Coin's underground card tournaments in the past week than she had from all her other jobs put together. Unfortunately, without the discount Old Sue had arranged for doing their landlord's laundry, Rory needed twice that much just to cover the rent. If she couldn't settle up on collection day, she might have bigger problems with the Coin than losing out on future jobs. She doubted there was much difference between their treatment of gambling debtors and rent dodgers.

Handing over the exorbitant amount of money would have been more tolerable if her landlord spent any of it repairing the cracked windows or fixing the steam pipes. Without the constant roaring of a fire intended to dry laundry, Rory noticed firsthand the problems other people in the building had been complaining about for years.

She reached for a worn brown sweater hanging on the back of a three-legged chair, grimacing when her shirt pulled tight across her back. Working the worn material free from the dried blood, she tugged the shirt over her head, careful of any further places it could be stuck to her elbows or shoulder blades. The cloth brushed against raw skin on Rory's jaw, igniting a prickling, burning itch. She pressed a handful of slush from the bowl against her cheek. Cold numbed the sensation enough to keep her from tearing at her face. These patches of flaky, cracking skin had been a constant feature of Rory's life since she was five. She knew all too well that scratching the unbearable itch would do more harm than good.

Most of the blood on her shirt had already dried brown. Rory tossed the cloth into her bowl to soak. The cold air on her skin sent shudders down her spine and gooseflesh rising on her bare arms, but at least it quieted the ache in her back and shoulders. She picked up a clay jar and ran her fingers around the inside, scraping out a bit of the caribou tallow to smear over her raw skin. Years of scouring cloth with hot water and harsh lye soap had turned Old Sue's hands as cracked and battered as lichen fever had left Rory, and the washerwoman had perfected a salve years ago to soothe both ailments. Rory didn't miss lying in a chilly bath, waiting for dried patches of blood to dissolve so she wouldn't start sobbing and screaming when the stiff fabric was removed.

The scent of rich poplar buds, sharp pine sap, and salty seaweed stung Rory's nose as she tentatively touched her salve-coated hand to her back, brushing away flakes of black and brown blood and gray, ruined skin. Her fingers came away with only a few bright red streaks. Rory rummaged through the heap of blankets on the end of the bed until she found the spare shirt she'd tossed there a week ago. The cloth was threadbare, cuffs and hem tattered, but it would keep any more blood from seeping into the thicker shirt and sweater she wore over top. Those were much harder to wash, never mind the time they took to dry.

Rory blew on her fingers, frowning at the layer of charred wood and ash covering last night's smoldering coals. She counted the concerningly small stack of split logs next to the hearth and pushed more ashes over the coals with a bent poker, hoping a few would survive until evening. She'd need to ration what was left in her woodbox to keep some embers alive through the storm blowing in.

A small heap of cloth next to the chimney burbled, and a bright pink eye blinked at Rory from the tangle of scraps. Blizzard tilted his head and cooed inquisitively as he emerged from the makeshift nest.

Still shivering, Rory shook her head. "I turned out my pockets for you last night. No crumbs left."

The pigeon ruffled his feathers in disappointment, then began searching the floor around the hearth for any bugs seeking the warmth.

Rory unwound her fraying braid and ran a carved antler comb through her coarse hair. After tugging the mostly untangled mess into a serviceable new plait, she shook a handful of loose, ashy-gray strands onto the floor. The hair growing out of the lichen scab behind her left ear was a colorless, brittle stripe winding through the length of her dark blonde braid, broken strands sticking out of the otherwise smooth rope at every twist.

The water in her basin was already forming a tiny crust of ice at its edges. Rory quickly scrubbed the stained shirt against itself until a majority of the blood tinted the water and not the cloth. Her fingers ached, then turned numb. She wrung out the wet cloth and tucked her hands under her arms, shuddering.

As soon as Rory could halfway feel her prickling fingers again, she draped her damp shirt over the rope stretched across the room. She'd pulled all but one of the drying lines down days ago, ending years of ducking beneath cords low enough for the stooped old washerwoman to reach. Despite being hung as close to the fireplace as possible, the shirt was already freezing into stiff wrinkles. Rory's job didn't require keeping her apartment warm all day and night, and she couldn't justify wasting expensive fuel to dry one shirt. Ever since the last of the forest near Rime was clear-cut the previous winter, the price for a cord of wood had tripled.

Rory pulled her knife out from under her flattened feather pillow, the blade slipping partially free from its too-large sheath as she did so. The starsilver alloy glimmered, its glowing blue patterns mingling with the reflection of orange lamplight. Rory shoved the blade firmly back into its sheath and secured the strap to her belt. The weight against her hip and thigh was familiar and comforting, oiled leather rasping against the worn spot it had formed on her pant leg. Her blade and her instincts for what jobs to walk away from were the only things keeping her from ending up wounded or worse. Trusting the wrong person in Rime, letting your guard down for even a moment, could easily cost your life.

Wind howled through the cracked window casings, louder than before. Tiny fragments of snow spattered against warped glass like chattering teeth. Rory took her worn coat off its peg and wrapped her scarf around her face. Reaching down to Blizzard, she snapped her fingers. The pigeon fluttered as he climbed up her sleeve to her shoulder, leaning slightly to compensate for the twisted stub of his left wing, then tucked himself inside Rory's hood, his tiny heartbeat thumping in her ear. She dug a pair of gloves from her pocket and pulled them on.

She was as ready as she could be to face the world outside. The wards kept out sunlight, but never the storms.

Rory hung her lantern on its nail beside the door, then flinched as her boot crunched on a shard of dark-glazed clay. Even after sweeping every inch of the floor twice in one week, Rory kept finding stray fragments of Old Sue's favorite mug. She kicked the piece toward the door, wishing it was that easy to sweep away the memory of pottery crashing from slack hands and lifeless, filmy eyes staring into her own.

Rime had killed Old Sue, even if not so clearly and violently as a victim of one of its desperate cutpurses or syndicate squabbles. She'd grown up in a house built with shattered stone from the Starfall site, and the poisonous magic seeping from its foundations had twisted her up like the city's caribou or pigeons. When Old Sue had taken Rory in fourteen years ago, the washerwoman's hands had already been warped and gnarled, back bent nearly double, and voice rasping in her throat even though she was no older than Rory's own mother. Rory had known for years that Sue's health was failing, but there was a difference between expecting to wake up and find her cold in the bed and the startling shock of watching life leave her mid-step.

Rory snatched her father's messenger bag from its hook by the bed and slung it over her shoulder. The guide magic she'd inherited along with his fair skin and gray eyes meant her best chance of making a living in Rime was to follow in his footsteps. As long as she didn't follow him to an early grave, that was fine by her.

Rory snuffed the lantern and stepped into the hallway without turning the rusty lock. She had nothing worth stealing inside her room, and if it ever took eight tries to undo the latch again, Rory wouldn't be responsible for her actions. She left the key in the inside pocket of her coat, next to her disappointingly light purse, and stepped out into the howling cold.

Snow drifted in swirls past the street lamps' glow. A trash cart rattled up the street, the crunching of iron-rimmed wheels on ice and the clatter of studded horseshoes echoing off the buildings. The driver halted his pony and tied the reins to a lamppost, then climbed down and began picking up the waste bins and slop buckets left along the street. When he dumped the pails in front of Rory's building into the metal tub inside his cart, the frozen contents clanged almost as loudly as the city bells. Empty buckets toppled over in the wind, and one rolled away down the street in a lopsided arc. Rory kicked it back toward the building.

The driver stacked the battered metal buckets one inside the other, then hung them all by one handle on the rusting hook near the door before climbing back onto his cart. He untied the reins from the lamppost, then slapped them against the pony's back to force it into a shambling trot.

Rory followed him as far as his next turn. The stench from the cart burned her eyes, but the wagon's high sides provided a vague shelter from the biting gusts that stung them just as badly once the meager windbreak was gone.

The edges of Rory's vision sparkled when she stepped out into the brighter square along the riverfront, her eyelashes already crusted with frost in the few blocks she'd walked. The cold was so bitter that the snow still falling had become icy shards instead of puffy flakes. All around her, people's heads were bowed against the wind, scarves wrapped around their faces up to the eyes, hands shoved deep in pockets.

Shabby storefronts around the riverside square drew in shoppers trying to escape the brutal weather, but there was still plenty of bustle in the rows of tiny pushcarts that covered the open cobbled space. The spicy, warm smell of their wares almost drowned out the fishy stink from the riverbanks and the odor of hundreds of rarely-washed bodies crowded into a small space. The chatter of bargains and the rattle of money changing hands was nearly louder than the wind howling through the alleys.

The first pale green glow crossed the wards at the far east side of town, over the High Quarter's roofs. The light shimmered and faded again as Rory stepped into the chaos around her. It would be some time until the deep reds appeared, and even longer before they lit the River Quarter more clearly than its street lamps.

The only morning Rory had ever known was those shimmering curtains of color that flickered across the wards when the sunlight outside struck the magical barrier. The lights came out, the city woke up, and people went about their lives and their jobs and their petty arguments under the glittering, ever-changing glow.

Some claimed the lights were spirits of those who died in Rime, trapped forever in the afterlife, unable to escape the city's confines even in death. Rory's father had said they were the sun breaking through the wards the only way it could, like someone beating on the Bastion's stone walls with their fists to let a prisoner inside know they weren't alone and forgotten. His version was more sentimental than the ghost stories. No one outside the city cared about Rime, least of all an indifferent, distant sun.

Raised voices drifted across the square, and Rory instinctively glanced toward the source. A man darted out of one of the shops but was halted on the threshold by a massive hand closing on his coat collar. His captor's broad shoulders were wider than the doorframe.

When the hulking figure turned sideways to pass through the door, Rory caught a glimpse of the syndicate emblem stitched into the back of his coat, a vivid yellow star. Shoppers who'd stopped to gawk at the scene ducked their heads and scurried off. Even two Cohort guards who'd been shouldering through the crowd toward the commotion removed their hands from their weapons and turned aside.

Blizzard chittered anxiously from Rory's shoulder, and she stroked her hand soothingly over his head and back. "I see him too. But he won't bother us today." The first year Rory had taken to the streets with her father's gift and his messenger bag, Trey had been a competitor who wasn't above stealing jobs from his fellow messengers by threats or force. Blizzard's warnings had helped Rory avoid the wrong side of Trey's meaty fists more than once. But after he'd begun working for the Star Syndicate, he was bound by their exclusive contracts. He was no threat to a freelancer like Rory.

The captive started to say something, but his voice was cut off by Trey's fist slamming into his mouth. The man crumpled to the ground, and Trey grabbed him by the legs and slung him over one shoulder as if he weighed no more than a sack of pinecones. Trey walked off with his limp burden toward the bridge that led to the High Quarter.

Rory made her way across the square to a pushcart with a small oven in its base, smoke rising above its lopsided chimney and fire gleaming through cracks in the metal container. The owner, a man with flamelike orange veins flickering under his skin and in his dark eyes, looked up and waved a hello, eyes locking onto hers. Most likely, Rory's red coat had caught his attention. Color was a luxury in Rime, usually only worn by those who could afford lighting enough candles or oil lamps to properly see and appreciate it. The cart owner probably assumed she was rich enough to buy something hot out of the oven.

He didn't know her by reputation or by experience, which made him a perfect mark. Judging from the way his wares were openly displayed on his small cart, he was new to the city.

Tough luck. Magic is less regulated here, but so is everything else. Eternal winter nights brought out the worst in everyone.

Rory perused the vendor's offerings. His cart was stacked with small loaves of coarse bread made with nut flour and gull eggs, pastries stuffed with caribou, trout, or salmon meat mixed with dried berries, and thin biscuits with crushed pink shore lichen sprinkled on top. Like most vendors, this man was selling cold food at half price.

Rory took a single small loaf from the hour-old stack, its surface already slightly frosted despite the warmth rising from the oven underneath. She had a coin in her purse worth the bread's exact value, but she fished out the next largest denomination instead. She hadn't seen the cart owner slip a tray into his oven the entire time she'd been crossing the square, and his stock of hot biscuits was fairly depleted. She was betting a batch would be done any second.

As the vendor took the coin and fished through the leather pouch attached to his belt for her change, his gaze drifted to the oven and the faint smoke trail escaping it. "One moment, I'm sorry," he said, bending down to pull out the tray of biscuits before they scorched.

The instant he took his eyes off Rory, her hand darted out, slipping one of the freshly baked meat-filled pastries into her pocket. It was still a bit warm, and the weight was comforting. By the time the vendor looked her way again, her hand was waiting, open and empty. She slipped the few chilly coppers he dropped into her palm back inside her purse and melted away into the crowd.

Rory devoured her ill-gotten breakfast in the shadow of a tattered awning. Wanted posters for criminals and rebels fluttered next to her, corners tearing free of their nails. She gave the sketch of Jax a small salute with the meat pie in her hand. The cat-eyed rebel was the one who'd taught her how to size up an opportunity and when to make a move. He'd meant her to use those skills for more than petty theft, but joining up with him would almost certainly have been a one-way ticket to the Bastion or an early grave. Jax's ragtag band pushed boundaries without considering the consequences, and the Cohort retaliated with sweeping vengeance. Avoiding the cycle of rebellion and reprisal entirely was Rory's best chance of survival.

The only powerful players in the city Rory was willing to take jobs for were the syndicates. They had plenty of money, unlike the rebels, and they didn't mind parting with it nearly as much as the Cohort. Rory had never attached herself to any one employer, preferring the risks of freelancing to being a casualty of a syndicate squabble. Only the Star demanded exclusivity, and there were plenty of other syndicates willing to trust an unaffiliated messenger.

Rory broke off some of the singed pastry crust and held it out to Blizzard. Uncharacteristically, he ignored it, staring down the street. Rory followed his gaze to a cloth marker fluttering from a door handle two houses down. Most people sought out messengers at the market or in their regularly-established haunts, but the very busy or the very ill sometimes used the riskier method of hanging a summons cloth. Blizzard cocked his head and ruffled his feathers, waiting for Rory to start walking before accepting the treat.

She gave him a second, larger piece. He'd earned it.

Rory stuffed the rest of the meat pie into her mouth and wiped her lips on the back of her sleeve before stepping up to the door, knocking, and announcing herself as a messenger answering the marker.

There was no reply.

Rory moved to the window, rubbing away frost with her sleeve. Most of Rime's deaf people lived in neighborhoods near the bell tower, undisturbed by the hourly clanging. Rory might need to visually catch her client's attention.

As she leaned toward the window, the door creaked open. Rory frowned at the empty space in the crack before looking down, expecting to see a child.

A wizened old man, back bent nearly double, stared up at her. The eyes that met Rory's were entirely black, the pupil swallowing up whatever color there had once been. Overgrown silver fingernails clicked like metal against the doorknob.

A starsilver miner.

The fragments of a fallen star that had buried themselves in the ice and stone outside Rime no longer had enough power to grant new gifts, but they still contained the most valuable resource in the Altrenean Empire.

The first gifteds to be arrested en masse had been shipped north to become forced labor in the starsilver mines. But the prisoners could withstand the mines' dangers better than the guards stationed to keep them in line, most of whom fell victim to twisted monsters and poisons in the air that coated their lungs and rotted their bones. Even though centuries had passed since Starfall, magic remained concentrated and volatile in the mines.

Eventually, the government turned their efforts and their labor force toward constructing the Bastion, a prison built on their own terms. The mine and its contents were technically still owned by the empire, but without a way to control the miners' actions underground, the government chose to incentivize delivery of the ore. The prices they offered had encouraged some of Rime's residents to exchange one sunless existence for another.

The miners had built an entire underground society, complete with secret exits for meeting syndicate buyers with even deeper pockets than the Cohort and elaborate burial chambers for the many who never left the depths. Those who did return to the surface never came back the same.

The old miner coughed, stumbling forward and barely stopping himself from falling on his face in the street slush.

"You wanted a messenger?" Rory asked.

He nodded, then pulled a bulky envelope from the pocket of his thick robe. The package had no address, but that didn't matter. Attached to the string wrapped around it was a single curl of reddish hair. "Take this…to my son," the man rasped out. "Please tell him…that his father regrets…wasting so many years."

When he placed the packet in Rory's hand, she felt something heavy beneath it. Rory removed the hair from the twine tie, slipped the package into her messenger's bag, and inspected what was left in her hand. Two gold coins, more than triple the normal rate for this kind of delivery. Rory slipped the coins into her purse. Almost no one paid for a messenger upfront. With any luck, she'd be able to convince the recipient that there was a balance owed. She'd gained a reputation for honesty by always following through on her deliveries and never once breaking a seal on the correspondence she was entrusted with. It had nothing to do with her business practices in regards to payment.

She pulled off one glove, wrapped her fingers around the curl, and closed her eyes. A memory that wasn't her own flooded through her. Gloved hands shaking off smaller fingers, then lifting a pickaxe leaning beside a door frame.

Rory shook her head to dispel the images her own mind was attempting to add to the scene. A swirl of white poppy smoke from a battered pipe, stained fingers curling into a fist to pound against a familiar apartment door.

Memories similar to her own past were the hardest for Rory to keep a grasp on. She clenched her own hand into a fist around the hair so tightly her ragged nails dug into her palm. The stinging ache pushed away the true memories, and she sank back into the vision of someone else's history.

A man's back, only beginning to develop the stoop it carried in the present, disappeared onto the street. The door slammed shut in his wake, plunging the room into total darkness.

When Rory opened her eyes again, the ground in front of her sparked to life as brilliantly as if someone had poured a line of molten metal into the cracks in the flagstone. The lights slowly creeping into view overhead painted the icy streets with white and green reflections, but the thread of her destination stood out against them, a bright gold that didn't exist outside the flames in a hearth or street lamp. The trail wound away from the square, deeper into the heart of the River Quarter.

Rory was carrying an apology to a neglected child from a father who had cared more about making money than spending time with his family. Likely, a few lines explaining that the dying old man had realized his wealth was a poor substitute for being surrounded by family.

Sentimental old fool. The rift he'd created with his son couldn't be mended in the few weeks he had left. Still, if the dying miner was willing to part with his coin out of some belated need to atone for his past choices, Rory wasn't going to be the one to stop him.

She dropped Blizzard off at the windowsill of the Wolf's Den pub as she passed. Anyone who wanted to engage her services while she was busy on a delivery could leave a note with the pigeon, tucking it into the leather harness across his back.

Snow continued to fall, sharp fragments that stung Rory's face wherever they reached her skin. Between the squalls, wickers hustled past with their short ladders, moving toward the harbor in tandem with the lights overhead spreading west. They dropped their ladders against the lamp poles, turning down the wicks as soon as the first streaks of pale green appeared directly overhead. In the River Quarter, street lamps were snuffed once the lights rose, no matter the weather. The price for a barrel of whale oil had gone up nearly as much as a cord of wood, and the Cohort would never spend money on anything but absolute necessities.

The streets got dingier and the houses more crowded the deeper Rory wound along her route, alley walls covered in twisting mazes of old, blackened bloodbriar vines. Many of the buildings were nothing more than reinforced workers' shacks from the original construction of the Bastion. No one had bothered to knock them down and replace them with anything sturdier before the wards had gone up and the city had been flooded with gifteds.

Some had come following an incarcerated family member. Others, like Rory's parents, had been lured by the lies the Altrenean government fed the outside world. Gavin Blake had truly believed Rime would be a place a gifted child could grow up safely.

When Altrenean troops began combing the Iron Peaks for gifteds and imprisoning any they discovered, Gavin had chosen not to follow the rest of his family further up into the untracked wilderness. He'd voluntarily entered Rime with his pregnant wife in search of sanctuary. Instead, they'd found a slum town ravaged by twisted magic, devastating winters, and diseases no scientist bothered to study or cure.

Once they'd come through Rime's gates, Gavin's gifted status had been recorded, and there had been no way for him or his child to leave.

The trail Rory was following, its light now burning like the white-hot heart of a fire, slipped under a door hanging loose on one hinge. Rory let go of the curl of hair and blinked a few times until her blurry vision started to clear. She'd learned a long time ago not to simply arrive at her destination and walk up to the door with her path's glow still burning behind her eyes. Everything from being handed the wrong denomination of coin to missing the glint of a weapon in her recipient's hand was a potential hazard until her vision returned to something approaching normal.

Once she could see well enough to be reasonably sure she wouldn't be cheated, stabbed, or unlucky enough to slip on black ice, Rory stepped up to the door of the dilapidated house and knocked, then took a few steps back. A man with red hair a few shades darker than the curl Rory was still holding shoved open the door. He wore a smith's apron, and behind him, coals in an open hearth swirled into a spurt of flame from the door's draft. His skin was flushed from the heat, and his arms, bared by sleeves rolled to the elbows, showed a mixture of lichen scabs and old burn scars.

"What's your order?" he asked.

Rory shook her head, reaching into her bag and pulling out the envelope. "I have a message for you." She held out her empty hand while keeping the package tucked near her side. "There's a silver piece due for delivery."

The man scowled, grubbing around in his apron pocket. "Shoulda known Luko would make me pay postage when he sent me his designs. You wait and I'll send him back my estimate for these cart wheels so he can see how it feels." He held out a tarnished coin and Rory lifted the envelope. The moment payment was in her palm, the package was in his hand.

The package wasn't the only thing Rory needed to deliver. Verbal messages were just as much a piece of a messenger's duty. "Your father also asked me to tell you he was sorry for wasting so many years."

The man's face shifted from annoyed to enraged. With a speed Rory wouldn't have expected from his bulky frame, he turned and flung the package into the center of the hearth's blaze. A moment later, he slammed the door in Rory's face.

Rory barely flinched. The letter her mother had sent on Rory's eighteenth birthday had met the same fiery end. No parent who chose their own profit above their child could say anything that mattered anymore, although Rory would have advised the smith to open the package before burning it. The coat currently snug around her shoulders had been part of the same birthday parcel. Words could be discarded, but in Rime, coins or a coat were much too valuable to waste out of spite. She tucked her payment into her purse and set off down the street.

Blizzard wasn't on the windowsill when Rory got back to the Wolf's Den, but a soft coo drew her eyes up to his perch in the low gable of the pub's entryway. As soon as he'd been given a message, Blizzard would make his way up to the rafters, protecting the note from both the elements and any would-be thieves. Rory held out her arm, and Blizzard fluttered down awkwardly, listing to one side as his bad wing struggled to hold him up.

"It's time for another one to die," Batty Bower singsonged from his corner. He pushed himself up the wall to lean against the front door, rhythmically slapping the wood with an open hand. Charlie must have kicked him out to sober up. More often than not, Bower moped around the

Wolf's Den in an ale-soaked haze, muttering about Cohort conspiracies. Most of his fellow patrons were used to it, but if he got in anyone's face, Charlie would oust him. Unfortunately, Charlie kicking Bower out of the Den meant Rory had to deal with him.

"Another month, another heart," he continued.

As if Rory should care about some specific death out of the dozens that would happen in Rime today because it was supposedly more magical than the rest. She'd heard the rumors that there was a heart thief active in Rime again, someone who could kill with a single touch. Still, syndicate thugs, Cohort officials, and desperate or insane people were just as dangerous. The chances of meeting a violent end in Rime were high. The odds of dying by having your heart stolen were almost laughably low. If Bower had really wanted to change something, he might have done better ranting about people who let slush freeze in front of their doorsteps. Rory had fallen more than once in the past few months and narrowly avoided cracking her head open. Messengers ran far more risks than simply encountering disgruntled recipients.

Rory pretended Bower's ramblings were a shrieking, hungry seagull and pulled the note from Blizzard's harness. The shaky scrawl belonged to Gia Carerra, a stonesmith from Jasper Lane.

Must see you in person. Urgent message for Katya Roland.

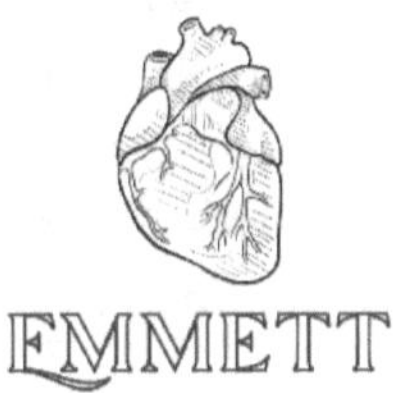

EMMETT

8 BELLS

Emmett closed his book and gently moved Carlo's arm off his chest when he heard the knock at the door. He stood up, tucking the blankets closer around his son.

Carlo mumbled something unintelligible, curling up into a tangle of limbs under the covers as soon as his father's warmth vanished.

The craftsman who'd modified their door had done a shoddy job. The joints connecting the swinging panel to the rest of the door were uneven, and the metal scraped against the floor each time someone opened it and again when the panel dropped back into place.

Emmett winced. He'd been listening to that sound for five months, and he was tired of it.

If the door was still the wooden one their room had when he and Carlo were first brought here, Emmett could have found the life left in the boards and reshaped them enough to let the panel clear the ground. He couldn't do anything about metal plates and flagstone floors. Marcus wasn't taking any chances on Emmett using his gift to attempt another escape.

Emmett picked up the dishes from the floor and brought them back over to the bed, sitting down on the edge with a plate in each hand. The food was still warm enough to give off a little steam, even if it was severely overcooked and bland. It had been ages since Emmett had tasted pepper or ginger root. At least the plates had been piled with enough chopped meat and shredded potatoes that neither he nor Carlo would be hungry before the next meal appeared at twelve bells.

Carlo's head appeared from under the covers, his curly hair a hopeless mess. Emmett waited for him to wriggle out from under the blankets far enough to sit up before handing him one of the plates. Carlo grimaced as he took the dish, and Emmett gently rested a hand on his son's shoulder, working his fingers into tense muscles. "Does it hurt?"

Carlo nodded. Storms had always made his bones ache, as if he were a poorly crafted chair with joints improperly fitted to move with the seasons. At least he was alive. Rime's poisoned magic infected any children born in the city and became more dangerous with each generation. It had taken Carlo's two older siblings before Emmett and Theresa even had a chance to choose their names. The way things had turned out, Emmett wondered if they'd been the lucky ones.

Emmett ran his hand down Carlo's arm, rubbing his elbow. His own fingers looked unfamiliar against Carlo's sweater.

Maybe it was because the scars were months old now, fading or vanished altogether. No bandages covered splinters or scrapes from a slipped tool. Once-thick calluses on the tips of his fingers and crossing his palms had softened. Even the raw places where cinderpine dust had slipped inside Emmett's gloves, leaving sores between his fingers whenever he worked with the volatile wood, had long since vanished.

Or maybe it was because Marcus had turned those hands into weapons. Carlo only trusted them to comfort him because he didn't know what they'd done.

Carlo leaned against him, breakfast forgotten in his lap, and Emmett caught the plate with his free hand just before it slid to the floor.

"Tell me about the dolphin," Carlo whispered.

Emmett smiled. Carlo had heard the story hundreds of times, but he always asked for it again. It was certainly better than the bloody legends from the books that had been in the room when they'd arrived here. Emmett had tried to soften those when he'd read them, although sometimes he skipped too many words for the tale to make sense. Carlo was learning to notice when Emmett glossed over the brutal aspects, and eventually he'd ask questions Emmett couldn't avoid.

Emmett set the plate he'd originally given to Carlo down on the floor, balanced the other on his lap, gathered a forkful of food, and held it close to Carlo's mouth. In stormy weather, even the motion of lifting a fork could hurt Carlo's joints, and while he'd feed himself without complaint if he had to, Emmett saw no reason to make him. There was little enough he could do for his son in this place.

Once Carlo had swallowed a bite, Emmett took a deep breath and began the tale. "A long time ago, far away from here, a family of dolphins lived in the sea."

He waited for Carlo to chime in, as always. "A cold sea like ours?"

"No. A warm sea, where the sun shines and the ground is made of sand that looks like someone poured gold over everything." Emmett had never seen the places his parents described. They'd arrived in Rime before he was born, and all he'd ever known of the outside world came from the stories he'd been told over three decades. He wasn't at all sure he was doing them justice, but his versions enthralled Carlo all the same.

The story had been a good one for the nights they'd huddled together on a thin mattress listening to the cold wind howl, with the few coals of their fire banked under ash to keep them alive until morning, and Emmett and Carlo wrapped in every blanket they owned to do the same. Nights when the only warmth they'd had was the dream of standing under the sun. Emmett had thought that was the coldest anyone could feel. But Marcus's house, despite its dozen fireplaces and tightly sealed windows, was filled with a chill no flames could drive out.

Emmett continued before he could get lost in the shadows in his own head. "One little dolphin was more curious than all the rest of his family. He swam along reefs covered with all kinds of sea plants and deep down into caves where things lived that had no eyes."

Carlo shuddered and wiggled closer. "Like cave bears?"

"Like cave bears." Emmett had only ever seen the corpse of one of the twisted monstrosities that lived in the starsilver mine. The eyeless creature with a nose that looked like fingers and claws as long and sharp as kitchen knives had haunted his dreams for years.

Now the monsters he was most afraid of had human faces.

"One night, the little dolphin was swimming close to the surface of the sea when he saw something shining. Like someone had dropped a bright round silver coin on top of the water." Emmett had no idea why a dolphin would know what a coin was, or care if it did, but that was how his parents had told the story. "When he swam up to catch it, the bright thing disappeared as soon as his nose touched it."

"Where did it go?" Carlo bounced slightly on the bed.

Emmett raised an eyebrow. "Do you know?"

"Into the sky!" Carlo giggled, pointing up to the ceiling.

"That's right." Emmett let his gaze follow Carlo's finger. "The little dolphin looked up, and there was that bright, bright circle in the sky. Now this dolphin was very good at jumping. He used to leap out of the water to say hi to his friends the, um..." His parents had always said seagulls, but Emmett had seen plenty of those around the docks, and he'd never found them particularly worth knowing. "Puffins." He tried to change birds every time he told the story so Carlo could never be quite sure which one Emmett would pick.

Carlo laughed, then took the fork from Emmett and shoved a heap of shredded potatoes into his mouth, puffing up his cheeks.

"Well, the dolphin figured the bright shiny thing couldn't be any higher up than birds were. So he started jumping and jumping." Emmett used his now-free hand to imitate the arcing leaps. "Higher and higher. But he couldn't quite reach it. Finally, he swam all the way down to the bottom of the sea." Emmett held his hand beside the bed, below the level of the mattress. "Then he swam up, up, up as fast as he could. And he leaped out of the water—" Emmett's hand shot as far up as he could reach. "And pop!" He splayed his fingers open, pulling his hand back a bit as if it had struck some invisible obstacle.

"Where was he?" Carlo asked.

"Inside the moon!" Emmett replied. "The little dolphin was swimming around in a big white bubble. He could look down and see the waves underneath him, and his family circling down below. But when he tried to tell them where he'd gone, they couldn't hear him."

"Poor dolphin." Carlo's shoulders slumped.

"He started jumping up and down inside the moon. When his family looked up, they could see him in there, a gray spot instead of all the white. So they started leaping up themselves, trying to bring him back down. But none of them could jump quite as high as that little dolphin. And ever since, dolphins jump out of the sea at night, trying to reach their lost brother in the moon. If you look up at the sky, you can see the little gray shape of him still inside."

Emmett had no idea why his son was so fond of a story that ended with a little creature separated forever from its family. He also couldn't bring himself to change the tale and end it any other way.

"We don't have a moon," Carlo said.

"Not here. It's outside the wards. People who don't live in Rime can see it." Emmett shrugged. "But we have the lights."

"I like the lights." Carlo set his fork down, his plate empty. "Do you think there's any dolphins in them?"

Emmett had no intention of telling him about trapped spirits.

The knock at the door came again.

Emmett startled, then froze, stomach sinking. There was only one reason his room was visited aside from food being given and the pot under the bed being taken out each night.

He ruffled Carlo's hair. "I have to leave again for a bit, okay?"

Carlo nodded.

"I'll be back before you know it."

The latch rasped with a horrible screech of metal on metal before it clicked open. Another poor alteration to the original door. The catch that had once been inside had been removed and turned around so the door could only be locked or unlocked by someone standing in the hall. Emmett and Carlo were no less prisoners than anyone in the Bastion.

Emmett stepped into the hall, glancing at the stony-faced guards waiting out of arms' reach. They nodded toward the stairs, then moved to walk one in front of him, one behind, hands on the knives sheathed at their belts.

He was doing this for Carlo. At least, that was what Emmett had been telling himself for the past two years to justify every choice he'd made.

He'd only wanted to put enough food on their table to keep his son from asking what had happened to his father's plate. To keep Carlo from finding him bleeding on the floor next to his workbench again, after Emmett had stood up too quickly and the world had spun and gone black. The faint scar on his temple from the corner of the bench was a constant reminder that he'd been literally inches from death, from leaving his five-year-old son with his body and no one in the world to look after him.

Instead of condemning Carlo to an orphan's life on the streets, Emmett had dragged his son with him into the home of a vicious monster.

He passed another two guards on his way to Marcus's office. A third opened the heavy oak door for him, and Emmett stepped out of the chilly hall into a room where a fireplace burned so hot his eyes stung and watered.

Despite the blaze roaring behind him, Marcus Deahl wore a heavy robe as he slouched in his massive chair. Papers covered the desk, but rather than scratching away at the documents, Marcus had tucked his hands together in front of him. A single flickering candle cast strange shadows on his hollow cheeks.

Emmett stepped forward, into Marcus's line of sight.

Marcus looked up with obvious effort. Thick, ropy veins stood out on his pale forehead. Cold blue eyes bored into Emmett's before flicking down to his chest and the starsilver locket hanging there, shaped like a human heart. "It's time."

Marcus stood slowly, trembling hands braced on the chair's arms. He pulled the key on its chain around his neck free of the folds of his robe and opened a tall cabinet next to the fireplace. One by one, he removed the canvas coat, battered boots, and walnut-colored scarf Emmett had worn when he and Carlo first arrived. Behind them, Emmett could see Carlo's rabbit-fur-trimmed boots and patched jacket.

"I need you to take care of Katya Roland." Marcus dropped the bundle of clothing and shoved it across the floor with his foot. "Head of the Rapids Syndicate."

Emmett nodded. Nothing good could come of telling Marcus he wasn't stupid; he knew who the powerful people in Rime were. Besides, it was only half true. If he'd been a little better informed, he never would have gotten involved with Marcus in the first place.

Instead, he picked up the pile of winter clothing while Marcus unlocked a desk drawer and removed a long roll of paper.

The office door swung open, banging against the wall.

Emmett flinched, dropping the bundle in his hands. Only a few syndicate members would dare enter Marcus's office so violently, and none of them were people Emmett wanted to be anywhere near.

Trey's massive frame filled the doorway. "Caught your little runaway trying to get in touch with a Quill forger," he said, nodding over his shoulder to where two guards were hauling a struggling, bloody-faced man down the hallway toward the courtyard.

Marcus scowled. "Take him out back and teach him what happens to people who double-cross us."

Trey nodded, eyes glittering with vicious glee. "My pleasure." He slammed the door behind him.

"Now, where were we?" Marcus continued as if he hadn't just condemned a man to an excruciating death. He untied the strings around the paper and spread it out on his desk.

Scrawled notes and a crudely sketched partial map of the High Quarter filled the stained, ink-smudged sheet. "My scouts inform me that Roland's vulnerability is the route between her house and that bathing establishment she owns on the riverfront." Marcus traced a line on the map with one shaking finger.

Emmett shrugged his coat around his shoulders and tucked the scarf into his pocket. He shoved his feet into his boots blindly. He didn't dare risk missing Marcus's instructions by bending down to tie the laces.

"Roland travels with only two trained guards and leaves her High Quarter home at ten bells each morning. You will be waiting for her when she does. The best place to intercept her will be almost directly outside her gate, at a crossroad here." Marcus indicated the location with a sharp fingernail that had turned an unnatural shade of blue. "Both streets are busy. An accidental brush with someone in the crowd should barely be noticed."

Marcus rolled up the map and replaced it in its drawer. He knocked twice on his desk and the doors opened, guards stepping in beside Emmett as he finished lacing the boots he'd mistakenly put on the wrong feet.

The guards' sleeves were still smeared and spattered with blood.

Emmett wished he could go back to his room long enough to tell Carlo he should cover his ears. Better yet, he wanted to sit with his son, holding Carlo's head against his side, reading yet another story as loudly as he dared to drown out what was going to happen in the courtyard below.

But if Emmett didn't want to be the next person facing Marcus's rage, he had a heart to steal.

Marcus slumped back into his chair. His voice was a shadow of its usual self, but no less disturbing for its whispered tone. "Do your job, and do it quickly."

RORY

9 BELLS

Jasper Lane, where Gia Carerra had set up her workshop, was a side street mostly populated by stonesmiths. Its window displays advertised everything from pocket-sized whetstones to lucky amulets. Rory had no use for impractical trinkets, but there were plenty of superstitious people in Rime, and even more outside the wards. Most shop owners who created carved charms did a decent trade with the wider world. Outsiders were willing to pay a steep price for magic, as long as it was something small and safe they could lock away in a drawer if they became uncomfortable with it.

Gia made her living repurposing slag from the forges, polishing it with seawater and sand in a series of rotating barrels. The dross left over from starsilver refining processes was brittle and worthless in Rime, but outsiders prized anything that had so much as come in contact with the magical metal.

Rory stepped into the entryway of the stonesmith's shop, wincing at the clatter. It nearly drowned out the whistling of the small woman rapidly pedaling the machinery that kept the polishing barrels spinning.

Gia waved Rory in, then slid off her stool, letting the whole contraption rattle to a stop. "Be with you in a moment!" she shouted. Years of running the barrels had ruined her hearing, despite the tiny cloth rolls she plucked from her ears and set on her workbench next to a half-finished necklace.

Whenever she saw Gia's work, Rory could almost understand why outsiders would find the dross fragments elegant. The necklace looked like Gia had torn down a piece of the warded sky. Bright, polished pieces, shimmering green and gold in the low firelight, were mixed in with less refined ones, tumbled only enough to put a gloss on the sooty black.

Gia picked up a folded paper from the table and handed it to Rory, then wiped her black-creased fingers on her leg, smearing dust across her pants.

Rory accepted the note, her fingers closing on awkward lumps that meant the paper had been folded around some small, solid items, then waited. Gia had always preferred dictating her messages, since her handwriting turned out garbled no matter how much she focused. Rory had only been able to decipher the note she'd left with Blizzard through years of familiarity with the misplaced letters and barely-legible script.

"This needs to be delivered to Katya Roland, as soon as possible." Gia cleared her throat, then took a deep breath, fingers twisting in her leather apron. "The dross I received from the Black Spark was low quality this past delivery. I found traces of moss lines when I tried to polish it. Whatever ore the forge master's using, his source wasn't the Rapids."

Katya Roland had turned the Rapids Syndicate into more than a ragtag collection of gifteds peddling their services from riverside huts by cornering the market on smuggling raw starsilver. The Rapids' divers bypassed the Cohort's gate patrols when the river thawed, swimming beneath the level where the wards weakened and dispersed in the water. Rory didn't envy them the plunge into the frigid river, or the risks of poisoned magic and detection by patrols, but the full purses they earned for a few months' work would have been a tempting trade.

The forge master at the Black Spark could have decided to supplement his ore stock mid-winter by hiring a new supplier, one who cut corners at that. Moss lines meant the ore had been scavenged from the surface, where it had fused with groundcover when the falling star exploded on impact. Dealing with the outlaw miners who worked the underground caverns was more expensive, but it ensured the quality that had built Katya's reputation.

Rory made a mental note to be prepared to run as soon as she handed off this message. Katya wasn't the sort to stab a messenger for delivering bad news, but Rory didn't intend to risk being injured by stray shards of glass if the syndicate leader threw another decanter across a room.

Gia grimaced. "I've heard no rumors that the Flare is changing suppliers, and I can't imagine they would want one who offered such poor quality ore. But even if Kaden made a deal on his own initiative, I'm worried. Whoever brought this ore into the city is willing to risk circumventing the miners as well as crossing Katya." She swallowed, fidgeting with her apron again until Rory could hear metal tools clinking together in her pockets. "I would have reported it to the head of the Flare, but I couldn't be sure how they'd react."

Rory nodded. Gia made her living off a contract with the Flare Syndicate. If she'd appeared to be questioning their decisions by complaining about quality, she could lose her entire business overnight. Instead, she'd been shrewd enough to make it another syndicate's problem.

"I'll see to it Katya gets this," Rory said, then stepped out of Gia's shop and headed for the crowded bridge that led to the more affluent side of the river.

This deep in midwinter, the river was frozen thick the whole way across. Dozens of people were using the ice to avoid the bottleneck on the bridge, but Rory hadn't trusted it since she was twelve. She'd watched a boy swallowed by a weak place and woken up screaming from nightmares for a month afterward. The thought of being trapped under the solid gray surface, slamming her hands against it in a futile attempt to break free, screaming silently until she sank to the bottom like a stone, was terrifying.

The city bells rang out as Rory stepped off the end of the bridge. This close to the tower, the sound was overwhelming, a harsh clanging that shattered like ice off the nearby buildings before rippling through the city and dissolving into the wards. The bells had been cast from pure starsilver, and the magic emanating from them reinforced the impenetrable inky wall around Rime. Since the city's founding, the sole condition for employment as a bell ringer was profound deafness. Rumor had it the bells' magic would drive any ringer who could hear them to madness, although the ear-shattering reverberations inside the tower would probably be enough to make someone insane even if the bells hadn't been saturated in the power of a fallen star. Every aspect of life in Rime, from shifts at the factories to curfew hours for the High Quarter, was marked out and bounded in by the ringing of the bells. Rory had grown up with the echoes in her bones as deep and constant as the unflinching cold.

Rory counted the chime in her head, up to its tenth and final toll, matching her steps to the beat rolling through the earth underneath her. She stopped at the foot of the bell tower. Now that she'd crossed the river, she would either need to turn left toward the bathhouse Katya managed or right toward her house in the High Quarter. At this time of day, Katya was probably somewhere on the route between the two, but there was always the chance she'd arranged for an early meeting with a supplier or another syndicate. Rory wasn't about to waste her time walking all the way to the wrong place.

Gia hadn't given Rory anything to trace, but that wasn't a problem when the delivery was intended for Katya. Rory slipped off one glove, reached into her bag, and wrapped her fingers around a smooth gray stone tucked into one corner.

This memory it pulled to the surface was hazy around the edges, worn smooth just like the often-used stone that summoned it. A girl in a muddy-hemmed dress crouched on the riverbank, boots sunk ankle-deep in the slimy thaw mud, flicking her wrist to send flat stones skimming across the rippling surface. She blew a loose copper curl out of her eyes and then placed another stone in a smaller, paler hand whose knuckles were caked with red sores and gray scabs.

Rory opened her eyes. The bright gold line rippled out from her feet, then veered right.

Rory took her hand out of her bag, put her glove back on, and followed, blinking away the afterimage of the glowing trail. If she stayed on Riverfront Street, she'd intercept Katya and her guards somewhere in the middle of their route to the bathhouse. She didn't want to be so blinded by her gift that she let Katya walk right past her.

There was less reason to hurry on the rich side of the river. More lamps, still lit, hung over the street on each block. This close to the Cohort headquarters, the street patrols were more focused on guarding the politicians going to and from their offices than accosting ordinary citizens.

Rory sidestepped the two guards clearing a path for a Cohort official forcing his way through the crowd. The man's clothes gave off the sickly-sweet odor of burned poppy even from a distance.

It smelled like willful ignorance. Rory pulled her scarf a bit tighter around her nose.

Technically, possession and use of the flowers that had earned the Red Meadows province its name was illegal, but those who enforced the laws could bend them with little consequence. If anyone bothered to ask about the poppy smoke permeating this man's surroundings, he'd probably claim he'd been supervising the destruction of a seized shipment. As if the Cohort bothered stopping a trade that benefited only themselves.

Inhaling the smoke from poppies grown in the ash of a fallen star was said to be as close to the experience of magic as anyone without a gift could achieve. Rory had tried her mother's pipe once, out of sheer curiosity. All she'd gotten for her efforts was a coughing fit and her mother's hand across her cheek. Poppy had no effect whatsoever on gifteds. If it had been capable of offering them some respite from Rime's endless misery, the Cohort would have done their best to be sure not one petal crossed through the wards.

Katya's house was only a short climb into the hills that gave the High Quarter its name. The city's wealthiest residents usually preferred homes high above the water to avoid the river's stench and the swarms of mutated midges and mosquitoes that plagued its shores during the melt months. Katya had made the Rapids profitable enough to afford a house closer to the overlook, but she would never have chosen to move so far from her river.

Although Rory rarely saw any of the High Quarter elite out and about before twelve bells, almost every house had servants to do the shopping. They were expected to put a meal on the table or bring a tray to bed the moment their employers woke. Rory had missed the worst of the bustle that tended to happen around seven bells, when walking through the High Quarter resembled trying to swim in a salmon river. Now she was fighting her way through the smaller stream of desperate servants who'd overslept or were overburdened with tasks, scrambling to get to Market Row before all the fresh breads and best cuts of meat were sold.

Someone bumped up against Rory in the crowd, their hand pushing her sleeve up her arm. She pulled away from the touch, instinctively reaching for the strap of her messenger bag. She wove through the crowd at a faster pace for a few moments, muscles tense and heart fluttering. Too close a call for her taste. The enchanted starsilver buckles her father had purchased for the bag would prevent anyone from pickpocketing it, but that didn't mean the strap couldn't be cut. And if Rory lost a message, especially one intended for one of the syndicates, she'd be finished in this town.

Rory shoved her sleeve back down, shivering at the momentary contact with the chill, and hurried on. Whoever her would-be pickpocket was, without gloves, they'd lose some fingers to the weather today. Not a very smart thief, risking their most valuable tools.

A woman bustling by with a large basket on her arm caught Rory with an elbow, spinning her into a wall and knocking the wind out of her. She didn't even apologize as she rushed past. If Rory had been feeling a bit more charitable, she might have let herself assume the woman had a harsh master waiting at home who'd made a demand she needed to rush to fulfill. Today, she wasn't in the mood to give anyone the benefit of the doubt.

As much as she scanned the crowd, Rory saw no sign of Katya's red curls or blue clothing. It was unusual for her not to be at least on her way to the bathhouse, but every time Rory checked her path, the bright line led her in the same direction. According to her gift, Katya was still at home.

When Rory approached Katya's house, one of the guards was pacing up and down in front of the gate, breath fogging in clouds. The other leaned against the wall outside the guardhouse door, hand resting lightly on the grip of a knife tucked into his belt. Rory recognized the leaning guard. Griffin's hooked nose had been broken several times, a scar ran along his right cheek, and his beard was more silver than blond these days. If he was waiting outside the guardhouse instead of next to the hearth to chase aches out of his bones, he was worried about something. Something he felt would be given an insurmountable advantage by the few seconds required to unlatch a door.

"What's going on here?" Rory asked, trying to catch her breath. The storm's icy wind had left her dizzy and a little faint. Before she left, she'd go down to Katya's kitchen and get a cup of tea from the cook.

"An assassin came after the boss." Griffin's frost-caked scarf muffled his voice.

Attempts on the lives of syndicate leaders were a familiar reality in Rime's underworld, both from rival syndicates and unofficial Cohort attempts to keep power in their own hands. Katya was one of the few people Rory could honestly say she'd be sorry to hear was dead. The Rapids boss had as much blood on her hands as any syndicate leader, but she refused to have anything to do with trafficking in living things, human or creature. She was as close to a legitimate businesswoman as anyone who illegally breached the wards could be.

Rory leaned forward to open the gate latch, removing one glove to press her thumb against the cold starsilver. The enchanted latch would stun unwelcome visitors with power like a crack of lightning, but Rory had been delivering messages for the Rapids on a regular basis for long enough that Katya had given her standing permission to pass shortly after the latch was installed.

Griffin grabbed Rory's wrist. "The boss isn't going to see any visitors today," he said sharply.

"Griff, you know me," Rory snapped back.

"But I don't know what you're deliverin'." Griffin frowned at her messenger bag. "Could be some trick. Rigged to explode in her face when she opens it. I'll inspect it before I hand it over."

Rory shook her head, pressing her free hand over the flap of the bag. "This message wasn't sent to you. I need to hand it directly to its rightful recipient."

Griffin scowled. "Even if it could kill her?"

"That's not my concern." Rory's duty started and stopped with the item that had been placed in her hands or the message she'd been told to repeat. She wasn't responsible for its contents. "Let me deliver it. Then it's up to Katya whether she chooses to open it or not."

Griffin sighed. "Maybe you ought to open it yourself."

"That's the one thing I'm even less likely to do than give it to you." Rory shook her hand free of his and opened the latch, stepping into the courtyard and up the front stairs.

The house was nowhere near as massive as those built on the overlook, but it was still the size of two whole floors of Rory's apartment building, and all for just one person. Or at least that was the intention when it had been built. The many-sized footsteps crossing the path and the remains of a snow fort assailed by handfuls of snowballs were the work of a revolving trail of strays and orphans Katya recruited from the streets. She wasn't taking them in out of the kindness of her heart, though. Katya carefully selected children with gifts that might be useful to her syndicate.

When Rory knocked, a young woman with a vivid blue headscarf opened the door. Katya's people all wore the Rapids' color. It could be on something as simple as a braided cloth band around the wrist, or as eye-catching as this scarf. In the hall behind her, voices echoed and footsteps clattered as a pair of dark-haired boys raced through, skidding across the polished floor before vanishing into one of the rooms, still yelling and laughing.

"I'm delivering a message for Katya Roland." The words were an effort to get out. Rory blinked, shaking her head slightly, and stepped inside once the feeling that she was about to fall face-first in the hallway had somewhat faded.

"I'll tell her to meet you in the guard room." The woman stepped away, and Rory turned to her left and entered the narrow stone chamber that ran the whole length of the housefront. The two guards inside eyed her suspiciously, but left their weapons sheathed.

Rory frowned. Almost all of Katya's people recognized her well enough to know that their boss didn't consider her a threat. Usually, when Rory came to the house with a delivery, she was invited into the sitting room. Katya had dealt with attempts on her life before, but something about this one had clearly left her whole household seriously rattled.

A few moments later, Katya swept in, wide wool skirts brushing the floor, hair tied back with a ribbon dyed her signature blue.

Rory remembered the days when they'd dug rocks out of the mud and pretended they were starsilver miners, earning themselves endless scoldings for coming home in filthy clothes. Katya had shed that life as easily as if she'd slipped out of a dirty shift, but Rory would always see her as the person she'd raced stone crabs with on the riverbanks. When Rory had first become a messenger, Katya's confidence and patronage had given Rory a certain standing with the other syndicates and helped her build the reputation she traded on now.

None of that meant Rory trusted the woman in front of her. It did mean when she removed the letter from her bag and motioned Katya to speak privately, the woman dismissed her guards without question and leaned in, just out of reach of the ten-inch blade sheathed at Rory's hip. Katya reached into her pocket, pulled out a small coin, and dropped it into Rory's outstretched palm. Rory was about to object to the amount when she noticed it wasn't a coin at all. This was a token for Katya's bathhouse, worth about a dozen times the value of a coin the same size.

"A message sent to you by Gia Carrera," Rory said, handing over the folded paper. "The dross she received from the Black Spark forge in its last delivery was not to its usual caliber. She believes they may have a new supplier."

Katya took the envelope gingerly. She didn't look angry or worried, only irritated, as if she'd found a loose thread unraveling in a glove. When she unfolded the paper, two shards of black dross fell out. One, hard and glossy, glittered in the candlelight from the sconces. The other was dull and crumbling, dust sifting out of the paper after it and covering Katya's hand.

Rory started to step out of the room, taking Katya's silence as dismissal. If the syndicate leader had wanted to craft an immediate reply, she would have asked Rory to wait while she did so. Katya likely intended to take some time before answering the message in any way. Or she had a response that required a bit more hands-on approach than a messenger could provide.

Another wave of dizziness hit, and Rory pitched forward, catching herself on the doorframe.

Katya's brow furrowed. "Is something wrong?"

"No." Rory knew better than to show weakness to anyone. Katya wasn't a friend anymore. Just an ally, as long as Rory stayed useful.

"Watch your step. There was a heart thief in this neighborhood not long ago. A messenger who knows syndicate leaders' locations as well as you do would be a decent catch for someone targeting us."

The heart thief was the assassin who came after Katya. Rory had assumed it was the usual fare: a knife drawn in a crowded street but blocked by a guard's swift hand or an arrow fired from a rooftop taken astray by the wind.

Rory blinked away the glittering sparks at the edges of her vision. She was imagining things, the same as when Old Sue used to complain about her knees or wrists and Rory felt phantom aches in her own body. If Katya hadn't mentioned the heart thief, Rory would never have assumed the lightheaded feeling was anything other than cold and hunger. One meat pie couldn't undo nearly a day without a proper meal. She'd intended to save the loaf she'd purchased for later, but she might need to eat it so the dizziness would stop making her worry about something that hadn't even happened.

Besides, Rory told herself as she removed her gloves in Katya's kitchen, wrapping still-pale fingers around the mug of tea the cook had poured her, there was no way anyone could have taken her heart. Heart thieves had to feel someone's pulse before they could rip it out, and no one had come close enough to Rory to manage that since Sue had collapsed.

Only when Rory handed back the mug, her coat sleeve sliding up her arm from the motion, did she remember the pickpocket.

Bare-handed in the frigid wind. Reaching not for Rory's bag, but for her wrist. Chilled skin pressing against her own barely long enough to sense the flutter under the surface.

Rory waited until she was two blocks from Katya's house to turn aside into an alley, pull away her scarf and one glove, and reach for the pulse in her neck with shaking fingers.

She couldn't blame the trembling in her fingertips for the normal steady rhythm having become a faint murmur. After what she'd just learned, her heart should have been galloping like a spooked caribou.

The fact that it wasn't could mean only one thing.

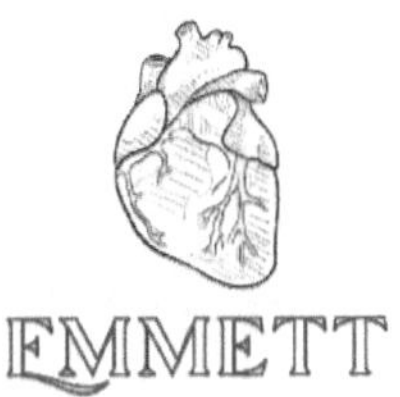

EMMETT

10 BELLS

If Emmett got caught, he was going to die.

He dodged the grip of one of his target's angry bodyguards, shoving between a servant carrying a basket on each arm and a washerwoman with a heavy bag slung over her shoulder. Both cursed at him for jostling them. When Emmett ignored them, they turned to take out their frustration on the person behind him, giving him enough time to dodge into an alley. At the first turn, he tucked himself behind a stack of crates, crouching low and pressing himself to the cold stone wall.

The slatted boxes were far from a suitable hiding spot, but Emmett was counting on that.

Heavy booted feet rushed down the alley, headed for the far street where a clever person could have already lost themselves in the crowd.

As soon as his pursuers vanished into the moving sea of people, Emmett stood up and walked back to the street he'd left. He'd survived this long by knowing when to run as far and as fast as he could and when the better part of wisdom was doing the unexpected, like hiding in plain sight. No one would expect him to come back to the street where he'd almost been caught.

Unfortunately, he'd probably only bought himself a few more hours. When he went back to Marcus without Katya's heart, he might end up wishing her guards had caught him after all. Katya was probably already safely sequestered in her house, guards on high alert. Emmett couldn't try to steal her heart again this soon.

He couldn't go back empty-handed either. Judging by Marcus's condition when Emmett had left, he urgently needed a new heart. Given how volatile he could be at the best of times, it would be beyond dangerous for Emmett to go back without one.

Of course, it would also be risky to stay away too long. Marcus would suspect Emmett was stalling, or, worse, trying to escape. If Emmett wasn't around to be punished, more than likely, Carlo would be the one to suffer.

Emmett glanced up at the swirling lights overhead.

"Dwellers in the stars, hear my plea…" His whispered, nearly reflexive prayer for divine assistance died on his lips halfway through the first line.

Many Seachosen believed their gods had abandoned them when their island home had flooded. To them, Starfall had signified the death of the deities who'd made their home in the skies, danced with the planets, and placed pieces of starlight itself into the first people to form their souls.

Emmett's family had been more optimistic, clinging to the idea that Starfall was a gift from the heavens, the powers it offered an echo of the gods-touched heroes in their earliest histories. They'd believed the gods still gazed down from the skies, waiting in the stars to welcome their people home at the end of their lives.

There were no stars in Rime.

There had been a time when Emmett had spent hours begging for help from anyone who might have been capable of hearing him through the wards, be that the Seachosen gods or the local fate deity his family had thought it wise to reverence as well. He'd offered them almost anything he could think of to spare his family, or to get him and Carlo away from the monster holding their lives in his hands.

Now, Emmett was almost certain any god who might take notice would see the blood on his hands and decide the world would be better off without Emmett in it. That might be preferable to the life he was trapped in, but he couldn't leave Carlo alone with Marcus.

Emmett bit back the words that still wanted to spill out. He had no right to ask for help, and he'd learned the hard way that attracting the attention of anyone powerful only ended badly. If he couldn't find a way to fix the mess he'd made of this job, all he'd have to look forward to was pain at Marcus's hands.

Instead of praying, he forced himself to think.

He couldn't go back without a heart for Marcus. With a heart as used up as the one currently beating in his chest must have been, the Star leader couldn't wait for Emmett to get another chance to slip past Katya's protections. That left one option; not a good one, but the least likely of Emmett's limited choices to get him or Carlo seriously hurt or killed.

He needed another heart. One Marcus might deem an acceptable substitute for a powerful syndicate leader's.

Unfortunately, most of the desirable targets were either still asleep or sending out expendable underlings to do their bidding. In a few cases, after word of the assassinations started spreading around Rime, syndicate leaders were even employing doubles. Emmett wouldn't be surprised if a few takeovers happened soon. The lackeys, trusted enough to act in their masters' places but still treated as disposable, could easily decide it was time for them to wrestle control into their own hands.

That was the kind of chaos Marcus wanted. Suspicion and infighting in the syndicates made them vulnerable to another coup like the one that had brought that monster into power over a decade ago. Now Marcus had the men and weapons and resources to crush any syndicates that refused to fall in line. He wanted to fan the simmering rivalries in the city into a destructive blaze and rebuild the Star Syndicate's empire on the ashes left in their wake. And he'd found a perfect weapon in Emmett.

A patch of color caught Emmett's eye. Someone in a dark red coat, moving purposefully through the crowd.

That particular shade of red came from one source: bloodbriar. The only plant that could flourish under Rime's sunless sky sprouted anywhere spilled blood had soaked into the ground. Thin vines could be found in nearly every River Quarter alley and creeping up the walls of syndicate mansions, but the only place it typically grew in quantities large enough to harvest was the Bastion's courtyards. The plant's poisonous thorns made it dangerous to gather and process, and the dye extracted was used for clothing intended to be worn by the Cohort. Technically, no civilian could wear bloodbriar red, but after it became a status symbol among wealthy syndicate leaders flaunting their untouchable status and the blood they'd spilled to cultivate the plant on their own grounds, the Cohort relaxed the regulations rather than risk direct confrontation. Still, it was uncommon to see that shade of clothing anywhere other than mansions at the top of the overlook or the city offices.

The woman didn't appear to be a Cohort employee or a wealthy homeowner. Judging by the leather bag slung across her chest, she was a messenger. Messengers knew the ins and outs of the city, including the locations of even secretive syndicate members, and often they weren't above taking a peek at what they delivered. The secrets they traded in meant they could be influential in their own way, but they weren't the sort of people Emmett would have expected to own a bloodbriar-dyed coat. There were only three ways someone like this messenger could have gotten a coat like that: someone powerful gave it to her, probably as payment for an important delivery; she'd bought it herself, which would take more money than any honest messenger could spend on something so frivolous; or she'd stolen it, which meant a former owner with money and status either hadn't been able to take it back or had decided not to. Unless she'd acquired the coat recently, she hadn't yet sold it in desperation or been successfully threatened by someone wanting to steal it. Whether this messenger had the patronage of someone powerful or simply the cunning and blackmail material to survive the cutthroat streets of Rime, what she knew could be useful to Marcus.

The potential for mishandled correspondence with freelance messengers was serious enough that Marcus didn't use them, instead employing two or three who worked exclusively in the Star's interests. This one wasn't wearing Marcus's signature yellow on an armband or scarf. She was fair game.

Emmett wove his way through the crowd to the messenger, then pretended to stumble, catching himself against her shoulder. His hand slid the worn, frayed cuff of the red coat up her arm far enough for his fingers to find the pulse in her wrist.

One beat, and her heart was his.

He closed his fingers around a startling gleam that appeared in his palm and pulled away, melting into the crowd. He kept his hand clenched until the brightness slipped under his skin. His gift wrapped itself around the heart, tugging at it for a brief moment before the starsilver locket around his neck ripped it away.

Emmett kept to the side streets, slipping his gloves back onto his hands and tucking them into his pockets. The familiar ache gathered behind his eyes, his gift demanding the price of using it, but he had nothing to offer. As long as he wore the locket, forged by Marcus's smiths to make sure Emmett kept his end of the bargain, his gift couldn't absorb any heart he took. The enchanted starsilver drew them and contained them until he could hand them over to Marcus.

Emmett hunched his shoulders against the chilly wind that always bit a little sharper when he was tired. The auroras had just begun swirling brightly overhead, but he wanted nothing more than to crawl back into bed, pull the blankets over his head, and sleep until the next day.

Still, he appreciated being outside the mansion walls, surrounded by people who didn't know who he was or what he could do. Out here, people didn't flinch from Emmett's touch or snap at him to keep his distance. He was just another stranger on the street, not a dangerous, valuable weapon too risky to trust but worth too much to discard.

The warm, savory scent of roasted nuts wafted over from a street vendor's stall, making Emmett's stomach snarl. For a moment, he could almost feel Carlo's hand snug in his own, and hear his hesitant voice asking if they could stop.

Emmett slipped a hand into his coat pocket, gloved fingers closing around the grubby coin he'd found on the street that morning.

Marcus hadn't given Emmett any money since he and Carlo were brought to the mansion. Food was all provided by the cooks, and whatever new clothing Emmett and Carlo needed was bought and paid for by Marcus directly. Emmett had no chance of hiding away even a small amount he could use to make an escape.

As if he'd have taken the chance of trying to run again. He'd thought it through a hundred times, trying to find a way where Marcus wouldn't kill him, where he could get Carlo out of the house without the guards stopping them, but he'd reached the same conclusion every time. It couldn't be done. He'd learned that the hard way, too.

There was no point in saving the coin, no chance it would do him or Carlo any good if he managed to smuggle it into the mansion. He might as well spend it on something Carlo would appreciate much more than a shiny but useless copper.

Emmett turned around and walked back to the vendor, doing his best to rub a little shine into the metal with the corner of his scarf. "How much will this get me?" he asked, holding out the coin in his palm. The vendor looked from it to him, then scooped out a handful of nuts from his roasting pan and dropped them into a cone made of dried, flat seaweed.

Emmett handed over the coin, took the small, warm cone, and shook a few salty nuts into his hand as he walked away from the vendor's cart. He crunched them gratefully as he started in the direction of Marcus's mansion, licking the remaining salt from his palm and hoping it would help stave off some of the dizziness. He'd learned a few thefts ago that he felt better sooner if he ate heavily salted things, like the dried salmon that appeared on the dinner plates when the head cook was busy with her second job: inventory of smuggled goods. The nuts weren't quite as salty as preserved meats, but maybe Emmett would have less of a headache for the next few hours.

Once the first few nuts were gone, Emmett hesitated. Trying to bring anything other than the clothes he'd been sent out in and the hearts he'd been sent after into the Star's headquarters was risky. He'd be thoroughly searched at the door, and even something as innocuous as a packet of roasted nuts could raise questions. It might be safer just to eat them all rather than take the risk. With his gift screaming for the energy imprisoned in the starsilver locket and warm, salty food in his hands, it might be easier, too. But he wanted to bring some back for Carlo.

Emmett folded the seaweed cone over the rest of the nuts, then tucked them inside his coat. The opening wasn't a pocket, just a tear in the lining, but it might keep the food a little warmer on the rest of his walk back. Better yet, the door guards didn't know about it, so they might not notice Emmett had anything inside it when they searched him.

The crowd thinned out once he passed Market Row. When he finally turned down the road whose weathered sign still read Brick Street, he found himself alone in the shadow of the house that took up almost the whole block. Whatever the Cohort-installed sign claimed, everyone simply called this Star Street.

Most syndicate leaders liked to show off their wealth and power with large houses, and Marcus's mansion was no exception. Various shades of pale stone covered the façade: the center dark and weathered, the middle sections showing some wear, and the furthest wings still bright in the perpetual twilight. Most builders tried to cover up the obvious signs a house had been expanded. Marcus preferred flaunting the steady growth of his power and influence.

Emmett walked to the massive front door and pulled the chain with its locket from under his shirt. The faint glow shining through the starsilver meant there was a beating heart trapped inside, the only reason Marcus had to permit Emmett back into his headquarters.

One of the guards swung open the heavy door, allowing Emmett inside. Emmett's breath still fogged in the air, the anteroom chilly despite the fires burning in the hearths on each side. The four guards inside wore heavy jackets covered by thick leather vests with padding and plating that could stop a blade or a crossbow bolt. Their gloved fingers rested in easy reach of sheathed blades.

Steps above told Emmett the guards overhead had left their alert posts to return to their own fires. Unlike many High Quarter houses, Marcus's defenses covered the entire front of the building, rather than stopping at the ground floor. In the narrow second floor rooms, the syndicate leader had stationed guards wielding crossbows they could fire at a moment's notice through the small windows. Anyone who tried to get into the house uninvited would leave it in a death cart. Break-ins happened from time to time in the High Quarter, but even the most desperate people knew better than to risk a confrontation with Marcus. The guards were such a deterrent that in the six months Emmett had been imprisoned in the mansion, no one had made a burglary attempt.

Emmett turned out his pockets and removed his coat, sweater, and boots in response to the guards' orders, proving he wasn't carrying any contraband or weapons back inside with him. He wasn't sure if it would have been more or less humiliating to be pawed over the way the guards would have searched an ordinary visitor than to stand half-dressed and barefoot, shivering in the chilly room until the guards were satisfied he was no threat. At least considering that distracted him from worrying about what would happen if he was caught trying to smuggle in food. Or *when* he was caught trying to substitute a random messenger's heart for Katya's.

The guard who'd opened the door jerked back when Emmett stepped toward him. The one who'd been inspecting his clothes dropped them to the ground in a heap rather than handing them back.

Their concerns were unfounded. With a heart already in the locket, Emmett couldn't steal another one. He'd have to be touching someone's skin to even try, but people never seemed inclined to trust he wouldn't use his gift on them. He collected his clothes, shaking off slush previous footsteps had left on the floor before slipping his feet back into his boots and tugging the sweater over his head.

As soon as Emmett stepped into the hall, two more guards moved in behind him, blocking his way to the door. Their presence felt like a solid weight on Emmett's shoulders, the hands resting on their weapons an ominous warning of what he might face when Marcus realized he'd brought the wrong heart.

When the guards at Marcus's office opened the door, Emmett flinched back from what felt like a physical wall of heat. The fire was burning even higher than before, flames roaring white and blue in the center. Acrid smoke hovered in the air, twisting in black swirls as the storm wind forced a draft down the chimney. Immediately, sweat began dripping down Emmett's neck and back under the layers of clothing he'd needed to brave the outside weather.

Marcus tucked an elaborately carved pipe into the pocket of his robe. His fingers shook violently, and the pipe slipped from his hand and tumbled to the floor. Emmett took a single step forward, reaching to retrieve it like he'd done for his father when his gnarled hands struggled to grip the carved handle of a chisel or awl.

"No." Marcus's order, though raspy, was barked out. He raised a hand in warning, then bent over, coughing, to pick up the pipe and replace it in his robe. Emmett waited, hands clenched in front of him, until Marcus looked up. When Marcus's bloodshot eyes met his, Emmett unwrapped his scarf and gestured to the locket around his neck.

Marcus nodded.

Emmett walked up to stand beside the chair, slipping off his gloves and tucking the locket back under his shirt. The locket's enchantment could absorb the hearts Emmett stole no matter how many layers of clothing lay between the metal and his skin, but retrieving the heart to hand over to Marcus was much less exhausting if Emmett's body was in direct contact with the starsilver charm. He closed his eyes, focusing his gift on drawing out the heart once again.

Just because pulling the heart back out was easier with the locket against Emmett's skin didn't mean it was simple. His gift fought him the entire time, battling to pull the stolen life further into him instead of pushing it outward. Emmett bit his lip until he tasted hot, salty blood. He breathed out, imagining the exhale forcing the heart away from his chest and into his hand.

Finally, his gift obeyed, relinquishing some of its grip on the heart's energy. Warmth moved from Emmett's chest, down his arm, and into his palm. Emmett didn't open his eyes until it had settled, hovering over the center of his hand like a bird unsure whether it had found a safe branch on which to rest.

The heart fluttered in his grasp, the light of its energy pulsing and flickering in shades of green, blue, and magenta like the auroras outside. It was the most brilliant heart Emmett had ever seen. The ones he'd stolen before had been darkened and twisted, damaged by their owners' cruelty and greed. This one had its shadows, and a sharpness that stung his fingers as it fluttered, but its vivid light shimmered around the room, illuminating even the dark corners.

Emmett's gift continued to surge through his veins, reaching for the heart in his hand. He swallowed hard, shaking his head to dispel the urge to close his fingers around the glow and hold it close. He couldn't take the heart for himself, no matter how much his gift wanted its vibrant energy. It would only return to the locket, and he'd need to start over, draining more of his own strength in the process.

Emmett turned his hand over and dropped the heart into Marcus's outstretched palm, then drew his fingers up the stark blue veins on the inside of the man's thin, pale wrist. The light followed his fingertips, sinking into the skin, running along veins and vanishing under the rolled-up sleeve of Marcus's shirt. A moment later, Marcus gasped as the heart's energy reached his own. He smiled, a crimson flush taking the place of the grayish pallor on his cheeks.

Most people who relied on stolen hearts were already dying, desperate to extend their lives at the price of someone else's. Marcus was merely greedy for the secrets he could extract from his competitors' hearts. There'd been no reason for him to resort to such drastic means of gaining an advantage over the other syndicates. Emmett had tried to warn him that taking others' hearts too often would cause his own to wither and decay, leaving him reliant on more and more to survive. The faint scar Emmett saw every day on Carlo's throat was a constant reminder of what Marcus had thought of his advice.

As long as Marcus kept getting what he wanted, he'd pay any price for it. That ruthlessness had turned the Star into the most powerful syndicate in Rime. Emmett had made the mistake of getting on the wrong side of it.

Marcus's predatory smile turned to a scowl. His eyes grew stormy, like the sea in a gale. A hand flew out, gripping Emmett by the shoulder of his coat and throwing him backward with such unexpected ferocity Emmett stumbled over his own feet and fell onto the thick bearskin rug.

Emmett scrambled to get his feet under him, flinching. Enough memories must have filtered in from the new heart that Marcus had realized it didn't belong to his intended target, and Emmett was about to suffer the consequences of his mistake.

"This isn't what I asked for."

"She was a messenger. She must know things you could use."

"You found the only honest freelancer in this town," Marcus snapped. "She doesn't read what she delivers. All I know from her is trivial gossip. One of my people could hear what she has at the Wolf's Den over a pint that would cost far less than the money I shell out to keep you and your son around."

Emmett flinched involuntarily. He couldn't afford to make a mistake, especially not one Marcus could claim had been deliberate. There were plenty of ways Marcus or his guards could hurt Emmett without needing to lay a hand on him.

"You have a heart. Give me a couple days, let things quiet down out there. I'll get you Katya's." There'd been something about this heart that worried Emmett, the way it prickled his fingers like he'd grabbed hold of a bloodbriar vine.

That hadn't been the heart of someone who would go home and curl up and wait to die once she realized what had happened. A messenger who knew the city might stand a chance of tracking Emmett down before her time ran out. If she found out her heart was gone for good, she'd probably kill him out of sheer spite.

If he could buy himself two days, she'd be dead and he'd be free to try again to take Katya's heart. By that time, the Rapids' guards would be exhausted from their constant alertness, which might mean an opening he could exploit.

Marcus shook his head.

"One thing I did learn from the girl. Someone has discovered our dealings with that Flare foundry. Her contact knew only that the Black Spark was working with a new dealer during the frozen months, but Kaden likes to boast, whether it's about his blades or his alliances. My men will deal with him and the informant. But if word of who he's working with is already circulating, I need Katya out of the way as soon as possible. Bring me her heart, and we won't need to discuss your punishment for this…lapse."

Any argument Emmett would have wanted to make died in his throat. There was no winning here. He'd be facing someone's ire whether he agreed to Marcus's terms or not, and an unknown messenger's anger didn't hold the same weight as a vindictive syndicate leader's. She certainly wouldn't have as many resources to track Emmett down. Most importantly, she didn't have Carlo to hold over his head.

If Emmett went back out willingly, neither he nor Carlo would face Marcus's attempts to force Emmett's hand. The only thing that would placate Marcus's fury was Katya's heart. The sooner Emmett retrieved it, the sooner he could be back in the relative safety of Marcus's house, instead of hiding from all the people who wanted him dead, including his latest victim.

"Your messenger grew up with Roland, along the river."

Emmett winced. Katya's guards hadn't been able to get a good look at him, but if she and the messenger were on friendly terms, or worse, if *she* was the wealthy patron who'd given the messenger the expensive coat, Katya could be throwing the entire weight of her syndicate behind a dual effort to punish the assassin who'd made an attempt on her life and to avenge a friend or valued associate.

Then again, staying closer to his target than anyone would expect had saved him after this morning's failure. Maybe the best place Emmett could be if he had the Rapids Syndicate hunting him, short of Marcus's mansion itself, was near Katya Roland.

"It appears Katya has always wanted to be as close to water as possible if she feels threatened. Most likely, that means she will risk making the trip to her bathhouse again for its proximity to the river." Marcus opened his desk and pulled out a small bag. He shook a coin-sized brass token stamped with the design of a crashing wave into his palm and handed it to Emmett. "Go and get the heart I asked for, and don't come back without it."

Emmett nodded, tucking the token into his pocket as he backed out of the room into the hallway. He ignored the guards' smug smiles as he passed, walking back to the door instead of up the stairs to the cell that could, if someone was feeling generous, have been called a bedroom.

Emmett wrapped his scarf around his face and stepped out into the bitter cold again.

RORY

12 BELLS

When Rory lowered her hand from the point of her pulse for the tenth time, her fingers came away stained with red. She'd picked off the scabs on her chin and jaw, a habit she thought she'd broken years ago. She wiped the blood on the hem of her coat, wrapped her scarf around her face again, and stepped back onto the street.

She stopped at nearly every alley she passed, partly to catch her breath, partly to check her pulse. Trying to convince herself she'd misunderstood what she'd felt the first time was a lost cause. Her heartbeat had remained slow and halting, and the dizziness she'd been attributing to cold and hunger left her stumbling over even the High Quarter's level cobblestones. She couldn't imagine how bad it would get once she reached the River Quarter's frost-heaved streets.

No matter how much Rory searched her memory, nothing stood out to her about the heart thief she had assumed to be a common pickpocket. Like everyone else braving the storm, they'd been wearing a hat and scarf obscuring most of their face. Rory couldn't identify the person, and they hadn't left anything behind for her to trace. She needed another solution.

At best, she had forty-eight hours before her body shut down. She needed to find the thief and get her heart back. Fast. Until she did, she was a dead woman walking.

Rory gripped the wide stone railing as she crossed the bridge, her normally sure steps faltering. Halfway across, she stopped and leaned against a lamp pole to catch her breath. A paper fluttering from one of its notice hooks slapped her cheek. Rory ripped it down with a sharp jerk, tearing a corner away in the process. She balled the poster up to throw it over the side of the bridge, even though it would only skate along the river ice, when one of the words caught her eye.

She slowly uncrumpled the paper, smoothing it out on top of the railing to read in the flickering lamplight. It was a wanted poster distributed by a syndicate, not the Cohort. Most often, these rewards were offered for the capture of disloyal former syndicate members or the whereabouts of people with large balances on the books. If Rory had crossed her landlord, she could easily have found her own face and name on a Coin Syndicate debtor's notice, courtesy of his nephew.

This one had been posted by the Ravens. They were offering seven hundred gold coins to whoever could bring them the heart thief they claimed killed one of their lieutenants. There was no description on the paper, no sketch approximating the thief's features. Rory shoved the flyer into her pocket anyway. The fewer people who were looking for the heart thief, the less competition she'd have. Rory was the one person in Rime who had a reason to kill the thief that went beyond revenge. The Ravens were out for blood, but the same would be true if anyone else had attacked their syndicate. Killing the heart thief wouldn't bring back their lieutenant's life, but it might save Rory's, as long as her own hand dealt the finishing blow.

Rumors about how to deal with heart theft had been floating around the city since the deaths started, in the same way sleazy cure hawkers did a roaring trade when fever season began. People wanted to believe there was some way to control their fates and protect themselves and their loved ones. One of the most prominent theories claimed using a starsilver blade to stab the heart of a thief who'd taken your own would allow your life's energy to flow back along the metal into your own body. That solution might have been as worthless as the bottles of flavored alcohol sold at cure-all stands, but whether or not it was true, Rory didn't plan on dying without taking her killer down with her.

She hoped the success of that method didn't depend on the blade having a specialized enchantment. Anyone who'd gone to the trouble and expense of acquiring a starsilver weapon must have taken advantage of the metal's capabilities, but Rory doubted returning a stolen heart was the specific quality forged into her knife for its original recipient. As far as she could tell, the owner had asked for some form of protection on the blade itself: a mundane enchantment that kept the knife's edge sharp without a whetstone or prevented nicks and damage.

Hopefully, the presence of starsilver alone would be enough to take back her heart.

Between the howling wind Rory was fighting through and her heightened awareness of the weak pulse in her ears, she nearly missed the rhythmic hoofbeats that should have warned her to move off the main street. She felt the rumble under her boots just in time to dodge a herd of tri-antlered caribou being driven down to the wharf. Necks permanently bowed by the added weight, the caribou stumbled along the street in front of a group of whip-wielding traders. At the docks, they'd be loaded into ships that would take them to foreign lands, where new owners would keep them in tiny paddocks for people to gawk at. Unlike one-winged pigeons or razor-clawed snowshoe hares, the caribou were a valuable export. Whole herds were driven close to the city during breeding season to encourage as many altered calves as possible.

Caribou weren't the only magically-twisted creatures that turned a profit. The rainbow flesh of thousands of Rime salmon was packed in ice in the rambling six-story building at Dock Twelve. The few times Rory had been given a fillet as payment for hand-delivering an outstanding bill to the High Quarter, she'd found it tasteless at best, or bitter. She preferred the ordinary salmon and trout that were sorted from the nets, salted and dried, and sold in the market at two for a copper.

Nothing Rime's magic touched was ever truly bettered. Batty Bower claimed the government had designed the city to kill off gifteds without having to get their own hands dirty. Some of his theories were outlandish, but the fact was two-thirds of children born in Rime died before they turned five. Those who survived often developed deformities like Old Sue's. The only reason Rime hadn't overflowed the wards with the constant stream of gifteds arriving was because almost every family died off in one or two generations. Rory had met very few adults whose parents were born in Rime.

Few people would have chosen to come to the city knowing the truth, but Altrenea continued to claim Rime was a refuge because the use of gifts had been outlawed anywhere else in their empire. Even those who chose never to use their magic were considered dangerous for the potential in their blood, and if found, they'd be locked away as a precaution. Anyone who escaped Rime and didn't leave the country altogether would risk their freedom if they revealed the city's true conditions.

Even the Cohort members were, by and large, serving their own sentences. Corrupt officials from all over the empire were often given the choice between stepping down or relocating to Rime, which meant the worst of the worst were handed the reins of power in the city. But according to Bower, the bigger threat was those who hadn't been relegated to Rime by scandal but had come of their own free will, convinced they were doing the world a favor by creating a place that could stamp out gifteds altogether.

If Bower was right about Altrenea's intent for their city, his ramblings about the new heart thief might also contain some grain of truth that could help Rory track her killer down. Of course, Bower also claimed the wards had been created by burying gifteds alive under each of the city watchtowers. Rory would have to take anything he told her with a healthy dose of skepticism.

Rory's breaths puffed out harshly in pale clouds by the time she reached the Wolf's Den. Blizzard cooed from the windowsill, his harness empty. Normally, Rory was annoyed when she was gone this long and no one had left a delivery request, but right now, it was a relief. She didn't need any unfinished jobs hanging over her head.

Rory stepped into the pub, and the warm air hit her like a wave. She stumbled, catching herself on the back of a chair, then pulling it out as if she fully intended to take a seat right there with her back to the door. Scanning the room slowly, Rory blinked against the blurriness that filled her vision like clouds of smoke. Charlie was arguing with someone at the bar, and for a moment Rory wondered if Bower was about to be kicked out again.

"You've had enough for three people for three days. Now get out before I throw you out." Charlie lifted the hem of her sweater, showing off the ragged, ropy scars on her stomach. "I wrestled the cave bear who gave me these to the ground. I can take you."

The voice that replied to her from the slouched heap at the bar definitely wasn't Bower. "Know how I got this?" a raspy tone slurred, as the drunk woman pushed back her hood and pointed to her forehead. She laughed, the sound wet and humorless. "Tell everyone I got it in a brawl, but I walked into my mother's open cupboard door. I was twelve."

Rory knew exactly what scar Elena was talking about: a gash through her right temple that twisted her eyebrow out of line. She'd had it ever since Rory had met her, when Elena had tied her hair back to show it off and acted like it made her the toughest kid in Jax's band of teenage rebels.

"We're not swapping scar stories, Elena." Charlie reached for the old pickaxe hanging behind the bar.

Apparently, the dried bloodstains mixed with dust from starsilver ore got the message across loud and clear. Elena stood up as unsteadily as Rory had walked in and stumbled to the door.

"Sometimes I think I should move down to the waterfront," Charlie snapped, cracking a rag in the air before scrubbing it along the bar. "Sailors coming into port can't be worse than bounty hunters who just finished a big job." The whole building rattled slightly, and dust sifted down from the rafters. Charlie always struggled to control her gift when she was angry.

A waitress with clawed fingers clenched around a pitcher stepped up to Rory's table. Rory accepted a glass of water, although she refused to order a stronger drink. She needed a clear head. Sipping the water slowly, she glanced into the dark corners until she saw a familiar crushed wool hat, its owner resting facedown on the table.

Rory drained her glass, then stood. The dizziness rushed back, and she grabbed the edge of the table for support. Fortunately, no one paid any attention to her moment of weakness. Rory could probably have fallen on her face in here and no one would have questioned it. She took a few deep breaths and waited until her feet felt attached to the rest of her before walking over to Bower's table.

She didn't sit down at one of the empty chairs. Instead, she stood next to the drunken man, shaking his shoulder roughly.

Bower woke with a start, drool stringing from his mouth to his coat sleeve, eyes bleary. "Wasn' makin' no trouble, Charlie."

"It's Rory." Rory sighed. "How about I buy you another drink, and you tell me everything about that heart thief you were talking about earlier?"

The mention of more ale, and permission to repeat his acquired gossip, replaced the hazy look in Bower's eyes with eagerness. "You bet I will," he said, grabbing her hand before she could take it off his shoulder. "Now what's this about buying me a drink?"

Rory used her free hand to wave down the waitress who'd poured her the glass of water. The woman looked less than enthusiastic about serving a customer who hadn't paid for anything yet. When Rory dug a coin from her purse and told the woman to give Bower another tankard, she looked even more put out.

When the waitress returned and plunked the full mug down with a scowl, Bower downed half of it before she'd taken four steps away from the table. Only then did he look up at Rory, his beard covered in pale foam, liquid dripping from the end of it onto the sticky tabletop.

"This ain't just a dyin' fella tryin' to keep breathin'," he whispered. "This is an assassin. They're goin' around pickin' off Syndicate members, and it's got everyone on edge." Bower coughed, spitting black phlegm onto the floor, and Rory's boots in the process.

Rory grimaced, not from the added filth on already dirty leather, but from the reminder of how fragile the peace in Rime was. She only vaguely remembered the citywide riots and bloody takeovers that had taken place fifteen years ago, after the new leader of the Star dissolved the longstanding syndicate alliance. For a ten-year-old, her father's recent death had been the more relevant tragedy. Still, she'd heard enough stories over the years to know her chances of survival if the simmering resentments and power struggles reignited were slim to none.

Bower blinked at Rory. "You thinkin' about goin' after them for the reward? Hear the Midnights are offerin' five hundred gold coins to the person who brings them the thief. Ravens put up seven."

There was often good money in tracking bounties. Far better than what Rory earned as a messenger, although rarely as high as the prices being offered for the heart thief. Still, Rory had never taken a bounty job in her life. Part of it was her disdain for the profession as a whole. Most bounty hunters were as bad as Elena, drinking away their reward as soon as they had it in hand and then needing to round up a new job.

A much larger reason was the only thing Rory knew about her father's last job. He'd been paid to track someone down, and it had ended with him dead.

Bower belched loudly, then wiped his lips with his sleeve. "That's about all I know."

Rory left him to his ale, pulled up her hood, and stepped out the door into the wind.

The last heart thief who'd made a real stir in Rime had been active when Rory was starting out as a messenger. He'd been hunting in the rich sector along Market Row, stealing a heart almost every day. People had worn thick gloves in the middle of thaw, and crowds had thinned out to the point that Rory could complete deliveries in half her usual time. It had been a tense two weeks before the thief attacked an off-duty Cohort guard; it was an incident that ended with the thief dead and the guard lauded as a hero until he keeled over two days later.

Those attacks had been random and unpredictable. The thief had supposedly been the victim of a starsilver mining accident, stricken by poisoned magic consuming him from the inside out. Grisly rumors had circulated that his corpse decayed in front of the witnesses, leaving only rotten bones for Cohort inspectors to retrieve. Whether that was true or not, he'd been stealing hearts to survive the way a fox hunted down hares. There'd been no calculated goal, and no way to predict who the next victim might be.

If Bower was right, a risk Rory would need to take, this heart thief was more cunning, using their powers as a weapon rather than a means of survival. Someone specifically targeting Syndicate members while avoiding capture had to be deliberate and strategic. If Rory could figure out their plan, she stood a chance of tracking them down.

Rime had killed her father and twisted her mother into something as unrecognizable as a cave bear. Rory wouldn't let it take her too.

Rory checked three of the neighborhoods Willow favored before she found both a seller's mark on the window and a tiny twig tucked into the doorframe. She leaned against the gate, trying to catch her breath. Her scarf clung damp against her chin from the panting that had accompanied her attempts to climb the last few hills, her temples throbbed, and a lightheaded nausea that felt like she hadn't eaten in days churned in her stomach, draining the strength from her limbs. She hadn't been worn out from walking six blocks since her first day delivering clean laundry for Old Sue.

Rory pulled the loaf out of her pocket, breaking off a chunk and warming it in her hand before sticking it in her mouth. Even if hunger wasn't her real problem, she needed to keep up her strength. Her third bite of the crusty, dry bread caught in the back of her throat when she swallowed, and she coughed.

She scooped up a handful of snow from the top of the fence. The cold made her teeth ache, but at least it was something to wet down the tickle in the back of her throat.

She gently stroked Blizzard's head, trying to settle him. He'd been fluffing his feathers nervously and hadn't begged for a crumb once. Rory wondered briefly what would happen to the crippled bird once she was no longer around to take care of him, then banished the thought to the dark corners of her brain. She couldn't let herself accept her death yet. She still had a chance of taking her heart back if she could talk to Willow.

While Rory practically carried a street map in her head, Willow had the equivalent of a notebook filled with the secrets of everyone whose skin he'd ever touched. It was a powerful gift, capable of making him plenty of enemies, so he moved constantly between vacant houses. Creditors were always trying to make a profit off places they'd snapped up as collateral, and the semi-legal Bone Market, basically a syndicate itself, set up auctions when no heirs could be found after an owner's death. Willow knew plenty of people in both trades.

Willow may have been a repository of secrets, but he'd never divulged his own, not even his real name. Even to his closest friends, he was known only by his calling card, that single branch. It was currently tucked into the latch side of the doorframe, which meant he was out somewhere in town.

Rory saw the lanky figure walking up the street, bundled in an overly large gray jacket, before he saw her. When he looked up, he stopped short, then moved forward again. "Gave me a scare there for a bit," he said, stopping at the gate next to her. "Thought for sure one of my clients tracked me down."

Because by 'clients' you mean the people you blackmail by promising you'll keep their secrets safely in your own head.

"Then I saw the coat, and your bird pal cinched it. Someone coulda knifed you and taken that jacket, but Blizzard wouldn't go with anyone he didn't trust, would you, boy?" He ran a finger over the pigeon's head.

Blizzard snapped his beak at him.

Willow smiled. "See, my point exactly."

"He's just afraid you'll find out he's been sneaking food from my cupboard behind my back and tell me all about it."

Something in the attempted joke must have fallen flat because Willow looked at her searchingly, head tilted. "What's going on, Rory?"

"Not here."

Willow nodded and opened the gate. He didn't bother moving the branch before she stepped inside the door. Rory appreciated his intentional offer of a private conversation.

The house was pitch black indoors, windows covered by heavy curtains that served a dual purpose of blocking the cold and preventing any curious passers-by from glimpsing light or motion inside a building that was supposed to be empty. Without any fire in the fireplace, the room felt nearly as cold as the outside.

Willow hadn't needed to risk the visibility of a smoking chimney since he blackmailed a syndicate lieutenant out of the coat he was currently wearing, its material laced with threads of starsilver enchanted to provide permanent warmth to the wearer. The victim had probably decided losing a few fingers or toes to frostbite beat losing his head if his boss found out he was shortchanging the books.

"I need to find a heart thief," Rory said as soon as the door latch clicked behind them.

Willow froze in the middle of lighting the lantern hanging over a rough table in the middle of the room, then cursed when his cinderpine match burned down to his fingertips. He dropped the charred twig, hissing and sticking scorched fingers into his mouth. "You know that kind of magic is illegal, right?" he mumbled.

Rory sighed. "I don't want to *use* it, Will. I need to find the person responsible for stealing *mine*."

"That's a really bad joke, Rory." Willow struck another match and this time succeeded in touching it to the lantern wick. Rory shucked off one glove and held up her hand, showing him the purple taking over her fingertips. In the lantern light, it almost looked like her skin was blackening.

"Fate's Hand," Willow cursed.

At least, Rory hoped he meant the phrase that way. Old Sue used to say the same words almost reverently, quietly accepting Fate's workings even as its hand did nothing but strike her cruelly. She may have been content to surrender to Fate, but Rory didn't intend to go down without a fight.

Willow reached for her hand.

Rory yanked it back. One person using their gift on her was more than enough for one day. Willow was an expert at maintaining a facade of concern to get close to his marks. Even if he'd only intended to make a closer inspection, Rory wasn't in the mood to satisfy his curiosity. She was the one who needed answers.

Willow looked from her fingers to her face. "Who wants you dead that badly?"

"Unlike you, I'm not exactly walking around with a target on my back." Rory didn't mention that she already knew the assassin was after Katya. Willow didn't need any help extracting more leverage on people. "I've heard some rumors that make me think this is someone with a specific plan. If you know where the other victims died or who they were, I might be able to figure out what the thief is doing and catch up to them."

"As you might have noticed, heart thefts take a while to, ah, to kill people," Willow said, scratching self-consciously at the lichen scabs crusting the tip of his ear. "Where the victims died has nothing to do with where the thefts actually happened."

"Yes, but I'm dying here, so humor me a little."

"Doesn't mean I won't charge you."

Rory sighed. "I'm not giving you a copper until I decide if what you know is worth it."

"You know perfectly well it will be." Willow held out his hand, beckoning with the tips of his fingers. "Besides, if it's not, you won't be needing money anyway. Might as well give it to a friend as have a stranger take it off you, right?"

"Fine. Half now, half after." Rory had known she'd get nothing from Willow for free, but she wasn't going to hand over her money without some protest. She pulled out her purse, counted out three silver coins, and dropped them into Willow's hand, her own fingers held half an arm's length above his.

Willow shook his head and began digging through a pile of papers on the end of the table. He untied a large, stained roll and spread it out under the lamp. Brightly colored spots crossed a detailed, hand-drawn city map. "Red dots are all the people who've died of magical causes in the past year, at least the ones I know of." He pointed out tiny letters written inside the ink splotches. "S is starsilver toxicity, B is bloodbriar poisoning, and the H here is heart theft."

There were several H markers on the outskirts of the River Quarter. Heart thieves weren't common, and the few that existed tended to keep to the slums, where they could hunt without raising the attention of the Cohort. Using gifts was legal in Rime, but murder technically wasn't. When someone's gift had become capable only of killing, they were no longer afforded protection. Rory had to assume the markers on Willow's map were only a fraction of the true death toll. In that part of town, almost no one noticed one person less on any given day.

The unusual activity was a cluster of deaths concentrated in the triangle where the affluent High Quarter, the port companies, and the shady portion of Market Row intersected. Willow recited the names, alliances, and death dates for each of the heart thefts as Rory pointed out the markers. The victims so far had been a low-level enforcer for the Star, a senior longshoreman who kept Horn cargo off the official books, a negotiator from the Midnights who regularly brokered deals with the Cohort, a Ravens lieutenant, a High Quarter businessman suspected of handling and pocketing money from a few different syndicates, and, last month, the Horn boss himself. Without their leader, the Horn Syndicate had been crumbling from the inside. Rory hadn't delivered any envelopes with a green wax seal in the past two weeks, and she was none too sorry about that. Their main trade, shown in their sigil of a mountain sheep's head and curling horns, had been trafficking magical creatures.

Aside from the last one, these deaths had been hushed up and glossed over. There was a reason Willow's gift made him feared and powerful in Rime. The syndicates kept their business close to their vests, and hated revealing anything that made them look weak. Rory would have bet the Midnights and Ravens had only posted their rewards after the Horn boss had died.

Willow glanced at Rory with a raised eyebrow once she was finished. "Up until you, they were all criminals. Well, known ones, anyway."

Rory rolled her eyes at his clarification. Petty theft hardly put her on the same level as extortion, bribery, and smuggling. At least it explained why the authorities hadn't gotten involved, even though the killings were in the High Quarter. The Cohort generally kept their hands off crime in the city unless it impacted them or their business allies. Life was cheap in Rime, and justice reserved for those with deep pockets. Whether the crime was robbery, rape, or murder, retribution was the only closure most people could ever hope for.

"Does this help?" Willow asked.

"Maybe."

"What are you going to do now?"

Rory slipped her rarely used knife from its sheath and inspected the tarnished blade. The rippled pattern in the starsilver alloy was faintly visible, resembling agitated water on the river's surface where it flowed over buried stones. "I'm going to test an old legend."

Willow grimaced. "So you're going to murder somebody?"

"*They're* the murderer. Without my heart, I'll be dead in two days." Rory shrugged. "It's them or me. And I know who I'm picking." She slipped the knife back into its sheath and walked out the door before Willow could recover enough from her declaration to ask for the second half of his payment.

That bravado carried Rory about two blocks from Willow's house before the dizziness struck again. She stumbled to a stop against the wall of a shabby three-story apartment building, narrowly avoiding crushing Blizzard between her shoulder and the stone. Rory propped herself a bit more firmly against the wall, hoping she wouldn't slide down into the stinking slush in the gutter. She tried to focus on what she'd learned from Willow, not the erratic heartbeat thumping in her ears.

Willow's map had corroborated Bower's assassin theory. Syndicate members weren't someone's victims of convenience. Even if the thief lived in that area, they'd have been much safer picking off household servants or wickers or trash cart drivers. Someone had wanted those specific, often high-profile, people dead.

It was unlikely that so many people, from such a variety of syndicate circles, had directly wronged any one person enough to be killed over it. Besides, the thefts had started with syndicate members fairly low in their respective hierarchies and gradually moved up. That didn't seem like a personal vendetta.

More likely, the assassin was a contract killer working for the syndicates in some capacity, either freelancing for each job or following a single employer's hit list. The variety of syndicates the victims had come from suggested a freelance killer, but it would be risky for an assassin with such a specific trademark to hire out their services to syndicates they might previously have attacked. Judging from the Ravens' wanted poster, the only reason they'd want to find the heart thief was revenge. A syndicate with a more subtle approach, or anyone looking to collect on the reward money, could pretend to be interested in the assassin's services, then set a trap under the guise of handing over information or payment. Freelancing was a risk Rory didn't think fit the thief's cautious nature or their continued survival.

But if the heart thief was working for one syndicate, the deaths so far had already eliminated a majority of the large players in Rime as potential employers. The thief obviously wasn't working for the Midnights or Ravens, and the Horn wouldn't have killed off their own leader unless an underling had planned to step up and take over the reins. The Coin had the money and power, and no deaths in their ranks thus far, but they preferred brutal punishments that sent a message. Heart theft was too bloodless for their taste. Katya could conceivably have orchestrated a 'failed' assassination to throw suspicion off herself, but her guards had been legitimately disturbed. Also, while Katya certainly wasn't above lethal manipulations of people and power, Rory didn't think she would let anyone working for her attack random people on the street. The Star underling's death could have been a sanctioned punishment, but as the first kill it could also have been a test of the thief's skills, since Star employees tended to be almost as notoriously paranoid as their leader.

Rory swallowed hard as a wave of nausea swept through her, trying to keep her breakfast from ending up on her boots.

There was one other possibility for the motive behind these deaths, and that one worried Rory most. Someone targeting so many different syndicates could have been getting their orders from people who wanted the whole underground magical power structure of Rime to collapse. The Cohort wasn't above secretly employing gifteds when it suited their purposes, and they had the most to gain from the syndicates turning on each other out of suspicion. If the thief was operating under their sanction, with their protection, they'd be untouchable.

A loud clanging that wasn't the bells drew Rory's attention out of her thoughts. Several men in heavy coats, dented metal pails swinging from their gloved hands, walked past. Probably a crew on their way home from a Smoke Quarter factory shift. Rory kept her hand on the grip of her knife until they'd turned a corner. Nothing good could come from them assuming she was a drunk, too uncoordinated to get up the steps and through the door of her own apartment building.

Once the clatter of their pails, the crunching boots on ice, and their muffled chatter faded, she turned her attention back to dealing with the person who'd already made the mistake of thinking Rory was an easy target.

If the thief had been sent to kill Katya specifically, their failure this morning would have left them with a serious problem. A freelance assassin would have taken a major blow to their reputation. A killer on payroll would probably, at best, find themselves out of work. In either case they'd have provoked the wrath of an employer who had paid to have someone murdered and made themselves a potential loose end. Every minute Katya wasn't dead put the thief's livelihood and life at risk. Doing the sensible thing and holing up somewhere until their current victim keeled over was no longer an option. At the least, they'd probably be staking Katya out, learning how alert and thorough her guards were, finding out how many had been added since this morning, and determining the best way to get past her defenses.

Having Rory's heart, and thus her memories of Katya's tendencies and mentality, would be an advantage for the thief. But it was also working in Rory's favor. She knew what the thief wanted and where they would be most likely to go.

Rory took a shaky breath and began walking. She wouldn't become another red dot on Willow's map if she could help it.

EMMETT

13 BELLS

Emmett rubbed the back of his neck, wincing as the persistent headache became a stabbing pain behind his eyes. He could barely stay on his feet, let alone think clearly enough to plan a second attempt on Katya.

His route from Marcus's house had taken him far closer to the Bastion than he was comfortable getting. The huge building at the center of the city, round walls permanently encased in a layer of gray ice, was a stark reminder of Rime's purpose. The Bastion was the official prison, but the city itself was a fortress, designed to keep its inhabitants inside rather than protect them. The outside world moved forward, but none of its progress could ever reach into Rime. Everyone here lived in the same endless round of routine, serving a life sentence just for being different.

And somehow, there was still room for prisons inside prisons. Even in Rime, the threat of being sent to the Bastion held weight; a reminder that even when your life was terrible, it could get so much worse. Emmett grimaced as another dizzying wave of agony crashed through his skull. He didn't need armed guards or a frozen tower to know that life could always find a new way to tear you down, even once you thought you'd fallen as far as you could go.

Emmett ducked his head and shoved his hands into his pockets when two Cohort guards appeared. There was no reason for them to know anything about his gift, but he couldn't help feeling like they'd see through his coat to the locket against his skin and haul him off in chains.

The slavering malamute leashed between the guards threw back its head and howled. The sound raised the hair on the back of Emmett's neck.

The former sledge dogs were remnants of the beasts of burden that carried the first Altrenean expeditions into the province to claim the site of the fallen star as a government mine. When the pups born near the city began showing the effects of magic, their role shifted from sledge haulers to guards. The Cohort bred Rime malamutes specifically to encourage the most intimidating qualities, like this one's saber fangs and porcupine-quilled curving tail.

Somewhere deep in the city, a sickeningly warped howl rose up in reply to the leashed dog. Emmett had heard horror stories of the Cohort's malamutes being unleashed to quell the citywide riots that had followed Marcus's rise to power. In the aftermath of those bloody encounters, not all the dogs were recaptured. Those that escaped formed packs that terrorized neighborhoods and attacked lone travelers.

Without new blood, the feral packs had all but vanished in the last decade. The dogs that still roamed the streets were so twisted and malformed by generations of magical poisoning that most pups died at birth, and those that survived were often too hobbled and weak to give chase. Surprising one while it fed on a carcass or rooted through trash was still a good way to get bitten, but people were unlikely to be chased through alleys by seven or eight snarling, vicious beasts.

The howl from the depths of the city died off in a choked whine. The feral dog was probably in its death throes, wailing for packmates already gone. Still, hearing the sound chilled Emmett to the bone. There was something uniquely horrifying about a creature that had once been loyal and trustworthy becoming a mangled, vicious predator.

He dug into the lining of his coat for the package of roasted nuts he'd hidden there. He needed the salt to clear his head, or he was going to make a mistake. He finished off the meager handful of cold nuts left in the cone, then broke the dried seaweed into pieces, chewing each one slowly. The leathery plant was the same one his father had collected when he'd gone to the docks to barter with incoming ships. Emmett's mother had wrapped the red-veined leaves around small fish the sailors exchanged for repairs to railings and hatches before baking them in the hearth coals. The taste of brackish water and the feeling of tiny fragments catching in his teeth were achingly familiar.

Emmett sighed, leaning back against a tavern wall where he could get a decent view of the bathhouse. He flinched when a vivid magenta swirl overhead illuminated the words on posters tacked to the wall of a shop across the street. The Midnights and the Ravens were both offering sizeable rewards for his capture. He wasn't sure whether he was more disturbed by the callous 'dead or alive' at the bottom of the poster the Midnights had distributed, or the ominous 'alive for gift to be proven' the Ravens demanded. There was no known way to tell if someone was a heart thief until they'd actually taken a life, but some legends claimed their hearts would appear black if the thief's chest was cut open while their own heart was still beating.

At least none of them had even an approximate sketch of his face, or any description beyond a poor estimate of his height. So far, he'd done a good job covering his tracks, concealing his features with his scarf during every attack. He wouldn't be able to if he went after Katya in her bathhouse.

Marcus had been convinced by the information he'd gathered from his new heart that Katya would be here, in the low rounded building at the end of the street that rested partially on heavy pilings sunk into the riverbed. Two guards stood at the front door. Emmett would need to get past them, as well as however many more were inside, and into Katya's notoriously well-defended inner circle, a place where hiding his face would be impossible.

The token Marcus had given him was stamped with two concentric rings, meaning it only allowed access to the second level of the bathhouse. Tokens for the third ring couldn't be purchased. They were only given to people Katya trusted or needed to hold a face to face meeting with. To steal Katya's heart, Emmett needed to get inside that third level, which meant stealing a token from someone with access. The best way to find out who had it was by watching the people who were able to go in and out. Then he could pick the one who seemed like the best mark. He hoped being a heart thief somehow extended to making him a decent pickpocket.

The wisest choice would have been to wait until Katya had relaxed enough to resume business as usual. If Emmett waited too long, though, he'd have to steal more than a third level token. Marcus had told him in no uncertain terms not to come back without the heart, and once again, he hadn't given Emmett any money. The more petty thefts Emmett needed to make to survive, the greater the risk he'd be caught.

Katya would do one of two things today. She might bar all visitors and refuse to allow even her most trusted people to enter her safe space. Or she might call in every favor she was owed, reaching out to her contacts across the city in the hopes one of them would know why she'd been targeted or who'd tried to kill her. Emmett hoped the latter was the case. Katya had always been a bold businesswoman, taking the kind of chances that had allowed her to build the Rapids into a major player in only a few years.

Emmett couldn't stop thinking about Carlo, sitting on the edge of their bed tonight, watching the last flickers of pink and green in the sky. He'd wonder where his dad had gone, and why Emmett wasn't back like he'd promised. Emmett didn't want to leave Carlo alone with Marcus any longer than absolutely necessary. Unfortunately, the alternative was taking a risk that could mean Carlo lost him forever.

"I'm sorry," he whispered, looking up as a tangle of green and white danced across the wards. He wasn't speaking to any deity this time, but to someone he was equally uncertain would hear him. Someone he couldn't be sure looked at him with any more compassion. "I've ruined everything. I've put Carlo in danger, and I don't know if I'll ever see him again." He sniffled, tear-blurred vision and streaming nose no longer due entirely to the chilly air. "If you're watching us up there, I want you to know—" He took a shaky breath. "I want you to know I tried. I just wasn't good enough."

Rime's cruel winters and unfamiliar diseases were particularly brutal for the Seachosen. Emmett's parents had lived longer than most in their small community, but that was hardly a consolation. Only one generation removed from the warm southern shores, they'd both died within a few days of falling ill during the Winter of Graves.

Theresa had held on three days longer, but the strength that carried her through burying her parents and two children, as well as a difficult birth the midwife said should have killed both her and Carlo, finally failed her. Emmett had been the one left to pick up the pieces, the least prepared of them all to deal with so much loss, so much grief. So much responsibility.

Emmett hoped his family had at least found peace in the afterlife. The Seachosen believed their souls would be guided home by the stars, the same as sailors at sea. When Emmett's infant sister died, some of the neighbors who'd come to sit with the family had whispered that Rime's lights could confuse souls, dooming them to forever wander the wards, looking for a path in the constantly shifting glow.

Emmett's parents had reassured him as long as someone's body was buried outside the wards, their soul would follow and find the stars overhead. For all their sakes, Emmett prayed that was the truth, not just his father's way of placating a distraught five-year-old boy wondering where his baby sister had gone.

The wards ensured that every time Emmett looked up, he was only reminded of who controlled his life. He couldn't be certain any god could hear him, and it was hard not to wonder if the cruel magic that kept his family prisoners in their lives would cling to them even after death.

If the next few hours went wrong, he might find out firsthand.

RORY

15 BELLS

The section of Riverfront Street that housed Katya's bathhouse was mercifully smooth and level. Katya didn't allow animals into the building, so Rory stopped across the street, consigning Blizzard to a relatively sheltered nook with a clear view of the bathhouse door. It took him longer than usual to leave her arm, claws digging into her jacket. When she managed to detach him, he burbled softly, tilting his head to study her with those too-bright pink eyes. Maybe he could sense Rory was running out of time. Or maybe he just didn't like being left outside in the increasingly bitter wind.

Normally, Rory would have waited to use the token Katya had given her that morning until she couldn't stand being around herself. Rory's deliveries didn't earn her second-level access often enough that she could afford to squander it. But the bathhouse wasn't just a source of income for the Rapids while the river was frozen; it was Katya's primary base, the center of her empire. The outer levels turned a respectable profit from people willing to part with their coin for the luxury of warm water, and the inner circle provided a level of security that little in Rime could match. In the aftermath of an assassination attempt, Katya would almost certainly be in her bathhouse, and if Rory knew that, the thief did too.

Besides, if Rory couldn't find the thief, at least she could enjoy a last bath. There was no sense letting the token go to whoever went over her corpse.

Rory showed her token to the doorkeeper, who let her into the first level of the building. She passed a series of taps and basins where people handed over a copper in exchange for a small allotment of warm water to wash their faces and hands. The two circles stamped on the disk in her hand meant the next doorkeeper allowed her past him into a space with small curtained-off alcoves and attendants who handed new arrivals a pail of hot water, a folded towel, and a sliver of bittersweet juniper berry soap.

The second level was much warmer than the first, and Rory usually relished stepping through the door. Today, the warm, moist air was somehow even harder to breathe than the bitterly cold wind outside. She waved off the attendant and stood still, forcing her lungs to draw in the deepest breaths possible, until she was reasonably confident she could carry a heavy pail without dropping it to the wet stone floor and possibly following it herself. Steam turned the loose strands escaping her braid into curled tangles that brushed against the raw skin on her cheek and jaw, igniting an aching itch she tried to ignore. It was her own fault for clawing at it earlier.

Rory chose an alcove where, if she adjusted the curtain properly, she had a clear view of the end of the room and the two guards flanking the thick cedar door leading to the third level. Tokens with three circles stamped on them were handed out sparingly to Katya's most valued associates. Anyone granted access was required to leave their clothing and weapons in the anteroom directly behind the door before entering the central baths, a set of deep pools cut directly into the rock floor. In the third level, Katya was surrounded by the water her gift controlled, and anyone who wanted to approach her directly was incapable of hiding a weapon. Not that it would do her much good against a killer who was coming after her with magic.

Few people ever went through that door, and even fewer were handed back their token by the guards when they left.

Rory had only been given a token with three circles once. She'd delivered a letter from one of Katya's scouts, a servant working in a Cohort mansion. The moment Katya had read it, she'd begun ranting about gifted traitors who sold out to the Cohort for a few coins, then flung a decanter across the room so hard that glass shards had hit Rory's boots. One of her suppliers had been compromised, and if Katya and her people had arrived as planned to pick up their shipment, they'd have walked into a trap. The information had been valuable enough for Katya to allow Rory a chance to access her inner circle, even if on a one-time basis. Soaking her whole body in the warm water had been a luxury. It was one of the few times Rory hadn't been perpetually reminded of her raw and chapped skin.

If she could catch the assassin, Katya might decide that was worth a permanent third-level entry token. Rory would consider that almost as valuable a reward as the money the other syndicates were offering.

Rory set her bucket, towel, and soap on the stone bench at the back of the alcove, then sat down in the space left, collapsing gracelessly onto the stone shelf as soon as she bent her knees. She slumped against the wall, dizzy and panting.

Her heavy outdoor clothes in the warmth of the bathhouse probably weren't helping. Rory struggled out of her coat and scarf, hanging them on hooks in the wall, then peeled her sweater and both shirts over her head together.

Rory watched the third-level door and the attendants and patrons she could see through the gap in the curtain until she could more or less breathe again. She dipped one side of the towel into the pail of warm water, rubbed the soap into one corner, and washed her face and neck, avoiding the scabs on her shoulders and the area around her eyes. Scrubbing at the lichen patches when they were already bleeding would only do more damage, and she had no intention of closing her eyes, even for a few moments.

A heart thief who'd killed six people without revealing their own face wouldn't be easy to catch in the act of surveilling Katya. But if they were desperate enough, they might start to make mistakes. That could give them away, but only if Rory kept her eyes open.

Rory cupped some water in her hand and gently rubbed the lichen patch on her face to remove the blood and dead skin, then did the same for any other scabs she could reach, glancing out the curtain each time she heard footsteps pass. She scrubbed under her arms with the soapy section of the towel until her skin tingled and turned red. After a moment's consideration, she rinsed any remaining soap off her towel in the pail. She'd cleaned up as well as she could without compromising her ability to quickly catch the thief if they appeared.

Washing her feet wasn't worth the risk of taking off her boots. Her hair could have used a good rinse, but she couldn't be sure she wouldn't have to chase her quarry out into the storm. Old Sue had always claimed Rory would catch her death if she went outdoors with wet hair, and it would be just her luck to steal her heart back and die a week later of some illness.

Then again, it could just as easily happen next month, a knife to the gut from someone desperate enough to steal her meager purse. There was no real future in this city. Rory probably had another one or two years, if she was lucky. The life expectancy in her profession was twenty-five and she'd passed that mark last thaw. She was always one angry message recipient away from being tossed into the river or the bay in pieces.

So why was she fighting so hard to get her heart back?

Maybe it was the same reason the beggars on street corners dragged themselves to their place day after day. Why the prisoners Rory had seen hauled away to the Bastion still struggled against their guards. Why Old Sue kept gasping in each labored breath, even as her body failed and crumbled like she was already in her grave. Something inside all of them wanted to live. Kicking, clawing, fighting for one more breath, one more touch, one more smile, one more day watching the lights come out.

Rory bent forward to dip her cloth back into the pail, glancing at the nook across from her own. The alcove's curtain swayed slightly, pulled back like hers in a way that implied casual oversight but almost certainly wasn't. It would take some nerve for the heart thief to get this close to their target so soon after a failed attempt, but the unexpected audacity might have worked.

At least, it might have worked if the thief hadn't been taking their plan right from the heart they'd stolen, whose owner was still very much alive and wanted it back.

Rory scrubbed water off her skin with the dry piece of the towel and pulled her shirts back over her head, watching the curtain. There was no reason not to check on her suspicions right away. At worst, she would disturb one customer, and at best...well, it wouldn't be the first time someone had been stabbed in Katya's establishment.

If Rory could slip around the back of the room and come up from behind the alcove, she might be able to take the thief by surprise, since they were probably focused on the third-level door. She slipped on her coat, pulled the hood over her hair, and wrapped her scarf loosely around her neck. Sweat started to trickle down her back under the heavy clothes.

Rory untied the straps securing the hilt of her knife and wrapped her hand around the grip as she ducked back out into the steamy room. She made her way towards the door, then turned just before reaching it and retraced her steps carefully, avoiding splashing through the small channels that fed water from the alcoves to the floor drains. She rolled the soles of her boots so there would be no distinct sound of footsteps. Raising her free hand, she prepared to yank back the curtain and surprise the person inside. Just a few steps more.

Someone walked in front of her, and Rory's purposeful momentum carried her directly into them. The pail they held swung into the wall with a metallic clang and a loud splash before rolling away along the floor.

"Watch where you're going, would you?" its holder snapped.

Rory tensed, pivoting on her heels as the curtain flew open and a tall, slender figure bolted past. She cursed under her breath, trying not to slide on the slick floor, boots splashing through trails of water making their way to the drains. The thief had the advantage now, and by the time Rory reached the exit, there was no sign of him in the room beyond. The door to the street swayed slightly back and forth.

The thief was taller than Rory, with longer limbs and the advantage of a heart that wasn't slowing with every beat. She couldn't catch him if she tried to outright chase him down, but that wasn't her only chance at finding him. She stopped short of walking past the startled attendant at the second door. Ignoring the confused stares of several bathhouse patrons, she walked back to the alcove the thief had vacated, pulled back the curtain, and stepped inside.

The thief had taken Rory's life, her future, her memories. But no one could steal your gift by stealing your heart.

Rory ran her fingers over the rough fabric of a canvas coat, a knitted scarf, and a greasy-edged hat.

Whoever he was, the thief confused her. He was smart enough to use Rory's heart to sort out Katya's most likely hiding place, but if he could see her memories of Katya, he would also have been able to watch how her gift worked. He should have known letting her get her hands on something that belonged to him would draw her a map straight to him. Either he'd panicked and bolted without thinking of what he was leaving behind, or he wanted Rory to follow him.

Either way, Rory didn't have a choice. The longer she waited to confront the thief, the weaker she would get. In a fight, right now, she might get the upper hand. If he'd intended for her to find him, he was going to regret it.

Rory picked up the scarf, the brown yarn faded and fraying, and focused.

The memory that flickered through her thoughts was a picture of herself, seen from afar, pushing her way through the morning's High Quarter crowd. To the scarf's owner, her red coat was vivid, and she stood out in the hurrying shuffle like an ember in a grate full of ash and coals. If she'd had any doubt this man was the heart thief, the vision of his fingers pushing up her sleeve would have instantly quelled them. A startling, vivid flare of light appeared in his hand, a physical heart glowing blue and green and purple. Rory blinked on instinct, the afterimage still burning behind her eyes, and the vision dissolved into smoky shadows.

When Rory opened her eyes again, the floor ignited in a line of fire. She tucked the scarf into her pocket and followed its trail out the doors and into the street.

Rory stopped by Blizzard's windowsill and held out her arm. He scrambled up, then tucked himself inside her hood and shuffled around to face forward. His heartbeat pumped fast and loud against Rory's ear, drowning out the fading stutter of her own. She wrapped her fingers around the scarf and took a breath that felt worse than useless in the frigid wind.

The light tracing along the cobblestones led toward Bell Square, the third and largest collection of street vendors in town. While Market Row catered to the rich, and the River Quarter's square offered goods the people near it could actually afford, Bell Square housed merchants who sold items imported at the shipyards. Traders there offered pigments and dyes for weavers, exotic spices for cooks and bakers, and the most valuable commodity of all: news from the world outside the wards.

Three ships had docked in the port yesterday. The market would be chaos.

Rory once again had to admit a grudging respect for her quarry's skills. Trying to lose himself in a crowd was smart. But he was also walking into a place where one shout from her could have him dead on the pavement in seconds.

Cohort law required all out-of-town sellers to do business in Bell Square, under the shadow of their own offices. Officially, it made policing the market easier and prevented people like Rory from stealing the traders' expensive wares, although more likely the Cohort officials just didn't want to walk far for their cut of the goods and profits. Either way, there were at least ten Cohort guards scattered around the square at any given time. But Rory wouldn't let the patrols kill the thief for the same reason she hadn't shouted his identity in the bathhouse. It had to be her knife through his chest, or her heart would be gone for good.

Rory's gift led her down a shortcut, which ran through an alley closer to the bell tower than most hearing residents were comfortable walking. Rory would have taken the potentially mind-bending notes of the bells over the chatter and shouts that slammed into her like a wave as she turned the corner and faced the square. She grimaced, trying to block out the sounds and focus on the bright line cutting across the cobblestones in front of her.

Her quarry couldn't be far. The light from her gift was nearly blinding.

Rory wove her way between haggling merchants and buyers with baskets and bags draped over their arms. One of the bell ringers was engaged in an energetic, silent conversation with the current apprentice, hands flying. The child, so small Rory doubted she could pull the rope hard enough to coax any sound from the bells, rubbed her shoulder and pointed in the same direction Rory's gift led.

Rory let go of the scarf and tucked it into her pocket, blinking away the light behind her eyes. If she was going to stand a chance of winning a fight with this thief, she needed her vision clear. And she'd rather have her head up, looking for a person's face, than have her eyes on the ground. The thief had already taken her by surprise while she was distracted, twice over. She wouldn't give him a third opportunity.

A bright green swirl crossed the sky overhead, and even the far side of the square was visible in its glow. In a spot where two carts blocked some of the bitter wind, Rory caught a glimpse of a figure taller than most of the others around him. His dingy white shirt stood out among the sealskin coats or sooty smocks most of the square's patrons wore. He glanced over his shoulder like a skittish caribou being herded through the city gates. His eyes met Rory's for a fraction of a second.

Then, he bolted.

Rory pushed through the crowd behind him. She was smaller, able to squeeze between people faster, and for a few moments she was gaining on him.

He turned away from the packed center of the square and broke out of the crowd, ducking into an alley that led toward the Smoke Quarter.

Rory's legs and lungs burned fiercely as she continued her pursuit, her vision dark and blurring out around the edges. She blinked, trying to keep the pale gleam of the thief's shirt in view. Running did him no good in the long term, but she preferred not to let him get to the part of town where he might be able to acquire a weapon.

She was so focused on not losing sight of the thief through the odd sparkle clouding her vision, like snow in a streetlamp's glow, that she didn't notice the wall in front of her until she'd crashed into it.

Rory dragged herself up off the ground, panting so hard she could taste blood in the back of her throat, and stumbled around the turn she'd failed to make.

The thief was still in view, running down a long, narrow alley.

She couldn't keep up this pace without her heart. There was no way she could catch up to him. But they were far enough from Bell Square that the Cohort guards, if they heard any scuffle at all, wouldn't consider it their problem. Rory had seen them walk past houses with the audible screams and shattering dishes of a domestic dispute and ignore muggings down side streets. If the guards couldn't line their own pockets well enough from the gratitude of the rescued victim, they couldn't be bothered to intervene. Neither Rory nor the thief would be worth their time.

If she could slow him down, she'd have a chance to take back her heart.

Rory's gift showed her the most direct path to her destination, but that didn't mean she had to follow it herself.

Rory planted her feet firmly on the ground beneath her, taking a deep breath and blinking away the residual specks of light that had invaded her vision. She pushed back her hood to keep it from interfering with her view and her sense of the wind's speed and direction, ignoring Blizzard's indignant cooing at being subjected to the storm again. Breathing slowly in and out, she wrapped the fingers of one hand around the grip of her knife.

When Jax had taught Rory how to fight, he'd instructed her not to aim her initial attacks for the chest or throat. Instead, he showed her how to slash her attacker's arms or legs, slicing through the muscles that let them hold a knife or stand to face her. Rory bit her lip, focusing on the place in the thief's leg that made the difference between him running away from her and crawling.

He'd almost reached the end of the alley. She had one chance to get this right.

She closed her free hand around the thief's scarf.

In the moment between a hazy vision of the Bastion's walls and a brilliant flash of light at her feet, Rory snapped her arm forward and let go of the knife.

The only sound that followed was her blade clattering against stone. Rory blinked away the afterimage behind her eyes, squinting to see the results of her throw. The first thing she noticed was her knife spinning to a stop on the icy cobblestones, silver blade glinting green and purple under the lights flickering overhead.

A moment later, the thief stumbled, catching himself clumsily on a wall before sprawling onto the ground. His hands clutched at the wound spilling a bright stream of crimson into the drifted snow. He struggled to stand, then collapsed again to the snowy street.

Rory frowned. His clumsy, panicked gait must have taken him out of the direct path of the knife, or he wouldn't be able to move that leg at all. Still, if the wound she'd managed to inflict was keeping him on the ground, Rory couldn't complain.

She calmly stalked past him and picked up her knife, then spun around, holding the point over his chest. As Jax had reminded her several times, the heart wasn't an easy thing to strike. It might take a few tries to get her blade through the thief's ribs in the right place.

His bloodstained hands flew up between the knife and his chest. "Stop! I don't have it!"

Rory paused, the blade an inch from his fingers. Not because she believed him, but because this would be a lot easier if she cracked him over the head with the knife handle first. He couldn't fight her if he was unconscious.

In the moment it took her to change the position of the knife, the thief had clawed at the neck of his shirt to reveal a locket on a long chain. It was about the size of Rory's thumb, shaped like an anatomical heart. The metal glittered and sparkled in the dim light like her starsilver blade.

"What is this?"

The thief winced. "It holds the hearts after I…after I take one."

Rory had never heard of heart thieves needing a container for the lives they stole. She lifted the locket with the tip of her knife. There was a small catch on the side, and she unlatched it carefully, paying just as much attention to the thief's hands and feet as the locket. The inside was tarnished and stained with what almost looked like soot, as if the thief had been carrying tiny flaring bits of cinderpine inside. But the metal was cold to the touch.

"It's empty! See? I already gave your heart away!" The thief's eyes darted between Rory's face and her knife, the lights overhead reflected in wide pupils surrounded by only the narrowest ring of brown.

Last month, Rory had watched a cart driver put his pony out of its misery when it slipped on icy cobbles and snapped a foreleg. She'd skirted the animal's scrambling legs on her way to a delivery, but she caught a glimpse of rolling, white-rimmed eyes before the owner pinned the pony's head down to finish the job the street had started. That was the most abject terror Rory had witnessed in another living thing, until today.

She scowled. Whoever this thief was, he was a poor excuse for the monster she'd been expecting. He'd been basically incapacitated by a wound that, by Rime's standards, was little more than a scratch, and reduced to wild-eyed, helpless fear by his own victim.

Then again, she had nothing to lose. His only weapon was the magic he'd already used on her. She was the one with a sharp blade.

"You'll understand if I don't take your word for it."

Blizzard chittered from Rory's shoulder, fluffing himself up menacingly.

"I wasn't taking your heart for me," the thief gasped, hands pressed against his leg again. "I swear."

"Then who do I need to kill?" Rory didn't really expect an honest answer. The thief could give her the name of anyone he'd like dead. Still, she'd have a lead to follow up on if she didn't get her heart back when she put her blade through his.

"You can't." The thief winced. "Won't get it back that way."

Rory shrugged, tilting the knife so the lights overhead reflected off the rippled pattern of metal in the blade. "My knife is starsilver. All I need is this, and two minutes alone with whoever has my heart."

"You might be able to get it back from a thief that way. But he isn't one."

"Give me a *name*. Because all I'm hearing right now is you trying to pawn off my anger on some unspecified third party."

"Marcus Deahl. Head of the Star Syndicate."

Rory scowled. "How convenient. The only syndicate leader who never leaves his fortress. The one no one has seen in twenty years." No one who wasn't a loyal subject or who had lived to tell the tale, anyway.

"If I didn't give him a heart every month, he said he'd kill my son!"

Rory looked down at her blade.

Her fingers closed around the horn handle.

Jax's catlike eyes gleamed in the single candle lighting the room. "He was holding that knife, must have wrestled it away from his killer somehow. At least he went down fighting."

Rory swallowed the sick feeling burning the back of her throat. She squeezed her eyes closed to block out the red swirling through her vision.

Instead of comforting blackness, a dim room appeared. A figure paced back and forth along the length of it before stopping in front of her. Its harsh voice whispered, "After he finds the mark, finish him."

Rory blinked, then gasped, nearly dropping the knife as the world around her burst into glowing sparks.

"We don't want that horrid thing." Mom tried to snatch the blade away with the hand that wasn't holding the carved grip of Dad's

wedding knife, a bloodsoaked mate to the one sheathed at her own waist. Rory clutched the rough horn handle tighter.

The light she'd seen was the same glow that sparkled in Dad's eyes when he was on a trail. He could find anyone if he had something that belonged to them. And she was holding the knife that could tell her where his killer had gone.

She closed her eyes again.

Her father's face appeared in front of her, cloaked in shadow, lined with fear.

"Please, don't do this," Dad whispered.

And then Rory's hands plunged the knife into his stomach.

A glittering golden trail ignited under Rory's feet, stretching out across the floor, under their door, into the city. It went dark the moment her mother yanked the knife from Rory's hands and shoved it back into Jax's, so sharply and carelessly it drew a bright line of blood across his palm.

"Get it out of my house."

At ten years old, Rory had been ready to follow her gift's trail to the man who'd murdered her father so she could put his own blade straight through his heart. Killing this man might make his son want to put it through hers.

"Let's say, for the moment, I believe you. Why did you take *my* heart?"

If the thief was telling the truth, Marcus had likely been sending him after people who had double-crossed him or were a threat to his power. Rory didn't think she fell into any such category, but if there was a reason she'd been targeted, she wanted to know. It wouldn't do her much good to get her heart back and then have an arrow put through it because the Star still wanted her out of the picture.

"I missed the mark this time. I got desperate." The thief swallowed hard. "I was supposed to get the head of the Rapids. She had better security than I was expecting."

"So not only did you take my heart, but you did it as an afterthought to save your own skin?" Rory had more or less known that already. It still stung to hear it from her killer. She was seriously considering stabbing him whether that could return her heart or not. But there was a small possibility that someone who could get in and out of the Star Syndicate's stronghold, who had the capability to take Rory's heart out of her chest, might be able to put it back.

"Do you want to live?" Rory asked.

The thief nodded.

"Then you're going to steal my heart back for me."

The thief shook his head. "Please," he whispered. "Please don't ask me to do that. I don't know what Marcus would do if I betrayed him like that."

"Then there's no point in me not stabbing you, is there?"

"Please, don't!" he gasped. "Please. If it was only my life at stake, I'd try. But Carlo. Please. You can't ask me to risk my son's life." His voice was drowning in the same cornered panic threatening to bleed into Rory's own words.

She sighed, letting the tip of the knife drop. "You should have thought of him before you got involved with the most ruthless syndicate in Rime."

"I…please. Just put the knife down." He shivered harder, curling in over his wounded leg. "Could we talk about this somewhere warmer?" The bitter wind tore at his thin, damp shirt, and frost had collected at the tips of his hair. His hands, where they weren't stained with the blood still seeping from his leg, were turning blue.

"You can freeze for all I care."

"If I do, you'll never get your heart back."

Unfortunately, he had a point. Rory scowled. "Then you'd better come up with a plan, thief, or you're still no good to me."

"Emmett."

"What?"

"My name is Emmett. Not thief."

Damn him. He knew enough about manipulating people to know that giving her his name would make him a little more human and a little harder to kill.

"This isn't a dance in a Cohort ballroom. I don't need your name; I need a solution." Rory tilted the knife in her hand for emphasis, dragging in another difficult breath. "You're the reason I'm dying. So you're going to fix it."

"There has to be a way we both get out of this without putting a syndicate target on us. What if I get you someone else's heart?"

Rory scowled. Without her own heart, she'd slowly be changed into the person whose life he put inside her. Someone else's memories, feelings, thoughts, hopes, dreams, crowding out her own until there was nothing left of Rory Blake. It sounded like nothing more than a different way to die. "No. I want mine back."

Emmett swallowed. "If you think you can get into the Star's headquarters and take your heart back from their leader, maybe it's your brain that's gone missing."

"Don't play games with me. You're just trying to stall until I run out of time." She looked from the blade to him. "I know what your priorities are."

"He's just a kid. Please."

She blinked against a wave of dizziness. "I know. He doesn't want to die. Neither do I."

"I c-can't help you if I die in th-this alley." Emmett's voice had fallen to a shuddering whisper. "Can we please talk about this s-somewhere better?"

Rory nodded, but it was less a concession to him than a practical choice on her own behalf. She was already struggling to breathe, and the icy wind was stealing even more of her precious air. She slipped the knife back into its sheath, taking the extra moment to wrap the leather cords around its grip so no one could easily pull it back out. If she was going to be spending any amount of time around this man, she needed to be sure he couldn't double-cross her. This had been a lot easier when she'd been planning to kill him.

She pulled Emmett's scarf out of her pocket. He blinked, but didn't have time to say anything before she wrapped the cloth around his leg and knotted it tight. He yelped like a kicked dog.

"Do you want to bleed to death?" she snapped. "Shut up."

He didn't. "Why do you have my scarf?"

"How do you think I found you? I'm a guide." It was starting to make sense that he hadn't known what Rory was. It was Marcus who'd gotten her heart and all her memories. Who knew all her strategies. That could be a serious problem. "When you left behind half your clothes in the bathhouse, you basically gave me a path right to you."

Emmett winced and gasped as he struggled to stand. Rory didn't move to support him until he was on his feet. If she'd bent over to try and help, she might have found herself on the ground next to him.

"You couldn't have brought my coat, I guess," he mumbled.

"I thought I was going to have to kill you. You weren't going to need it. And the scarf was easier to carry."

Emmett stumbled over a loose cobble and nearly dragged Rory to the ground. She yanked him back to his feet, ignoring his pained yelp. Blood continued seeping through the brown cloth knotted around his leg. Even if the wound wasn't quite as deep as Rory had intended, her knife had done damage that required more than a makeshift bandage to repair. And unfortunately, she needed Emmett alive.

"We need to find a healer," she muttered.

Most of the healers in Rime would be at work in the Smoke Quarter, treating injuries at the factories and forges who had contracts for daily assistance. This time of day, they'd have their hands full. Freelancers charged a small fortune, but there was one who lived only a few blocks away.

"What is your name, anyway?" Emmett asked. "Marcus never told me." Apparently, he was under the impression that having given Rory his name meant she needed to return the courtesy. Knowing it might make him feel a little more guilty about what he'd done to her, though.

"Rory." She shook her head, trying to clear the sensation that someone was packing snow into her ears. Emmett's next stumble nearly took them both to the icy cobblestones. "Now stop asking me questions and pay attention to where you're walking."

The house Rory stopped outside had a row of small, slightly worn stones at the beginning of the path to its door. Rory grimaced, stepped over them carefully, then let Emmett brace himself on her shoulder to get past them as well. A faint orange glow spread over the path, and Rory looked up to see an open door and a figure standing in it, holding up a lantern.

Tal had known Rory was coming since she'd stepped over the threshold stones. His gift was more than simply healing; he could sense a tragedy before it occurred. In a city like Rime, that could easily be overwhelming, so he'd shut himself away in this little house, the stones surrounding it veined with enough starsilver to create a miniature version of the wards around his life.

Rumor had it the stones were a gift from the master of the forge where Tal had once been under contract. Tal had been dismissed from that position when he became increasingly tormented with visions of fire and death. A day later, the entire building had exploded. Tal had returned to pull as many of the injured as he could save from the flames, and the guilt-ridden forge master had given him the ore as a parting payment.

Of course, another rumor said Tal had stolen the ore while pretending to assist the workers, but Rory didn't care which was true as long as she could consider him an ally.

Since Tal hadn't slammed the door on them by the time Rory half-led, half-dragged a severely limping Emmett up the front walk, he still considered her an ally too.

Emmett slumped against the doorframe, and Rory made sure he was somewhat balanced before shifting his weight off her shoulder, rubbing her aching muscles. "Tal, I'm gonna owe you for this one, but I need some help."

"I think he needs it, actually." Tal looked at her with a frown. "What you need, I can't give."

Rory had no idea whether the tragedies Tal saw could be prevented, or if once he had the visions it meant the future was set in stone. He hadn't been able to stop the forge fire, but maybe it wouldn't have happened if Tal could have convinced someone there to believe him. The idea still left a cold pit in Rory's stomach.

If she let herself give in to the fear and believe she was doomed, she'd simply lie down and die. She'd rather spend her last hours fighting for her life, even if it was a lost cause.

Tal held out a pair of gloves to Emmett. "Put these on," he insisted, and Emmett did. Once Emmett's hands were covered, Tal helped him in the door and sat him down on a rough wooden chair near the fireplace. Rory stood close to the fire, peeling off her gloves and holding her hands out to the warmth. Her fingers had turned purple to the first knuckle.

Tal unwound Emmett's scarf and examined the wound dispassionately. "I can't fix this completely," he said. "But I can buy a little time before it starts to unravel."

"I know." It wasn't the first time Rory had needed the services of someone with a healing gift. The ability to repair damage done to another person's body was almost as rare as Emmett's power, and it came with a steep price for the wielder. Healers absorbed a part of whatever injury they treated and rarely tackled more than minor and surface level damage. Going deeper could kill them, with no guarantee the patient would survive either. Rory had only seen that once. A woman who worked at a Flare foundry tried to save a smith who'd been crushed under a falling crate of ore. Neither of them had survived.

Of course, the price in pain and risk that a healing gift exacted from the wielder was passed on to those who sought it out. Tal's services would cost almost everything left in Rory's purse. At least he asked for a bit less than the ambitious and greedy gifteds who'd taken up residence in the High Quarter, who charged the rich a fortune for alleviating hangovers and calming ulcers.

Tal spread his hands over the gash, wincing.

Emmett grimaced, head thrown back over the chair, teeth gritted against the pain of muscle and skin and nerves knitting themselves back together in moments instead of days. Rory'd felt it herself, but she couldn't summon much sympathy for her would-be killer. He was the reason she'd be dead in two days. The least he could do was suffer a little first.

When it was over, Emmett slumped forward, panting. Tal stumbled a few steps back, leaning on the fireplace mantel and rubbing his own leg. He turned to Rory, looking from her face to her fingers.

"I'll make some tea for you," he said. "You'll need to stay here until he's feeling up to walking, anyway."

Rory nodded. The cold in her fingers was worse than frostbite. No matter how carefully she protected them, no matter how close to the fire she stood, the chill only spread.

Emmett, on the other hand, looked healthier. The paleness under his copper skin had mostly vanished, replaced by a warmer flush. His eyes were still squinted closed, and sharp lines of pain creased his forehead. Their depth made them seem less connected to his injury and more of a permanent situation. At least he no longer looked like he was going to crumple to the ground at a moment's notice and force Rory to drag him through the streets.

Not all the silver in his hair had been frost. Rory couldn't see any lichen marks on his skin, but all along his temples and in the patch at his forehead that stuck almost straight up, a scattering of icy gray was picked out by the firelight.

Emmett's eyes began to blink open.

Not wanting to be caught staring at him, Rory looked into the fire.

A log fell, sparks crackling and swirling upward. A small chunk of embers tumbled out onto the hearth, the bright orange and red glow rapidly turning to charred black as the stone leached out its warmth.

As Tal returned with her tea, Rory kicked the lump of wood back into the heart of the flames. She wrapped her fingers around the mug, breathing in the steam and watching the tiny coal catch fire again, pulsing with the glow.

EMMETT

18 BELLS

Emmett had seen healers work before. Once, when his father's drawknife slipped and sliced deep into his thigh, his mother had foregone the usual bandages and bottle of alcohol. Emmett had watched curiously while she moved her fingers slowly and carefully over the wound. The muscle and skin in his father's leg pulled together and closed over, with only a faint pinkish line to show for the trouble.

Emmett's mother had never advertised her healing. Even when money was tight, when the pay could have put enough food for three families on the table, none of them ever discussed the possibility. His mother's gift wasn't something to be sold.

Aside from his father's leg wound, Emmett only remembered his mother using her healing one other time: during Carlo's birth. She'd trusted the midwife not to reveal her secret, and the situation had been dire enough to warrant magical intervention. If Theresa hadn't stopped bleeding, if Carlo hadn't started breathing, Emmett knew his mother would have let her own gift tear her to pieces trying to save them. After that night, Emmett and Theresa had agreed Carlo would be their last and only child. If his birth had been any more dangerous, they could have lost three family members in one night.

Emmett's normal scrapes and bruises had always been allowed to heal naturally, so no one would become suspicious if his injuries disappeared overnight, and he'd never broken a bone like some of his friends. He had no idea it would hurt so much when a healer used their gift on someone. His leg still ached, even though the damage had been more or less repaired. A residual tingling tug of magic held the wound closed, like invisible threads.

He'd considered trying to escape once the healer was finished. Rory was obviously feeling the effects of her missing heart, and he'd hoped to be able to outrun her. With Emmett's leg in the shape it was in, however, their chances remained even.

Rory leaned on the fireplace, occasionally frowning at him over the mug of tea she was sipping. If she could have stabbed him with her eyes, he'd have a dozen gashes worse than the one that had just been repaired. Her pigeon, perched on her shoulder, gave him an equally disturbing glare. The fact that Rory had brought Emmett to a healer was only partially comforting. She still looked like she wanted him dead. If he wanted to survive long enough to escape once Rory's heart gave out more completely, Emmett needed her to believe he was cooperating, and that keeping him alive was still in her best interests.

Tal grimaced and rubbed a hand over his leg as he re-entered the room. A lifetime of using his gift had left a landscape of scars on the healer's arms and face, glinting against his brown skin in the firelight. He set down a clay cup on the small table beside Emmett. "Drink this. You'll need it after losing that much blood."

Emmett forced himself to swallow a few sips of the bitter liquid. Even though the taste made him want to throw up, he couldn't afford not to drink something while he could get it.

Rory set down her mug on the mantel and took the small pouch Tal held out as he turned to her. The tips of her pale fingers were still blue, despite the steam rising off the drink she'd been holding.

"This won't cure you, but it might help with the dizziness," Tal said.

Rory took the bag from him and opened it, sniffing the contents. She stuck one finger into it and tasted the powder she pulled out.

"How much will I owe you?" she asked.

"Make it three more silver and we'll call it even."

"For salt?"

"And some herbs that help people who come to me with less magical heart problems."

Rory sighed, then counted out the extra coins. Once Tal left with his payment, she leaned back against the mantel and looked out the window, where the sky had darkened to indigo twilight. She picked up her mug again and took another long sip, draining it to the dregs. "We should be going."

"We can't stay here?" Emmett wasn't looking forward to going back out into the frigid city.

"I've put Tal through enough trouble. I'm not going to risk getting him on the wrong side of the Star because someone saw us here. As long as you can walk, we're gone."

Emmett looked from the windows to his leg, then gingerly stood. Rory watched him with no attempt to help. Maybe she was making sure he could stand on his own and she wouldn't have to drag him across town, or she just didn't care if he fell on his face in the middle of the floor. Fortunately, his leg took his weight with minimal protest.

Rory picked up Emmett's bloodied scarf from the floor. "Just in case you get any funny ideas about running off," she said, rolling it up and shoving it into an inside pocket of her coat, where Emmett had no chance of casually retrieving it. "It doesn't matter how attached you were to this. Now that it's got your blood all over it, I can track you anywhere, anytime. So don't try and run, and I won't have to slice your leg open again. Understand?"

Emmett swallowed and nodded.

"Good. Now let's go." Rory opened the door, and a swirl of snow whipped in. The chill slapped Emmett in the face. He shuddered and wrapped his arms around himself, already feeling half frozen and not at all looking forward to searching for a place to stay in the miserable storm.

Rory glanced at him, then turned away from the door to the small kitchen where Tal was preparing some sort of ground herb mixture. "Tal, can we borrow a coat?" she shouted over the rasp of a stone pestle against the sides of a bowl.

"We?" the healer asked, frowning. "Borrow?"

"By 'we' I mean him, and by 'borrow' I mean you might get it back if we live through this, which we probably won't."

"Kind of figured as much. Well, I don't guarantee clients once they walk out my door. I fixed his leg. Deal said nothing about making sure he didn't freeze two bells later."

"Let me guess. I've got to pay."

"You got it."

Rory grumbled under her breath as she opened her purse and fished out more coins.

Tal looked them over, and after pocketing them, reached for the coats hanging on hooks near the door. He pulled down a worn brown canvas jacket, by far the oldest one hanging there, and handed it over. Tal looked from the coat to Emmett's hands. "You want to take my gloves too, that's extra."

Rory grabbed Emmett's hands, pulling the gloves off and tossing them onto a rickety shelf nailed to the wall beside the coathooks. "Coat's all we need."

As much as Emmett would have liked to argue that point, Rory didn't need protection from his gift anymore. And he couldn't think of any other reason she'd spend even more money on him.

Emmett shrugged the coat over his shoulders and slipped his arms into the slightly too short sleeves. Rory opened the door again, and they both stepped out. The night's chill settled in Emmett's bones immediately, and the snow squeaked underfoot with every step.

The streets were fairly busy with soot-stained forge laborers on their way home, and factory workers headed to evening shifts, but almost no one looked up against the howling wind. Even the pair of Cohort officers on patrol passed by them without a glance. Emmett and Rory were two more nameless figures in an unconcerned crowd.

Rory led the way toward the River Quarter. Emmett trailed behind her, close enough she wouldn't need to wonder if he'd slipped off down an alley, but not so close he'd make her nervous. At least more nervous than she already appeared. One hand was always on the grip of her knife, and her gaze flickered constantly across the housefronts, down the alleys, and over her shoulder to him.

Rory was moving quickly, her heart apparently bolstered by the powder the healer had given her. Emmett doubted she'd believe he legitimately lost track of her if she had to hunt him down again. He would have been worried about getting separated from her if not for the fur that gleamed like a beacon on the hood of her coat under each streetlamp she passed. The rest of her clothing was serviceable shades of brown leather and gray reindeer-hair knits, so the coat stood out. Even with several years' wear on it, the dark purple-red had remained vivid, and the tattered wolf's fur around the hood was nearly pure white.

Her satchel's buckles gleamed with starsilver's inherent glow, most likely infused with a pickpocket-repelling charm. That sort of enchantment made sense for a messenger, the way a smith might purchase a hammer that dulled the sounds of its use. Emmett's father had owned a small saw that would cut only wood. Emmett used that tool when he was first learning his family's trade and put it in Carlo's hand once he was strong enough to draw the jagged teeth through a plank.

Small items like a buckle or practical ones like an alloyed saw blade were common enough to own, but the knife Rory had threatened him with in the alley wasn't the sort of thing carried by anyone less than a syndicate lieutenant. The large, heavy blade would have cost a small fortune. Emmett couldn't imagine Rory having that kind of money, or spending it on a blade like that if she did. A starsilver knife was a status symbol, unless someone wanted it for a specific job, like stealing back a heart.

He would have assumed she'd bought, borrowed, or stolen the blade that day, but she'd had the sheath on her hip when he'd seen her in the morning. The leather was tooled with motifs from Iron Peaks lore, a scene of Starfall creating the crystal-blue lake at the heart of the mountains. Most of the color had worn away, although a bit of gilding clung to the falling star's trail, and flaking teal blue coated the lake.

Rory was a strange collection of contradictions and incongruity. Not the kind of person Emmett wanted to be trusting with his life or Carlo's safety. Unfortunately, he didn't have much choice in the matter.

Usually Emmett didn't envy Marcus whatever he learned from the hearts Emmett gave him. Now, he wished he knew more about the person he was trapped with. He didn't like the idea that Marcus could find some thread of a memory that showed him Rory's weak points. If she kept up her strength long enough to actually attempt a break-in, Emmett was well aware she'd take him down with her if they were caught.

At least Marcus couldn't see through Rory's eyes. Only the Star's founder had been a bloodspinner, capable of that level of control over his victims. If Marcus had inherited that gift at its full potential, he wouldn't have needed Emmett or his heart thefts, only a single drop of blood from whoever he wanted to bend to his will. Once Emmett gave Marcus a heart, its owner died, and Marcus absorbed their memories and knowledge, but that was where it stopped. Marcus couldn't puppeteer people from his mansion, twisting their limbs into doing his bidding.

Whatever the syndicate leader's gift was, he'd kept it secret for decades. Not knowing what the man was capable of was almost more terrifying than whatever power he might possess.

Eventually, they stepped out from between buildings onto the riverbank. Ice creaked and crackled in the cold, deep fissures showing pale white against the blue-gray surface. Rory tapped one foot against the ice multiple times before stepping out on it gingerly.

The wind kicked up, driving eddying swirls of snow along the surface of the river. Emmett followed Rory's steps across the open ice and onto the other side, into the part of town he'd left behind months ago. The buildings only blocked some of the wind, and he wished he had his own coat. The lining in the one Tal had given him was shredded, and most of whatever had been stuffed between it and the canvas for warmth had long since fallen out. Both elbows and the cuffs were tattered, and a long tear marred the left side, a suspicious stain circling it. Whether the coat was left behind as collateral for a healing job, or taken off a body when Tal's gift wasn't enough, Emmett didn't want to consider. He buried his hands in the pockets, grime from the seams catching under his nails, and hunched his shoulders against the chill.

In the River Quarter, fewer lanterns lined the streets, and half were smashed so badly the wind had blown out their flames. The only people on the streets at this time of night were drunks stumbling home, prostitutes in ribboned jackets headed for the gambling halls, and shadowy figures slipping in and out of alleys.

And Cohort patrols, whose actions under the cover of darkness were hard to differentiate from those of the cutthroats and robbers.

After the streetlamps were lit, respectable citizens locked their doors, banked their fires, and settled around the table with whatever food they'd prepared and whatever family they had.

A few blocks from the river, Rory stopped, looking over her shoulder. Emmett forced himself to walk a bit faster. His leg ached fiercely, but he wasn't sure if that was all due to his wound or partially because this was the furthest he'd walked in months. Aside from his trips into the High Quarter to retrieve hearts for Marcus, Emmett was restricted to pacing around his small room. He'd known doing nothing and letting himself weaken from sitting still would make escaping after heart thefts much more risky, but being in good enough condition to walk a few streets in the High Quarter without getting exhausted was different from traveling halfway across the city, some of it in a panicked chase. He'd definitely be feeling the sore muscles in the morning.

When Emmett caught up to her, Rory didn't keep moving. Instead, she looked down the street, then back at Emmett.

"Marcus will know where I live." Rory swiped a loose strand of hair away from her face. "We can't go back there."

Emmett could only nod. He wasn't looking forward to spending a night somewhere in an alley. The first and only experience he'd had with that was about six months before, during thaw. He and Carlo had still felt like they were freezing to death in the night chill.

"Any place I know to hole up is no good." Rory rounded on Emmett, her voice as sharp as the knife at her side. "The only thing working in our favor is that Marcus doesn't know you're with me. So you're going to need to find us something."

The only place Emmett had in mind, Marcus knew about too. But he'd probably never expect Emmett to willingly go there. In that respect, it might be the safest house in town. "I think I know a place."

Breaking a trail through the drifted snow was far more exhausting than following Rory. The wind had turned even colder, slicing through Emmett's coat and cutting his skin to ribbons. Rory kept trying to take back the lead, pushing past Emmett, then dropping back when she remembered he was the one who knew their destination.

"Just tell me where it is?" she finally asked.

"We're almost there." Emmett turned another corner, and the ramshackle building loomed up ahead of them. His throat tightened, and he shuddered, shaking the invisible weight off his shoulders before taking another step.

Rory looked up at the warped siding and twisted window frames. "What is this place?"

"It used to be home."

"And no one's moved in since?" Rory asked, frowning at the boarded windows. "What do they know that I don't?"

"We're in the middle of a Seachosen neighborhood. Very few people would move into a house where…" Emmett swallowed, remembering his parents' fingers joining with his own and Theresa's, tracing the grain in the support beams' wood. Superstitions about houses with their residents' lives woven into them ran nearly as deep as the magic itself. Few people wanted to risk inviting the same tragedy that had befallen the home's previous inhabitants into their own lives. "The whole neighborhood knew my family kept this place standing with our gifts. Houses like this…even the most desperate people prefer not tempting a curse."

"Except for us." Rory pulled out her knife, and Emmett stepped back as she started to pry one of the boards away from the closest window.

Emmett reached for the other end of the wood, fingertips tracing the grain. The board twisted around the nails and fell free with a clatter, revealing a cold, empty room beyond. Patches of snow had drifted in the corners, and the air carried the stale, damp scent of moldering wood.

He and Rory pulled away the rest of the boards, then Emmett pushed the warped window frame out of the way with a groaning creak.

He stepped in and turned to give Rory a hand. She'd already scrambled through the window behind him, standing in the back of the room and looking around with a distinctly unimpressed expression. Emmett wasn't sure what she saw. His view of the room wasn't colored by the weak light from the street lamp outside, but by decades of memory.

The house looked the way it did when he left, although neglect had left its mark on everything. Tools were scattered on the workbench and hanging from their hooks on the wall, metal covered in a scum of rust, wood handles swollen and split. They were coated in a thick layer of feathery frost, as were the walls and furniture. Even the plates sat where he'd left them, resting on the workbench that served a dual purpose as a dining table. They'd been picked clean by whatever took up residence after Emmett and Carlo left, and dust and ice had obscured the painted designs on the earthenware. The chipped rim of a bowl made him suck in a shaky breath. Carlo had always insisted they couldn't get rid of it just for having a little crack.

Emmett kicked the snow off his boots where a drift had collected near a gap in the doorframe. At least they were protected from the bitter wind. Emmett already felt a little warmer. Nowhere near enough to consider discarding his coat or removing his boots, but not actively freezing to death, which was something.

His leg ached, a deep, searing pain that left him reaching for the nearest available support, which happened to be the back of a chair. Emmett recognized the twisted top board immediately. The lumber he'd used to construct his own chair had been cut from trees deformed by a heavy snowstorm years before. The trunks had warped themselves into unrecognizable shapes to survive. Emmett couldn't bear to let the wood go to waste, even after his father had warned him that working with stressed timber was risky, and they couldn't sell any piece that used it. He'd kept correcting the emerging twists and bends with his gift for the next five years.

The chair wobbled under the added pressure, legs uneven from six months of being allowed to reform themselves in the damp and fluctuating temperatures of the abandoned house. Emmett grimaced and shifted his weight back onto his own body, ignoring the pain that stabbed through his only partially healed wound. His father had been right. Such badly damaged wood couldn't be trusted.

"Nice place." Rory's voice dripped sarcasm. "Is it going to fall down on our heads and kill us both? Save Marcus the trouble?"

"It's a lot sturdier than it looks. Or sounds." Just reshaping the window boards had sapped Emmett's strength dangerously. He wasn't strong enough to offer any more of his energy to reinforce the heartwood in the support beams, but there were years of love and dedication running through the frame of this house. It probably had at least one more night left in it.

"That's supposed to make me feel better?" Rory ran a gloved finger over the windowsill. Her pigeon hopped off her arm and settled on the small ledge. "You could have brought me here knowing it's a deathtrap."

"If you die in here, so do I," Emmett said. "That would be a little counterproductive."

"Point taken." Rory looked around with a sigh. "Well, it's better than nothing. We're still going to need more than just our coats for the night. Are there any blankets around here?"

Emmett nodded to the heap next to the fireplace where he and Carlo had spent most nights once it was only them in the house. Rory picked one up by its corner and made a face when the cloth separated into shredded strings.

"Any that haven't been totally destroyed by mice?"

"There's a trunk in the bedroom upstairs." It held the extra winter blankets Emmett had put away once thaw came. He didn't move any closer to the steps stretching up into total darkness. He couldn't go back up there, not to the silence and emptiness that felt so wrong after years of chatter and laughter and breathing and heartbeats.

"Great. I'll go find some, then." Rory brushed past him. "If you're gone when I come back down, you'll regret it." She pulled his scarf out of her pocket and waved it in front of him. "You won't get far."

"Believe me, I know." Emmett swallowed. "I'm going to see if there's anything down here we can use." The mice had probably already found any scraps of food, but Emmett would feel a lot better if he had a weapon himself. There were plenty of chisels and files on the walls, and probably a couple decent sized knives in the kitchen drawers.

For a brief moment, he entertained the idea of grabbing a blade, hiding in the shadows, and making his move when Rory came back down the stairs. She was dying anyway, slowly and painfully, and going up against Marcus was suicide. Emmett would be saving her the trouble and protecting himself and Carlo from the brutal wrath that would come down on both of them when Rory's plan inevitably failed. He could go back to trying to find a weak spot in Katya's defenses without watching his own back for a knife.

He reached for one of the chisels hanging over the workbench. The wood and metal were heavy in his hands. He'd never hurt anyone with the tools his family used to create. It had always been his gift, the subtle trace of fingers over skin for a fraction of a second. Instinct, something dark inside him uncurling itself and striking, then retreating.

If he had to choose between Carlo's life and a stranger's, he was going to choose Carlo. He always had. The last time he'd been in this house, he'd killed to defend his son. *And look where that's gotten you,* a bitter voice in his head reminded him. *Standing here with a weapon in your hand, waiting for the person whose fate you've already sealed, so you can finish the job a little faster.*

Emmett turned the chisel over in his hands. He knew how to use it to shape wood, but he wasn't so certain he could stab it into someone's body. Heart thefts were bloodless, and Emmett was always gone long before his victims succumbed. There was something entirely different about killing someone face to face. Rory's sharp gray eyes were pure steel, but even she'd hesitated to bring her knife down on Emmett's heart. If he couldn't kill her in the first blow, she wouldn't give him a chance to try again. Even if she eventually bled out, she'd do it on the floor beside his corpse.

The pigeon burbled from its place on the windowsill, and Emmett glanced from the chisel to it. Those too-bright pink eyes were watching his every move, and the soft coo sounded like a warning. Rory might have left Emmett in a room full of weapons, but she didn't leave him unattended.

He set the chisel on the bench and turned away as footsteps echoed on the stairs. Rory emerged into the faint light, carrying a bundle under her arm. Her eyes followed Emmett's to the wall of tools, and her free hand drifted to her knife. He stepped back from the wall, not wanting to risk her coming to the conclusion that he'd been searching for a weapon, even if that was the truth.

Rory dropped her bundle on the table, then wiped her dusty hands on the front of her jacket. More smears of grime streaked her pale cheeks, and a single cobweb had draped itself over her hair. "Well, the mice made a nice mess of the beds, but there were blankets in the trunk, and some clothes." She threw him a battered gray sweater Emmett had kept for the days he stained furniture. The sleeves were patched with brown yarn darning, and the front was a mixture of wood finishes, speckled with wax blotches.

Emmett slipped off his jacket long enough to tug the sweater over his thin, bloodstained shirt. He ran a finger along the ragged edge of the sleeve, where the cuff must have snagged on a stray splinter. No one had ever gotten around to weaving it back in neatly. He tugged on the thread, twisting it and balling it up between his fingers, even though he knew it would only make the problem worse.

When he looked up again, Rory was in the process of changing sweaters herself. The brown one she'd chosen was a few shades darker than the worn sweater she tossed onto the table, the wool still thick and warm instead of frayed and thinning from too many washes. Theresa's family's cable pattern ran down the arms.

Those designs used to be owners' marks woven into the edges of fishing nets, when the Seachosen still lived in their archipelago kingdom. The Starfall refugees who'd found themselves in Rime had altered the stitches to make clothing suited to the chill of their new home, while clinging to whatever pieces of their heritage they could.

Emmett squeezed his eyes closed as a memory washed over him with the devastating force of the waves that buried the Drowned Islands.

Theresa sat next to the fire, humming an old Seachosen sailors' tune as her fingers twisted a cable pattern that blended Emmett's and her own into the edge of a small hat. One-year-old Carlo was perched on her lap, chubby hands tugging at the yarn and batting the knobbed ends of the knitting needles Emmett had carved. Emmett and his parents had tried to take the boy to give Theresa a little peace, but Carlo cried whenever he was separated from his mother for more than a few minutes.

Emmett blinked, and the figure by the fireplace shifted from black-haired to blonde. The sweater's sleeves fell halfway over Rory's hands, visible even when she pulled her coat back on over top. Emmett thought about snapping at her for taking a dead woman's clothes without any thought of asking permission, then changed his mind.

"So what happened to the rest of your family?" Rory asked bluntly. "At least five people lived here, but you've only ever talked about your son."

"They're dead," Emmett said sharply.

"That's what I thought when I couldn't find them from anything up there," Rory said, starting to unfold a blanket on the floor.

She'd chosen a spot where she was blocking Emmett's access to most of the tools, and where he'd have needed to step over her to get to the kitchen. She twisted her old sweater into a nest on the windowsill for the pigeon. It was a surprisingly thoughtful gesture for someone as practical as Rory. Possibly she just didn't want the pigeon to become agitated in a place it didn't recognize, but the way she ran her fingers over the bird's head as it settled in suggested otherwise. Emmett had been wondering if he was wrong about what the light Rory's heart gave off meant about her character. But she did seem to care about something. She was a better person than she wanted Emmett to assume.

The bird looked at Emmett one more time before tucking its head under a wing. Emmett was convinced if he so much as breathed in Rory's direction too loudly, the pigeon would wake up and screech a warning.

Rory tossed Emmett another blanket.

When he shook the dusty cloth out, something it brushed against rattled on the floorboards. He fumbled around under the rough wool until his hand came to rest on something hard. Emmett didn't particularly want to lay down on an awl or a chisel blade. He grabbed the wood and started to toss it aside when his fingers brushed over a familiar curve.

It was the carved dolphin Carlo used to hold every night when he fell asleep. He must have dropped it the night they ran, when Emmett grabbed his hand and pulled him out the door. Emmett tucked the figure into his pocket. Carlo might still want it back.

When Emmett lay down, wrapping his blanket around his shoulders, Rory seemed to take that as her cue to do the same. For a long time, he listened to the sound of their breathing; his steady but wet with swallowed tears, Rory's halting and a little too shallow. Snow spattered the windows and door like tiny knocks. The house beams creaked and moaned, and wind howled through the cracks like a hungry wolf. Emmett curled a bit deeper into the blanket, willing himself to stop hearing footsteps on the stairs, the swing of a door—hollow, mocking echoes of the life that was once here. The storm slowly died down, no longer screaming and wailing all around the house. Only whispering.

"Emmett."

He flinched. Hearing his name in the wind's wordless tones was nothing new. It only meant he needed sleep. He squeezed his eyes closed and covered his ears with his hands, but that only made it worse. The creaking wood and moaning wind were replaced with Emmett's own heartbeat echoing in his ears. He swallowed the ache in his throat, breathing shakily. There was no one in the house but him and Rory.

The thudding inside his head was overwhelming. He slowly uncovered his ears, tucking his freezing hands under his arms. The echo changed from a swishing, liquid sound to the solid thump of boots on wood. The footsteps were clear. Familiar. Descending the stairs, crossing the room. Stopping behind him. He didn't dare open his eyes and turn around to see what the shadows had become.

The air smelled like warm wool and ginger. Emmett tried to tell himself it was just the stain on his sweater sleeve, where Carlo had spilled broth while learning how to manage a spoon, but the scent was fresh, not faded.

Theresa shouldn't have been there. Her soul should have been dancing in the stars alongside their parents and the children she and Emmett never had the chance to raise.

"You should not have come back." Theresa's voice was a hiss, cold and vindictive. The tone was jarring, at odds with the soft cadence of her Archipelegian words. Emmett was far more familiar with her using their native tongue to sing lullabies and encourage Carlo's clumsy attempts at wobbling around a room. *"You doomed our son."*

He couldn't argue with her. All of this was his fault. *"I'm sorry. I'm so sorry."* The words choked on swallowed tears.

"I trusted you."

Emmett stifled a desperate sob. The memory of Theresa's paper-dry hands in his own, her brown eyes glassy with fever, her cracked lips trailing blood down her cheeks as he promised her he'd take care of Carlo, was still too fresh. His own voice wavered, no longer from a fever burning through him, but from the guilt tearing him apart from the inside out. *"I tried."*

"This should be you." A cold hand touched his shoulder, fingers sliding toward his neck. He flinched, pulling away, a hoarse yell escaping his throat.

Emmett looked up into the eyes of a dead woman walking.

RORY

23 BELLS

"Please. Don't do this."

Rory flinched, the hushed voice freezing her to her bones.

It was nothing more than a squall of wind. Rory's half-asleep mind had turned it into her father's voice, feeding off the dreams that had haunted her since Sue's death. The lingering echo of her father's last moments had burned itself into Rory's memory the moment she'd touched the starsilver blade and watched what amounted to her own hands driving it through his body.

It might have been easier to move on if her father's assurance he'd be home in time to sing her to sleep that night had been the last words Rory heard him speak. Any parent could make a promise and then break it. But Rory had always found it admirable that her father's last words had been a plea for his killer to reconsider. It might have made him sound like a coward to some, but it was what he hadn't said that Rory appreciated.

He'd never told the person who killed him that he had a child. Even faced with death, even when his fatherhood might have been a sentiment that could have swayed a halfway-decent person, he'd kept his family safe.

He'd never given any client his name. Never let them meet him anywhere near his home. Never let them fully see his face. Gavin Blake had known Rime was no place to have a weak point and his family could be his. He'd done everything in his power to keep them from being used against him as a bargaining chip or a threat, then carried their existence to the grave, leaving the syndicate who killed him none the wiser.

Which made the dead man whose voice Rory heard in the wind a far better person than the living one sleeping across the room.

A dog howled in the alley, breaking through the chilly silence and startling Rory fully awake. Yelps and snarls, accompanied by hissing and a blood-curdling screech, followed the sound. Feral dogs and wildcats fought over food all the time, but Rory hadn't lived on the ground floor of a building for over a decade. There had always been stairs and doors between her and whatever racket ensued in the alleys. She kept her eyes on the half-boarded window until the scuffle died off into whines and whimpers.

It took a few moments for Rory to realize those sounds weren't coming from outside the windows, but from the other side of the room.

She rolled over for the third time and sighed. The last time she'd woken up to hear someone else crying in the dark, she'd still been living with her mother. Old Sue had always worked herself to exhaustion, falling into a deep, dreamless sleep night after night.

It was probably for the best Rory didn't sleep too long. Forty-eight hours to live without her heart was an optimistic timeframe, how long people tended to have when they'd accepted their fate. When they went home and said their goodbyes and settled in to let the darkness take them. Rory was probably using up her heartbeats even faster, running all over the city trying to get her heart back.

She didn't have enough of a plan to feel like she and Emmett stood a chance going up against Marcus. As long as she was awake anyway, sorting through the contingencies would be the best use of her limited time. That was becoming increasingly hard to do with Emmett mumbling and thrashing and carrying on. Rory sat up, wrapping her blanket around her like a cloak, and walked across the room.

Emmett was curled in on himself, tears tracing down his cheeks and choking whatever he was whispering under his breath. Rory didn't understand the words, but she could pick out the accent and cadence of Archipelegian. Rory had met several of the Seachosen divers Katya employed, and she'd learned to recognize the general sound of their language, as well as a few relevant words and phrases. A second whisper came out a bit clearer. An apology.

Rory reconsidered her plan to kick Emmett in the back of the leg to wake him. It wasn't out of any feeling of sympathy; she just didn't want to risk interfering with the healing magic. Tal's work would wear off soon, and speeding up the process by kicking Emmett in his bad leg wouldn't help. She bent down to shake his shoulder instead.

Emmett yelped, jolting awake and scrambling away from her. He blinked a few times, rubbing his eyes. Rory crouched down beside him, turning her back to the wall and pulling the blanket a little closer around her.

"I can't sleep with you thrashing and moaning and talking to ghosts," she snapped.

Emmett turned, the faint light picking out tears trailing down his cheeks. "You're the one who wanted me to stay close." He probably meant that to come out bitter and snide, but his voice was too choked for it to have that effect.

Emmett took a shuddering breath, running a hand over his face and then pushing his fingers through his hair. He flinched as a gust howled around the corners of the house.

Rory shook her head. "It's just the wind." She was trying to convince herself as much as Emmett. The superstition that hearing lost relatives' voices meant the listener would soon join them was probably nothing more than a myth. It would have been easy enough to believe in Rime, where the wind howled nightly and death was as common as snowfall. "It doesn't bother me."

"Lucky for you," Emmett mumbled under his breath.

"People die all the time," Rory said, looking around the room at the neglected tools and abandoned dishes. "It's how life here is. What's haunting you so badly you're apologizing to your dead family in your sleep?"

Rory wasn't sure she believed the stories of spirits being trapped in the wards any more than the tales of wind voices as death omens. If it was true, it was oddly comforting to think her father got to see her picking up where he left off. Emmett obviously didn't find the potential continued presence of his deceased relatives reassuring. He seemed to think his family would be angry with him. Maybe for good reason.

"Did you steal their hearts too?"

"No!" Emmett glanced up sharply, meeting Rory's gaze and holding it until she looked away.

Maybe Emmett hadn't murdered his family, but something about their deaths had deeply unsettled him, and the apologies he'd been whispering suggested he felt responsible. It was possible Marcus had killed them to force him into compliance. If that was the case, Emmett's insistence the syndicate leader would do the same to Carlo was based on more than just a spoken threat. Rory couldn't compete with such cold-blooded intimidation.

"Was it Marcus?"

Emmett shook his head. "They died in the Winter of Graves."

"I remember that year." Rory's hands were freezing, even tucked into the blankets, and she rubbed them together briskly to get a little feeling back. "It hit the River Quarter hard."

An unfamiliar disease had spread rapidly through the crowded tenements. Old Sue had fallen ill a day before Rory herself, and by the time either of them was well enough to leave the apartment, half the doors in their hall had black quarantine marks scrawled on the doors. The closest Rory had come to dying during that winter had been tripping over the bodies piled in the stairwell on her way to fetch water, but almost half the families in the building had lost a member by the time thaw arrived.

For some reason, those who actually died from the illness were often people who'd never had lichen fever. It was the one time Rory had actually been a little grateful for her scabbed skin. Better in pain than in a death cart.

"I had to move them." Emmett sniffled softly, wiping a hand under his nose. "Both my parents and Theresa, after they died. I could barely stand, but no one would come in the house to take them." His voice cracked as if his own heart had been ripped from his chest. "I kept thinking if I had to carry Carlo down there, I'd just lay down in the street with him and give up. Let it take me too." Emmett blinked hard, and two tears slid down his cheeks, freezing in the stubble on his chin.

Rory looked at the coat hooks by the door, the chairs around the table. Four large chairs, four tall hooks. Then the smaller but longer-legged chair tucked in at a table corner, the peg in the wall only half as high as the rest.

"I couldn't…" Emmett curled his hands into fists. "I couldn't keep up, after. Working, making meals, looking after Carlo. I had to choose between putting food on the table each night or buying the supplies to make another set of furniture to sell in a week. We needed more money than I could make any honest way." The rest of his words were muffled as he buried his face in his hands. "I was just trying to protect Carlo from this city. And now, if I can't deliver what Marcus wants, he's as good as dead."

"So you offered Marcus your gift in exchange for protection for you and Carlo?"

"No!" Emmett's voice sharpened with anger. "I never would have voluntarily killed for him. The only way I got mixed up with the Star at all was their smuggling. They could sell the furniture I made outside the city with less money taken off the top than if I went through the Cohort's legal channels. I'd rather have gone to the Rapids but they couldn't move anything larger than a few carvings. That wasn't going to put food on the table."

"And you somehow let it slip you were a heart thief."

"I hadn't even realized I *could* steal a heart until—" Emmett swallowed hard. "Last thaw, when the Cohort started sending more patrols into the River Quarter."

Rory nodded. The effort had been a short-lived attempt to round up some rebels who'd sent threats to several Cohort officials. None of them had actually been apprehended, but a lot of small gambling operations and black-market dealers had been shut down.

"I almost got caught doing a handoff to my smuggling contact. I got scared and tried to back out. The Star sent someone to make sure I couldn't talk."

"And you used your gift to stop them."

"The first time was an accident." Emmett looked down at his hands. "I didn't realize what had happened until I was shoving him backward and his heart was crawling into my chest. I wasn't good at subtlety then, and it knocked him unconscious. I grabbed Carlo and we ran."

"And he went back to Marcus, dying of a stolen heart, and told him exactly what happened. Marcus saw an opportunity." Rory took a shaky breath.

Emmett wasn't the only person with a gift that had suddenly strengthened in the face of overwhelming fear or anger.

When Jax put that starsilver knife in Rory's hand, she'd wanted, *needed,* to find and punish her father's killer. The bone-deep pain had ignited the glowing trail of a true guide power in a child with only one gifted parent. If not for her father's murder, Rory could have spent her whole life feeling only the most subtle internal tugging toward her destinations.

Emmett's gift, on its most basic level, sensed the life force in things around him and drew it to the surface. The capacity for heart theft had been a part of him all along. It simply hadn't appeared until he'd been faced with a threat to his life. And to Carlo's.

"I knew what my victim knew about Marcus and the Star, but in the end, it didn't help. They still found us."

Rory nodded. The Star kept their own guides on payroll, and the dying man could have given them the location of Emmett's house. Something as simple as a well-worn tool or a battered boot would start the trail, and all the knowledge in the world wouldn't have kept Emmett and his son safe.

"Marcus's people knew what they were up against the next time they came for me. They wore gloves and scarves and I didn't have a chance to touch any of them." He took a shuddering breath. "They hauled us both to Marcus's house, and he insisted I use my gift for him." Emmett grimaced. "When I tried to refuse, he put a knife to Carlo's throat. Cut deep enough to scar him. That's the kind of man we're dealing with."

Rory sighed. "I see what you're doing. Trying to convince me to do the noble thing and let myself die so I don't put your kid's life at risk." She frowned at him. "You dragged him into this. Just like you dragged me into it."

"I didn't mean for this to happen," Emmett whispered. "I was just trying to keep us alive."

It was hard to blame him for trying to survive. Rory knew all too well the city didn't give people many options. Even fewer were good ones. Rory had chosen to trust no one: Cohort, syndicate, or rebel. Emmett made a deal with a monster. In the end, both of them had made the choices they believed would protect them.

"Nothing I said to Marcus made any difference. I tried to explain that my gift would never let go of a heart once I had it inside me, but he hired a smith to forge this locket and enchant it." Emmett rubbed a hand over his chest, above where Rory knew the starsilver charm rested. "Now I can't steal hearts for myself, only hold them until I can hand them off to him."

Rory could see why Emmett believed going against Marcus was a lost cause. Casually assuming control of one of the most powerful gifts in existence and redirecting it to suit his own purposes definitely made the syndicate leader look invincible.

"He's gone to a lot of trouble and expense just to get my gift into his own hands," Emmett said.

Rory glanced at him. "Well, you are the only one who can keep him alive."

"I wasn't always." Emmett frowned. "Marcus wasn't dying when he found me. I would understand all of this if he was. He wants the hearts for their secrets. To get an edge on his competition and get them out of the way at the same time."

"So he doesn't actually need them." She shouldn't have been surprised at a syndicate leader's greed. Still, hearts were a different thing than a house bigger than Rory's entire apartment building or more money than anyone but Elena on a never-ending drinking binge could spend in one lifetime.

"He does now. Once you start using stolen hearts to keep yourself alive, your own adapts. It stops doing its job. Even after just one, I can feel it. He's had…" Emmett frowned, counting on his fingers. "Six now. And hearts don't last as long outside the person they belong to. He needs a constant supply."

Rory took a breath, wincing at the crushing feeling of choking even as she knew, logically, air was finding its way into her lungs. "Is there some way we can use that? Marcus may control where the hearts go after you steal them, but he still needs your gift. He might give my heart back if he believes the alternative is me killing you."

Emmett would still need to take her heart back for her from Marcus, which would complicate that bluff, but she'd figure out how to keep the threat viable, and make sure both Emmett and Marcus held up their ends of the bargain, if they got that far.

"He'd let you kill me and find himself another thief," Emmett said quietly.

Rory hadn't really expected him to approve of a plan that used him as a bargaining chip, but he did have a point. Willow's map was proof Emmett wasn't the only heart thief in the city. He'd just been the easiest for Marcus to find.

"I thought about refusing to steal hearts for him anymore, but he'd just replace me." Emmett shook his head. "As long as he has Carlo, he knows that will keep me in line."

Rory nodded. Emmett might be a killer, but he wasn't heartless himself. If it came down to Marcus testing Emmett's resolve, he would have chosen Carlo's survival over any scruples about murder.

"There has to be a way where neither of us dies." Emmett looked from Rory to her knife. "If there is, we can find it in the morning." His eyes were half closed, his head slumped forward.

"Without my heart I may not make it through the night, not here." Rory gestured vaguely to the room, watching her weak breath fog in front of her. "It's too cold."

"We can't light a fire. This building is supposed to be abandoned. A patrol might notice the smoke and stop to find out who's broken in." Emmett blew on his hands and rubbed them together. "We just have to tough it out."

"Or we can keep each other warm." Rory shrugged. "We'd have double the blankets and body heat. It's what Old Sue and I used to do." Rory missed that warmth beside her more than she wanted to admit, although she wasn't sure a murderer who'd condemned her to a slow, painful death was a better bedfellow than an annoyed pigeon who no longer wanted to be held after Rory had rolled over on him in her sleep.

More importantly, she'd rather have Emmett where she knew what he was doing than wake up to find one of those rusty chisels at her throat. Or not wake up at all. Rory had almost expected Emmett to try and kill her when she left him alone with a room full of potential weapons earlier. It made her more nervous that he hadn't. "I'm keeping you alive. You can return the favor."

"You're doing what?" Emmett barked out a laugh even as she could hear his teeth chattering.

"I got your leg patched up."

"After you sliced it open."

"After you ripped out my heart and then tried to run from me."

Emmett couldn't argue with that. "Most people don't…" He trailed off. "No one wants to be anywhere near someone who can steal their heart in one beat."

"Well, mine's already gone, so I've got nothing to worry about." Rory stood up. Before Emmett could react, she grabbed his tattered blanket off his shoulders and crossed the room to the space she'd already claimed as hers. She wasn't giving up her view of their only viable exit for the rest of the night, even if Blizzard was keeping watch.

"Hey, no." Emmett rubbed his hands up and down his arms. "Give it back."

"Nuh-uh." Rory grinned at him, the way she'd seen wildcats bare their teeth defending their kills in the streets. "Not gonna happen."

"Fine. Fine." Emmett crossed to her side of the room. "You're not going to cut my throat in my sleep, right?"

"That would be counterproductive."

"You could decide you'd rather see me dead than risk me double-crossing you." He winced as he settled onto the single quilt she'd spread over the floor, facing her.

"You thinking about doing that?" Rory shifted the blankets around them, capturing the most warmth she could with the tattered cloth. At least if she died tomorrow, her last night wouldn't be spent as alone as the past few weeks had been.

"No." Emmett curled in on himself, arms crossed tightly over his chest, hands tucked under them. "You'd make sure I was dead if it was the last thing you did."

"Damn right." Rory moved closer to Emmett, pressing herself up against his chest. He'd left his jacket closed, blocking some of the heat, and she reached for the first button.

Emmett winced again when her numb fingers missed his collar entirely and accidentally grazed his jaw. "Your hands are cold."

"Your fault." Rory continued to fumble with the button at his collar.

"I deserved that." Emmett sighed, and Rory felt the warmth of his breath on her cheek. "I-I'm sorry."

He took over undoing the buttons, and Rory tucked her hands in between her own chest and his. If she was lucky, she'd get through the night without more than two frostbitten fingers.

"No you're not. You wouldn't really be sorry about anything you did to protect Carlo." She couldn't hate him for it. At least he tried to take care of his kid, even when things got tough. He didn't run away and start over and pretend they didn't exist. She took a slow, shaking breath.

"Well, I'm sorry I hurt you."

"I bet you are." Rory shook her head. "Of all the hearts you've stolen, how am I the first person to hunt you down and try to get theirs back?"

"I'm sure the others tried. But even if they connected me to Marcus, even if they tracked me down, they couldn't take on the Star. Before this I've been able to stay inside his headquarters for the two days it takes them to…to die." Emmett flinched at the last word.

He's not the one it should be bothering.

Actually, what concerned Rory wasn't the final word, but everything before it. "If Marcus already has my heart, why did he send you back out so soon? Do hearts only last days for him now?"

"He wants Katya's heart specifically. Told me not to come back until I had it with me."

Emmett sighed. His breathing slowed and evened as he drifted off to sleep. Rory couldn't afford to do the same. Emmett might have thought Marcus's demand for a specific heart was a problem, but she could see an opportunity. Marcus's insistence had revealed a vulnerability he shouldn't have shown. Wanting anything in this town was dangerous.

It meant you could be tricked. It meant you could be beaten.

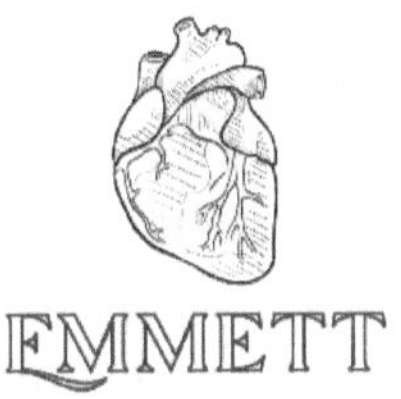

EMMETT

6 BELLS

Emmett woke up to an elbow jabbing him in the ribs. "Hey," he mumbled sleepily. "Carlo, it's still dark."

"Not your son," a voice he wasn't awake enough to place replied. "And we do have to get up. Right now."

The day before came flooding back the moment Emmett opened his eyes. The failed attack on Katya. Marcus sending him to try again. Rory. The healer. Emmett's old house.

Rory was sitting up with a blanket still draped over one shoulder. "If you gave Marcus a heart, could you take mine back while you were still touching him?"

Emmett shook his head. "I've given him enough hearts by now he'd notice if anything felt different."

Rory frowned. "You told me last night that you can knock someone unconscious when you pull a heart out of them."

Emmett's leg twinged painfully when he sat up. He should have been resting and letting his body heal the damage Tal couldn't. "I was taking the only heart he had. I don't know what might happen when two hearts are involved. If it doesn't work and Marcus realizes I'm double-crossing him he'll slit my throat."

Even if Emmett could knock him out, Marcus would eventually wake up, and Emmett would only have delayed paying the price for a betrayal of that magnitude. But Emmett's fate after he returned Rory's heart wouldn't be any of her concern. If he wanted her to come up with a plan that didn't leave him to deal with Marcus's retaliation, Rory needed to worry about Emmett while she was still relying on his gift to save her.

"You're too valuable to kill. He might knock you around a little."

"More likely, take it out on Carlo."

Rory shook her head. "He knows if he kills Carlo he loses his leverage. How stupid are you?"

"Marcus doesn't have to kill him, Rory! How stupid are *you?*" Emmett couldn't stop thinking of what could be happening to Carlo right then. The longer he stayed away, the more time Marcus had to get angry, to want to punish Emmett somehow. And he knew the best way to do that would be hurting Carlo.

It would be a last resort, Emmett hoped, knowing what he did about Marcus's plans for Carlo's future. But the more hearts the syndicate leader acquired, the more unstable he became. He might sacrifice an uncertain future for a more predictable present. Carlo's gift could take years to manifest, and there was no guarantee he'd share Emmett's power. Marcus wouldn't last that long without a heart thief keeping him alive. "Just let me get you someone else's heart. It'd be a whole lot easier."

"For you, maybe. I don't want to find out what it feels like to turn into some other person in my own body. I want *my* life back." Rory started to stand, then wobbled and sat back down hard. She dug into her pocket for the small pouch from the healer. Her whole hand was a deathly shade of purplish gray. It trembled slightly when she shook some of the powder into her mouth.

Emmett had never watched one of his victims die.

"Marcus wants Katya's heart. If we brought him that, do you think he might consider returning mine in exchange?" Rory asked.

Emmett blinked, not certain he understood Rory's meaning correctly. "You want to help me steal Katya's heart?"

"Marcus won't even let you through his doors if you don't have the one he wants, right?"

Marcus wouldn't know that until Emmett had already given him the heart. But Emmett didn't bother to correct Rory's assumption. The only thing that could save him from Marcus's rage was following through on the job he'd been sent to do. If Rory could help him get Katya's heart, he had to let her believe it would save her too.

Emmett nodded. "It's worth trying."

"This is the only way I see that both of us get out of this. Marcus gets what he wants, so do I, and neither of us kills you over it. And if he doesn't agree to the deal, we can fall back on the plan of trying to incapacitate him." Rory stood up, this time without losing her balance, and waved her hand at Emmett in a 'come along' gesture.

He reluctantly crawled out of the blankets.

"I delivered a message to Katya yesterday from someone who implied a Flare foundry was using ore that had been smuggled in by a syndicate other than the Rapids. Katya might agree to a face-to-face meeting with someone claiming they can explain the situation."

"You think she's going to fall for that?" Emmett started to check the coats on the hooks near the door. Maybe one of them was better than what he was currently wearing.

"I think the Flare is the one syndicate she might open her doors to right now. And she's never seen you. Some of her door guards have, after you showed up there yesterday. That's a risk we'll have to take."

"But—" Emmett swallowed. Marcus would kill him without a second thought for revealing the truth, but every detail mattered when planning a heart theft this elaborate. He'd already told Rory plenty of things Marcus didn't want any outsider learning, starting with who Emmett was stealing hearts for. And if he couldn't get Katya's, that would be the least of his concerns. "I know who the Flare's new supplier is. It's the Star."

Rory raised an eyebrow.

"Marcus was trying to undercut the Rapids' pricing, but his ore doesn't match quality. That's part of the reason he wanted Katya out of the way. If the Flare can't rely on the Rapids anymore, they'll have to come to him. And he knows if Katya finds out someone is going behind her back, she could pose a real threat."

Rory chewed on her lip for a moment. "That might actually be a good thing for us. Marcus will be putting pressure on the Flare not to go any more public than they already have. There's less chance we'll show up only to find out the Flare actually sent someone to talk to Katya."

Emmett nodded. He was fairly sure, from the way Marcus acted when he found out about the information leak, the Black Spark Forge would be looking for a new master soon, if they weren't already. Rory turned away from him, taking some of the chisels off the wall and laying them on the workbench.

Emmett looked from her to the tools' rusty, but still sharp, edges. "What are you doing?"

"We need to convincingly pass you off as a Flare member," Rory said. "They use the rust from their own ironworks as a base for dyeing their markers."

Syndicate dyes were one of the best kept secrets in Rime. Marcus had one person who knew the Star's mixture and dyed the markers for new members or repaired faded ones. Losing your marker could result, at least in the Star, in losing your life. Emmett was almost glad he'd never been given one. He frowned. "How could you possibly know that?"

Rory smirked. "I figured it out by accident when I hung a sheet too close to the steam pipes and it ended up looking exactly like one of their scarves. Sue wasn't happy about that at all; it was impossible to get the stain out completely." She held up one of the shredded strips of blanket from the heap by the fireplace, then rubbed it against the rusted metal. "This should make a decent approximation of one of their armbands, as long as you don't let anyone take too close a look."

Emmett left her to her makeshift dye job and took his father's coat off its peg to check the lining. Two silver-furred mice with inch-long fangs stuck their heads out of a tear near the collar and hissed. Emmett dropped the jacket on the floor and jumped back, banging his shoulder on the lantern hanging from its hook near the door.

Rory frowned at him. "We'll also need to get our hands on a token for the third level of the bathhouse. If we hang around the place long enough, I should see someone I can pickpocket. It's pretty clear who has the prestige and power to get access. Between the armband and the token, you'll look legitimate."

"What if someone recognizes me?" Emmett gave up inspecting the coats. None of them were in better shape than the one Tal loaned him, and he didn't want to be in the middle of their scheme only to have an angry mouse crawl out of some hiding place and chomp down on his hand or neck.

"Tell them part of the truth. You were there yesterday hoping to find out how much she knew about the new arrangements." Rory held out the orange-tinted cloth strip. "We'll wrap this around your wrist. Flare members aren't required to wear their markers in any particular way, and it would make sense for you not to be advertising your syndicate allegiance too visibly when half the city is ready to go to war." She knotted the ragged ends and Emmett tugged his sleeve down to mostly cover the orange band.

He figured he was better off not thinking of the multitude of ways this half-insane plan could go wrong. Rory had an answer for all of them, and that answer seemed to be 'make it up as you go.' Not exactly the way Emmett liked to operate, but he had to admit it worked for her. She'd found him. Maybe they did stand a chance.

If Rory was right about Katya's willingness to talk to a Flare representative, and could find someone with access to her inner circle careless enough with their token to let it be stolen, and *if* Emmett could get close enough to Katya to actually take her heart.

Even if all of that happened, he'd still need to make it back out of that place alive. Rory hadn't said a thing about that part of the plan. She might not have even thought that far ahead.

Or she might not have expected they'd get to the point that they'd need to know.

Rory nodded to the window. "Come on. I don't have all day to wait around." She took a shuddering breath, then climbed out the window and dropped to the other side, holding out her arm to her pigeon.

Emmett tugged Tal's coat tighter around his shoulders, pulled on a pair of his father's heaviest gloves after shaking them thoroughly, and stepped out into the cold.

At least the storm had died down. There were several inches of fresh snow on the street, already churned up by people either leaving for their jobs in the dark or coming home from a night's work. Rory took the lead, turning down a winding side road so narrow that, with all the snow that had drifted into it, there was barely room for anyone coming the opposite way to pass them.

Emmett felt like they must have been going deeper into the quarter, but when the alley dead-ended into a wider, busier street, he realized they'd stepped out onto a main road that led directly to the market square.

When Rory stopped, turning to look into the window of a bakery that had just opened its doors, Emmett nearly ran into her back. The pigeon ruffled its feathers and gave Emmett a head-tilted glare.

"Do we really have time to stop for food right now? I thought we were in a hurry," Emmett said, looking up at the swinging sign overhead, carved into the shape of an extremely plump bear.

"Shh," Rory hissed. "We're being followed."

Emmett glanced behind him, and Rory smacked his shoulder. "Don't *do* that." She scowled at him.

"I'm not stupid. You're just wrong." Emmett wouldn't have lasted long as Marcus's assassin if he didn't know how to tell when he was being watched. He'd been checking on instinct and hadn't seen anyone behind them.

Rory shook her head. "Blizzard's been fussy since we turned down this street, and he just nipped me. He doesn't bite my ear unless there's something he's worried about."

A pigeon didn't exactly seem like a failsafe method of noticing danger. Still, it wouldn't hurt to be more cautious than necessary. "Okay. What now?"

Rory nodded to the bakery. "We'll go in here and then slip out the back kitchen door. By the time whoever's behind us catches up, we'll be long gone."

Emmett wasn't sure Rory's concern was justified, but he still didn't like the idea of anyone trailing them. Marcus shouldn't have been concerned about Emmett's whereabouts after less than a day, but he had just acquired a new heart. Thoughts and memories got scrambled up and twisted when they were merging with new ones. Emmett had woken up the morning after he'd stolen his first heart wondering why he and Carlo were huddled up in an alley and not sleeping in their own house. Marcus might have forgotten he'd ordered Emmett to come back with Katya's heart or not at all.

Emmett shook himself out of his thoughts to find Rory already shoving her way through the line of people waiting for their breakfast, ignoring their angry shouts and ducking under a swung fist.

Emmett had a harder time getting past, and by the time he'd placated a woman whose foot he accidentally stepped on, Rory was standing near the staff entrance to the kitchen, one hand pressed firmly over her pigeon's head.

"Good. I wasn't sure how much longer I was going to be able to keep him away from the cranberry loaves," Rory muttered, then grabbed the pigeon in both hands as he squirmed out from under her grip and attempted a fluttering leap at the tray on a shelf. "Blizzard. No." Rory wedged the protesting bird under her arm.

Emmett chose not to comment on the round loaf shape in one of her pockets.

Rory pulled him through the staff door, narrowly dodging a young woman with a full tray on each hand coming out to replenish the stock.

As soon as they were inside the kitchen, Emmett felt sweat begin trailing down his forehead. The heat was disorienting, making the roar of the fire, the chatter of the bakers at work, and the thwack of dough being turned out on boards overly loud. Rory seemed equally affected, leaning on a counter and taking a few slow breaths before weaving her way through the room. She nodded to a baker with burn marks littered across his massive arms and the plump bear from the outside sign embroidered on his apron.

"Thanks, Bruno. I owe you one."

The man, wrist-deep in a thick dough, grunted. "Owe me five, actually."

"Put it on my bill."

"Right along with that loaf in your jacket."

Rory laughed and ducked out the door to the alley, dodging a mangy lynx that had been rooting through the trash bins. The wildcat looked up briefly, strings of saliva hanging from its too-wide mouth. Rory moved to the other side of the alley, and the animal went back to its meal.

"Do you know everyone in this town?" Emmett asked.

"Good for business," Rory replied. "You would not believe how many deliveries I made for him when I was starting out. If anything, he owes me."

She dodged down an even narrower alley, and Emmett was about to follow when the pigeon let out an ear-splitting screech. There was a quick, angry scuffle, then a distressed coo and hard thud, followed by a low snarl that didn't sound entirely human. He was pretty sure it was Rory, regardless.

"You're taking my job over my dead body." Rory snapped breathlessly a moment later.

"Fine with me." The new voice was familiar, but Emmett couldn't place it when his own heart felt like it was going to jump out of his ears.

Emmett stepped back and crouched down out of sight behind the corner of the wall, trying to avoid the thorny bloodbriar that had crept up its rough stones. The lynx continued digging through the crates behind the bakery, making a racket as it searched for scraps. Emmett hoped the sound would cover his footsteps if he bolted. He wouldn't have to lift a finger, and someone else would deal with Rory for him. He wouldn't have her help to get to Katya, but at least she wouldn't have the chance to realize he'd tricked her and kill him out of spite.

Rory's next words stopped him in his tracks. "I'm twice the guide you'll ever be."

Whoever was looking for Emmett had the same gift as Rory. That meant they had something that belonged to him. The Midnights and the Ravens didn't know who he was, so there was no reason anyone working for them should have anything of his to track. Only one person who would want to find Emmett would also know what to give a guide to accomplish that.

Stomach sinking, Emmett leaned forward enough to see around the corner. The figure looming over Rory had a bright yellow scarf wrapped around his throat, and the Star's emblem was sewn into the back of his gray coat in the same color thread. A coat that was stretched to the limits of its seams to cover broad, hunched shoulders.

That explained the familiarity of the voice. Marcus sending Trey meant he didn't particularly care if he got Emmett back in one piece. Trey would kill Rory to get her out of the way, then continue to track Emmett down relentlessly. Emmett's chances were better with Rory and her overly optimistic planning.

"Then how is it I'm the one with the knife to your throat?" Trey snarled.

"Maybe because I found your mark before you did?" Rory was goading Trey, which Emmett could have told her was a terrible idea. "I was always one step ahead of you."

"Which is why it's going to be so satisfying to not only finish this job, but get you out of my way in the process," Trey snarled.

Emmett picked up a chunk of stone, then flung it toward the scavenging wildcat. The lynx yowled as the rock bounced off the wood near its head. Ears flattened, it bolted down the alley, hissing and snarling.

"What the—" Trey snapped.

Emmett tugged off one glove as he pressed himself to the wall. He rounded the corner to see Rory already using the distraction to her advantage, struggling with Trey for control of her knife. Trey had a good head of height and a fully functioning heart on her, and it was showing.

Emmett stepped up behind the Star guide and slipped his hand between Trey's coat collar and the coarse beard on his jaw. Emmett's gift surged through his fingers, pulling them to the rapid beat under Trey's skin, just above a faint crust of old lichen fever scars. One pulse, and Trey's heart slipped up Emmett's fingers, a smoky shade of dark gray. Emmett's gift clawed desperately at the energy as the locket pulled the heart away and trapped it inside the starsilver.

Trey crumpled like a street performer's puppet whose strings had been cut. Rory wrenched her knife out of his hand, and in one swift motion, pulled it across his throat as he sank to the ground. Emmett stared at the rapidly growing pool of blood around the body. He choked back a sick feeling that had nothing to do with his gift rebelling at being denied another heart.

"Did you have to kill him?"

"What did you want to do, let him run back to Marcus and tell him we're working together?" Rory scoffed. Despite the bravado in her words, the knife in her hand was trembling. Emmett couldn't tell if that was because what she'd done had sunk in, or if her heart was struggling to handle the stress of her own near murder. "Besides, he hit Blizzard."

Rory crouched down and picked up the dazed-looking bird wandering around on the cobbles, depositing him in her hood. There were scratches on Trey's face that didn't come from Rory's knife. Neither she nor her pigeon had intended to go down without a fight.

Rory wiped her blade on Trey's jacket and slipped it back into its sheath, then took a deep breath. "All of a sudden you have a problem with killing people to get the job done? In case you forgot, we were on our way to take Katya's heart."

She was right, but watching someone bleed out on the snow felt different. Death was always worse when witnessed in person. Emmett blinked back memories of foamy blood on his mother's lips, his father's eyes going blank and glassy, Theresa's body already stiff before Emmett could gather the strength to lift her.

He fell back, panting, and slid down the wall. Using his gift twice in such a short time had been a mistake. He felt as weak and lightheaded as he had when he was giving all the food in the house to Carlo.

Rory held up a cracked wooden button. "Is this yours? Trey had it tucked into his glove. I think it's how he was tracking you." She dropped it into Emmett's hand.

Emmett did remember noticing the bottom button from his coat had gone missing at some point. He'd assumed he'd snagged it on something during one of his thefts, and would have carved himself a new one if he'd had access to any scrap wood or tools. He nodded and slipped the wooden disk into the pocket of Tal's worn jacket.

"Okay. At least no one else can find it and come after us, even if they find his body. Now what?" Rory asked, standing up and brushing off her gloves.

Emmett dragged in a few shaky breaths before he had enough air in his lungs to respond. "What do you mean?"

"You've got a heart in your locket, which I'm assuming means you can't steal another one." Emmett managed a weak nod. "And before you even suggest it, I don't want to become *him*. I'd say we should take our chances and go to Marcus with what we have, but since it's not the right heart, and worse, one of his own people…"

If Rory thought they were out of options, Emmett might join Trey bleeding on the ground. "It could still work."

Rory scowled. "What?"

"Marcus only sees who the hearts belong to when they're already in him. It took him a little while to realize yours wasn't Katya's." Emmett winced as a headache crashed into his forehead with all the force of a wave hitting the piers. "There might be enough time for me to pull yours out." He leaned against the wall. With what he'd just told Rory, it wouldn't be hard for her to realize he'd kept part of the truth from her and was using her convoluted plan to steal Katya's heart to save his own skin.

"I guess we're back to the plan where you knock Marcus out." There was no knife at Emmett's throat, no blinding pain other than the one his gift was inflicting. If Rory had put the pieces together and hated him for using her, she wasn't doing anything about it.

Emmett took a few shuddering breaths. This wasn't ideal, but at least he wasn't at the wrong end of Rory's knife again. He could figure out a better solution once his gift stopped trying to tear him apart from the inside out.

"Marcus sent a guide of his own looking for you. If he wants to know where you are that badly, we need to get moving. He won't believe you can evade Trey for long."

Emmett shook his head, even that motion making him feel like he might throw up. "I'm going to need a little time. To get my strength back."

"Well, in case you forgot, I'm running out of time. The longer we wait, the weaker I get."

"Then we'll split the difference."

Rory sighed. "Okay, fine. Until ten bells."

"Twelve bells." He thought that might be enough. Barely.

"Okay. Twelve. And let's get out of the alley with a dead man in it," Rory said, hauling him to his feet.

Emmett couldn't argue with that. He looked over his shoulder at the body on the snow and suppressed a shudder. "Sounded like you two had history," he observed.

"We were rivals when I was starting out as a messenger. Trey played dirty, though. I'm not surprised the Star got him in their pocket." She shrugged. "Well, he's not our problem anymore."

"You're welcome."

Rory glared at him. "I had it under control. Didn't expect to have backup. I figured you'd run while you had the chance."

"Did I have a choice? He'd have hunted me down like you did."

Rory sighed. "Assumed you'd try and talk your way out of it with Marcus."

Emmett winced at the thought of how things went the last time he tried to talk his way out of anything there. "Figured I was better off with you."

"Thanks for the vote of confidence."

A street and a half away from Trey's corpse, Rory stopped outside a small, sagging building that looked like its owners might once have optimistically referred to it as a market stand. "This should be as good a place as any." She pried the latch off the door with her knife, letting them both inside. The tiny shack was drafty and sounded like the next strong gust would knock it over. At least it provided some shelter, and more importantly, would keep them hidden from anyone who happened to walk past.

Emmett slumped down against the rough, splintery wall, and Rory followed him after lifting Blizzard out of her hood. She set the bird in her lap and started stroking his feathers, whispering to him softly.

"You really were willing to help me kill Katya to get your heart back, weren't you?" Emmett asked.

Rory looked up at him. "I want to survive. I'll go through anyone and anything I need to. You ever hear trappers talk about wolves chewing their legs off to get out of traps? Everything wants to live. So do I."

"But you won't leave the city." Someone like her must have had favors she could have cashed in with forgers and smugglers.

"Where would I go?" Rory pulled her knife out of its sheath, rubbed a bit of dried blood off the handle with her sleeve, and inspected the blade. "This city is all I know. Besides, I can't use my gift outside the wards without risking being hauled back in chains or outright killed for it."

"Your gift isn't exactly visible."

"Yes, it is." Rory reached into her pocket, holding up one end of Emmett's scarf. She closed her eyes for a moment, and when she opened them again, gold flecks danced and whirled in them, swallowing up the usual color. Her pupils had all but disappeared, the pale glow resembling the bluish cast of a blind person's.

She tucked the scarf back into her pocket, blinked again, and her eyes returned to their normal gray, pupils once again black.

"Even if I chose never to use my gift again, it would be hard to hide this." Rory pointed to the scabbed marks on her cheek. "Lichen fever isn't very common outside Rime, especially not cases this bad. It's almost guaranteed to make people wonder where I came from." She shrugged. "I've learned how to survive here, and I don't want to start over in some new town. I'm not going anywhere." She slid the knife back into its sheath and shifted slightly, so Emmett couldn't reach the handle, then pulled the edge of her jacket over it. She took a dark metal flask from her pocket.

"What's that?" Emmett asked.

"Don't know. Trey had it in his jacket." Rory opened the top and took an experimental sniff.

"So not only did you kill him in cold blood, but you stole from him?" Emmett hadn't even seen her take it.

"He was dead. He wasn't going to be using it." Rory shrugged and took a small sip. "Not great, but it's still a little warm. Want some?" Emmett shook his head. "Suit yourself."

Rory pulled the loaf of bread out of her pocket, tore it in half, and offered him the smaller piece. Emmett shook his head again and wrapped his arms around his knees. Rory took a massive bite, washing it down with another swig from the flask. She ate in silence for a few minutes before turning to look at him again.

"Look, Trey had it coming. Work for the Star, you get burned sooner or later. If it wasn't my knife that got him, it would have been someone else's." The flask shook slightly, her hand still trembling. "I just saved him from the same slow death as me. If anything, you're the one who really killed him."

Not exactly a sentiment Emmett could argue with. "So," he asked, hoping to change the subject, "how'd a River girl like you get a coat like that?"

Rory's face hardened. "It was a gift." The words were clipped and angry. She must not have been too fond of whoever it came from.

"Oh."

Rory swallowed the last of the liquid in the flask. "My turn. What's with the hair?"

"Huh?"

"You don't have lichen marks, but you've got as much gray in your hair as I do."

Emmett shrugged, running a hand through the tangled mess. "Each time I take a heart for Marcus, I get more. Stealing a heart takes a lot out of me, and the energy my body absorbs is supposed to replenish that and then some. But I have to give the hearts away, so my gift feeds on me instead." Emmett was taking a loan on his future with each theft. He wasn't sure how many years he'd given up by this point. Not that it mattered when he was already living on borrowed time.

"Did Marcus ever think about what happens to him when he finally pushes you too far? I know you said he'd replace you, but he can't guarantee he'd be able to recruit another heart thief before he ran out of time, especially when most of them are stealing to survive." Rory stopped. "Oh. He thinks your son inherited the same gift, doesn't he?" Clearly, she'd managed to put together the pieces of what he'd said, and hadn't said, when she'd asked whether Marcus would consider Emmett's death inconvenient enough to make a deal with her.

The words he couldn't choke out in the emptiness of his old house and the echoes of his nightmares weren't much easier to say in daylight. Emmett swallowed. "I'm a stopgap until Carlo's gift manifests." Aside from that first moment with the knife at his throat, Marcus had treated the boy with disturbing fondness. "He wants Carlo to do this for him voluntarily."

"That's ridiculous." Rory grimaced. "He's using the kid as leverage against you, then wants to turn around and ask him to steal hearts for the person who ruined his life and yours?"

"All Carlo knows is that this man gave us a roof over our heads when we were sleeping in the street, and more food than he's seen in his entire life." Emmett winced. "Marcus has done more for him than I was ever able to."

"It's harder than it seems to buy a kid's loyalty." Rory sighed. "My mother gave me this coat when I turned eighteen." She shook her head. "She thought it was a nice gesture. She'd spent so long in a Cohort mansion she forgot life was different down here."

"Your mother is—" Emmett hadn't seen that one coming.

"She married Howe about a year after my father died. The Cohort can't have gifteds in their households, so she left me with Old Sue." Rory tugged at a loose thread on her coat sleeve. "She could have up and left Rime altogether, I guess. She kept saying she was going to, before she met Howe. He offered her the kind of life a former barmaid could never have gotten in the outside world." Rory looked up to the brighter patch against the wards where the High Quarter's lamps sent up a glow. "She even gave Old Sue an allowance to take care of me. I think she was afraid if she didn't send the money, Sue would come knocking on Howe's door with a half-gifted child and tell him whose daughter I was."

"Howe doesn't know about you?"

"I can't imagine she would have told him. He probably wouldn't have married someone with such potential for scandal. She always hid the money for Sue in the bundle of laundry. Probably made some excuse that the washerwoman charged a small fortune but it was for a job well done. She did better by me than she might have. She couldn't buy back my love, though. And she was my own mother."

"You kept the coat," Emmett said with a shrug.

"Thought about tossing it in the river at first, to be honest. But it's good quality, and it's warm. I wasn't going to throw it away out of petty anger." Rory grinned, something feral and dangerous in the expression. "I don't waste opportunities, no matter where they come from."

Emmett swallowed and leaned back, closing his eyes. Rory kept things around, no matter what her emotions were, as long as she could find some practical use for them. Emmett needed to make sure her plans never shifted far enough that she thought she didn't need him.

RORY

11 BELLS

Rory waited until Emmett had dozed off into a fitful sleep before letting herself break.

She scrubbed her hands hard against the leg of her pants, but the feeling of Trey's blood staining them was impossible to remove. She couldn't let Emmett see that killing Trey had shaken her. If he realized it was the first time she'd intentionally taken a life, he might think he could convince her to back out of the whole idea.

No matter how many times Rory told herself it was Trey or them, all she could see was the same knife that took her father's life used to end another. The vision of her own hands holding it and standing over her father's corpse felt less like a glimpse of the past, and more like her future.

It was one thing to consider sending Emmett to steal a heart from someone who used to be a friend. It was one thing to believe she could get her heart back by driving a knife through an unknown thief's chest. Knowing how it felt to be responsible for taking the life of even someone as despicable as Trey, Rory was grateful she hadn't needed to do either of those things.

She might have tricked Emmett into believing her cold, callous front, and she'd even fooled herself for a little while. She'd thought she was fully willing to hand over Katya's heart as a bargaining chip. But Rory knew now that it would never have been as easy as she'd pretended. Even though the blood on her hands would have been a little less literal didn't mean she wouldn't have been just as horrified when the time came to let Emmett steal Katya's heart.

Some part of her was still desperate and clawing to live. That hadn't changed. But the part asking why, asking what she was going to live for if she did manage to pull this off, had gotten louder. It was asking if success was worth the price Rory had already paid, and the price she was going to before it was over.

At least one more person had to die. Marcus wouldn't let the double-cross they had planned go without retaliation. The only way to keep him from coming after both Rory and Emmett with the full weight of his syndicate was to take him out of the picture entirely. Knowing Marcus was responsible for so many murders, even if he'd had Emmett doing his dirty work for him, made the thought a little easier to stomach, but not much. Rory knew better than to hope it ended there.

The Star might crumble without Marcus's iron-fisted authority, but some of his loyal people would be out for blood. Rory wasn't sure if she was more afraid of hesitating when someone confronted her, or of the person she'd become if she had no more qualms about taking another life.

She glanced at Emmett, who looked tired and pained and sad even in his sleep, where he should have been able to escape for a little while. Rory had killed only one person, and it was so much worse than she'd ever expected. Emmett had killed seven, and if they failed to get Rory's heart back, which in all likelihood they would, Rory would be the eighth.

The fact that he was still acting as Marcus's assassin, that he was even still alive, meant he'd figured out some secret to burying the guilt. But asking him how he coped with the blood on his hands would mean admitting Rory *wasn't* dealing with her part in Trey's death well.

Emmett shifted slightly, leaning further into Rory's side and mumbling something unintelligible in Archipelegian. He'd probably mistaken her for Carlo again, like he had when she'd woken him that morning. Rory could barely remember what it was like to have a parent whose first thought was of their child.

Maybe the only reason Emmett could live with himself after everything he'd done was because it wasn't his own life he was trying to save.

Rime hadn't broken Carlo yet, but Marcus was going to put blood on his hands sooner or later. If Rory did nothing else with the last day of her life, she should at least get Carlo out from under that man's thumb. Otherwise, this city would take his heart the way it had Rory's, long before Emmett had ever pulled it out of her chest.

Alone, Emmett couldn't save Carlo. Even with both of them, they'd probably fail. It was still worth the risk. No one could turn back time, not with any gift in existence, but this was Rory's chance to fight for the tiny girl with the too-big eyes and the too-small boots who learned too early that the only person she could count on to protect her was herself.

The bells chimed out, twelve echoing peals that sounded dull and hollow by the time they reached this part of the Quarter. Rory dug her elbow into Emmett's ribs hard enough to wake him.

"Huh?" he asked groggily.

"Twelve bells. That was the deal. We've got to go." Rory stood up, catching herself on the wall when her head spun and her body felt as if it wasn't actually connected to her efforts. She dug out the packet Tal had given her and shook a small amount of the salty mixture onto her tongue, hoping it was enough to help. The pouch had gotten disturbingly light. She took a few deep breaths and waited for the dizziness to fade.

"You okay?" Emmett asked, standing slowly and looking a bit like he might be sick on his own boots. His eyes tracked the bag in Rory's hand the way Rory would size up a vendor's stall for easy pickings.

"Just sat too long in the cold." Rory tucked the pouch back into her inner pocket. She might have gained a little more sympathy for Emmett, but not enough to share her precious cure with him. He'd recover, eventually. She would need whatever was left when she inevitably got worse. The lightheadedness eased after a few breaths, and she pulled herself upright.

"Are we going to Marcus now?" Emmett asked.

"No. Still Katya's first." Rory looked at him. "We don't need her heart, but we do need her help. We're getting Carlo out of Marcus's headquarters before we try to steal back my heart."

Emmett stared blankly at her.

"Look, I know you care more about Carlo than me, so the only way I can be sure you're not going to double-cross me is if we save him first." She took a shaky breath as she stepped out into the cold. "But the guards aren't exactly going to let us go retrieve him before escorting us to Marcus if we approach them with a deal like we'd planned. We need a way to get Carlo out of the house before then."

"And Katya can do that?"

"One of her people might be able to help." Rory hoped Brook would be willing to talk about the Star, even though she still carried its scars. "And whatever happens to us, Katya will make sure Carlo is looked after." Rory sighed. "He wouldn't be the first orphan the Rapids has taken in."

She didn't mention that Katya didn't do charity cases. The son of a heart thief would be extraordinarily powerful when his gift did manifest, whatever it turned out to be. Katya would definitely keep him around until then, and after that, well, it would be up to him. At least he wouldn't be starving on the streets or working for a monster like Marcus if Rory and Emmett messed this up and died, which was the most probable outcome. She doubted Emmett was capable of pulling off a convincing enough bluff in front of Marcus.

"Marcus probably has his people watching Katya's place. Especially if he sent a guide after me."

Rory shrugged. "I know ways around that." A lower-level door that wasn't public knowledge gave Katya direct access to the water if she ever needed to make a quick escape. Getting to it by crossing the frozen river was possible, if they didn't mind taking the risk of breaking through the ice around the bathhouse.

The best place to cross would be the steps at the river square.

Instead of sticking to alleys and skirting the more crowded center of the market square, Rory walked directly into the chaos when they arrived.

A child, clutching a small pastry, crashed into Rory's leg when she turned to look for Emmett. The kid grabbed the fallen food off the ground and rushed off.

Rory could hear a vendor shouting from somewhere to her right, but the man probably wouldn't leave his cart unattended for anything less than his coin purse being cut from his belt. The kid vanished down an alley after jumping up and ripping one of the wanted posters off the wall, and Rory's chest tightened. She'd done the same when she was with Jax, taking a perverse delight in tearing up Cohort posters for his arrest, like she was doing him some huge service.

She wanted to yell after the child what she'd learned just in time. *Kid, I hope you figure out those rebels won't take care of you. You need to watch your own back. You might be loyal to them, but it doesn't go both ways.*

"Shouldn't we not be here?" Emmett asked, trailing behind her and pushing through the flood of people.

"Crowds are better right now. We'll hear people cursing out anyone pushing through them to get to us, and we can lose ourselves in the chaos."

"Or get lost," Emmett grumbled.

It was easy for Rory to forget he wasn't like her. Dragging him halfway across the city by circuitous routes had probably left him totally confused and disoriented. Rory stopped in front of a vendor selling chunks of roast caribou meat on sticks, partly to let Emmett catch up, and partly because the smell made her stomach snarl. "I'm hungry."

Emmett dodged a short woman with a scowl on her face that looked disconcertingly similar to the turned-down lips of the salmon hanging over the edge of her basket. "I'm not."

"Suit yourself." Rory nodded to the vendor, who was taking a handful of skewers from the flat rock where they'd been searing. He dropped a fresh batch onto the stone, and the hiss nearly drowned her next words. "You stole my heart. You can pay for what might be my last meal."

Emmett turned out his coat pocket as an answer.

Rory sighed. "Okay. I'll buy my own last meal. Not like I'll be needing the money much longer."

"You're just giving up?"

Rory handed over the few coins, picked up a skewer from the stack, and turned away from the vendor's stall. "Going up against the head of the Star Syndicate is suicide. I just happen to be dying anyway. I'm not giving up, I'm being realistic." She'd lowered her estimation of their chances since Trey had gotten the jump on her in that alley. He shouldn't have had such an easy time turning her own knife against her. But her hands had been so numb and tired she could barely hold the blade.

Food might help. She picked a chunk of meat off the stick and chewed on it as she walked. The meat was stringy and tough, but that was usual during the lean winter months. Whatever mixture of fermented fruit it had been soaked in before cooking was just as delicious as it had smelled.

"You should have had some. This is amazing." Rory licked stray juices off her fingers. She held out a small piece. "Sure you don't want a bite?" Emmett hadn't eaten since they met. She'd rather not have him getting dizzy from hunger while they were in the middle of stealing her heart back. And the more she ate, the less her stomach agreed that food was a good choice. She didn't think she could eat the rest on her own.

"I don't think I can." Emmett grimaced. "You can finish it."

When his back was turned, glancing for the third time at someone Rory had already deemed not a threat, she handed the rest of her skewer to a kid sitting on the steps of one of the buildings. While they'd been crossing the square, she'd seen the girl walk away from a pickpocket attempt with her hands empty. The girl grinned at Rory, a broken tooth showing, before grabbing the rest of the meat off the skewer in one scab-covered, dirty hand and cramming it into her mouth. Rory felt a tiny smile of her own flicker at the corner of her lips.

She stopped at the stone stairs leading to the riverbank. The worn steps were familiar; she and Old Sue used to come every day to retrieve water for the washing. Rory's shoulders ached with the phantom weight of the buckets that had hung from the pole she'd carried each morning. Old Sue had always led their way, ax slung over her warped shoulders, a stave pail on each end.

Rory had been thrilled the first time Old Sue handed her the ax's worn handle. Sue had probably been trying to make a point about how difficult it was to get water, and how if they were going to waste it getting Rory out of bloody clothes she had to pull her weight in retrieving it. That hadn't occurred to Rory then, and if it had, she wouldn't have cared. There was something satisfying about pounding the tarnished metal into the frozen surface, letting shards of ice skitter halfway across the river. Hauling full pails all the way back to the apartment was the torturous part, especially after the lichen patches had crept so far up Rory's shoulders the pole chafed them with every step.

None of the people currently chipping away at the ice or hauling up dripping pails paid Rory and Emmett any attention as they stepped down onto the river. Rory tested the gray-white ice with one foot to be sure it didn't creak or groan before placing her weight on it. She avoided the black patches where the ice had been opened, although there were few and most of them were in use. People preferred breaking the spots where someone had already done the hard work for them.

Emmett followed Rory with significantly less caution. When he put his foot inches from one of the thin places, Rory turned around.

"Haven't you ever seen the river take people under?" she scolded.

"In thaw season, sure. Which this isn't." Emmett drew up nearly level with her.

"Well, you ought to be more careful." Rory breathed in and out slowly. She might throw up if she thought about the churning in her stomach. "Once we get to the bank by Katya's, the ice is a lot weaker because of the hot springs." Katya had redirected most of the water inside, but there was still a permanent melted place where the drains ran off, and the heat from underground made that portion of the river the last to freeze. "We'll be lucky if we get to her door without breaking through."

Emmett frowned. "I thought your gift tells you where it's safe to step."

There was so much wrong with that assumption Rory almost laughed. While she did technically have a way to point her gift in Katya's direction with the stone in her bag, Emmett couldn't have known that. Besides, even her tether to Katya's location didn't do her any good at the moment. "Guide gifting only works on solid ground," she explained. "The water running under the ice seems to confuse it. My gift doesn't think anything about the river is safe to walk on."

"Oh."

Emmett thankfully stopped talking. Rory picked her way toward the opposite bank, moving slowly despite everything inside her screaming for contact with firm ground. She didn't like relying on her physical senses to find her path. It was taxing and stressful, both of which weren't good for her deteriorating condition. Maybe this was how people felt trying to navigate the chaotically tangled streets of Rime without a magic map in their heads. Rory didn't envy anyone that situation.

It was a relief to be able to lean on the solid stone and frozen earth once she'd reached the other side. Katya's bathhouse was unmistakable, jutting out over the river on wide tree-trunk pilings that kept it steady even as portions of the bank had crumbled beneath it.

The riverbank had been unstable since a thaw flood five years prior that left the shoreline in a tangle of half-standing houses, water-logged shops, and plots swept completely clear. Lots had sold for less than half their real value, owners desperate to make any money they could from the ruin left behind. Katya had snapped up everything surrounding the natural hot spring, then combined her gift with some retired miners' abilities and the Flare's knowledge of pipes and mechanics to construct her bathhouse.

There was a small bend in the river's flow between them and the building, and Rory gestured to the overhanging bank. "Can I trust you to stay put here until I come get you?"

Emmett didn't respond.

"No sense risking someone recognizing you and putting Katya's people on edge when we need her help."

Emmett nodded and ducked back into the shadowed gap.

"If you run, I'll find you, and all you'll have done is slow us down," Rory said, waving his scarf at him again before tucking it back into its hiding spot.

She stepped out toward the building. The ice around the drain chute was black, and slush had overflowed and covered even the thicker ice under her feet. The wetness soaked into the seams of her boots and through her socks.

A shuffle of steps on rock drew her attention. *Really, Emmett? You're going to make me chase you again, after I promised to help you rescue Carlo?* Rory turned around, ready to shout at him. It would be his own fault if Katya's guards came running and remembered him from yesterday.

Emmett wasn't climbing up the bank. Someone was coming down. A pale goldenrod-dyed scarf peeked out from the collar of his coat. A hacksaw in one hand was visible in the faint gleam from the shuttered lantern in the other. His path would take him straight to a long, thin pipe that had been partially exposed when the bank crumbled during the last thaw.

Flare smiths hadn't only made a system to move water through the bathhouse. The same seepage from the fallen star that heated the underground pools gave off a gas that ignited at the merest spark. The Flare used it to fuel their forges, maintaining the intense heat needed for starsilver smithing without paying for cord after cord of expensive wood.

When Katya's efforts to redirect the natural hot springs had uncovered a vein of gas alongside the water, she'd seen an opportunity. She'd bargained with the Flare to reduce her prices for starsilver smuggling in exchange for them installing and maintaining a secondary pipe system to channel the gas for heat and lighting. Her concern about an exclusive deal had also taken into account the consistent repairs and replacements needed on the pipes. Without those, Katya's system could decay and corrode, posing a risk of the gas escaping or a stray spark turning the place to ash.

But there was always the much more immediate risk of sabotage.

Marcus wasn't content sending one of his people to check on Emmett's progress. He'd gotten tired of waiting for Katya's heart to be stolen and taken matters into his own hands. If Rory didn't get to him first, this man might kill two birds with one stone. The route he was taking down the bank led him right past Emmett's hiding place, and the small overhang wouldn't be enough cover once the man set foot on the ice.

Rory ducked back under the drain chute to stay out of sight, trying to ignore the faint creaking under her boots. Wasting more heartbeats by panicking about potentially falling through the ice wasn't an option. If she could circle around, she might be able to come up behind the saboteur and catch him unaware. Emmett had surprised her when he stole Trey's heart, but he wouldn't be able to do that again with one in his locket.

As soon as the man's head dropped below the overhang, Rory shuffled along the ice and started climbing. Chunks of earth and stone shifted under her hands, but none of them dropped to the ice below. She moved as quickly as she could once she reached the top of the bank. Whispered voices drifted up from below.

"I'll get her heart. That's why I'm here right now. I found a way in," Emmett said, his voice the same tone of tense desperation as when Rory was about to stab him.

"Boss is tired of waiting. He'd rather make sure it's done fast and done right." The unfamiliar voice was laced with menace.

"Just give me a few more hours," Emmett pleaded. "I'll get him exactly what he wants."

"Then you're going to do it with me watching you the whole time. Come on, then, get busy."

Rory was far enough down the bank that she could see the stranger standing behind Emmett and a bit to his side, out of easy reach of his hands. The hacksaw had been replaced with a small, glinting blade.

The man shoved Emmett's shoulder, and Emmett stumbled forward. The locket fell free of his coat, glittering brightly against his chest.

"Hold on a minute. You already got a heart. What's this game?"

Rory didn't want to wait for Emmett to fumble his way through some half-true explanation. She dropped the last few feet to the ice and locked her arm around the stranger's, pinning his own knife and laying hers across his throat.

"Well, I think we just got a pretty decent bargaining chip to convince Katya to open that door," Rory said, relishing the way the man's shoulders stiffened.

The three of them tracked around the river's edge to the escape hatchway, a small door cut partly into the rock and partly wood-framed like the rest of the building.

"Emmett, you're going to need to knock pretty hard," Rory said.

Emmett slammed a fist against the wood, and the sound echoed under the pilings.

It took only a few minutes for someone to answer the door. Wolf opened it a crack, his dark hair curling from the steam slipping out behind him, sharp eyes scanning the three of them. A pen was tucked behind his ear. He had probably been busy doing Katya's books and happened to be the closest person to answer the door.

Four years ago, Katya had won ownership of the gambling debts Wolf owed the Coin Syndicate when their leader put them up as collateral in a high stakes game. Wolf had been working off the balance ever since. He excelled at mathematics, and he probably would have won ten times what he'd lost if the Coin didn't rig all their games. Katya just happened to be slightly better at cheating. And a much more tolerable employer.

Rory shoved her prisoner a few steps forward. "Go tell Katya that Rory Blake is here with a warning. Caught this fellow snooping around the bank, and I have it on good authority he was planning some kind of sabotage."

Wolf tilted his head, looking them over. "That's all?"

"All I can tell you. I need to speak directly to Katya. And I have someone I need to bring with me. We need invitations to her inner circle for two, or what I know stays with me." Rory raised an eyebrow.

"I'll pass that along." Wolf closed the door, and Rory glanced at Emmett, who looked extremely confused.

"I can't leave you out here," Rory said, nodding to her prisoner. "These people are determined. The only place they can't get without raising an alarm is into Katya's inner circle. You're going to have to come with me."

Her captive attempted to say something, but Rory shut it down with a slight tightening of her blade against his throat. He swallowed, a streak of blood running down his skin, and stayed silent.

The door opened again after a few minutes, and this time, Wolf wasn't alone. Rory recognized the two people with him as the twins Katya had recruited from a street-fighting gig where they went head to head in performative bouts that nevertheless had kept the crowd amused. The woman had a band of Rapids-blue paint running down her face through her left eye, and her brother wore two stripes across his nose. They'd kept their flair for the dramatic and their menacing presence. Good choices to deal with the would-be saboteur.

Once they'd taken her prisoner off her hands, Rory turned to Wolf. "Did she agree to meet?"

As an answer, Wolf held out his hand, two shining tokens pressed between his fingers. Rory rolled her palm over, and he dropped them into her glove. "She says you'd better make it worth her time."

"I already have." Rory held out her arm, letting Blizzard perch on the rocky bank next to the pipe, then stepped through the door. Emmett followed, closing the door behind him, and Wolf locked it. "Oh, and you might want to put a few people outside keeping an eye on that gas pipe," Rory added as she started down the hallway. "Blizzard's great at sounding the alarm, but he's not really in any shape to take on a saboteur solo."

"You couldn't have told us that a bit sooner?" Wolf asked.

"I wasn't inside the building then," Rory replied. "Now it's my life on the line if they try again." Wolf sighed and hurried off toward the door where Rory assumed some of Katya's guards spent their spare time.

She handed Emmett one of the two flat disks with the three-circle design stamped in the center. "Let me do the talking, and whatever you do, don't tell her what you are, unless you want to join the Star guy we brought in. I doubt Katya would be particularly forgiving if she finds out what you were going to do to her."

"You were going to let me."

"She doesn't need to know that."

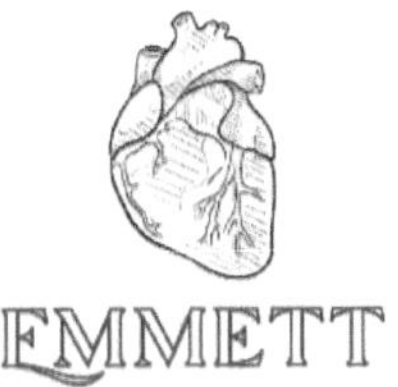

15 BELLS

The last time Emmett was at Katya's bathhouse, he'd been wondering how he was going to palm a token to get through the secured doorway when not one single person with access to Katya's inner circle had gone in or out the whole time.

He didn't have *that* problem anymore, but he did have a new one. Access to the third level of the bathhouse meant leaving any weapons and clothing in small cubbies built into the wall in an antechamber. Flickering flames in smoky-glass globes lit the room instead of candles. Narrow pipes ran along the wall below the sconces, miniature versions of the one the Star saboteur had tried to cut. Emmett had no idea what Katya planned to do to the man. He could only assume he'd find out for himself as soon as they came face to face.

He'd removed the fake Flare band around his wrist with the help of Rory's knife, but he couldn't take off the locket. The enchantment on it meant only Marcus himself could do that. Katya knew an attempt had been made on her life yesterday by a heart thief. To show up at her headquarters a day later, wearing a heart-shaped locket, would be far too much of a coincidence for him to pass it off as anything other than the truth.

"Are you sure we both need to go in?" Emmett asked in a low voice, running a finger around the collar of his sweater. There was no guard in the anteroom, probably because the ones outside either door were on alert for any sign of trouble.

"Unless you want to wait outside and hope none of the guards recognize you from yesterday. Where Katya's concerned, you're safer the closer you stick to me." Rory had already put most of her clothing away. "Besides, I don't know about you, but I intend to enjoy the baths while we're here. Might as well not waste the opportunity. It's rare enough." She rubbed a hand over a rough, reddish-gray lichen scab on her shoulder. Her whole back was a mosaic of half-healed skin and dried blood. "Almost worth dying for."

Rory's sleeves had hidden the purple shade that now crept halfway up her arms. Her feet and legs, too, were purplish-gray almost to her knees, a dead color that belonged on a corpse, not anything still living and moving and breathing. Emmett shuddered and turned away.

He'd killed a lot of people. Rory was the first of them he'd actually regretted.

He removed his sweater and the bloodstained shirt underneath it, folding them up small enough to fit into the box in the wall. Rory started to say something before her voice trailed off in a startled gasp. The room fell into uncomfortable silence.

"That was Marcus being reasonable. Or so he claimed." Emmett didn't turn around. He didn't want to see whether Rory pitied him or thought he deserved those scars and more for what he'd become. "I tried to escape after the first

time he made me steal a heart. I should have known better."
He shuddered. "He told me the next time, it would be Carlo
he punished."

"We're going to get Carlo back," Rory said quietly.
"We're going to do it right, and Marcus is never going to be
able to threaten either of you again. Once you incapacitate
him and have my heart, we're going to kill him."

That bothered Emmett less than it probably should have.
What did concern him was the fact they would most likely
never get close enough to succeed.

Rory didn't know Marcus like Emmett did. The memory
of how he got those scars was ragged around the edges, hazy
from cold and misery, but a few things were painfully clear.
The sharp blade at his throat that had stopped him and Carlo
both only a few steps from what Emmett had hoped was
freedom. The chill seeping into his hands from a rough stone
wall competing with fiery lines crossing his back from each
fresh lash. Marcus's hands firm on Carlo's shoulders, fingers
digging into his tattered sweater, forcing him to watch.

The worst of it came after Trey had coiled up his whip
and walked away.

*Emmett took one step away from the wall, and agony seared through
his back and shoulders. He crumpled to the courtyard's blood-streaked
cobblestones. The shivers that racked through him the moment his skin
touched the icy stone set every lash on fire all over again.*

*Footsteps clattered in his direction, and Emmett forced his eyes open.
Carlo crashed to his knees beside Emmett, eyes wild and frightened,
sweater still twisted out of shape at the shoulders from Marcus's grip.
Blood left crimson smears on the knees of his pants.*

*Carlo's hands hovered inches from Emmett's arm. Seeing his son
afraid to touch him, even if it was most likely an attempt to avoid
causing even more pain, made Emmett's heart twist in a way his gift
never could.*

Carlo's lips moved, but no sound escaped them. Emmett still recognized the shape. "Dad?"

"I'm..." He couldn't tell Carlo he was alright. He couldn't even promise things would be okay. "I'm sorry."

Carlo rocked back and forth, arms hugged around his chest, before a torrent of words spilled out so fast Emmett struggled to understand. "He said this only happened because you wanted to leave. Why did we do that, Dad? Why aren't you happy here?"

Emmett knew how poisonous Marcus's words could be. It had been the same convincing promises, false concern, and tempting reward that had gotten Emmett mixed up with the Star in the first place. Hearing how deeply they'd infected his own son was a worse punishment than the lashes.

"Emmett."

Rory's hand on his arm jarred him out of the memory. It was only sweat rolling down his back, not blood. The air was stealing his breath with its humid warmth, not its frosty chill.

"Marcus wants Carlo to trust him. He won't hurt that boy unless you're there to witness it." Rory broke off, taking a few deep, shuddery breaths before continuing. "It does him no good to be cruel when you can't see it. He's counting on you to come back because you're afraid he'll hurt Carlo. If you don't, Carlo is his best chance of living longer than a month."

Emmett shook his head. "Marcus doesn't need to persuade Carlo to his side by pretending to be kind. He can get what he wants by force just as easily. He could be torturing Carlo right now and telling him it's my fault, that if I come back I can stop it, but I don't care enough to do that." He coughed, choking on fear and the heavy scent of damp cedar.

"Then you're going to prove him wrong. Either way, you aren't going to make this better by giving up and going back and caving to Marcus all over again. You're only going to draw things out until either you get desperate enough to try to escape on your own again, or Carlo ends up like you, stealing hearts for that monster to stay alive. Is that what you want?"

Emmett swallowed and shook his head.

"This is your best chance to get both of you out of that place and start over. I have connections and a vested interest in taking Marcus off the board." Rory sighed. "There's nothing we can do about Marcus right now except worry, and that won't help anything. If you're scared of what he might be doing to Carlo, you need to focus that into something productive, like retracing what happened when you got caught, so we don't make the same mistakes. Okay?"

With that mentality, it wasn't surprising Rory had survived Rime so long. No regrets, no second-guessing herself, only determination to work with the situation at hand. She was as hard and sharp as her own blade, honed to a deadly edge by the way she'd learned to live. Emmett couldn't help but wonder if he was looking at Carlo's future. Emmett had dragged him into a life that made survival the only priority, no matter the cost. The legacy he'd left his son thus far was desperation and bad decisions and blood on his hands. He had to make it right.

"Okay. I can do that."

"Good. Because if Katya smells a moment of weakness, she will hold your head underwater until you stop breathing," Rory said with an entirely too cheerful shrug. She slammed the door of her cubby and locked it, then removed the key and hung the leather cord attached to it around her neck. She took a few steps toward the far door. "Come on. You're wasting time, and I'm getting cold."

The room was so hot Emmett had been afraid he might fall asleep on his feet. Losing her sense of temperature couldn't mean anything good for Rory's chances of staying alive long enough to get her heart back. She was using up the few heartbeats she had left traveling all over the city. There was no way to know if she would run out of time before her plan fell into place, but at the rate her body was failing, her odds didn't look good.

Emmett stuffed his pants and boots haphazardly into his own space and hung the key around his neck. The metal clattered against his necklace, and Emmett flinched. He couldn't remove the locket, but he could make it a bit less visible. He slid the heavy, glowing heart along the chain to the back of his neck, where it would be more or less hidden under the rough edges of his hair. The chain itself he tucked under the strap holding the key. The leather cord wasn't wide enough to totally conceal the starsilver, but Emmett would have to take his chances.

His leg ached when he took a step toward Rory. Emmett looked down at the wound. It was still closed, but the skin around the gash was red and swollen, starting to pull away from itself at the center. At the rate the healer's work was unraveling, Emmett's leg might give out before Rory's heart.

Rory knocked sharply on the door as soon as Emmett joined her. The guard on the other side opened a small slot near the handle and accepted Rory and Emmett's tokens. "Step back from the door, please," he said gruffly. A key turned in the lock, and the man stepped inside. He wore only a loose, knee-length sleeveless shirt, but a curved knife was attached to the belt around his waist. Leather wraps covered his wrists, neck, and chest regardless of the heat that followed him through the gap.

Emmett suppressed a shudder. If the locket gave him away, they'd fail before they even walked through the door.

He tensed, preparing for the edge of the guard's blade across his throat.

Instead, the man took two clay cups and a pitcher from a shelf. "Drink up," he said, filling the cups and handing them over.

Rory swallowed hers immediately, and Emmett followed suit, the water a relief to his dry throat but sitting uncomfortably in his empty stomach. Once they handed the cups back, the guard opened the door and waved them on.

Rory descended carved stone steps into a room so full of steam that despite dozens more gas lamps flaring on the walls, Emmett could barely see an arm's length in front of him. He stepped carefully, not wanting to walk off the edge of one of the deep pools. Rory's voice was oddly muffled and distorted when she called back to him to turn left before he ran into a wall.

Katya's design allowed a certain amount of anonymity for her prestigious guests. Sudden movement of any kind was liable to pitch someone into the nearest bath, and it was impossible to see anyone in the room through the heavy clouds of steam. There could be ten of the Star's people in the room, and Emmett would have been as safe as he could be anywhere in Rime.

He felt a lot less secure when he considered the possibility that Katya could control the water in the air as a weapon. Emmett swallowed and moved toward Rory's voice.

Once Emmett caught up, Rory began winding her way between the pools, her steps faltering and a little uncertain, still moving faster than Emmett thought was safe on the slick stone. She stopped at a door that appeared out of the haze as if it was solidifying into existence. When she knocked, the sharp staccato deadened into nothing almost before it reached Emmett.

The door swung open. A tall woman appeared in the opening, water trailing down her body and splashing onto the stone around her. Her red hair was piled into a straggling mass of curls that still managed to appear elegant, her pale skin flecked with coppery marks and an assortment of livid pink lines crisscrossing her arms and chest. Katya Roland wore the scars life had dealt her as both a badge of honor and a tacit warning.

"I was told you had news for me," she said coolly, folding her arms and frowning.

"I think you'll find it both valuable and timely," Rory replied.

"I certainly hope so. I trust you, but your companion…" Katya's gaze drifted to Emmett's chest.

He winced at the familiar weight resting there. The locket must have slid back to its usual position while he was stumbling through the room.

The syndicate leader's eyes narrowed, the fingers of one webbed hand drumming a sharp rhythm against the other arm. "He waits out here."

"Not the terms of my deal." Rory spun halfway around on her heel, wobbling and catching herself on the doorframe as she did.

"Is there a problem?" Katya asked.

"Less of one than you'll find yourself having if you decide not to listen to me."

Emmett couldn't imagine intentionally agitating a syndicate leader that way. Rory's actions felt more like a dance or a game than a negotiation. She seemed to be on, if not friendly, at least comfortable terms with Katya. And she'd still been willing to let Emmett take the woman's heart if it would keep her alive.

"If anything happens, both of you will pay the price."

"I understand." Rory's voice was breathless and somewhat choked.

Katya moved out of the doorway, and Rory stepped in. Emmett followed her before Katya could change her mind.

If possible, there was more steam inside the tiny compartment. Emmett jumped, startled, as Rory sank into the floor in front of his eyes. It took him a moment to realize she was descending a set of steps into another pool, this one taking up nearly the entire room. Emmett followed, wincing at the water's heat against his skin. He was sure he'd get used to it, but the first touch felt like he was being boiled alive.

Emmett could barely make out Katya's red curls through the steam, even by the light of tiny jets of flame set in a low circle behind the pool. The water came up to his chest when he stepped off the last of the stairs, and he moved slowly toward Rory, who'd thrown one arm over the edge to hold herself up in water lapping at her chin.

On the other side of the pool, Katya leaned both elbows on the smooth stone, her posture relaxed and at ease. She was literally in her element. And she'd forced both Emmett and Rory into it, the same as she did to anyone who wanted a personal audience with her. Emmett had no doubt if either of them tried to harm Katya, the water itself would kill them without the syndicate leader doing more than raising a single finger.

"Start talking. I didn't let you in here to trick a free bath from me," Katya said. There was no real edge to her voice, despite the words.

"The man we caught was headed for the gas pipe."

A loud splash came from Katya's direction, as if she was bodily hauling herself out of the water.

"Give me some credit," Rory continued. "I warned Wolf before he sent us in here." She paused and took a halting breath. "I wasn't keen on walking into a building that might blow up at any second."

The chaotic ripples in the bath stilled. A circle of wood, the cross-section of a tree trunk, glided across the surface. Two clay mugs rested on top. Rory took one and handed the other to Emmett. He eyed the reddish-brown liquid inside with concern. Drinking water the guard handed him had been one thing. Accepting an unknown beverage from a syndicate leader seemed like a risk he'd be better off avoiding.

"Drink it or you'll get lightheaded. Trust me," Rory said. Her voice had an undertone of strain, and she sounded like she was choking on a mouthful of water from the bath. Emmett hoped that didn't mean Katya was strangling her with the dense steam. "It's just tea. Katya doesn't need to poison us."

Emmett took a tentative sip. The liquid was almost overpoweringly bitter, but it did make him feel a little less disoriented.

"That man was here because the Star is behind the Flare's supply chain discrepancy," Rory continued after draining her own cup and taking a few deep breaths. "Marcus Deahl was keeping his involvement a secret. Now he's concerned the letter I brought you yesterday contained enough for you to suspect him."

"That scum. As if he doesn't have his fingers in enough of this city," Katya snarled. "How do you know all this?"

Rory pulled herself a bit further up on the edge of the bath so her neck and collarbones were above water. "Because Marcus is the one who tried to have your heart stolen yesterday. My friend here works for him and heard why." Her words still sounded too wet and strangled.

Katya's voice dropped into a threatening snarl. "Don't pretend with me, Rory. Your 'friend' *is* the heart thief."

Emmett's own heart plunged down through his feet into the stone underneath them. He waited for water to surge over his head, flood his lungs, wrap itself like fingers around his throat. Nothing changed.

"And my guess is, from the look of you, he took yours instead." Katya's snarl faded out, replaced by a tone that conveyed more concern for Rory than herself.

"Marcus isn't going to stop trying to kill you." Rory was still projecting a confidence Emmett had left behind in the anteroom with his clothes. "You're a threat to him. And the Star doesn't allow threats to survive." She broke off, coughing, and Emmett could hear harsh, panting breaths she tried to muffle. "If Marcus can't take your heart, he'll hire someone to put a blade or an arrow through it, or to burn this place and everyone in it to the ground. Unless we stop him."

Katya leaned forward, her eyes sharp even through the hazy steam surrounding them. "No one gets close to that man. Certainly not close enough to hurt him."

"You're wrong about that. Marcus does let one person close, but only out of necessity." Rory closed her eyes for a moment, shook her head, then continued. "Emmett is the only one who stands a chance of stopping him."

Katya swirled one finger in the water, forming a tiny whirlpool beneath it. "Then what could you possibly need from me?"

"A second way in. I know Brook used to work for the Star." Emmett barely held back a startled gasp. When he hadn't seen Brook with Marcus after he'd been forcibly relocated to the syndicate headquarters, he'd assumed she was dead. "I want to talk to her. And I know you vet anyone you let close to her. Even me."

"You can speak with Brook. He goes nowhere near her. For all I know, Marcus could have found out she's here and sent him"—her hand poked out of the mist uncomfortably close to Emmett's chest—"to collect her heart and punish her for her betrayal."

The last thing Emmett would do was hurt a childhood friend he'd given up for dead months ago. "That's not why I'm here. I—"

He broke off as Rory slapped his arm, her wet palm making a damp smacking sound. He winced, rubbing the spot she'd hit.

She scowled at him. "I told you. Let me do the talking."

"He hasn't learned yet, has he? Rory Blake gets what she wants, and no one had better get in her way," Katya said with a chuckle. "Well, I know you a little better than he does. I'll give you two a chance to talk to Brook, but only on her terms. And if I hear even a whisper that Marcus knows she's alive, you will pay dearly for it."

"When we're through with him, she'll be able to walk the streets a free woman again. And so will you." Rory pushed the round slab of wood back into the steam toward Katya.

"The guard at her door will permit you to pass only with the words 'the river has no end or beginning,'" Katya said. "And he has full authority to end your lives if she orders it."

"I understand." Rory moved toward the steps, pushing Emmett away from the wall so she could keep a grip on it to pull herself along. "We're no threat to her."

"That will be up to her to decide."

Rory climbed out of the water, reaching for the door handle. She stopped, hand falling to her side, and a moment later she was lying on the ground beside the pool. Emmett scrambled up the last few steps. Rory's eyes flickered open, and she glared at Emmett when he bent down beside her. Her breaths were shallow, but he didn't see any blood on the stone or in her hair.

Katya crouched down on the opposite side from Emmett, remaining out of his reach even as she inspected the person who'd collapsed in her private bath.

"You should…do something about…these slick spots," Rory managed, pushing herself up on one elbow shakily. She was panting as if she'd run miles, chest heaving violently with each breath. "Unless you're…trying to kill everyone who comes in."

Katya's amused smirk didn't reach her eyes. "I don't think the stone is to blame for this one, Rory."

Rory shook her head, then glanced at Emmett. "Watch your step."

Rory hadn't slipped on anything, but if she wanted to deny that her body was failing her, Emmett wouldn't argue the point. He held out a hand in case Rory needed some support getting to her feet. She slapped it away and pulled herself up, somewhat unsteadily, with the doorframe. Emmett heard Katya slipping back into the water as they walked out.

When they stepped out the door, Emmett shivered. The air in the third level actually felt chilly after the overwhelming heat of Katya's private bath. Rory led the way back to the antechamber, steps still shaky and off balance. Emmett stayed close behind her, a hand out to catch her in case she fell again. One bad tumble into the pools beside them, and she could hit her head and die before her heart had the chance to give out.

Back in the antechamber, Rory snatched a folded towel from a shelf under the cups and tossed Emmett another. She leaned against the wall as she dried the end of her braid and rubbed the towel down her arms and legs. She looked at her feet, then shuddered and glanced away. Emmett didn't blame her. If anything, the purple shade had gotten worse since they'd gone inside.

Emmett winced when his own efforts to get the water off his skin reminded him of the rapidly forming bruise on his arm. "Why did you hit me?"

"Because unless I'm very much mistaken, you were about to tell Katya we needed to get your son out of there," Rory hissed back.

"Why is that a bad thing?"

"Letting her know she's the key to something you want that badly gives her the upper hand in a negotiation. She could already tell I was on borrowed time with a stolen heart." Rory winced. "No sense giving her anything more to hold over us. She had to believe we could walk away at any time without caring about the outcome."

Emmett didn't have an argument for that. Letting desperation get the better of him was how he'd gotten into so much trouble in the first place. It wouldn't help him get out. "Actually, I was going to tell her I knew Brook. We grew up together." The Seachosen community in Rime wasn't large, and most of them had been clustered in Emmett's old neighborhood. Before the Winter of Graves took some families whole and shattered the rest, they'd been a tight-knit group who spoke the same language and shared the same customs and let little come between them. But as soon as Brook had left to live with Marcus, everyone who'd known her had acted as if she'd died. Emmett hadn't heard or spoken her name in years. "Last I knew, she was Marcus's lover."

Rory sighed. "Until he got tired of her or something she did pushed him over the edge. Marcus beat her within an inch of her life. He must have believed she was dead, because his men threw her body in the river. Katya found her washed up against the bathhouse pilings. She's given Brook sanctuary ever since in return for what she knows about the Star. If Marcus found out she was alive, he'd put a bounty on her head bigger than all the syndicates put together have on yours."

"So how do you know she's here?"

"Katya sent me for a healer she could trust when it happened. And there were some rumors floating around town about Marcus and his lover having a falling out that didn't end well for her." Rory swallowed. "A few months ago, Katya asked me to deliver a message to a woman in the Seachosen district. Between all of that, I pieced together the story."

Rory pulled the sweater she'd taken from Emmett's house over her head. Emmett forced himself not to wonder if it was some kind of omen that the last woman who'd worn it had died.

Rory led the way down a hall that branched off from the main bathhouse, repeating the phrase Katya gave her to a stoic-faced guard outside a heavy door.

The man opened the door and motioned them inside. "If she says you leave, do it before I need to take you out by force."

Rory nodded and stepped through the door.

Emmett followed her into a room that was cooler than the third level baths, but still hazy with steam rising off a shallow pool in its center. A young woman sat on the edge of a low bed, her bare feet under a long brown shift dress dangling into the pool. When Brook looked up, Emmett tried not to flinch. Half her face was covered in shiny scars, a missing eye mostly obscured by falling curls. She'd braided her long, dark hair back on the comparatively less damaged side of her face, and that sharp dark eye studied both him and Rory with mistrust.

Emmett would barely have recognized Brook if it wasn't for the tattoo on her left hand and arm. Intricate swirls of ink ran from her knuckles to her shoulder, depicting a Seachosen legend that predated Starfall. Unlike the dolphin story, this one had a happy ending; after a pearl diver rescued a sea monster from a net, the creature had used its ink to paint the letters of the Archipelago's alphabet on the diver's skin, giving the Seachosen the gift of written language. Tentacles spiraled out from the creature's body tattooed on Brook's hand, each carrying one of the twelve base letters up her arm. Accents and additions swirled around them as if tossed by waves and whirlpools.

Emmett's mother had sung the rhythmic verses of the ballad as she painted the same letters onto the back of his arm in clay slip. He'd done the same for Carlo, because Theresa had claimed his handwriting was neater than hers. Every Seachosen child learned the language of their ancestors that way. Brook had made hers permanent about two years before she left to live with Marcus, when she'd still been telling everyone she wanted to open a school in their district and teach the Seachosen children about the world they belonged to, where ice and snow were only a legend.

Rory had insisted on doing the talking. But Emmett thought it might be him Brook would trust. The same heritage that made them outsiders in this part of the country made them allies, if only in a shared history.

The Archipelegian words slipped off his tongue with an ease he couldn't feel in any other language. *We're not here to hurt you.*

Brook's hands unclenched slowly.

Rory glared at Emmett.

He ignored her as he took a few steps forward and crouched to one knee, level with Brook's gaze. *"Do you remember me? From when we were kids?"*

Brook shook her head.

"Emeterio Santos. Lia and Ramón's son?" Emmett dredged his memory for something that might have survived Brook's harrowing experiences. *"I tried to make your spoon fit your hand and all it did was throw broth all over your face."*

Recognition dawned in Brook's eye. *"That was a lifetime ago. That Brook is dead. You should go."*

"I can't. I got mixed up with the Star, like you, and now I need your help."

"Whatever it is, I want no part of it."

"You don't need to do anything. We just need what you know about Marcus—"

Brook's shoulders tensed, and a shudder ran down her arms, tossing the letters on their waves like a storm had rolled in. *"Never say that name."*

Emmett nodded. He didn't like hearing it himself, and he'd suffered less than half of what the woman in front of him had at that monster's hands. *"He has my son. We want to get him out of that house and safe."*

If Rory spoke fluent Archipelegian, she was going to kill him.

"You ask for the impossible." Brook clenched a fist in the fabric of her dress. Her voice wavered.

"There's no way to get into the house unseen?" Emmett frowned, trying to reconstruct his own mental framework of the mansion. He'd only seen pieces, but he understood the logic of constructing a building. *"The kitchens?"* Food deliveries had always come to the rear of the house.

"No one is allowed into the house from there. Cart drivers knock at the doors, and the guards unload their goods. And before you ask, nothing large enough to hide a person is ever carried in without

inspection."Brook paused for a moment, then shook her head. *"There was a secret entrance to allow the Cohort officials he has in his pocket to come and go in private. The latch was inside, and only he knew the secret to releasing it."*

"But there is a door."

"You would never reach it. It's in the back wall of the house. You would still need to pass the courtyard gate."

Emmett knew the wall she meant. That explained some of the strange night sounds below his and Carlo's window that he'd been attributing to the wind.

"If we could open that door, where would it lead?"

"To a passageway behind the walls that connects to his private study." Brook shrugged. *"As I said, it does you no good."*

"It's still more than we knew before. Thank you." Emmett nodded to Rory. "We can go."

"Not before you tell me what she said," Rory whispered back as he joined her at the door.

"There's another way into the house besides the front gate. Marcus had a secret door built." Emmett grimaced. "Unfortunately, it only opens from the inside."

Oddly enough, Rory smiled. "Then we're in." She glanced from him to Brook. "How do I tell her thank you?"

"She understands just fine," Brook replied. "You shouldn't do this. The only way you'll survive is to stay as far away from that man as possible."

"Normally, I would agree with you. But this time, we have no choice." Rory looked at Emmett. "Now we can go."

RORY

18 BELLS

"Where are we going?"

Rory ignored Emmett's question as she concentrated on placing her feet firmly on the ground in front of her. She hadn't been confident in her own body's ability to function since her unfortunate tumble in Katya's bathhouse. Every breath felt like lifting an anvil off her chest, her stomach churned sickeningly, and her feet felt only distantly related to the rest of her. Even her thoughts were scattered, floating in a hazy mist, like the steam from Katya's pools had snuck inside her head and followed her out onto the street. When she'd lifted Blizzard from the riverbank to set him back on her shoulder, the small bird had felt as heavy as if he were made of lead.

"Rory?" Emmett stepped up beside her, head bent against the wind, gloved fingers beating a rapid pattern against his leg.

Rory shook her head. She had bigger problems than his nervousness.

She stopped at the next street corner to catch her breath. Her pulse swished in her ears, a sound she could almost have mistaken for water left over from Katya's bath. She wished it was, but she knew full well her head had never been deep enough in the water for that.

"Rory!" Emmett's voice was low, but insistent and distressed, cutting through the haze and the echo of her blood. Rory looked up at him.

"There's someone following us again."

When Rory shifted her position under the guise of checking her boot laces, the figure behind them was already slouching against a wall. As Rory watched, the person pulled out a pipe and a small bag from a pocket. A few moments later, a match scraped down the rough stone wall and flared to life in cupped hands.

She'd have been annoyed with Blizzard for not catching sight of their pursuer first, but he was still recovering from the knock he'd taken when Trey flung him across the alley. Rory couldn't blame the pigeon for being snuggled as far into her hood as possible. If she'd had the option, she'd have gone home and curled up under the covers a long time ago.

Rory nodded at Emmett. "You're right."

Emmett tensed to bolt.

"Emmett, don't," Rory whispered, grabbing his coat sleeve. If he ran, she couldn't hope to keep up, or catch up again in time to have any chance of getting her heart back. Rory straightened, pulled Emmett around the corner into the side street, then ducked into the closest shop's door.

Or tried to. The handle was locked. All the buildings across the street were private houses, as were the next three buildings in the row down from the shop. Worse, the street she'd chosen at random was a dead end. A defunct tavern stretched across it, windows boarded and doors nailed shut.

A peeling sign hanging by one chain advertised the name as the Slag Dump.

Emmett took two steps up the crumbling stone stairs outside the tavern. He grabbed one of the boards nailed over the windows, then stumbled backward like someone had pushed him.

"What happened?" Rory asked, as Emmett leaned his hands on his knees, panting.

In answer, he pointed.

Rory winced. The Cohort seal had been branded into all the wood nailed over the openings, as well as the doors themselves. This place hadn't just gone out of business; it had been shut down by the government. There was no getting past enchanted starsilver nails designed to thwart squatters.

Rory's luck was running out along with her time. They needed to get back on the street and take their chances. Rory reached for her knife, her arms weak and shaky. She'd need her target to be much closer than Emmett had been yesterday. She ducked her head back around the street corner to see the formerly slouching person approaching at a rapid pace, leveling a miniature crossbow at Rory's head.

So much for taking out their pursuer with her knife. Rory would be dead before she got her arm in position. She caught a glimpse of the face behind the scarf and hood. The green eyes and black hair could have belonged to half of Rime, but Rory only knew one person with a huge twisted scar through her left eyebrow.

"I'd advise against either of you running," Elena ordered in a raspy voice, pipe smoke hanging in her lungs. She looked from Rory's hand hovering near her knife to the pigeon fluffed up and hissing angrily on her shoulder. "Hand over the mark, Blake, and you walk away from this."

"I thought you'd know better than to squabble over a job I beat you to."

"Last I heard, Rory Blake didn't do bounties." Elena shrugged, crossbow still leveled at Rory's chest. "If you've decided to change professions, I might as well get rid of the competition." Elena tilted her head to the side. "But you look like death already." She smirked. "So I shouldn't have any trouble taking him off your hands."

"Listen to me," Emmett said. "Whatever the Star offered you, it's a lie. You can't trust them. They'll double-cross you the second you bring me to Marcus. You'll be lucky to walk away empty handed at the end of the day."

Elena laughed, the sound like a death rattle in her throat. "I'm not taking you to the Star. I don't want their blood money. But that Ravens lieutenant was my cousin." The tip of the crossbow moved from Rory to Emmett. "And you're going to pay for her death."

"If you want the person responsible for that, killing him isn't going to help you," Rory said. "He's been working under the orders of Marcus Deahl."

"Nice try. If he was, he wouldn't have attacked the Star last night."

Rory looked from the crossbow's aim to its owner's face in confusion. Trey's death shouldn't have been traceable to a heart thief, not when Rory had finished the job with a clean slice across his throat.

"You can't not know about that. It's their wanted posters that finally gave us all something to be looking for." Elena frowned. "How'd you find him without one?"

Rory had very little to lose. "What are you talking about?"

Elena, her weapon still pointed at Emmett, pulled a sheet of paper from her pocket and held it out to Rory. "I got lucky. I was already hanging around Bell Square looking for another mark when a couple Star people came through.

They were handing these out to the crowd. Trailed my mark to the bathhouse and happened to see you two come out, before he put up his hood to hide that hair."

Rory leaned forward, as if to get a closer look at the paper. Then she threw herself directly at Elena's waist, shoving her crossbow hand up as she did. The bolt flew wildly off to the side, and Rory landed on Elena's chest in a heap, grappling for her knife. Elena kicked and struggled, trying to fend off both Rory and Blizzard. The pigeon flapped around Elena's face, trying to get past her scarf and hood, and his beak already had a bloodstain smeared across it. Rory was wasting more heartbeats fighting, but she couldn't let Elena take Emmett.

Elena gasped and went still. Rory looked up, wondering what threat larger than her had entered the fray.

Emmett's hand had closed on Elena's wrist, just below her glove. "I don't want to kill you," he said quietly. "But if you don't let us walk away, I will."

He kept his hand on Elena's wrist while Rory tied the bounty hunter's hands and feet, snapped the crossbow string and tossed Elena's bolts and backup knife down the street, and snatched the now-torn paper from the gutter. Rory stuffed the wanted poster into her pocket and stood up carefully, not wanting to topple over into the street. She nodded to Emmett, and he released Elena's wrist and joined Rory.

"We're just going to leave her?" Emmett whispered once they'd rounded the corner and Elena couldn't hear.

"She saved my life once. I owed her one. Now I don't." Rory shrugged. "She's probably got two more knives on her I couldn't find. She'll get free before the weather gets her."

"Doesn't that mean she'll come find us again?" Emmett asked, looking over his shoulder.

"Elena's not a guide. Her gift is sensing people's presence when she's close to them, like if someone's hiding in a building." Rory even knew the exact night Elena's gift had manifested. The memory materialized as clearly as any her gift called up.

Rory glanced up at the blackened walls of the burnt-out house. The stained red rag Jax hung from the window to announce a meeting was still fluttering in the wind. To a random passerby, it looked like a shred of scorched curtain from the house had slipped through a gap in the window, but to the teenage rebels, the ragged cloth was a clear message.

Rory took another step toward the house when a shadowy hand emerged from an alley and clamped down hard on her arm. Another slapped itself across her mouth, muffling the startled yelp Rory had been about to release. She grappled for her knife with her free hand, but stopped when her attacker stepped out into the glow of the corner streetlamp. Light caught on the twisted red scar disappearing into the taller girl's hat.

"Shh."

Elena turned Rory around, dragging her down the alley. Rory tried to pull away, the awkward grip on her arm and face wrenching her into an uncomfortable position, but Elena didn't release her hands until she'd hauled Rory across another street and into a second alley. Rory twisted free of her grip when Elena finally stopped, rubbing her sore shoulder.

"What are you doing?" she hissed.

"There's someone in there," Elena said, her voice trembling.

Rory frowned. "Of course there is. We're meeting tonight."

"I can feel them, Rory," Elena whispered. "Whoever they are, they're not our friends." She looked over the buildings beside them to the blackened, burnt walls barely visible through swiftly falling snow. "Go home, Rory, and don't come back."

Rory found out the next day, from a boy with a gash in his shoulder and a haunted glaze in his eyes, that it had been a whole unit of Cohort guards, tipped off to the rebels' meeting place by someone inside the group. They'd swept up almost half the kids Jax had called in, although the rebel leader himself slipped through their hands.

Elena wasn't the only person Rory stopped speaking to after that night. She'd waited three days to see if Jax would come to Old Sue's to check on her. In the end, she'd tracked him down herself, relying on her knife sheath, a family heirloom of Jax's that he'd given her along with the starsilver blade. What she'd found at the end of that search had severed any ties to the rebels Rory might have clung to.

Rory moved her hand away from the worn tooled leather and blinked a few times until the boarded-up door in front of her swam into focus. The building had been condemned and sealed by the Cohort, but Rory was willing to bet if she climbed up to its cedar-shake roof, she'd find a section missing.

She'd never realized Jax avoided the Cohort's searches by hiding in the buildings they'd already secured and written off. His boasts about the government's confidence in their own methods becoming their undoing had apparently been based on personal experience.

Rory curled her chilled fingers into a fist to gain some feeling in them before she slipped a glove over her hand and began scaling the crumbling bricks.

When she dropped through the gap in the roof onto a snowdrift, the sharp point of a knife dug into her spine between her shoulder blades.

"You shouldn't be here."

Rory didn't dare try to turn around. "You never came. I could have been arrested, I could have been dead."

She wasn't sure she was surprised anymore. Not when the echoing memories from the knife sheath had shown her Jax crouched on a rooftop in the shadows of a chimney, looking down at a blood-soaked alley. Waiting until her father's killer rushed off before approaching the dying man. Jax had told Rory and her mother that he'd stumbled across Dad's body after he was already dead, when the truth was, he'd hidden like a coward until the danger was past. Just like he was doing now.

"If you had, what good would me coming around have done you?" The chill in Jax's voice rivaled the wind whistling through the gap in the roof. *"I've been betrayed by one of my own. It's not safe for me to go anywhere in the city right now, let alone get near any of your homes. I have no idea whose houses the Cohort could be watching. You shouldn't have come here, Rory. You need to go."*

The Rory who'd naively believed Jax would take her father's place died that day. It looked like the Elena who'd risked her own freedom to warn Rory about the ambush had too. Rory couldn't see any part of her in the woman she'd left in the alley. Both of them had come to believe the same thing Jax had. The only way to survive Rime was to stop caring about the fate of anyone other than yourself.

Rory waited until she and Emmett had doubled back on their own trail twice to actually look at the paper. It was a wanted poster almost exactly the same as the ones the Ravens and Midnights had tacked up all around the city. But in the section between the headline and the reward, this one had two paragraphs and a crude sketch.

Heart thief wanted for attempted assassination of Star lieutenant. Consider highly dangerous and apprehend with caution.

Male Seachosen, approximately thirty years old, dark hair with multiple stripes of gray, dark eyes. Last known to be wearing a tan coat and brown scarf.

The sketch was barely passable, but it picked out Emmett's deep-set eyes and straight nose unmistakably. Rory shoved the paper back into her pocket. "We need to get off the street."

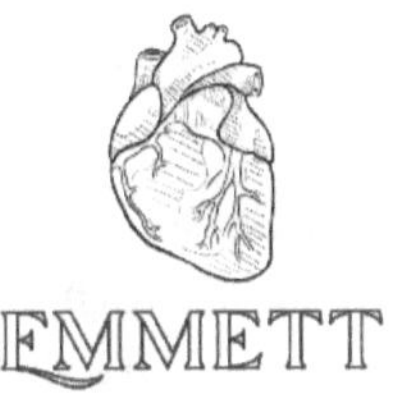

EMMETT

19 BELLS

Emmett swallowed down the terror threatening to freeze him in place. His stomach churned, and even though there was nothing left in it, he thought he might throw up. Marcus had given his description to every bounty hunter in Rime. Even the ones who wanted nothing to do with the Star would use it to find him for the Ravens or the Midnights or any other syndicate that decided it was time to put a price on his head.

"Why would Marcus reveal you?" Rory asked. "You're his weapon. Keeping you anonymous was in his favor."

"I don't know," Emmett said. "Marcus is always more unstable when he has a new heart. His mind is trying to wrap itself around your lifetime of memories on top of his own and five others'. It's entirely possible he doesn't remember having told me not to come back without Katya's heart." He swallowed. "I want to rationalize it somehow. Because the alternative is that he's finally snapped. And Carlo is still in there with him."

"He won't be for much longer," Rory replied.

Emmett was trying not to think about the worst reason Marcus might have decided his current heart thief was expendable. Carlo's gift shouldn't have been ready to manifest yet, but there were stories of it happening to children as young as five. Usually, that was under extreme circumstances, like someone's control of water appearing to douse a fire spreading through their home or a child tearing the earth apart under the feet of someone who had been tormenting them. Emmett didn't want to know what Marcus could have done to Carlo to turn him into another heart thief. Or what he would do if he thought he needed Carlo more than he could trust Emmett.

Marcus had already given Emmett a second chance, something he wasn't known to offer lightly. Another botched escape attempt would almost definitely end in far worse than a whipping. "What if we only make things worse?"

Rory responded by drawing her knife. Emmett flinched back, heart racing in his ears. He shouldn't have said anything. If he'd made Rory question his determination to see this through, she might have assumed he'd double cross her to put himself at least partially back in Marcus's good graces.

Then he heard the whining howl.

Rory leveled her knife at the shadows in an alley. A malamute limped out, head tilted heavily to one side, fangs bared. The tooth-edged tongue lolling between its lips almost touched the ground. Bony protrusions had sprouted from its shoulders and spine like spikes on a fence, and its patchy tail still carried enough quills to make encountering it an extremely unappealing thought. Blood oozed from raw wounds on its ribs and one foreleg.

The dog whimpered, low and pained, its quilled tail tucked between its legs.

"Easy, there," Emmett said quietly, hoping his tone settled the animal a bit. "What's the matter with you?"

"Emmett, back up," Rory hissed. Her knife hand shook. "It shouldn't be approaching us like that."

"It might think we have food." Feeding stray malamutes in the city was as illegal as owning them. Some people did it anyway, and dogs that learned humans could be kind to them might seek people out when they were hungry or hurt. Emmett had nothing to throw to distract the animal, but maybe Rory did. "Do you have any of that caribou meat left?"

Rory glared at him for a moment before turning her attention back to the dog. "More likely, it's got bite sickness."

Emmett flinched. Diseases from the outside world rarely infected Rime's creatures, but sometimes the animals on ships brought outbreaks of a sickness that made animals mindless and vicious. Being bitten by one was a death sentence. Emmett stepped backward toward a side street one foot at a time, hoping he wouldn't trip and fall flat on his back.

Rory followed, her gaze still locked on the shambling, half-dead animal facing them. Just as Emmett reached the corner of the alley, the dog's uninjured foreleg collapsed underneath it and it tumbled to the ground with a quiet whine.

Rory let out a shaky breath.

Emmett looked from the knife in her hand to the dog. "Should we…should we do something?" He didn't like the idea of leaving the creature to attack the next person who walked past. And he hated letting even a sick, mindless animal die alone and agonized in the middle of the street.

"I'd have to get closer to it than I want to be." Rory grimaced. "If it's not dead already, a Cohort patrol will put an arrow in it when they come across it. And we need to be gone before they come around," she said, slamming her knife back into its sheath with a metallic clunk.

Emmett looked back once at the crumpled form before turning and following Rory down the street. He couldn't blame her for not wanting to get close to the dog and risk infection, although it probably wouldn't matter in a few hours. She was as much a walking corpse as anyone bitten.

"We're here," Rory said as they rounded the next corner, nodding to a forge with an intricate wrought-iron door. "There's only one person in Rime who can build a hidden door as sophisticated as the one Brook described, and this is his place." Unfortunately, the windows were dark, only a wisp of smoke rose from the chimney, and the door was locked with a collection of bars and gears and levers Emmett couldn't begin to sort out.

"Where is he?" Emmett asked.

Rory sighed, leaning on the doorframe. "I should have known." She slapped her forehead as if her brain had personally offended her. "Vero's an incurable card cheat, and there's a big game tonight at the Fortune's Favor. I was delivering invites all week." She frowned. "It's two streets back. I was hoping not to walk too much farther."

"I could go."

"No." Rory shook her head. "You are not walking in there. Do you have any idea how many people who have your description are going to be checking every seedy spot in this town right now?" She took a deep breath. "I can't leave you here either. We're going over to the Fortune, and you're going to wait outside while I get Vero."

"You're going to convince a determined gambler to leave a high stakes game?"

"Hopefully he's losing and will want an excuse. If not, I have my ways." Rory shrugged, then stumbled, barely catching herself on the windowsill.

"What's wrong?" Emmett asked.

Rory swallowed hard, pushing herself off the wall. "Just…just dizzy, that's all."

Her breaths were loud and shaky, and Emmett could hear a dry rasping in her throat. It was distressingly similar to the way Theresa's breathing had changed before her hand went limp in his. Maybe Rory's heart had finally given up. The strain of traveling all around the city must have taken too much of a toll.

Emmett winced. He was going to watch Rory fade away right before his eyes unless she agreed to the option she'd already dismissed earlier. "I still have Trey's heart," he said quietly. "It could at least buy you some time."

Rory looked up, glaring at him in the glow of the streetlights. "No." Her lip cracked and Emmett flinched at the sight of blood running down her chin. Rory wiped it away with one glove, wincing.

She was still panting, but Emmett wondered if a dry mouth was the reason for the harsh sound in her throat. He'd had the same trouble after heart thefts, his throat and lips parched and his tongue feeling as if it was wrapped in dusty cloth.

He glanced at the icy streaks that had formed on the window panes after the forge was banked. Snow that hit the windows had probably melted at first, running down the glass and eventually freezing as it cooled. Long icicles hung from the sills below. Dark sooty smears streaked the ice, and tiny black fragments of ash were scattered through it, but it looked more palatable than the filthy slush under their boots.

"I don't think we should go just yet." Emmett broke off one of the icicles. "Neither of us has had anything to drink since Katya's." He held out the icicle to Rory, but she broke off another from the windowsill instead, still frowning. "When I steal a heart, I get thirsty afterward, worse than usual. And we probably shouldn't confront anyone else without both of us being as ready as we can be."

Rory nodded, tucking a chunk of ice into her cheek. Emmett did the same, letting the chilly, ashy liquid slide down his throat. It wasn't ideal, but it was a solution Rory would at least accept, and it might buy her a bit more time.

Rory broke off a few more icicles and tucked them into an outer pocket of her coat. "Let's go. The more time we waste out here in the open, the more time someone has to find you."

Emmett winced at the twinge in his leg as they started back in the direction they'd come. Between that and Rory's failing heart, he wasn't sure they could survive another run-in with a bounty hunter. For a city with few laws about magic, Rime had a significant number of people who dedicated their lives to finding anyone with a price on their head. Some worked for the Cohort and were occasionally let out of the city on a short governmental leash to track gifteds who'd managed to escape Rime. Most, though, made their entire living finding people the syndicates wanted to silence.

Emmett could see why Rory would refuse to use her gift in the service of the Cohort's oppression, but a guide with her skills could have made a small fortune tracking syndicate bounties. She obviously had few scruples about working with the syndicates or about what happened to people when her job was done. "What did that woman mean, Rory Blake doesn't do bounties?" He'd rather think about anything other than what might be happening to Carlo. He snapped off another piece of ice and bit down on it hard, listening to the crack as it shattered between his teeth.

"I think that was fairly obvious," Rory snapped. She stopped at a cross street, glancing down the way that led to where they saw the malamute earlier, then turned in the opposite direction. Emmett wasn't sure if she'd picked a shortcut to the gambling hall or if she wanted to avoid another encounter with the animal.

"You tracked me down."

"Because I thought you had my heart and I wanted it back." Rory sighed. "My dad was a guide like me, and he took bounty jobs when money was tight. His last job was tracking someone." She leaned against a wall, taking a few shuddering breaths and pulling another icicle from her pocket. "He came home with a handful of coins, more than I'd ever seen at one time, and said he was promised ten times that when the job was done. All he got was a knife in his stomach." She snapped off a piece of ice, shoved it into her mouth, and pushed herself off the wall.

"I'm sorry." Emmett knew what it was like to have loved ones ripped away. He still vividly remembered the grief in Carlo's eyes when Emmett had told him Theresa was gone. It wasn't hard to imagine the same expression in the face of a much younger Rory.

"The people who hired him gutted him and left him to die in an alley." Rory's hand slipped to the handle of her knife. "We only found out because one of his friends found him and came to tell us." She looked up, eyes suspiciously shiny. "I learned my gift was the same as his that night. And I promised myself I'd never take a bounty and never let anyone come with me on a job."

Emmett didn't think it was wise to point out the obvious. Rory might have avoided following in her father's footsteps in her professional choices, but that hadn't saved her from what would most likely be a slow and painful death. And in trying to avoid that fate, she'd broken her two cardinal rules. Never track a wanted man, and always work alone.

RORY

21 BELLS

Rory stopped outside the spill of light from the Fortune's Favor's windows. The alley beside the building was full of empty ale casks waiting for a cart to collect them for refilling. It would make as good a hiding place as any. "Wait for me over there," she said. "Stay low, stay hidden. And remember, I still have your scarf. So no tricks."

Emmett nodded and ducked behind the casks.

Rory walked up to the door and knocked. The Fortune, like other Coin Syndicate establishments, was well-known as a gambling hall. Unlike the boarded-up tavern she and Emmett had passed earlier, it was never raided by the Cohort. The head of the Coin made sure a cut of his profits found their way into the city coffers, and in exchange, the Cohort ruthlessly eliminated his competition in the name of enforcing their laws against cash gambling.

A window in the top part of the door opened, and a thin-faced girl with bright pink lip stain and dark sooty eye shadow peeked out. "Invitation?" she asked.

Rory didn't have one, but she did know the password for the week. *"Gelid."*

"Sorry, but no one gets in without an invite tonight. Boss's orders."

Rory had never been to the Fortune on a big game night. She had no idea they were so exclusive.

If she couldn't get in to see Vero, maybe she could bring him to her. "I have a delivery," Rory replied, holding up the wanted poster, which she'd folded so only the blank paper was visible. "Need to hand this off direct to Vero Brae."

"One moment. I'll send him out to you."

The girl closed the panel, and Rory waited, leaning against the wall, until the door opened and a mountain of a man stepped out into the street, stretching and rolling his massive shoulders. Metallic clicks followed the motion as the gears and joints in his prosthetic left arm adjusted themselves.

"Delivery for me?" he asked, holding out a hand that was black to the elbow. His gift had replaced the skin with a char like burned tree bark, cracked and crumbling around each knuckle.

"Actually, I need you to find something for *me*," Rory replied. "At your place."

"Come back tomorrow. I'm on a hot streak." Angry breaths whistled through what was left of his damaged nose like a steaming kettle.

"Unless you want me to tell these people to start checking their cards for soot marks on the corners, I suggest you come with me now." Rory had played with Vero enough to know his trick. It was hard to accuse him of purposefully marking cards, given his perpetually char-coated functional hand, but if someone checked the deck carefully, they'd notice some of the smears were a pattern. And getting outed cheating at a Coin hall, in a game that big, wasn't something a person could walk away from, no matter how intimidating they were.

"Fine. What is it you want?" Vero asked. The burn scars on his cheek crinkled as he grimaced. Even a gift that allowed him to reach into a blazing forge and pick up red-hot metal with his bare hands couldn't prevent the effects of being splashed with molten starsilver when a crucible exploded.

He was lucky to have walked away with the scars and what was left of the arm now encased in a complicated mechanical cage of gears and joints. The enchantment on the starsilver components allowed Vero to use the arm for simple tasks like swinging a hammer. Rory had seen a variety of tools he attached to the end in place of a hand, as well as the six-inch blade concealed in a forearm brace. The expertise displayed in his replacement limb was the same mechanical skill he used to construct complex locks.

"I need to know about a door you built."

"Trade secrets, Blake. You know that."

"Door plans. Or—" Rory pointed over her shoulder and mimed thumbing a card.

Vero sighed. "At least let me go back and gracefully fold."

"Don't even think about double-crossing me. You won't outrun the Coin Syndicate." Rory waited until he'd gone back into the building, then walked over to the alley and thumped her fist on one of the casks. "You can come out now."

Emmett stood up, wincing.

If Vero had anything to say about the appearance of Rory's traveling companion when he returned, he kept it to himself. He led the way back to his shop at a pace Rory struggled to match.

She didn't think to warn him about the sick malamute until they reached the place where it had approached her and

Emmett, but the street was empty. A smear of blood had stained the icy cobblestones and turned the snow packed in the gutter a gruesome shade of crimson. Maybe a Cohort patrol had come along and put the dog out of its misery, or it had dragged itself away to die on its own terms. Rory still couldn't quite believe Emmett had actually been trying to make friends with the animal and had even wanted to feed it. Small wonder he'd ended up where he did, if he was willing to believe the best of even a snarling mongrel. Clearly, he hadn't learned anything from how poorly he'd misjudged Marcus.

Once Vero had unlocked his door and let them inside, Rory took a seat at a table covered with chunks of metal and various tools. She tried to force her brain to focus through the fog creeping around the edges of every thought. "We need to know anything you can tell us about the door you built for Marcus Deahl at the Star Syndicate headquarters."

Vero began sorting through rolls of paper in a cupboard. "One of the first trick locks I ever forged was for some little box for Feodor Deahl," he reminisced.

Rory had learned it was best to just let him talk. Trying to force him to get to the point was futile, and tended to make him take longer. Vero's stories were as elaborate and complicated as his metalwork.

"Turned out to be a fine little thing too. Still some of my best work if I do say so myself. Figure that's why his son hired me to do the door. First full-size door I ever made." He frowned. "Truth be told it was a bigger job than I was ready to tackle, but I needed the money."

If his gambling habit back then resembled his current one, Rory wasn't surprised.

"It was right after the big coup," Vero said, pulling a leather satchel off a shelf and rummaging through the contents. "Rush job. Guess Marcus figured when he'd murdered half the syndicate leaders and made enemies out of the rest, he needed a quick way to get out of that house with no one knowing."

Rory glanced at Emmett. He seemed absorbed in studying the construction of a door frame, but she could see the tightness in his jaw and the deep furrows in his forehead. He was probably as tired of waiting for Vero to get to the point as Rory.

She didn't have time to waste. It might be worth the risk to see if she could get Vero to tell them what they needed to know.

"What was the door actually like?"

"Nothing like what they tried to send me, I'll tell you that," Vero muttered. "Marcus was no hand at drawing a build. Kept sending his lackeys over with sketches I couldn't use. I had to redraw everything and then send it back to him to make sure he approved before I could so much as forge one bolt." He scowled. "For a man so bound and determined to have everything his own way, he sure didn't want to get his hands dirty. Sent everything with one of his people. Even his payment. Never did know whether he shorted me on purpose or if his runner just pocketed some of the cash for all his trouble, but he still owes me a hundred and fifty. Not that I intend to ask him to settle up any time soon."

Apparently Marcus's reclusive habits weren't a new development.

Vero retrieved a yellowed, water-stained schematic and unrolled it on the table. He pointed out a thin line where the door met the wall around it. "I built this door to be almost perfectly sealed, but the stone in that wall was so thick I had to bevel the edge so it could be opened without catching. There might be enough space for you to slide in your knife."

Vero traced the door's outline with one soot-caked finger, leaving black lines on the paper.

The catch of the lock was controlled from a mechanism inside, just as Brook claimed. But if Rory could work the tip of her blade into the tiny gap between the door and the wall, she could lift the latch with it in a way that should activate the internal release.

Vero flipped the drawing over. "Once you're inside, you'll be able to open the door with the latch. There's no key, but you need to move certain pieces in a specific sequence."

"Like a puzzle box," Emmett said, flattening out Vero's drawing with his own hand.

"Exactly," Vero replied with a hint of a smile.

"I made a box like that for…for my wife." Emmett swallowed.

Vero pointed to a smaller sketch in the top left corner. "The door that leads out of Marcus's study is hidden by a bookshelf. One of the books is the secret release. Third one from the left, on the fourth shelf, isn't real. Tipping it toward you will open the latch."

"Perfect."

"Won't do you much good though." Vero shook his head. "That's not the first door you've got to get through. Back of the house is a courtyard. Got a wall around it taller than my head."

Considering he towered over Emmett and had rebuilt every door in his forge to suit himself, that was saying something, but almost every High Quarter residence had something similar. Still, whether the wall was six feet high or sixty, Rory stood no chance of climbing over in her current condition. With the limp he was rapidly developing, Emmett probably didn't either, and Rory didn't want him going in first if she could help it.

Vero continued talking. "The only way in that doesn't involve you scrambling across spikes of metal on top is through a guarded gate. When I started working on that door one of the lieutenants gave me a piece of yellow cloth I had to show whoever was at the gate to prove I was there on official business. And every day I showed up for work, I still had to let the guards paw through my tools and my pockets to make sure I wasn't bringing anything dangerous inside."

"Let me worry about that. Just give me the drawing."

"Can't do that." Vero shook his head. "If you screw this up, and odds are you will, I can't have anyone catching you with the blueprints to one of my jobs. Even if the Star didn't dice me up over it, I'd never get another job in this town."

Rory clenched and unclenched her fists as Vero stood up. Her fingers had regained only a bit of their dexterity in the forge's warmth. To operate a door with such a complicated mechanism, she needed them functional.

"Whatever you're trying to steal from Marcus, you'll never pull it off," Vero said, opening the door to signal that their conversation was at an end. "Odds against you are too high. Best to forget the whole thing."

Rory couldn't walk away. She couldn't walk directly into Marcus's fortress either. To get through that gate, she'd need some sort of cover, and there was one service Marcus would most likely allow passage no matter how securely his mansion was guarded. Fortunately for Rory, the carts that collected waste in the High Quarter did so every day, unlike the River Quarter where the drivers followed a cycle that brought them to each street once a week.

"Thank you for your time." Rory slipped a hand into her pocket, feeling the folded paper of the wanted poster. "Emmett, we need to go. I've got what I need."

Rory couldn't let her facade of confidence slip for one moment. Her moose-headed determination that she and

Emmett would rescue Carlo from the clutches of the most ruthless syndicate leader in the city was probably the only thing keeping Emmett from abandoning the plan altogether. If he caught on to one moment of doubt, everyone else's insistence that they were doomed to failure would become louder than Rory's persistent claim that they could succeed.

Rory's toe caught on the lip of the door as they stepped out, and she grabbed the corner of the wall, leaning there until her head stopped spinning. If she took a step, she might end up on her face in the cobblestone street. When she'd been undressing at Katya's bathhouse, the sight of how far the purplish-gray, corpselike tint had crept up her arms and legs had unnerved her more than she wanted to admit. It was like seeing her future.

Emmett's reaction had concerned her too. Rory was used to her skin horrifying the people who saw it, but she had no way to know whether Emmett was just distressed by the lichen scabs, or if he knew enough about his gift's effects to have an idea of how much longer her heart would last. If she asked him, though, she ran the risk of showing him she was worried. She took a slow, measured breath. No sense using up her heartbeats any faster.

Emmett, thankfully, chose not to comment on her momentary show of weakness and fell into step with her as she haltingly moved away from the wall's support. Once they were a block from Vero's forge, Rory stopped under a street lamp's glow. The windows of the smithy in front of her were dark, but the snow landing on them continued to melt in the residual warmth, running down the glass and forming icicles like the ones at Vero's.

Rory shook out her hands, willing them to have some sort of sensation, even if it was pain. But the only way she knew they were moving was the shifting material of her glove. She clumsily fished the wanted poster out of her pocket, along with a charcoal pencil she'd palmed from Vero's drafting table, and handed them to Emmett.

"I hope you remember enough of that puzzle door to draw the latch mechanism."

Emmett looked from her to the paper. "Right now?"

"The longer we wait, the more chance you'll forget an important step." Rory blinked against the snow whirling down. The only places open this time of night were the taverns, the gambling halls, and the brothels, none of which were places she could guarantee they wouldn't run afoul of another bounty hunter. "If you use the light and one of those windows as a solid surface, I'll block the snow."

Emmett nodded, then wiped the glass mostly dry with one sleeve and flattened the paper against the window. He pulled off one glove to hold the pencil and began to sketch. Rory broke off a few more icicles and pocketed all but one. She snapped the ice into pieces and rolled them around on her tongue. The dead flavor of ash in her mouth was almost impossible to ignore.

"I need you to draw me a map of as much of Marcus's house as you remember, too," Rory added. "Show me where I need to go to get Carlo."

Emmett nodded, and below the rough diagram of the latch, sketched out a large box, adding a second one below it. The amount of rooms he filled in, and the lines between them, left gaps Rory wasn't comfortable with.

"You're sure this is accurate?"

"I was a carpenter. I know how to draw blueprints." Emmett swallowed. "Before we tried to leave, Marcus gave Carlo and me a little more freedom. We used to eat meals with him, and we were allowed downstairs during the day as long as he was close by. This is everything I saw of his house. I guessed on a few things, based on the size of the building." He pointed to the front door sketched on the paper. "He has several guards at the door at all times and others that patrol the halls. Even at night."

Rory sighed, taking the paper from Emmett and folding it up to tuck in her pocket. "This will have to be good enough. I'll take my chances."

"This might help," Emmett said. He held out some kind of carved wooden fish jumping into the air. "This used to be Carlo's favorite toy. I found it at the house when we stayed there. You should be able to use it to track him."

Rory took the carving from him and focused. A gold line, slightly faded but clear and unbroken, stretched out in front of her. "You're right. This will work."

Emmett took a shaky breath. "It might help him trust you a little more, too. If he doesn't believe I sent you, tell him the dolphins still leap into the sky at night, trying to play with their brother in the moon."

Rory had no idea what that meant, which was probably a good thing. It must have been a legend or a story Emmett told Carlo that only he would have known. She tucked the little carving into her pocket and turned her focus back to avoiding uneven stones in the road.

"I'm guessing you have a plan to get past that gate," Emmett said.

"I do, and that's where we're going."

At least Emmett hadn't contradicted her insistence that she'd be the one to find and rescue Carlo. In theory, either one of them could get inside, as long as they could get their hands on a tool similar to Rory's knife that Emmett could use to open the door. But if Emmett was the one who took Carlo to safety, he could disappear into the city with his son and leave Rory to die.

She knew all too well she was never anyone's first priority. Not anymore.

EMMETT

24 BELLS

"Is there anything else I need to know about Carlo?" Rory asked. "Besides your fish story?"

Emmett didn't bother to explain that a dolphin wasn't really a fish. "He might not talk to you at all if he's scared, especially since he doesn't know you. After we lost my parents and Theresa, sometimes he wouldn't even talk to *me*. And his elbows and shoulders hurt in storms like this. They slip out of joint easily, so don't grab his arm and yank him along if he's not coming with you."

Rory rolled her eyes. "I'll be careful with your kid. And the less he talks the better for all of us." She frowned. "Does he have anything that's been his for a few years, or might mean something to him? Trey probably isn't the only guide Marcus keeps around."

"We didn't have time to take much with us. Marcus took our coats and boots and keeps them locked in a wardrobe in his study. If Brook was right about where the secret passage lets out, it should put you inside that room. Carlo will need those when you leave."

"Okay." Rory was panting again. Even the ice she kept breaking off to put in her mouth didn't seem to be doing much good anymore, and she hadn't stopped to catch her breath or slowed her pace since the bells had sounded the midnight chime.

Emmett wanted to tell her to take a break, but he understood why she wouldn't. The bells were a somber reminder that in less than half a day, she'd be dead. And that was optimistic. At any moment, her heart could simply stop and she'd drop to the cobblestones.

Trey's heart beat a sharp, tense rhythm against Emmett's chest, clashing with Rory's hurried footsteps.

When Emmett had offered Trey's heart to Rory before, even as a temporary measure, she'd refused. But she hadn't been so obviously dying then. Rory had made it very clear how much she wanted to survive, and how far she would go to achieve that goal. If Emmett offered her the heart again when she truly was out of time, her immediate fear of death might override her concerns about losing herself in someone else's life.

But then there would be a new problem. Instead of Rory's body failing at a semi-predictable rate without her heart, they'd be racing against the unknown time it would take Trey's heart to override Rory's personality and emotions and choices.

Without her own heart to temper the influence of Trey's, Rory could shift from being Emmett's ally to his enemy halfway through their plan. She might end up siding with Marcus and turning Emmett in or using Carlo against him. Exactly how Trey's heart in Rory's body would behave, and how quickly the changes would take place, no one could know for sure until it happened.

Emmett and Marcus had both still had their own hearts when they'd taken in more, which was the only thing that had prevented them from turning into the people whose lives they'd stolen. The Star enforcer's heart Emmett had absorbed had been a dim background noise to his life, an annoying second voice in his head that felt like a reversed moral conscience. It had faded after about a month, although by then Emmett's own conscience had been stained as well.

It had taken a few hours for that heart to have any effect on Emmett, but he couldn't guarantee Rory would have the same amount of time. He hoped he wouldn't need to find out.

Emmett scooped a handful of snow from a windowsill as they passed. He'd run out of the icicles he'd saved from Vero's, and his mouth was dry from both fear and his gift's persistent snarling. The chill that spread through his body was less a reaction to the cold filling his stomach and more a sinking dread at the thought that Carlo's life would be in Rory's hands.

For the moment, Rory seemed personally invested in rescuing Carlo, but something about that didn't sit right with Emmett. Rory had been ready to kill him and anyone else who stood in her way to get her heart back. Altering her entire plan to make sure Carlo wouldn't get caught in the backlash didn't make sense.

Granted, Emmett had only known Rory for less than two days, during which she'd been slowly dying as a direct result of his actions. He of all people should know better than to judge someone based solely on their behavior in desperate circumstances. And he couldn't forget the radiant shimmer he'd seen when he'd handed her heart over to Marcus, much brighter than her callous attitude would suggest.

Rory had told Emmett not to let anyone see his weak points. Maybe she thought kindness was one of hers. In Rime, she might be right.

Emmett stopped when Rory abruptly halted, her head turning toward a crossroad where the street lantern had gone out. It was more common than not in the slums, but this close to the Commerce Quarter, smashed glass and a snuffed wick seemed out of place. "There's someone there," Rory said, nodding to a spot where the tattered awning of a building blocked the light from the street they stood on.

Emmett removed one glove. He'd gotten them away from one bounty hunter with a convincing bluff. He couldn't think of any other way to do it again. He and Rory were in no condition to outrun a threat, and Rory couldn't waste her heartbeats in another fight.

"Emmett, stop," Rory said. "Blizzard isn't worried."

The pigeon on her shoulder looked comfortable and relaxed. Whoever was hiding in the shadows, Blizzard didn't consider them a threat.

"I know you're there," Rory called.

A tall figure emerged into the streetlamp's glow. Emmett flinched at the way the light bounced off the newcomer's eyes. Some gifts took physical form in animalistic features and skills. Those were the eyes of a predator that could see clearly in Rime's pitch-black nights. Most likely, this was yet another bounty hunter.

The face that came into focus when the wind pulled a scarf away from a sharp nose and thin lips looked familiar. It took a few moments for Emmett to realize he'd seen sketches, badly done but capturing the essential features, on some of the wanted posters tacked up beside his own on building walls.

The reward for the rebel instigator rivaled the price on Emmett's own head, but because the Cohort was putting up the money, few bounty hunters were inclined to take them up on it. They'd likely end up right beside their quarry in the Bastion so the Cohort didn't need to pay.

Everyone in Rime knew trusting the Cohort was futile. Syndicates and rebel groups only had as much power as they did because no one expected the government to have anyone's interests in mind aside from their own. Unfortunately, that meant the standard anyone else had to improve on to draw people to their side was incredibly low. Emmett had learned the hard way the only thing syndicates did better than the Cohort was honestly admit their greed. Since wanted posters for rebels had been a feature of Rime all of Emmett's life, and virtually nothing had changed in thirty years, he imagined the rebels were probably just as corrupt and self-serving.

"It's been a long time, Jax." Rory's voice was flat and cold. Blizzard, picking up on her tone, began to fluff up his feathers.

"I ran into Elena," Jax said. He whistled, a low, warbling sound, and Blizzard calmed. "She told me Rory Blake was running with the heart thief and you two seemed to be working together." He frowned. "I wasn't inclined to believe her, but I also knew you weren't taking him in for the bounty. Figured I'd sniff you out and see what you were planning that was worth the risk of trusting a murderer."

Rory kept her hand on the grip of her knife. "My business with him is my own to worry about."

"Judging by the looks of you, he stole your heart," Jax continued. "And doesn't have it to give back. Or you'd have put that knife through his chest already."

Rory sighed.

"Planning to make him steal you a new one?"

Rory wasn't volunteering any information, so Emmett decided his best course of action was also keeping his mouth shut.

"Guess you're picky about what sort you want, or you'd have let him get you Elena's. You figure you'd rather take one from some High Quarter bastard? You want to turn into one of their greedy, worthless kind?"

"I'm getting my own back," Rory snapped.

"From who? My best guess, your thief's been taking them for a syndicate leader who wants to start a war. I'd have heard if the Cohort was using a heart thief." Jax raised an eyebrow. "You really think the two of you by yourselves can take on any syndicate boss in this town? All I have to do is give the word to my people, and you've got as much backup as you need."

"Don't try to pretend this is about old times' sake," Rory said. "You've wanted my gift since my dad died. Accepting your help means owing you." Rory's voice was fierce even as she leaned on the wall beside her to keep herself upright. "And if the Cohort catches me working with you, I'll die a lot worse than I will right now."

"I've been doing this a long time, and I'm still alive." Jax spread his hands, taking a step forward.

"How many of your people are?"

Jax didn't reply. Emmett got the feeling this was an old argument, something that had driven a wedge between them Rory couldn't forgive.

"You don't want my help, that's up to you," Jax finally said. He turned to Emmett and gave him an appraising glance. "But he might." The man reminded Emmett of a lynx: astute and dangerous. "Since you ran into Elena, you know every syndicate in Rime has your description. Whatever protection Rory's promising you in return for getting her heart back, she's just one person."

Emmett wanted to snap that she'd been doing fine, aside from the time she'd put a knife through his leg. The words stuck in his throat.

"The only thing the syndicates hate more than you right now is the Cohort. If you join me, use your gift to bring this corrupt government down, the syndicates will be free to run the city on their own terms. That's enough of a bargaining chip to get all but the most dedicated off your back. And those, my people can deal with."

It would have been a tempting offer, if Emmett hadn't thought taking it would put him right back where he was with Marcus. If he thought Jax would care about his son as more than a possible future recruit.

"No." Emmett shook his head. "After this, I'm done. I steal her heart back for her and that's the last one. No more." He wouldn't be a killer for anyone else, no matter how good an offer they put on the table. He'd already made that mistake with Marcus.

"Looks like you've got your answer," Rory said. "And don't even think about following us."

"I know when I'm not wanted." Jax raised an eyebrow as he turned away. "But if you change your mind about my help, Rory, you always know how to find me."

RORY

1 BELL

Rory heard Jaye's stable before she saw it. Ponies nickered faintly, their studded horseshoes ringing against stone. Pulling loaded carts up the High Quarter's icy hills required a solid foothold.

The shaggy ponies milling around the stable yard, native to the foothills of the Iron Peaks, were the only horses hardy enough to withstand Rime's weather. Cohort law required the stallions to be gelded before being driven to market. Breeding ponies in or near the city was strictly forbidden, although plenty of legends surrounded the true reason for that law. Old Sue used to break the monotony of pinning up sheets by reciting a folktale about carnivorous horses with teeth like wolves and a taste for human flesh. And scrubbing socks up and down the washboard had always gone faster when accompanied by the hoofbeat-echoing notes of a ballad about a snow-white stallion who could outrun the wind but could only be ridden by the child who'd raised him.

Rory pounded on the door, wincing at the way the vibration echoed up her arm while the hand hitting the wood felt like something separate from her own body. She leaned on the wall, glancing over her shoulder at Emmett. He looked as worn down as she felt, shuffling his boots on the icy cobblestones, head hanging. The longer this took, the more likely it was they'd start making bad decisions because they were exhausted.

Jaye opened the door, her short hair falling over her face in the same wild tangle as her ponies' forelocks. Rory knew full well she hadn't woken the woman, no matter what Jaye might protest to the contrary. In order to get the ponies harnessed, the carts hitched, and the routes for her apprentices assigned by the start of her day, she was certainly already on her second cup of tea.

"What could possibly be urgent enough that you come banging on my door at this hour?" Jaye asked, a heavy harness collar slung over her shoulder, the expected mug cradled in one palm.

"I need you to get me through a gate."

Jaye shook her head decisively. "I don't smuggle people past the wards anymore, Rory."

"I don't need to get out of Rime. I only need to get into a courtyard."

"What courtyard?"

"Marcus Deahl's mansion," Rory said.

"No way. His men already threatened to break my ponies' legs and mine if I didn't back off and let the Star take over moving people out of the city." Jaye shook her head violently. "If I cross him again, I'm finished."

"And if the Star is out of the picture, you get your side business back." Rory shrugged, looking past Jaye to the interior of the stable. "You can't seriously tell me you prefer digging through trash to walking around with a jingling purse of coins."

"I prefer walking."

Emmett cleared his throat behind Rory. "Sooner or later, Marcus is going to decide you're a liability whether he's threatened you into compliance or not. I used to work for him. He's unstable and it's getting worse. Any day he could send his men to slaughter every animal here and burn your stable to the ground. I don't think you want to take that chance." He swallowed. "You hear what happened to Garlin and his family?"

Jaye sighed and grimaced, the lichen mark in the corner of her mouth cracking and oozing a few drops of bright blood. "Turned my stomach, and that's hard to do."

"Marcus thought he might have been skimming from smuggling runs. No proof, but he decided to make an example of him regardless."

Jaye looked over her shoulder into the stable. "I won't have time to clean the cart out very well. I don't use the false bottom these days."

"I'll deal with it." Rory held up her scarf, pulling it almost completely over her face in demonstration.

"It's going to take me the better part of an hour to put it back the way it was," Jaye argued. "I took out the supports and the brackets and smeared mud over it all so there weren't any marks left."

"I can put the cart back together," Emmett offered. "I've done carpentry long enough."

Jaye raised an eyebrow. "Is he going too?"

"No, he's going to stay behind for a bit." Rory shrugged.

"Then he can mend those cart tongues and wheels I've got in the junk corner while he's at it." Jaye's meaning was clear. They had to pay for her services, one way or another.

Rory surreptitiously turned her coat pocket inside out, reminding Emmett they were out of other options.

"Sure." Emmett ran a hand around the inside of the cart and scraped a line in the grime coating the wood with one fingernail. He did the same seven more times, marking out what appeared to be locations of the brackets that would hold up the false bottom. It was the first time Emmett had looked anything close to calm since Rory had met him. He picked up some scrap wood laying near the broken wagon parts, took a saw from the wall, and went to work.

Jaye set down her tea to take a bridle off the wall, and Rory grabbed the still-warm mug, swallowing half its contents in a single gulp. The thirst she'd been holding at bay with the last of the icicles had returned, and if Emmett was right, the more water she drank, the longer she'd be able to keep going without her heart. She needed to buy herself all the time she could.

Jaye scowled. "Now you're going to steal my tea? On top of asking me to smuggle you into the headquarters of the most vicious syndicate in Rime?"

"You set it down," Rory said, hoping Jaye would chalk it up to her normal opportunistic nature.

"Then you can at least help me harness these beasts," Jaye said, then paused when Rory tried to pick up an armful of tack and almost pitched herself into the mucking pile. "Hold on." She frowned, tilting Rory's chin up with the heavy horse collar she was holding. "What's wrong with you?"

"Just a little under the weather," Rory said. "Nothing catching."

"Better not be," Jaye muttered. She looked from Rory to the still-steaming mug. "And you can have the rest of that tea. I'm not drinking it after you."

Rory just nodded. She grabbed the mug and drained most of its remaining contents, coughing when the tiny fragments of leaf and spice at the bottom caught in her throat.

Jaye watched her with pursed lips. "Also better not be letting your new friend over there do all the work on this deal while you fake your way out of it."

"You know me better than that," Rory argued, setting down the mug and swallowing the itch in her throat. "I can hold the horses while you harness them."

Jaye grunted under her breath, but brought the first pony in from the yard and strapped it into the crossties. Rory gently petted the animal's nose. The softness reminded her of the velvet clothing she used to run her fingers over when Old Sue got a load of laundry from the High Quarter. Eventually she'd realized dreaming about such frivolous things wouldn't ever put more food in her stomach or better boots on her feet.

Emmett finished replacing the brackets in the cart about the time Jaye's apprentices arrived. Several were new enough they'd never seen the original version of the smuggling carts with their removable false bottoms. A few stared in surprise and curiosity. Jaye cuffed them over the back of the head and sent them out to catch their own cart ponies while she finished harnessing her pair.

The apprentices drove smaller carts with single hitches. Jaye had been working long enough, and made enough smuggling runs, to afford the Cohort's working animal tax for two ponies. The payoff was a larger cart that let her make more stops and thus collect more money for her trouble. Until last year, it had also allowed her to move people past the wards undetected.

Rory had been skirting that particular tax by claiming Blizzard's stunted wing made him nothing more than a pet. She wasn't sure anyone truly believed someone like her kept a crippled bird around out of the goodness of her heart, but if she'd had to pay for him as a working animal, they'd both have starved. She moved the pigeon off her shoulder with a gentle hand. "This is where I have to leave you, okay? I need you watching out for Emmett."

Blizzard burbled in protest. Finally, he hopped off onto a support beam for the rafters and curled up, tucking his head under his good wing. Even in the faint glow from the stable lanterns, the pigeon's neck feathers glimmered purple and green like the lights. Rory ran a finger over his back, wondering if it was the last time she'd ever touch him.

She turned to Emmett and waited until he'd removed two chunks of a broken wheel from the heap of discarded pieces. "Leave here around three bells. That should give you enough time to walk to Marcus's while I'm getting Carlo out, even with your leg getting worse. I'm leaving Blizzard with you. He ought to alert you to any more bounty hunters. I don't like the idea of you walking all the way to Marcus's on your own with half the city after you, but there's not enough space in the cart for us both." She shrugged. "And if you try to double cross me, he'll peck your eyes out."

Emmett looked skeptically at Blizzard, whose chest feathers were still stained with Elena's blood. "Marcus will get suspicious if I walk in there with him."

"Leave him at the burned-out house on Silver Row." No one could miss that landmark. The destroyed stone mansion, gutted black walls standing starkly against the surrounding street, was a brutal reminder why all the street lamps in the city were lit with whale oil and not the gas the Flare and Katya used. When ordinary people tinkered with magical fumes, the result was total annihilation. The blast had killed the Cohort scientist who'd owned the house, and due to continuing seepage from the vein of gas he'd tapped into, no one had ever attempted to rebuild.

The house had a reputation for being dangerous and cursed, and people avoided it almost as strictly as the bell tower. After the ambush Elena had kept Rory from walking into, even the rebels had stopped using it as a meeting place. It would probably be safe enough for Emmett to leave Blizzard there, and Rory could pick him up afterward on their way to Katya's. If they didn't make it back, the house was close enough to Market Row that the pigeon could get fat in his retirement, eating off rich people's leavings.

Jaye pulled the cart's flat false bottom out from behind a stack of meadow-grass bales, setting it into place and pressing down on various parts with one hand. The wood never rocked or tilted, lying as firmly as if it were the actual bottom of the cart.

"Good work," Jaye said, glancing at Emmett. "Keep it up."

"You're not at all concerned with leaving me here by myself?" Emmett asked.

"Your gift has nothing to do with fire, so I don't have to worry about you accidentally burning the place down. And I'm a waste carter. Got nothing of value around here aside from my ponies and they're coming with me." Jaye shrugged. "I want those carts fixed and all my apprentices right now are lousy carpenters."

"Lousy drivers too," Emmett said, picking up a wheel. "What happened to this? Did someone try driving down an alley?" All the carts were narrow, but some alleys had barely enough space for a person to walk between the walls.

"That's exactly what happened." Jaye curled her lip in a disgust nothing from her actual job could have inspired. "That particular apprentice no longer works here." She lifted the false bottom and motioned for Rory to climb under.

Emmett set down the plane he'd picked up and rested one hand on Rory's shoulder. "Be careful," he said quietly, too low for the words to reach Jaye.

"Don't worry. I won't let anything happen to your kid," Rory replied.

Emmett swallowed. "You can't promise that. With Marcus…" He winced. "I wish I hadn't dragged you into all this."

Rory was sure Emmett would rather have anyone other than a victim of his own gift rescuing his son. But the fact remained, they needed each other. "Just get my heart back and we'll call it even."

Rory wrapped her scarf as tightly around her face as she could without struggling to breathe and lay down.

The scarf wasn't particularly effective at blocking out the smell. At least she was under the back half of the cart where food scraps, old clothes, and bones were thrown, and not the front, under the vat where Jaye emptied slop pails and chamber pots. Waste cart drivers had an unenviable job, but there was never a shortage of them. They were one of the few classes of ordinary citizens legally allowed beyond the wards. Even if only for a few hours under strict Cohort guard, seeing real sunlight was apparently worth slogging through the streets with a stinking cart and spending your days collecting everyone's refuse.

Despite its drawbacks, this plan had saved Rory a walk halfway through the High Quarter. She could slow her heartbeats and save them for when she needed them. As long as she didn't think about getting past the gate guard, that ought to be fairly easy.

At least, it would be if she didn't suffocate first. The air was thick and heavy, choking her and pressing down on her chest. Even though Rory knew the braces Emmett made for the false bottom were holding, her mind still told her it was caving in on top of her, crushing her. Nausea, a mix of the panic rolling in her stomach and the stench in the cart, rose in her throat. She rubbed her cheek against the wood to push her scarf down, rolling as far to one side as she could before the taste of bile and roast meat spilled into her mouth. The caribou skewer had definitely been a bad idea.

Rory spit a few times to get as much of the taste out of her mouth as she could, wincing at the worsened smell. The space under the false bottom was too narrow to move her arms, so she couldn't pull her scarf up again to block it. However, she was fairly sure her stomach had nothing left to throw up if the stench got the better of her again. Rory focused on running the steps of the plan through her head, touching her fingertips with her thumb for each one, breathing in and out as she went.

Get through the gate.
Slip out of the cart unseen.
Open Vero's door.
Find Carlo.
Get out of the house.
Hide Carlo in the cart.
Send Jaye to Katya's.
Wait until Emmett shows up.
Get my heart back.

It got a little hazy after that.

Rory used the rhythmic clack of horseshoes and the thud of trash being dumped into the cart to measure her breaths. *In. Out.* She could still breathe. Nothing was laying on her chest. The air wasn't any thicker. Her stomach rolled again at the memory of her father's body in a wagon not so different from this one. Now she was the one lying still with her corpselike skin, underneath the rest of the city's discarded refuse. Rory fought through each breath, trying to settle the panic and slow her heartbeat, until she heard a soft triple knock against the side of the wagon.

The next door was Marcus's.

The cart creaked to a stop at the gate, and Rory winced. Marcus was paranoid enough to lock himself away in his own house for over a decade. With his heart thief in the wind, he might have closed his gates to all but his own people.

The trash overhead muffled Jaye's voice as well as the guard's. Rory strained to pick out what they were saying, but only a word here and there filtered through clearly.

Schedule.

Boss.

Orders.

Heavy footsteps moved toward the wagon, boots thumping on cobbles and crunching through crusted snow. Rory took as deep a breath as she could manage, working her numb fingers down her leg until she could wrap them around the grip of her knife. She had no room to draw or swing the blade, but the solidity gave her something to hold onto as the panic building in her stomach and lungs threatened to suffocate her. Her heart was racing, and at that rate it might save the guard the trouble of killing her if it ran out of beats before he reached her hiding place.

Wood creaked, the cart boards shifted, and Rory braced herself for whatever trouble followed.

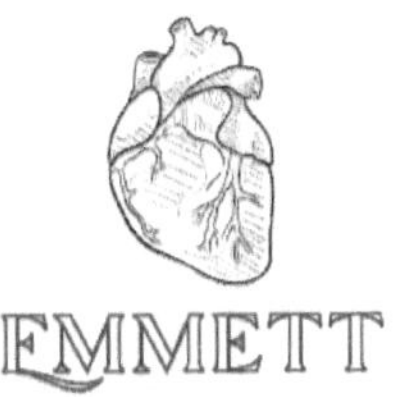

EMMETT

3 BELLS

When the bells chimed three times, their echo ringing through the empty stable, Emmett set down his hammer and ran a finger over the cart tongue he'd repaired. The joint had turned out smooth and neat, no edges sticking up at harsh angles. Tension on the tongue would only make the dovetailing pull tighter when a horse was hitched to it, a far better solution than the one an inexperienced apprentice had attempted.

Emmett replaced each of Jaye's tools exactly where he'd found them. She'd claimed she wasn't worried about him stealing anything, but she was a friend of Rory's, which probably meant she had the same sense of personally exacted justice. He held out his arm tentatively to Blizzard. The pigeon ruffled his feathers and cocked his head, then hopped down onto Emmett's shoulder. His claws gripped through the worn coat fabric more tightly than Emmett thought was strictly necessary for balance.

He was sticking to the plan Rory laid out, which meant he should arrive at Marcus's after she'd had time to rescue

Carlo. At least there had been work to do while he was waiting, or he would have been even more tempted to ignore Rory's instructions and set out right away. The familiar rasp of a saw blade against wood and the rhythmic thudding of a hammer in his hand had been a good way to drown out the voice in his head screaming that he'd left his son's fate in the hands of an amoral opportunist.

Rory's life was literally in Emmett's hands, and she knew that. He had to trust that she'd hold up her end of the bargain.

He also had to believe she'd stay alive long enough to succeed. The way she'd looked stepping into that wagon hadn't been reassuring. Her skin had been as pale as a corpse, her lips faintly blue. Emmett shoved down the sickening thought that his parents and Theresa had looked better when he'd laid them in the death carts.

He pulled his threadbare coat closer around him and stepped out into the frigid night. It felt strange to be alone, aside from the judgmental pigeon on his shoulder. Emmett had spent the better part of a day with Rory not taking her eyes off him for a moment, and he'd gotten oddly used to her presence, as well as her internal map of the city streets. Maybe he should have left earlier, to make up for the distinct possibility of him getting hopelessly lost.

A wicker, climbing his ladder to refill the reservoir of a corner lamp, frowned at Emmett's limping pace as he passed. When Blizzard fluffed up his feathers, the man turned back to opening and polishing the sooty glass. Emmett hoped the wicker, and anyone else who noticed him on the street, would assume he was a courier with an important delivery that couldn't wait until morning. The pigeon on his shoulder might protect him from anyone's scrutiny in more ways than one.

The side streets had seen little traffic since the previous night's snowfall. Emmett found himself slogging through knee high drifts in a few of the smaller lanes. He was wasting time he couldn't afford to lose, and his leg ached worse with every step.

Emmett seriously considered leaving the narrower roads and taking his chances on the main streets. Most people should have been asleep, he hoped, at that time of night. This close to the High Quarter, very few residents would be preparing for a shift at a factory, and it was still too early for the flood of house servants that would descend on Market Row in a few hours.

As he was about to turn down a road that looked fairly wide and probably led somewhere in the heart of the High Quarter, Blizzard cooed and flapped, beak bobbing concerningly close to Emmett's face. Emmett took a step back and continued on the narrow, slick street he'd been following, and the pigeon settled back into silence. Emmett didn't know if the warning was correcting his poor sense of direction, or if there was a bounty hunter or Cohort patrol ahead he didn't want to cross paths with. He was glad he didn't need to find out.

The lamps were brighter and more frequent the further into the High Quarter he and Blizzard went. The falling snow thickened, and the wind howled like a hungry wolf in the gaps between buildings. Emmett kept one hand clenched at the collar of his coat. The last thing he needed was his hood blowing back and someone who'd seen the wanted posters catching a glimpse of his hair.

There were few people going anywhere on the streets, but as the houses became mansions, guards were more and more common. Emmett tried to stick to the alleys and shadows, but even so, it was impossible not to pass several quiet sentries stationed in guardhouses outside their employers' homes. Thankfully, at this point in the night, most were too tired to pay attention to anyone not directly approaching the doors or housefronts. Some had even closed the street-facing windows of their shelters for a little more protection from the cutting wind and driving snow. Through one still-open shutter, Emmett even saw a guard dozing, head dropped down onto his chest as he leaned against the wall.

Marcus had always stationed multiple guards to prevent such behavior.

No guards Emmett passed, even the ones who wore dyed Syndicate armbands, paid any attention to someone walking alone and avoiding their employers' doors. Emmett's stomach sank at the thought that even when the syndicates knew a heart thief was targeting them, none were as paranoid as the person pulling the assassin's strings. Marcus knew he had nothing to concern himself with in that respect, and his guards still regularly accosted passers-by for nothing more than looking up at the house while they walked down the street.

Even in the middle of the night, Marcus never relaxed his security in the slightest. Rory could have gotten into the house through the secret passage, but once inside, she'd have to avoid the guards on patrol in the hallways. Emmett had laid awake too many nights, listening to the footsteps cross the corridor outside his and Carlo's room with each chime of the bells.

Emmett wished he'd warned Rory about the interior guards as more than a passing comment. He wasn't used to not being the one who needed to know every detail of a target's behavior and security. Every heart theft he'd made had been his job alone. Handing off responsibility for the job being done successfully would have been hard enough if it was just another assassination. But this was Carlo's life they were trying to save.

Snow began to fall again, deepening the drifts in the roads and glittering in the lamps' glow. Blizzard huddled further back into Emmett's hood, his feathers brushing Emmett's ear and tickling his neck. Emmett hoped the bird was still alert to potential danger. In this storm, he could probably walk right into a bounty hunter's chest before registering they were there in the first place.

The gash in Emmett's leg felt raw as each step rubbed his blood-stiffened pant leg against it. His limping steps turned his footprints into a collection of scuffs in the snow. It was only going to get worse as the road in front of him steepened. The High Quarter streets, rising into the foothills above the bay and the river, were a series of terraced levels with sharply inclined paths and sets of stairs connecting them. The Cohort mansions at the top were lit so brightly, Emmett could pick them out even through the driving snow.

For all its lights and mansions and clean, wide streets, the High Quarter was home to the worst of the worst in Rime. Emmett would be only too happy never to set foot in it again. Unfortunately, it wasn't the only quarter where he wouldn't be able to show his face after what he and Rory planned to do to Marcus.

Emmett had no idea how long he and Carlo could survive with half the city actively hunting them down. Rory had been disconcertingly vague with everything about her plan past the point where Emmett returned her heart. Probably because at that point, she'd no longer need Emmett's help, and his fate, and Carlo's, would be none of her concern. Whatever her plans were after she got her life back, they didn't include anyone else. Emmett was sure she'd disappear into the city for a few months, until the Star stopped hunting Marcus's killers and most likely disbanded entirely. She might even be counting on protection from Katya, given she'd planned to send Carlo there to wait for Emmett to collect him. He was surprised Rory had made any contingency for Carlo's safety if their plan got them killed.

It was possible she'd just wanted to make sure Emmett would never see his son again if he didn't show up with Rory right beside him. Katya hadn't directly threatened Emmett at the bathhouse, but the only reason for that was Rory vouching for him. Without her, he'd probably end up facing the consequences for his assassination attempt on the Rapids' leader.

All of it was likely a moot point, as Emmett highly doubted their chances of successfully tricking Marcus, retrieving Rory's heart, and escaping the Star headquarters alive were any better than the odds at a Coin Syndicate gambling hall. The dice were loaded and not in favor of the small players. Even Rory had acknowledged that the plan was likely to fail, despite the optimism she'd clung to over the past hours.

Rory seemed confident Katya would look out for Carlo, even if she and Emmett didn't come back. But Katya had a target on her back like any other syndicate boss. Few of them lived long, and the only reason Marcus was an exception was because he never set foot outside his own gates.

Emmett swallowed hard and looked up into the black, warded sky for a moment before returning his focus to keeping his balance on the slick streets. His father used to talk about a prayer Seachosen fishermen learned alongside tying knots and baiting hooks. It was meant to be used only in the worst extremity by sailors caught in storms actively sinking their boats. Knowing death was certain, the men would offer their lives to the god of the waves in exchange for sparing their families on shore from the same brutal weather.

Emmett wasn't sure there was a landbound version, but he whispered the words anyway, leaving off the usual address to the ocean god.

"To your waves I surrender my blood, my bones, my life."

If any deity could hear him, maybe they'd listen when they realized Emmett knew he deserved nothing better than death. It didn't matter what happened to him anymore, only that Carlo would be safe.

"Let your storm be satisfied with my life freely offered, and turn your wind and waves away from those I love. I can offer nothing less and nothing else to your—"

Blizzard's alarmed coo cut off the last few syllables of Emmett's prayer. He looked up, taking his eyes off the snowy cobblestones. Two figures had materialized from the shadows of an alley. The wind was whipping so much snow between them and Emmett that their shapes were indistinct, but a yellow scarf fluttered under one of the street lamps.

Emmett started to back up, hoping he hadn't been noticed yet. Taking another route to Marcus's would mean he'd arrive at the house a bit later than he and Rory had planned, but she might need the extra time if she had any trouble rescuing Carlo. He took a few careful steps backward, trying not to slip on the ice, but when one of the figures raised an arm and pointed directly at him, he realized there was no use. He'd already been spotted, and if he tried to get away, he'd raise their suspicions even more.

He couldn't outrun them, not with his leg aching more and more by the step, and there was no point in trying. If he did, they'd just chase him down, and probably take out their frustration at needing to run after him before they brought him back to Marcus. Hopefully by cooperating, Emmett could minimize the damage.

Whether he walked to Marcus's house of his own free will or was dragged in, Emmett would end up where he needed to be. He stopped for a moment, holding out his arm toward a windowsill. Blizzard quickly shuffled down onto the rough stone.

"Thanks for getting me this far. And for not pecking my eyes out," Emmett said. Blizzard gave him what looked like a nod.

Emmett started walking toward the silhouettes ahead of him. He hoped Rory was ready, and that by the time he arrived at the house she'd have gotten Carlo to safety. Because the timing wasn't up to him anymore.

RORY

4 BELLS

Rory kept her fingers clenched tightly around her knife's grip while the wagon creaked and swayed. But the sound was followed by hooves clopping heavily against the ground and a jolt of motion as the cart rattled through the gate onto smoother stones in the courtyard. Marcus wasn't so concerned about his safety that he was willing to let his house turn into a festering cesspool.

The wagon turned in a circle that made Rory's head swim. Footsteps moved around to the back, and the accumulated trash overhead was brushed aside. Jaye lifted the wooden panel enough for Rory to slide out. She'd parked the cart so the back faced away from the gate, and the snow was falling so thickly Rory could barely see the entrance when she glanced around the corner of the wagon. The guard leaned against one of the pillars, facing away from the courtyard, one arm over his nose. Apparently he wasn't inclined to get any closer to Jaye's cart than necessary. Rory couldn't blame him. She needed to visit Katya's bathhouse again as soon as possible.

She took a moment to dig out the tiny pouch from Tal and swallow everything left in it. If she wasn't at her best, she'd never get in and out of the house without being caught.

Rory felt her way along the back wall, avoiding thorns spearing outward from creeping tangles of bloodbriar, blinking in the flickering light from lanterns burning on each side of the kitchen door. She reached into the pocket where she'd tucked Emmett's carving, hoping her gift could feel it even if she couldn't. A trail of light appeared when her hand brushed against something solid, but it was trying to send her through the kitchen entrance. Rory sighed and pulled her knife from its sheath. Jaye began collecting the rubbish bins and slop pails set out for her, and the shuffling and thudding and splashing hid the sounds of Rory sticking her knife into every crack in the mortar. Finally, the blade moved upward past three separate blocks of the wall. Rory carefully slipped Emmett's diagram out of her pocket and blinked until the sketch swam into focus. The latch had been installed on the right side of the door inside, which meant it was on the left for anyone approaching it from the courtyard. She moved her blade a few blocks to the side, and it slipped into the door's left seam. She slid the tip of the knife deep into the tiny gap, wincing when the metal scraped stone with a faint rasp.

Then came the hard part. Rory slid the blade all the way up the door's edge once with no success. On her second attempt, she pushed it in a bit further, ignoring the resistance, and halfway up it caught on something solid. The lock disengaged with a soft thump. Rory pressed her hand against the far side of the door and watched the hidden hinge swing it outward. She ducked inside, pulled it closed, and re-engaged the latch, as Jaye cursed and a barrel rattled noisily across the courtyard.

So far, everything was going according to plan.

The hallway Rory had entered was pitch black. She pulled the carved fish from her pocket and wrapped her numb fingers around the wood. A shimmering golden glow ignited the passageway in front of her. Rory followed the light until it vanished into a solid wall on her right. In the faint glow of her gift, Rory shifted pieces of the latch until she heard a soft click.

She pushed the panel open a crack and rested her ear against the gap. Her erratic heartbeat thudded so loudly she doubted she'd hear anyone breathing inside the room, but she probably wouldn't miss footsteps or a creaking chair. No one approached to inspect the partly opened door, so Rory pushed it wide and stepped out.

On the other side of that door was a small but opulent study. Rory didn't close the panel behind her completely, even though she knew which of the heavy, leather-bound books covering the shelves was the secret to opening it, in case she needed to make a quick escape once she found Carlo.

A few red coals glowing in a banked fireplace gave the room enough light for Rory to see its contents. A desk and chair rested on a thick rug made from the skin of a massive snow bear. The walls were lined with shelves of old tomes and strange objects. More than a few gave off glints of starsilver in the dim light. The faint, cloying scent of burnt poppy hung in the air.

Some Cohort official had probably stopped in recently to test a fresh supply of the product before handing over payment. No wonder Marcus kept a secret back door. Bribery was one thing, but supplying Cohort members with illegal poppy flowers was an even better way to ensure he controlled their policies.

A large wooden wardrobe stood against the wall by the fireplace. Its lock was much easier to open with her knife than the secret door had been. The only winter clothes inside were a small jacket and a pair of fur-lined boots. Rory snatched them and tucked them inside her own coat.

The bells rang five peals, muffled by the heavy walls but nonetheless audible. She had to hurry. Jaye couldn't stall forever, even if she spilled every trash bin that had been left for her to collect. Rory cracked the study door open. The falling snow had dimmed the street lamps, but enough light still filtered in through a set of narrow windows for Rory to see she was alone in the hall. She followed her gift's glimmer to a set of stairs at the end of the corridor.

A door creaked open, and Rory barely had time to duck beneath the steps.

Four men stepped into the hall from the entryway, unbuttoning jackets and shaking snow from their scarves. Rory pushed herself as far into the darkness as she could, legs already cramped and aching. She breathed shallowly as the men milled around, complaining about double shifts and search patterns in raspy, congested voices. They shuffled slowly down the hallway, boots leaving clumps of snow on the slick slate floor. Finally, all of them disappeared through a doorway that, judging from the smell of pine tea and overcooked meat floating out, led to the kitchens. Rory slowly uncurled from her hiding place. Shadows crept in on the edges of her vision as she stood, and she caught herself on the stair railing. She couldn't afford to fall.

When Rory finally began climbing the worn steps, she placed her feet carefully at the edges of the boards. A dizzy spell hit her about halfway up, and she tightened her grip on the railing, taking shaky breaths until she could move her legs again. When she reached the door at the top of the steps, she listened outside it for a long time before she felt confident turning the handle.

The door opened onto a long hallway that closely matched the one below it. The line drawing her along glowed brighter. Rory watched it curve under the metal-plated door locked with an outside latch before she let go of the carving and allowed her eyes to adjust to the darkness in the hall.

Rory walked carefully to the door her gift had pointed out, expecting every moment for the others along the wall to burst open in some sort of ambush. The hall remained eerily silent even as she stopped outside Carlo's door. Two chairs rested against the wall nearby, both currently unoccupied.

All of this bothered Rory. Marcus had decided, in less than a day, that Emmett was no longer on his side and needed to be eliminated. She would have expected someone that paranoid to leave some of his people watching Carlo in case Emmett planned to return and rescue him before escaping the city.

Rory reached hesitantly for the door handle, half expecting to find a guard on the other side as soon as she opened it. She froze with her hand on the latch as the realization hit her in a wave.

It was thanks to her own heart this rescue was going to succeed.

Rory's heart may not have given Marcus her gift, but her drive to accomplish a clear, focused goal and her single-minded determination were at the core of who she was. Marcus was going on the offensive because that was what *Rory* would do, trying to get ahead of the problem exactly the way Rory had always dealt with her own. Any guard he could spare had been thrown into his citywide search effort as he tried to track down and eliminate the potential threat Emmett presented. Marcus had chosen one clear path of action, and it had blinded him to any alternatives.

Rory unhooked the door latch, wincing when the lower edge of the metal rasped sharply on the flagstone floor. She wrapped her free hand around the grip of her knife, braced for a flurry of voices and weapons to descend on her, but nothing moved. She carefully pulled the door wide enough to allow herself entry and stepped into the room.

Thick stone walls gave the impression they were slowly closing in, and Rory took a few shaky breaths. Like the study below, the space was lit by embers from a banked fire. This fireplace was much smaller, and the pail of wood beside it was nearly empty. A bit of light filtered in through a tiny slit of a window that looked out onto the courtyard. The storm, kicking up in earnest, spat snow against the walls. Rory couldn't see Jaye's cart through the blur of white.

In a wide bed in a corner, a small figure huddled up in tangled blankets was breathing softly. Rory crossed the room and gently shook his shoulder, hand ready to slip to his mouth and muffle a scream if necessary.

"Dad?"

The hopeful, sleepy whisper nearly sent Rory reeling backward, a startling reminder of how many times she'd woken from a dream where her father's death was just a terrible nightmare.

"No, but he sent me," Rory whispered back. She pulled the carved fish from her pocket and held it out to Carlo. "He told me to tell you dolphins still jump into the sky at night trying to play with their brother in the moon."

Carlo clutched the little carving to his chest in long, trembling fingers. The wide brown eyes looking up at Rory in a mix of hope and fear were all too familiar.

"Your dad is going to meet us when we get outside. We have to go now." Rory dug into her own coat for the clothes she'd found in Marcus's office. She held up the jacket and boots. "Are these all your things?"

Carlo nodded.

"You need to put them on and come with me."

Carlo shook his head.

"It's cold out there. You need a coat and boots," Rory said. She crouched beside the bed so she could look Carlo in the eyes.

"Can't leave," Carlo finally whispered.

"I know you're scared." Rory held out the jacket. "You have to trust me. Your dad is out there waiting to see you."

Carlo chewed on his lip. "Marcus said Dad would get hurt again."

Rory winced at the memory of the ugly, twisted scars crisscrossing Emmett's back and shoulders. She couldn't promise the next part of her plan wouldn't end with Emmett either tortured or dead at Marcus's hands.

She set the jacket in Carlo's lap and rested her hands on his shoulders. "My dad came to this town because he wanted me to grow up somewhere my gift wouldn't make people want to hurt me. And living here got him killed. All because he wanted a better life for me." She swallowed. "But I can't fix that. The only thing I can do is make sure he didn't protect me for nothing. Your dad loves you that much too, and he wants to keep you safe. The best thing you can do for him right now is to come with me."

Carlo took a shaky breath and nodded. Rory set down the boots in front of him, and he struggled to shove his feet into them. Given good food and plenty of it, Carlo had probably grown quite a bit in the past six months. When he pulled the threadbare jacket around his shoulders, he grimaced. The stitches in the sleeves were straining, and the seam in the back had frayed and begun falling apart. Carlo scrunched his eyes closed, the tiny lines at their corners nearly identical to Emmett's own pained expressions. He shook his head and began struggling to get the coat off. Rory helped as much as she could, remembering Emmett's warning about Carlo's weak joints. She didn't need him dislocating a shoulder from trying to squirm out of his own jacket.

Rory shrugged off her own coat, wincing when she moved one shoulder and felt the lichen marks crack and bleed. She took off her sweater and handed it to Carlo. "Maybe this will fit you better." And if it had belonged to his mother, the familiarity might be comforting.

Carlo ran his fingers over the knit pattern, then wrinkled his nose as he slipped the sweater over his head. Rory had stopped noticing the odor from Jaye's cart, but she was sure it had seeped into her clothes. She pulled her coat back on and stuffed Carlo's jacket into it.

"Is there anything in this room that's special to you?"

Carlo held up the wooden fish.

Rory touched the blankets, the pillows, the books on a shelf in the corner. None of them gave her more than a faint flickering gleam. Despite Emmett's concerns about what Marcus might have been saying to Carlo, the boy didn't appear to have any attachment to this place.

"Okay. We're ready. Stay close to me."

Carlo followed Rory out the door into the too-silent hall. She retraced her steps to Marcus's study, pulling Carlo into the space under the stairs when some noises came from the room the guards had disappeared into. No one stepped out, and after a few tense minutes, Rory led Carlo back into the corridor.

She half-expected the mysterious Marcus to be sitting in the chair in his study when they stepped inside, a gloating smile on his face. But there was no one in the room. She opened the hidden panel and stepped into the corridor.

Carlo's hand clutching her coat sleeve tightened when they entered the pitch darkness. Rory led the way down the passage by memory, released the door latch, then stopped short. Carlo slammed into her back.

Jaye and her cart were gone.

Rory couldn't blame Jaye for leaving. There was only so long she could stall without raising suspicion, and she'd already had enough problems with the Star.

Rory had already planned to wait for Emmett in the secret corridor, and she briefly considered keeping Carlo with her. But if she and Emmett failed, and Carlo was still in the house, she had no doubt Marcus would do something truly brutal to punish Emmett.

Rory looked up at the towering, frost-caked walls, blinking through the snow stinging her eyes. She hoped the guards were more concerned with people trying to get in than with anyone who might be attempting to sneak out. They probably didn't expect anyone to try scaling the courtyard walls, not with the absurd amount of sharp iron spikes and twists of bloodbriar running across the top. But given the outward-facing placement of those spikes, the threat they were meant to deter was someone entering the courtyard, not someone trying to leave. They would make getting over difficult, but not impossible. And the storm would help. Rory could barely see the gate from where she stood, and the wind driving toward the house would carry any sounds away from the guard.

"You have to climb over this wall," Rory whispered.

Carlo shook his head, arms wrapped around his chest, shivering.

"I'm going to help you. Okay?"

Carlo didn't strike her as the type with a lot of experience scrambling up walls for fun. Even if he had been, and if there were enough handholds in the relatively smooth stone, trying to make the climb in the middle of a blizzard, with only flickering lantern light, would be a disaster.

If Rory wasn't dying, she probably would have been able to lift Carlo onto her shoulders and get him high enough to pull himself onto the top of the wall. But moving her own body felt like every limb was made of iron.

Rory waited for a blinding squall of snow to die down, then looked around the courtyard. The flickering lamps on the house wall illuminated a woodpile near the kitchen door. The large barrels that held trash were lined up beside it, waiting to be taken back inside. The logs were all round, bark slick with snow and ice, and after an experimental shove, Rory could tell the barrels would be too heavy and noisy for her to move. Beside the woodpile, though, were a few crates, the emblem of the Red Meadows province stamped on the wood. Two had been broken apart for kindling. Three others were only missing their tops. Rory hooked her numb fingers through the slats of the most intact crate and lifted it enough to avoid dragging it on the cobblestones as she pulled it to the corner where the wall met the house, then flipped it over to make a step.

By the time she'd moved the other two, Rory was panting in earnest. She leaned against the wall for a moment to catch her breath, then pulled her knife from its sheath. Carlo cringed. Rory looked from the blade to the faint white scar on the boy's throat.

"I have to cut the bloodbriar away so the thorns can't poison you." Rory blinked away the flickers in the corners of her eyes and stepped up onto the crates. She sliced through the tangled, woody stems, trying not to wonder which ones had grown from Emmett's blood after his whipping. The alley where she'd tracked him down probably had its own twining strands by now. She used her knife to push the gnarled brambles aside, making a gap wide enough for Carlo to pass. Rory wiped the reddened blade on her coat sleeve and carefully stepped down.

The makeshift stairs had lifted Rory high enough to hack through the vines, but all three crates would only get Carlo's feet to the level of Rory's waist. If she made a step with her hands, she hoped Carlo could use it long enough to reach the top.

She swallowed. Getting him over the wall was only half the battle. Without Jaye to take him directly to Katya's, Carlo would be on his own in the city, with no way to defend himself. "Now listen to me very carefully. There should be a drift on the other side of the wall you can jump into so you don't get hurt. Once you're over, you run and don't look back."

Carlo looked from the wall to Rory and back again.

"If you go down two streets and then turn to your right, there's a big old house that burned." Rory took a shallow breath. "I need you to wait there. If anyone except your dad or I comes around, you hide. Be real quiet."

She flipped the knife in her hand, gripping the blade and holding the handle out to Carlo. "I'm going to give you this. If someone finds you hiding, do whatever you need to do to protect yourself."

Carlo gripped the handle gingerly.

"No, you need to hold it like you mean it." Rory put her hands over his, adjusting his grip. "You scream, you fight back. Make them more scared of you than you are of them."

Carlo nodded seriously. If it came to the worst, his survival instincts ought to take over. And Rory knew she'd back off fast from a panicking kid flailing a ten-inch blade.

The next part was the piece she didn't want to say out loud. It felt too much like accepting Fate's Hand would cut her down tonight. But she couldn't leave Carlo waiting for someone who was never going to come. "If your dad or I don't get there by the time the lights come out, go to the river. There's a bathhouse there. Tell someone at the door that Rory Blake sent you, and show them my knife. They'll take care of you." Rory unbuckled her belt, took the knife from Carlo and tucked it into the sheath, and strapped the whole thing around Carlo's waist. She took her own gloves from her pockets and pulled them over his hands. Her fingers were already purple and dead. A little more cold wouldn't make much difference.

Rory pointed to the crates. "Now you need to climb up these, and then step sideways into my hands so you can grab one of those spikes and pull yourself up on the top of the wall." She demonstrated interlocking her fingers.

Carlo stepped up on the first crate tentatively, then turned as if he was going to climb back down. He shook his head sharply, swiping a hand over his face as the wind whipped snow and loose curls of his hair into his eyes.

"You're going to be okay," Rory insisted, resting one hand on his back for a moment. "You can do this."

When Carlo stepped from the top crate into her hands, Rory realized she'd made a terrible mistake. The moment they took the extra weight, her numb fingers gave out completely. Carlo hung dangerously suspended by his grip on one spike, then let go of the icy metal. He tumbled down partly on top of Rory into a heap on the snowy cobblestones, and the ribs and leg she landed on seared in pain. She was fairly sure nothing was broken, but the fall hadn't done her injuries from Katya's any favors. Carlo gasped and whimpered, the hand that had been holding the wall spike clutched to his chest. Even through the layer of the bulky sweater, his shoulder looked wrong.

"I'm sorry," Rory whispered. She should never have assumed she could take his weight. This was her fault.

Carlo couldn't climb again unless Rory put his shoulder back into place. It wouldn't be the first dislocation she'd reset. Not even her first on someone other than herself. She was going to make it hurt more before it got better. And if Carlo screamed, the gate guard would definitely hear that, even over the howling storm.

She rested a hand on his uninjured shoulder, even as her own body protested every movement. "Carlo, I have to fix your arm, and it's going to hurt."

He nodded, biting his lip, eyes teary.

Rory took Emmett's scarf from her pocket and handed it to Carlo. "Put this in your mouth because if anyone hears you scream, they'll find us." She reached for his shoulder. "Okay. I'm going to put it back now."

She expected to hear the muffled buzzing of a yell against the fabric, but there was almost nothing. Carlo's silence was its own kind of pain.

"How does it feel?" Rory whispered.

Carlo moved his arm experimentally, grimacing, the corners of his eyes crinkling in pain. When he pulled Emmett's scarf out of his mouth and dropped it to the ground, Rory picked it up. She tied the bloodstained cloth into a makeshift sling that ought to keep Carlo's shoulder in place. Unfortunately, it would do nothing to solve their most serious problem. Carlo had only one usable arm for a second escape attempt.

Rory looked up at the wall. It was almost impossible to even see the top through the snow. "Do you think you could try and climb over again?"

Carlo swallowed, then nodded.

Rory bent over next to the crates, leaning her hands on the splintering wood. "When you get to the top of the crates, use my shoulders as a step." Hopefully, her legs and arms together would be able to support Carlo's weight longer than her fingers had managed.

When Carlo's boots landed on the raw lichen marks on her shoulders, Rory almost lost her focus. She breathed through the pain of rough cloth grinding against tender skin and squeezed her eyes closed, teeth clenched around a scream she couldn't release. *Don't fall. Don't fall. Don't fall.*

Even if Rory's heart had still been in her chest, it wouldn't have beat again until Carlo was perched on the top of the wall. She breathed a small sigh of relief. "Remember what I told you," she managed around panting breaths. "Burned house. Use the knife if you have to. Go to Katya's if the lights come out."

"What about you?" Carlo asked.

"I'm going to get your dad."

And then Carlo vanished over the other side. Rory waited, half afraid she'd hear a pained scream or shouts from guards who saw a small figure hop over the wall, but the only sound was howling wind.

Rory ducked back into the relative shelter of the house, moving along it until her hand brushed the edge of the hidden door. Only when she reached for the knife at her belt did she remember she'd let Carlo leave with what amounted to her key to get back into the house. Without a way to open the door again from outside, she had no choice but to give up and lay down right there and let the snow piling up bury her.

Fate's Hand.

Maybe it was always going to end this way. She dragged in a shallow, choked breath. The wind howled around her, whispering her name in her father's voice. She'd spent years trying not to die like him, and it had still ended with her sitting alone in the snow because she'd decided giving someone else a chance to survive was worth her own life. She'd always wondered if her father regretted his choice, in those last few minutes bleeding out in a freezing alley. If Rory was anything at all like him, now she knew he hadn't.

She wasn't sure if the pounding in her ears was the bells chiming the hour or her own heart counting out the few beats it had left. When it stopped after six, she half expected to collapse before noticing a quieter thump still echoing inside her skull. She leaned against the wall, the thudding, slowing rhythm of her heart drowning out the wind.

The hinges shifted with a faint creak and scrape as the secret panel opened partway. The door must have caught on packed snow and not closed completely behind her and Carlo. Rory straightened up slowly, bracing herself on the solid part of the wall, and slipped into the relative warmth of the passage.

She stopped with her hand on the latch of the study door. There were voices on the other side of it. One of them was Emmett.

The other voice was lower, quieter, but familiar too. Rory pushed the door open a crack. And then she froze as if the entire winter gale outside had ripped through the walls and into her skin.

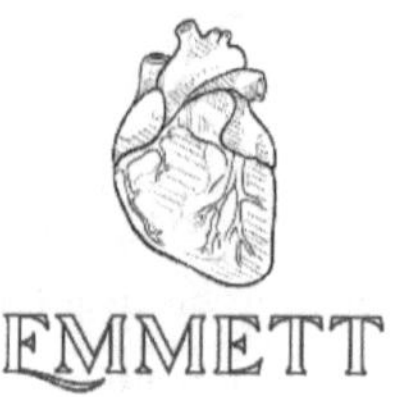

EMMETT

5 BELLS

Emmett grimaced when he recognized the approaching guards as two of Marcus's most ruthless. He stopped under a street lamp, pushing back his hood and letting the snow turn his hair even whiter.

"You've been a hard one to catch up with," Ara snapped, voice muffled by the scarf that protected all but her icy eyes from the bitter wind. Marcus's childhood bodyguard had long been suspected of having slowly poisoned his father so Marcus could inherit the Deahl fortune sooner. "I'd like to know why Trey didn't bring you in hours ago."

"I'd like to know why Marcus sent people looking for me when he'd barely given me enough time to do the job he ordered." Emmett was surprised at the sharp confidence in his own voice. He was starting to sound like Rory.

Pell snorted. "A job you seem uninterested in finishing, given you're nowhere near any place Katya Roland frequents." A former Horn lieutenant, Pell had secretly slipped information on his employer's weaknesses to Marcus before Emmett was sent to assassinate its leader. His reward had been a new position in Marcus's household when his former syndicate crumbled.

"It's done." Emmett held out the locket, faintly glowing with the heart trapped inside it.

"Then you won't have a problem coming back with us and settling accounts with Marcus." Ara's fingers dug into Emmett's arm through his coat. "And telling him everything that's happened since you left."

"Hope he's in the mood for a good story," Emmett said. "And a long one."

"What's gotten into you?" Pell asked. "You sound different."

Wonderful. Emmett was going to ruin the whole plan. He really should have left being Rory to Rory. "Got a decent night's sleep for once," he snapped back instead. "Didn't have to listen to you snoring like a rasp outside my room all night."

"I don't like that attitude," Ara said. "For all I know, you want us to walk you right in there so you can bury a knife in the Boss's chest." Her eyes flicked up and down his body. "Or in ours. I'm not taking you another step until I know if you're carrying any weapons."

Emmett hoped Pell and Ara wouldn't notice his coat wasn't the one he'd left in or ask about the dried blood staining his pants. He'd rather fumble his way through his story *once*. His leg threatened to give out as he unlaced his boots, and he stumbled, falling heavily against Pell's shoulder. The guard shoved him aside. Emmett barely managed to catch himself on a wall instead of falling on his face on the ice.

"Don't touch me," Pell growled.

Emmett wanted to remind him with a heart already in the locket he wasn't capable of stealing anyone else's, but he was afraid that might earn him a lot more pain. He pulled the top of his boots away from his ankle to show the absence of any blade. He unbuttoned his coat, shivering at the wind whipping it when he held it open, then lifted the hem of his sweater to prove he hadn't tucked a blade between it and his belt. Pell tugged at the bloodstained edge of his shirt, and Emmett winced.

"Looks like you had some trouble out there."

Emmett didn't reply. His own heart was clawing its way out of his chest, the echo of his pulse a choking lump in his throat. It was too late to have second thoughts. The only way out of this now was to go through with the plan.

A shove to the shoulder shook Emmett out of his panic. He buttoned his coat while he walked, then wrapped his arms around his chest. He hadn't bothered retying his boots, and they flopped against his ankles, rubbing the skin raw. Each time he stumbled into a drift, snow collected and packed in against his leg, melting and running down to soak his socks.

The guards kept Emmett pinned between them the entire time, whether that was walking one on each side on the wider streets, or putting him in the middle of the single file necessary to climb some of the narrow stairways. Even so, the snow was falling so hard and fast Emmett could barely see them if they moved more than an arm's length from him.

Their pace was excruciatingly demanding. Emmett's leg alternated between aching and burning, and he was sure the wound had reopened. He couldn't tell if the dampness he felt on his pant leg was melting snow or blood seeping from the gash.

The facade of Marcus's house loomed up in front of them as they turned the last corner.

"Well, well, look who's finally back," a guard snapped as Pell and Ara marched Emmett through Marcus's door. He held up a hand to halt Ara as she started to lead Emmett into the house. "I know you're in a rush to get that commendation from the boss and all, but we still have to search him."

Ara curled her lip in a faint snarl, clearly not appreciating the implication that she'd have let any risk come near Marcus. "Already done," she snapped. "Like I'd let you have half a chance of pretending you're the ones who caught him."

The door guard frowned, looking Emmett up and down. Emmett shifted from foot to foot, shivering, then stopped when his leg nearly collapsed underneath him.

"Guess he's in no shape to try anything anyway."

One of the guards, after a few whispered words, hurried inside, presumably to wake Marcus and tell him someone had brought Emmett back. When he returned, the guards opened the door and ushered Pell, Ara, and Emmett inside. Two more guards flanked all three of them the entire way to Marcus's office.

When Emmett opened the door, slowly and tensely, Marcus was already inside, waiting in his chair. Judging by the red crease on his cheek from a pillow seam, he'd been only recently awakened. Still, he'd slicked back his hair and put on a heavy dressing gown with the syndicate emblem sewn onto the chest. He looked dangerous, powerful, and distinctly curious. He also looked tired. After taking a new heart, Marcus was usually as vigorous and energetic as someone half his age. Tonight he was pale, eyes shadowed, skin sallow, as if it had been weeks instead of days since Emmett had handed over Rory's heart. Emmett had heard legends of stolen hearts rejecting their new bodies. Maybe Rory's knew it didn't belong in Marcus's chest and was making its displeasure obvious. Knowing its owner, Emmett wouldn't have been surprised.

"I must say, I'm impressed it took someone this long to find you. Not many people have the skill to outwit my best hunter." Marcus frowned. "I did not believe you were one of the ones who did."

"There was no need to send him after me. I did the job you asked." Emmett reached into his coat awkwardly with Ara's hand still holding his arm and fished out the glittering locket. Marcus smiled greedily, raising his hand and crooking a finger.

Something about the situation felt wrong. Probably because Emmett was on edge, about to do something he'd never attempted before. He had to act as if this was any other handoff. Marcus couldn't know anything was wrong until Emmett had Rory's heart back.

Emmett removed his gloves, shoved them into his pockets, and stepped forward. His gift curled around his fingertips, ready to extract the heart and offer it to Marcus.

When Pell coughed, Emmett realized what had been bothering him about the situation. Marcus had never allowed his guards to stay in the room when Emmett handed over a heart. He was already too close to Marcus to react when the man stood up and his hand flew out toward Emmett's throat.

Marcus ripped the silver chain from Emmett's neck and threw the locket to the floor, crushing it under his heel. Emmett stared in numb shock as the now uncontained heart shimmered for a moment above the shattered metal before dissolving into dark threads that curled upward like smoke from a snuffed candle.

Marcus waved to the guards. Ara's gloved hands closed on Emmett's wrists, then wrapped a length of sturdy cord around them, knotting it tightly into firm restraints. Emmett winced. Marcus was given to fits of passion, but he would never have wantonly ruined something as valuable as that locket. If Marcus had destroyed the means Emmett was using to steal hearts for him, it must have meant he had no further use for Emmett himself.

I'm sorry, Carlo. I brought you here and he's going to make you into a monster. Just like me.

"I know for a fact you never got close enough to Katya to steal her heart," Marcus snarled. "My men paid a visit to Kaden at the Black Spark Forge and found one of Katya's people delivering a very similar message. It took a few teeth to make him talk, but when he did, he boasted the Star would never be able to touch his boss. He said she took one of my men prisoner when he tried to sabotage the bathhouse and has been on her guard ever since." Marcus looked from Emmett to the locket. "I must admit, she trains her people well. Perhaps she ought to tell them to brag a bit less, though."

Emmett winced.

Marcus looked up at the guards. "Bring me the boy."

Ara nodded and shoved Emmett forward so hard Pell lost his grip, and Emmett landed roughly on his knees on the rug. Both guards stalked out into the hall, closing the door behind them.

Marcus faced Emmett with an angry snarl that twisted his gaunt face into something nearly unrecognizable. His hand flew to his chest, rubbing it as if in pain. "Do you know what makes powers like yours manifest to their full potential? It's fear. I've studied giftings a long time, and I've seen it. And if I have to bring that boy to the brink of death to turn him into the weapon I need, so be it."

Emmett closed his eyes. Marcus hadn't forced Carlo's gift to manifest yet. But if Rory hadn't done what she'd promised, Marcus would destroy them all.

Ara burst back into the room, doors slamming. "He's not there."

Marcus clenched a fist, knuckles whitening. Blue veins stood out along his forehead. "He can't be far. Search the house, search the grounds."

Ara nodded and retreated, slamming the door behind her.

Marcus stalked over to the door and locked it, then glared at Emmett. "I don't know which of my people is working with you, but I will find out." His fingers slid to a knife on his desk, spinning the blade around and around on the wood.

"It wasn't any of them."

Emmett hadn't said that, and neither had Marcus. The voice had come from the walls. Or rather, from the shadow emerging from them. It snatched the knife from the desk and turned the blade toward Marcus's throat.

Marcus caught the shadow's hand and threw the figure to the ground easily, where she landed awkwardly on one knee on the rug, red hood falling back from a frayed blonde braid.

Emmett couldn't make himself meet Rory's eyes. She had to know things went terribly wrong. The fact that Emmett was kneeling on the floor with his hands bound and Marcus standing over him gloating would have told her instantly.

Then Rory looked up at Marcus, blood redder than her coat dripping down the corner of her lip, and snarled. "You killed my father. And now, I'm going to kill you."

RORY

6 BELLS

When Jax had given Rory back the starsilver knife, after Mom left and couldn't argue about it, the trail the blade summoned had gone cold. Rory had followed a withering thread to the banks of the river, where it flickered out once and for all like a guttering candle. In the year and a half since her father's death, his killer had either drowned or been killed in turn, his body flung into the water. It was some kind of perverse closure.

Until now.

Even though it had been fifteen years since the night Rory first held that knife, even though the face in her vision flickered in and out of focus in a sea of sparks, Rory couldn't forget the voice threaded through that memory. She was looking at the man who gave the order to kill Gavin Blake. If it was the last thing she did, Rory was going to take that monster down with her.

She didn't look at Emmett. No matter what happened to them, they'd done their best for Carlo. And Rory intended to make absolutely certain not one more child would grow up without a parent because of Marcus.

The syndicate boss had wiped the shock off his face and replaced it with anger. He flung his knife back down on the desk, untied the belt of his robe, and grabbed Rory's wrists, twisting them behind her back and knotting the cord around them. He dragged her across the room and threw her down next to Emmett.

"So you really thought you could betray me and get away with it," Marcus sneered, glaring down at Emmett. "What did you do, convince the dying girl you could get her heart back if she helped you?"

"We've already gotten away with it." Rory smiled, bitterly defiant even as the room swayed and flickered around her. "You'll never lay your hands on that boy again." She hoped Carlo would follow her instructions if she and Emmett didn't come back for him. She'd done everything she could to make sure he'd be safe.

"As if my people wouldn't tear the city apart to find him."

The lack of a guard on Carlo's room meant Marcus wasn't concerned about whether or not someone tried to rescue him. If she had been Marcus—and thanks to her heart beating in his chest at the moment, she basically was—only one thing would have given Rory that much confidence about her ability to get the boy back. Once he'd become suspicious about Emmett's loyalties, Marcus must have taken something of Carlo's that could be tracked.

"I've just broken into your house and taken him from under your nose, and you think your people are smart enough to find him again?" Rory blinked a few times, forcing her eyes to focus long enough to see the results of her goading.

"I'm sure you've done your best." Marcus ran a finger over a small enamel chest on his desk. "But you of all people should know a guide will always be able to find anyone with a lock of their hair."

Beside Rory, Emmett slumped even more. A faint sound, something between a sob and a whimper, slipped out before he muffled it. Rory let her own distressed groan escape, hoping Marcus believed it was defeat instead of the chest-crushing pain from her rapidly failing heart.

For all his insistence that Katya's messenger had been foolish, Marcus was making the same mistake, rubbing Rory and Emmett's apparent failure in their faces and enjoying their reactions. Reminding them that when he'd finished with them, he could send his people out to find Carlo and finish the job he started. For Rory, all his gloating did was tell her what she needed to steal next.

Rory surrendered to the light flickering around the edges of her vision as Marcus opened a drawer and pulled out a pipe. He leaned on the desk and waved the item in Emmett's direction. "You're going to watch her die. Slowly. Painfully. And then you're going to tell me where the boy is before you condemn him to the same fate."

Rory heard the snap and crackle as Marcus struck a cinderpine match on the edge of the desk. A familiar smoke filled the air a few puffing breaths later. Rory blinked again, pulling the image in front of her into focus. In the smoldering glow, she could see a few unburnt red petals scattered across the desk.

No gifted would waste their money or their time smoking poppy. Marcus, for all his menace and power, had no magic. His choice to smoke in front of them told Rory, in no uncertain terms, that he had no intention of either of them leaving his office to let that secret be known. But if there was one thing Rory had learned from Willow, big secrets had a tendency to make people angry, whether they were revealed to the world or not.

"You're not really the Deahl heir." Rory fixed Marcus with the most accusing glare she could manage.

Marcus's hand trembled on the pipe stem as Rory's vision shuddered and fragmented.

"You haven't even got a gift." Rory took a shuddering breath, willing her voice to keep working long enough for her plan to fall into place. "You're a conniving opportunist who found a weak point and exploited it."

Marcus threw the pipe down on his desk with a clatter and stood up.

Beside her, Emmett tensed. Rory risked a glance at him. He was staring at her, raw confusion swirling in his eyes. Rory hoped he'd see the certainty in hers before she turned them back on Marcus. Everything she was about to set in motion depended on Emmett being confident enough to play his part when she gave him the opportunity.

"You murdered all those syndicate officers in your coup because they could have exposed you." The final piece of the puzzle slotted into place. "And they could have figured out you had the real heir killed."

Her father's last job.

Now the final words of the memory Rory had tapped into when she'd tracked her father's killer to the river made sense. *'Forget about him. We've got to take this one with us before a patrol comes.'* The knife's owner had abandoned the struggle for his weapon and left it behind in Gavin's body because his partner needed help disposing of the real Marcus discreetly. If the syndicate heir had been found dead, a substitution would have failed. But if he simply vanished, someone could step into the void left behind.

Rory wasn't surprised someone who'd been tasked with making the real Marcus disappear ended up dead as well. The imposter couldn't afford to leave anyone alive who could have linked him to the death of the Star's heir apparent. He'd bided his time, slipping effortlessly into his victim's shoes, hastening Marcus's father's death and blaming the old man's ravings on insane delirium.

"You won't live long enough to share your little theory with anyone else." Marcus's voice sounded oddly choked and pained, and Rory thought he was rubbing his chest. Then again, he could have been dusting ash off his robe. It was impossible to tell. Marcus picked up his knife again, and the glimmer of light it reflected exploded into a thousand different shards in Rory's vision. "Just like your father before you."

He was using the memories her heart held to antagonize her. For her plan to work, Rory had to make him the unstable, emotionally charged one. She couldn't let anger get the better of her. She needed Marcus to want to wipe the smug grin off her face.

But he still had to think he was in control of everything happening in this room. If Rory seemed too confident and defiant, Marcus might suspect she was scheming some way to escape.

"Why did you kill him?" she asked, letting a shudder slip through her voice. "He had no idea who he'd been hired to track."

"Unlike the real Marcus, I learned something from Feodor Deahl. Leave nothing to chance," Marcus snarled. "Which is why, as much as I want to hear you beg for the pain to end, that clever tongue will be the first thing you lose."

Marcus was calculating and determined, and Rory's heart in his chest had only emphasized it. Thanks to her memories, he knew the ways she'd survived Rime's dangers all these years. Rory didn't just need to outmaneuver Marcus at his own game. She needed to find a way past her own defenses.

Emmett had managed it when Rory cornered him yesterday. Rory glanced at him, trying to remember what he'd said instead of focusing on the wild panic in his eyes. He'd convinced her she needed him, and there was no chance she could do the same to Marcus. But at the root of Emmett's success had been the realization Rory hadn't wanted to admit. Her stolen heart made her vulnerable, and she couldn't afford weakness in Rime.

"You don't like being reminded that you're a powerless coward?"

"I hold the reins of the Star. The whole city moves for me."

"Because you have an entire army of gifteds under your thumb." Rory had done everything in her power to keep Emmett from realizing she wasn't physically able to follow through on her threats. She'd needed him to fear her, or her entire plan would have fallen apart. Marcus faced the same problem with his syndicate. "If half of them knew the truth, they'd turn on you. You're just a sham hiding from the world to keep his secret."

"A life in the shadows is the life of a leader," Marcus retorted. "I came into this house as Marcus's spare. Feodor plucked me off the streets to stand in place of his son. To risk death every day." He paused, coughing, and turned the knife blade over in his hand.

Rory let some of the anger that had simmered in her chest since crossing paths with Jax surface. Finding out she'd been expendable to a man she'd treated as a second father had turned a part of her heart to ice. Reopening that wound while her heart was in Marcus could serve her purpose. "You resented being placed in the line of fire on behalf of the pampered son."

"A foolish boy who never appreciated what he was given. Marcus argued with Feodor constantly over his future in the syndicate. The ungrateful wretch wanted to cut ties and labor for a living."

"The Star would have no use for a decoy without an original." Rory clenched a hand into a fist behind her back, trying to focus her flickering vision. She sucked in a labored breath, poppy smoke heavy on her tongue. "You could pass for the real heir and had access to everything he owned. You hired a guide to track Marcus down so someone loyal to you could kill him before Feodor killed you."

The man who'd stepped into Marcus's shoes ran a finger over the knife's blade. A single drop of blood fell to the floor. "He had his friends in this house, but they were few. All of them were weak like him. Easily *dealt with*." He hissed the last words, looking from Rory to Emmett.

Rory followed his gaze. Emmett was still kneeling, head down, eyes on his bound hands.

"Why go to all the trouble?" Rory shook her head. "Without a gift, you could have joined the Cohort or left Rime altogether. It would have been simpler."

"Simpler, perhaps, but not as satisfying." Marcus scowled. "Feodor found me in the gutter because my fool of a father thought the Cohort was the real power in this city." He clenched his fingers around the knife's grip until his knuckles whitened. "He was a port inspector with a weakness for card games he could never win. Eventually his coworkers got tired of his promissory notes. The one he owed most said he'd forget the debt if my father took his shift while he attended a Coin card tournament. He failed to mention he'd agreed to turn a blind eye to syndicate cargo." Marcus coughed, leaning against the desk. His voice was barely more than a strained whisper. "My father seized a large Horn shipment that night and reported it to his superiors. He thought he'd get a commendation. What he got was his door kicked in and his throat sliced. The dock master was in on the take and took offense to his deal being threatened."

"So he gave the Horn your father's location to avoid them taking out their revenge on him," Rory choked out. There was one thing her heart and Marcus's agreed on, and it was the injustice of their fathers' deaths.

"The Cohort is no more powerful than a toothless wolf. Their laws are a sham, twisted or ignored whenever it suits them and their comfort or their profits. They're puppets, and their strings are pulled by whoever wields the most true power in this city. The most coin, the most force, the most fear."

Rory smiled. Marcus would never have been any better at cards than his father. He'd shown her his whole hand. "And you think that's you? A grubby little street urchin without one drop of real magic in his veins, whose father died for someone else's petty ambition?"

Marcus crossed the room in three strides and backhanded her.

Rory barely saw Emmett move.

Marcus's face went slack, eyes dulling and sliding closed. His legs crumpled under him, and the next moment his deadweight landed squarely on top of Rory. At least the hand holding the knife was lying limp on the rug.

"Emmett," she hissed. "Get him off me?"

Emmett shouldered Marcus's body to the side, then pulled the knife from the man's hand with his own bound ones. "I'll cut you loose, then you can get my hands free." He winced. "Sorry if I cut your thumb."

"Didn't feel it," Rory whispered back.

When her hands were free, she beat one into a fist to curl it around the knife. Her fingertips weren't purple anymore.

They were turning black. That couldn't be right, but no amount of blinking and shaking her head helped. A dark haze hovered between her and her hands, shot through with floating, glimmering specks, like she'd walked into a forge with a plugged chimney. She was going to have to hope for the best.

Emmett's quiet "ouch" when she missed the rope on her first try made her wince a little. It took longer than she wanted to tentatively saw through the rope, but she was pretty sure she only cut Emmett's hands a few times. It was hard to be certain through the fog rapidly clouding her vision. The room was darker than it had been a few minutes ago, sparks whirling all around.

"Thanks," Emmett mumbled. She could hear him rubbing his hands together.

"You got my heart, right?"

Emmett nodded, then looked down at his chest. "I've never tried to give a heart back when it's already in me. I don't even know if I can. There might not be a way to, without…" He looked from her to the conspicuous absence of the sheath at her waist. "Where's your knife?"

"I couldn't leave Carlo with no way to defend himself."

"You gave him a *knife?* Rory!" Emmett snapped. Then his eyes shot to the door. Fortunately, it stayed closed.

"He might need it before this is over." Rory had given Carlo that knife to defend him from more than just the Star's people. She'd needed to protect him, and Emmett, from what she'd have been tempted to do now if she'd had the means. From the part of her that could justify plunging her blade into Emmett's heart in the name of her own survival. "So I guess you'd better figure this out."

Rory took another shaky breath. She was fading fast, the world narrowing to the echoing thud of each heartbeat in her ears. She slumped back against the desk.

Dying of a stolen heart felt almost like falling asleep.

But not the comforting collapse into oblivion after a long day's work. Death was the same weightless, unstoppable plunge that usually woke Rory gasping from nightmares where she'd tumbled off the top of the bell tower into the absolute blackness of a Rime night.

This time, the swooping vertigo wouldn't vanish as soon as she came back to reality in her own bed. She was already awake, heart stuttering, sweat trailing down her face. The rough rug under her back and the four walls closing in on her might as well not exist.

The emptiness in Rory's chest had swallowed her whole.

She was freefalling. There was nothing solid she could catch to save herself, even if she could have moved so much as a finger to reach for it. The only things that still existed were the roaring in her ears and the lights bursting in vivid greens and purples and pinks in front of her eyes.

There were worse ways to die. But Rory still wanted to wake up before she hit the ground.

The lights swirling around her flickered and spun, spiraling smaller and smaller until they were only a brilliant pinpoint. And then they exploded, a vivid, burning glow she would have squeezed her eyes shut to block out if they hadn't already been closed. Something strong and solid buried itself in her chest. An overpowering sensation of warmth burned through her like she'd swallowed a huge mouthful of scalding tea. Her body was covered in a million spikes of sharp agony, as if every inch of her skin had frozen and was beginning to thaw. Below the rush of blood in her ears, a low, insistent whisper repeated itself in words she lacked the strength to decipher.

The weight in her chest was choking, suffocating. If her arms could move, she would have pushed it off. She tried to lift a hand, but it felt as heavy as an iron bar. Not even a single finger obeyed her demands to move, to get away, to force this crushing thing away from her.

It was for the best they didn't, she realized slowly. Someone had taken hold of her failing heart and begun squeezing it, over and over. Pushing life through her in a way her own body could no longer manage for itself.

Each heartbeat was a wrenching ache. Blood seared through her limbs like liquid fire, igniting her fingertips, toes, and cheeks. Her ribs were ready to fly apart and shatter from the weight on top of them and the pressure inside. The pounding in her head echoed the rhythm of a pulse her body no longer controlled.

Coming back to life hurt so much more than she would have expected.

Rory dragged in an agonized, nearly impossible breath, and then immediately swallowed a cry of pain in her throat, the sound vibrating against her teeth and aching through her chest. The grip on her heart released, and the crushing weight faded away. Her pulse, unsteady and weak but finally her own, fluttered in her chest.

She lay there, breathing in the scent of poppy smoke, her twitching fingers burying themselves in the coarse bearskin rug, lungs aching and trying to convince themselves there was enough air in them to waste on a scream. Her eyes were still burning, even though the searing lights had faded away, replaced by a red-tinged darkness. Lines of what felt like pure fire tracked down her cheeks. Weight rested across her chest, crushing her lungs.

She rasped in another harsh breath and choked back any sound. She couldn't remember exactly why, but she knew she needed to be quiet.

"Go ahead and scream if you want. It'll just convince the guards he's torturing me," Emmett whispered.

Rory could barely hear him through the rushing in her ears, but his words brought the memories of the past few hours flooding back, effectively stopping any scream she might have considered allowing to escape. She'd just survived a stolen heart. She wasn't about to die at the hands of Marcus's guards. Besides, she needed all the breath she could get just to feel halfway alive. She gritted out a reply anyway. "As if you'd give him the satisfaction."

"Fair point." Emmett sounded like he was holding back a scream himself.

Rory blinked a few times and the room swam into a hazy view. Emmett was lying beside her on the rug, breathing shakily. One arm still rested across Rory's chest, his hand curled limp over the place her heart was rapidly but steadily thudding. Rory tried to raise her own hand to rub the blurriness out of her eyes, but her bones felt like iron bars, so she settled for blinking rapidly until the burning under her eyelids faded and the person beside her was more than a blur of brown, black, and gray against the white bearskin.

The silver strands in Emmett's hair had more than doubled along his temples and forehead. The rough stubble on his jaw had become more gray than black. If giving away a heart contained in the locket made his gift lash out, Rory couldn't imagine what handing over one his body had tried to assimilate had done.

"Guess we did it," she rasped out, voice weak and shuddery.

"I can't believe that worked."

Rory wanted to ask how Emmett had managed to return her heart, but forcing out even one more word felt impossible when every breath seared her lungs and every word stung her throat. Her ribs ached as if someone had slammed something down on her chest with all their strength.

Maybe Emmett had when he put back her heart.

After a few more half-satisfying breaths, Rory sat up slowly, pushing Emmett's arm off her chest. Flickering, blurred sparks appeared in the corners of her eyes, and she leaned against Marcus's desk, gasping. Her restored heart was pounding like it was going to leap back out of her chest any moment.

Rory slowly lifted a hand to the racing pulse in her neck. Her scarf had been loosened and her coat was unbuttoned, and her shaking fingers traced the line of her heart's fluttering beat. She winced and pulled her hand away when her fingers probed the edge of a forming bruise below her collarbone. Her layered shirts had been hastily yanked open and folded away from her left shoulder, and Rory felt through the folds of her coat for the buttons that had been snapped free. She doubted she had as much of an attachment to her shirt as Emmett had to the coat button Trey had used, but there was no sense in taking chances.

She reached up onto the desk, ignoring the way her ribs protested the motion, and swept her arm across the top, clumsily knocking everything to the rug next to her. She picked through a jumble of pens, matches, and paper scraps. There were two small enamel boxes, and Rory opened both. One contained a single black curl. The other was stuffed nearly full of poppy petals. Rory slipped both into her pocket, along with her loose buttons. She fumbled across the floor for Marcus's knife with shaking fingers.

The door rattled.

Rory jumped, and the edge of her hand smacked the knife handle, sending the blade spinning under the desk. She looked from it to Marcus and froze. The man's face was gray, black veins spidering across it, and a death rattle gurgled in his throat. His own heart must have been so deadened from surviving on stolen ones that without them, he didn't have days left. Only minutes. He'd be dead before they left the house.

She turned to Emmett and winced. His leg wound was bleeding again, a dark stain spreading sluggishly down his pants, a few drops falling to the rug underneath him despite the hand he'd pressed to the cut. Any of Tal's healing magic left must have repurposed itself into keeping Emmett from dying when he gave back Rory's heart. "Do you think you can run?"

Emmett grabbed the edge of the desk with his bloodied hand and pulled himself to his feet. "I think I'll have to."

"Then we're getting out of here."

Rory's vision was still swimming, and she wasn't sure she could count properly, so she ran her fingers over the books on the shelf until she felt the one that didn't move easily. She pulled harder, and the hidden door clunked softly as it released. Emmett stumbled inside, and Rory followed.

When she pushed open the door to the courtyard, the brisk, cold wind hitting her face was a relief, washing away some of the haze in her head. Which was good, because she needed a plan to get out the gate.

A shout echoed across the courtyard from inside the house, and the guard opened the gate and stepped through to see what was happening. That was all the opportunity Rory needed. The wind had knocked one of the trash barrels over, and Rory kicked it as hard as she could, rolling it directly into the guard's legs. Before he'd even hit the cobblestones, she'd grabbed Emmett by the arm and pulled him out the gate with her.

For once, Rory didn't want the fastest way anywhere. She couldn't risk leading anyone who might have started chasing them to Carlo. Instead, she wound deeper into the tangled heart of the High Quarter, hoping they'd lose any potential pursuers in the winding terraces and narrow alleys. Emmett struggled to keep up. As the distance between them grew, Rory finally stopped outside a courtyard where the curving wall offered a decent hiding place if the guards didn't turn down the small side street.

Emmett leaned against the wall beside Rory, panting breaths forming a frosty haze in front of him. He pulled his gloves from his pockets and slipped them on. Rory tugged her coat closed. She tightened her scarf around her neck, letting her fingers brush the thudding, rapid pulse pounding through her throat before concealing it under the rough, damp cloth.

"Do you think we're safe now?" Emmett asked breathlessly.

At first, Rory could only manage a hesitant nod. The frantic energy from their escape had faded, and she was painfully aware that getting her heart back didn't mean going back to the way she'd been before. Still, Rory was one of the luckiest people alive. She couldn't complain about exhaustion and short breath and dizziness.

Once she no longer felt like talking would use up all the air in her lungs, Rory cleared her throat. "Unless the Star can find another highly skilled guide on short notice, we should be," she replied. "They'd need someone with a stronger gift than mine to trace anything Carlo left behind, and you've been gone even longer." She grimaced. "Although you were bleeding all over the rug." She should have thrown some coals from the fire onto it before they ran.

"And a guide can track anyone anywhere with their blood, no matter how old it is."

Rory nodded. "But guides have some deep superstitions about that. My dad told me anyone who blood tracked would never work in this city again."

"Your father was the guide Marcus—well, whoever he was—used to find the real heir?" Emmett asked. He was still breathing hard, hands shaking where they rested on his legs.

Rory nodded. Her cheeks were cold, and when she touched them, she felt frozen tear tracks. She hadn't even realized she'd been crying. "All these years, I've wondered which syndicate did it. Whether I was delivering their messages. Whether I'd be next." She rubbed her fingers. The black had disappeared, the purple fading as well. She tucked both hands into her pockets before she traded the return of normal-looking skin for frostbite. "I've also gotten very good at making sure no one follows me." She glanced back the way they'd come. "I didn't plan to die like him if I could help it."

As if to prove her wrong, her body chose that moment to rebel. Her legs crumpled under her, and she started to slide down the wall.

"Rory!" Emmett didn't sound like he was faring much better himself.

"Just...a little dizzy." Rory gasped for breath, lungs searing from the cold air. She pulled out Tal's pouch and upended it over her mouth, but there was nothing left inside. She made a pathetic attempt to toss it across the street, but the pouch only landed a few inches from her hand.

"Do you have anything else salty?" Emmett asked. "It helps when I've taken a heart and my gift is hungry." A look Rory couldn't read flashed across his face as he sank down beside her.

Rory dug into her messenger bag and produced a waxed-cloth package. "Dried salted salmon. My emergency stash."

Emmett took the piece she offered him, chewing it slowly. Rory tentatively licked her own. She wasn't sure she could stomach eating anything without throwing it up again.

Emmett scooped up a handful of snow from the fairly clean drift they were sitting in, sticking it in his mouth. Rory copied him, taking a small bite of the snow and grimacing when it froze her teeth, then licking the strip of salmon.

"How did you do that?" she asked. "How did you put my heart back when it wasn't in the locket?"

Emmett looked down at his gloved hands for a long time before answering. "I…I thought you were going to be the next person I had to watch die in front of me. That I was as powerless to help as I was when I lost my parents and Theresa. And I remembered the last time my family was together and happy: using our magic to strengthen the house beams." He shuddered and coughed. "All my life, my gift could manipulate the energy in living things, or things that used to be alive. Even before it turned into this." He winced and pinched the bridge of his nose. "I put your heart back the same way we wove our lives into the heartwood. It seemed like the only thing that might work."

"Careful. You're starting to sound like me. Maybe you left a little bit of my heart behind," Rory teased. Her laugh was choked off by a sudden need for more air than her lungs could hold. It took several breaths for her to stop feeling like she was dying all over again. Talking probably wasn't in her best interest if she wanted to be back on her feet any time soon.

Emmett had been right. The salt wasn't a perfect solution, but after a little while, Rory's head began to clear and the dizziness started to fade. "We should probably get moving. Things went a little…sideways…getting Carlo out. I had to tell him to meet us at the burnt-out house." She reached into her coat for the jacket still balled up inside, and the trail of light led exactly where it should. "He made it okay, as far as I can tell. But if the lights come up before we get there, he's going to head for Katya's."

Emmett grimaced. "I see why you gave him the knife. We should go find him before he thinks he has a reason to use it."

Rory experimentally pushed herself off the wall. Her vision wavered and flickered, and she stumbled, toppling sideways. The drifted snow cushioned her fall, although not enough to smother the choked yelp when her aching ribs protested.

Emmett held out a hand.

Rory blinked in shock. Emmett had helped her get her heart back, but it was because she'd been doing the same thing Marcus had before her: using his son as leverage. Emmett had no reason left to care about her. He could have gone to find Carlo and left her there to fend for herself. Instead, he was holding out his hand.

He didn't look like he was in any condition to offer help. Sweat dampened his hair and slid down his forehead despite the chill, and he was leaning on the wall. The hand held out to her was trembling, fingers curled in awkwardly like he was trying to make a fist and only half-succeeding.

Rory reached up slowly. She didn't know how to grab onto Emmett's hand properly, ending up with her fingers wrapped around his wrist, very nearly pulling off his glove. Emmett didn't pull her to her feet so much as give her another point to brace herself against, but between him and the wall, she managed to stand without her vision going spotty or her legs giving out.

She took a few deep breaths. "Let's go get Carlo."

Emmett followed her through the narrow alleys, his boots scuffing like he was dragging his feet on the slick stones. "Do you regret not being able to kill Marcus yourself?"

"He ordered his men to gut my father and let him bleed to death in an alley. I saw it through the eyes of the one who owned my knife." Rory kicked a small stone down the street with such force it bounced off a wall. "Putting that blade in his chest would have been too easy a death."

The first faint gleam of the lights rose over the edge of town. Rory turned down the street where the ruined house stood. Hopefully Carlo hadn't left for Katya's already. Rory ducked into the blackened remains of the crumbling mansion, and Emmett followed.

"Carlo?" Emmett called softly. "Are you here?" A small shadow barreled out of the dark and slammed into Emmett with such force he stumbled backward. "Easy, easy, it's okay," he gasped breathlessly, voice tight with pain.

Rory smiled, even as the action pulled the gash on her lip and cracked it open again, coppery blood sharp on her tongue. She whistled for Blizzard, but there was no answering coo. "Blizzard?" she called softly.

"Had to leave him a few streets back, at some building with big iron balconies," Emmett said, voice muffled where his face rested against Carlo's hair. "Some of Marcus's people caught me. I don't know if he'll still be waiting on that windowsill."

Rory was fairly certain the answer was yes. With one good wing, in this storm, Blizzard wouldn't have gone far. "We need to go," she said. "The Star will be searching everywhere in this quarter for you both by now." She nodded down toward the river. "Once we get to Katya's, we can figure out what to do next."

Emmett smiled sadly and rested a trembling hand on Carlo's shoulder as he stood. "You promise me that no matter what, you listen to what Rory says, okay?"

Rory stopped mid-step. "What does that mean?"

Emmett continued to look at Carlo. "Can you go watch by the door and give us a wave when there's no one on the street who could see us come out?"

Carlo nodded solemnly, clearly proud he'd been entrusted with such a serious lookout task. Rory couldn't be sure if he also realized what she knew. Emmett wanted to talk to Rory. Alone.

Emmett waited until Carlo was leaning against the doorframe, eyes on the street. "I'm going to turn myself in to the Cohort."

"You're joking, right? Please tell me that was a joke." Rory couldn't believe they'd gone through so much to get Emmett out from under Marcus's thumb just for him to turn around and voluntarily walk into prison.

Emmett glanced over at Carlo. "You're sure that hair you took is the only thing a guide could use to find Carlo, right?"

Rory nodded, hand clenched so tightly around the tiny enamel box in her pocket that she was half convinced it would shatter in her grip.

"I can't take the chance that the Star won't find a guide willing to blood track me for the kind of money I'm sure they'd offer."

"Once we get to Katya's, her people will protect us."

Emmett swallowed. "This is where it has to end. Carlo's safe now. So are you. But I've killed people."

"So have I," Rory snapped back.

"Eight people are dead because of me. You almost were." Emmett looked down at his gloved hands. "I have to turn myself in before anyone else decides to take advantage of my gift. And before all the people who want me dead catch up. I can't ask the Rapids to risk their lives protecting me without giving them some reason to want me alive, and I won't steal hearts for anyone again."

"There has to be some other way. If you could get out of the city—"

"I'd never get past the wards alive. Every smuggler in Rime answers to the Star."

Rory hated it when he was right. The Star had systematically forced any competitors out of business or absorbed them into the syndicate to ensure they had the only reliable way of getting people in and out of the wards. Without Marcus, the Star's chokehold would eventually dissolve, but it would take some time for freelancers like Jaye to start operating again. Emmett and Carlo didn't have the money for forged papers from the Quill, either. Even if they managed to escape the city for a while, they could be caught without identification and brought back to both be imprisoned in the Bastion. But Rory wasn't sure Carlo would see the logic behind his father's decision.

"Do you have any idea what it's like to grow up knowing the one parent you had left chose something else over being there for you?"

Emmett swallowed hard, grimacing and squeezing his eyes closed for a moment before meeting Rory's accusing gaze. "This isn't the same, Rory. What your mother did was selfish, and you have every reason to be angry, but I'm doing this to keep Carlo safe. Being around me is dangerous. You know that better than anyone."

Rory shook her head. She did know Emmett, and she knew that the only reason he was dangerous was because other people had forced his hand. All she saw was a father about to leave his son behind forever out of some misplaced sense of guilt. "If you turn yourself in, this is a death sentence."

Emmett blinked, looking up at the sky for a moment. "The Cohort only gives those to gifteds who've hurt one of their own. Haven't you noticed?"

Honestly, Rory tried not to pay attention to those cases. But he could be right. There were plenty of killers locked up in the Bastion. The only ones she recalled being publicly executed were the ones who'd committed crimes directly against the Cohort, mostly rebels like Jax's crew.

"What are you going to do if they're the next ones to offer you a deal? You killed people they wanted dead. That's the only reason they weren't hunting you down themselves. You could end up working for them just like the Star."

"No. I'm done with that. No matter what they offer me." Emmett looked Rory in the eyes, his own shining with tears. "The only reason I agreed to the Star's deal was because Carlo was with me. I'll be turning myself in alone. The Cohort will have nothing I care about to hold against me."

Carlo turned around from the door, waving at them to come. Emmett limped over, and Rory followed more slowly. Carlo bounced up and down on his toes, not realizing that when his father walked out that door, it would most likely be the last time Carlo would ever see him.

Rory wished she'd known that the night her father died. "You have to tell him," she said, catching Emmett's shoulder. "He deserves to know what you're going to do."

"I know."

Rory sighed and looked up at the sky. Green and pink trailed across it in shimmering ribbons. "How is this best for anyone?"

"It's best for Carlo," Emmett whispered.

Rory shook her head. "You're all the family he has left."

Emmett looked from Carlo to her. "You had a plan for him if neither of us came back. Will you make sure he's taken care of now?"

"Of course." Rory pulled the boy in against her, resting a hand gently on his shoulder. Rime would be dangerous for Carlo even without Emmett, recognizable now thanks to

Marcus's wanted posters, attracting attention to them both. Many of the Star's people probably knew what he looked like. She swallowed hard and swiped a hand across her cheek as Emmett knelt down next to Carlo.

"I have to go, okay?"

"Why?" Carlo asked.

"Because I did something wrong, and I have to make it right." Emmett took a shaky breath. "I love you, kiddo. So, so much." His voice was choked, eyes squeezing shut as he rested his cheek on Carlo's messy curls. A few tears trailed down his face, silvery-green in the faint light, landing in Carlo's hair.

Emmett winced as he started to stand. Rory offered him her free hand, and he took it as awkwardly as she'd reached for his, fingers wrapped around her elbow for support. When she stumbled, trying to keep her balance, he pulled his grip away. "I'm sorry for everything," he whispered, looking down at his hands.

"I'm not," Rory said fiercely. She bit back her next words, painfully conscious of the small body pressed up against her. *Are you sorry for trusting me with Carlo even after you watched me slit Trey's throat? Are you sorry Marcus is dead and can't hurt anyone else? Are you sorry you put my heart back in my chest when it could have killed you?* Carlo didn't need to hear those things. "I don't regret what we did today." She swallowed. "Do you?"

"No. But…" Emmett glanced down at Carlo. He, too, seemed to have more to say than was meant for his son's ears. "I've put you and Carlo in enough danger. I can't stay." Emmett met Rory's eyes for a moment. "No matter how much I want to." Then he tucked both hands into his pockets and walked away into the shadows.

Rory tightened her grip on Carlo's shoulder when she felt him tense like he was planning to run after Emmett and beg him to change his mind. Carlo winced at the firmer grasp, and Rory remembered the fall he'd taken off Marcus's wall and the shoulder she'd slipped back into position. She kept one hand on his arm, holding him in place while she readjusted the scarf sling that had fallen loose when he'd careened into Emmett in that desperate hug.

Carlo sniffled, clutching his carved dolphin in both hands. The lights reflected on tears gathering in his eyes; whether from the pain of having his shoulder moved or the settling realization that his father was gone, Rory wasn't sure. She bent down, removing her belt from Carlo's waist and securing it around her own again. The reliable weight was the only familiar thing in her world at the moment.

Voices drifted on the wind. Still some distance away, but from the rapidly crunching footsteps accompanying them, the speakers wouldn't be far for long. Rory couldn't pick out individual words, but there was too much urgency in the overlapping chatter for her comfort.

"Come on. We have to go now."

She moved toward the door, and Carlo balked, shaking his head. "Can't leave," he whispered. Rory felt like she was trapped in an endless loop of talking this kid out of the same situations. "What if Dad comes back?"

"He's not coming back," Rory said as gently as she could. "He left."

"But he didn't say for forever," Carlo wailed. Before Rory realized what was happening, she was nearly knocked over for the second time by a surprisingly heavy, very distressed Carlo. This time, the pain in his tears wasn't something she could fix as easily as his shoulder.

Rory needed Carlo to stop crying so the Star's guards couldn't find them. She needed him to let go of her so they could move. She needed him to trust her.

She hummed softly, harmonizing with the wind that once again carried an echo of her father's voice. She hadn't heard his lullaby since he'd died, but she still recalled most of the tune and the story, a ballad from his native Iron Peaks. Rory couldn't remember all the words, but she couldn't forget the chorus.

She sang the last two lines out loud:

"For all I need is light to see
The path one step in front of me."

Carlo sniffled and wiped his nose on his coat sleeve. "What's that mean?"

Rory rested her hands on Carlo's shoulders. "It means that when something is really big and scary, the only way to get through it is to not think about all of it at once." Emmett had mentioned something about the wooden toy being part of a bedtime story he'd told Carlo, and even though Rory didn't know that particular tale, she hoped the familiarity of a story being told might reassure him long enough to get them on their way to safety. "A long time ago, there was a little boy like you, whose village was freezing. They sent him over the mountains to bring back fire."

Carlo stopped sniffing and blinking, which seemed like a good sign, so Rory continued.

"When he found an inn, he took just one coal from their fireplace, put it in a lantern, and started off back home. On his way he met a snow-white wolf, a mountain sheep with brass horns, and an eagle whose wings were so powerful he stirred up storms wherever he flew."

Carlo shuddered slightly. Rory wasn't sure if he was cold or if her descriptions of the animals had frightened him. Maybe the past few hours had shaken him enough that anything big and powerful sounded scary. Rory couldn't blame him.

"All of them asked the boy why he was carrying such a small coal. And he told them if he looked at the whole path, he'd see how far he had to go and lose his courage. He only needed enough light to see the next place to put his foot."

Carlo wiped his nose again, hand still clenched into a fist around his wooden dolphin. The sight of the carving reminded Rory she had one more thing to do once they left this ruined place to ensure she and Carlo would be safe. She wrapped an arm around his shoulder. "It's time to go."

Carlo looked over his shoulder once and then buried his cheek in Rory's coat, ducking his head against the wind.

The lights were shimmering brightly overhead by the time the two of them stopped outside the boarded-up building Emmett and Carlo had once called home. Thanks to a slight detour past the street where Emmett had left Blizzard, the pigeon was once again perched on Rory's shoulder, his head tucked uncomfortably under her ear, listening to her restored pulse. Rory didn't have the heart to move him.

Carlo had been quiet the whole time. His injured arm rested loosely in the makeshift sling Rory had made from Emmett's scarf, and his eyelashes were frosted with tears. Rory knew better than to say anything. Whenever people had tried to comfort her after her father died, she'd been furious. No words were going to make things better. None of them could bring her father back. The only thing she and Carlo could do was make sure Emmett hadn't turned himself in for nothing.

Rory stepped through the gap Emmett had made in the window boards when they'd spent the night and motioned for Carlo to come inside. He struggled over the high edge of the window, and once he was standing inside the room, his eyes welled up with tears. He reached for a broken chair with rockers on its legs that had been pushed into the corner near the fireplace, wrapping his fingers around the bowed rungs supporting its arms.

Rory rested one hand gently on his shoulder. "I know there's a lot of memories here," she whispered. "But that's why we need to leave soon. We can't let anyone else who wants to hurt you find this place."

Carlo nodded, even as a fresh streak of tears ran down one cheek. He sniffled, wiping the back of a hand across his nose, then let go of the chair and clenched his fingers into fists.

"Get anything you need that means anything to you, and do it fast," Rory said, slipping her satchel over her shoulder, unlatching the starsilver buckles, and folding the flap behind it before handing it to Carlo. As soon as Carlo started climbing the steps, Rory crossed the room to the hook by the door where she'd seen a lantern. The base was still half full of whale oil that had thickened and congealed. Rory turned the base over, spreading the liquid across the workbenches, the table, and a pile of scrap wood near the fireplace.

Once she'd emptied the lamp, she leaned on one of the chairs' warped backs to catch her breath. She moved to the cupboards, rifling through torn bags of what used to be flour, frozen jars of pickling liquid with fish bones at the bottom, and moldering wooden spice shakers, before finding a small tin container. The sea salt inside was freckled with kelp fragments and solid with moisture. Rory chipped out a chunk with her knife and popped it into her mouth. She crunched it between her teeth, feeling the kelp fragments tickle the back of her throat when she swallowed. She tucked the little box into her pocket.

Carlo returned from the stairs with Rory's messenger bag stuffed to bulging. The sleeve of a sweater and the corner of a small book poked out. Rory reached into her pocket for one of the matches she'd swiped from Marcus's desk. "There's too much of your life here, Carlo," she said quietly. "We have to burn it down so no one can find you."

He didn't answer.

 Rory must have been doing this wrong. Emmett had told her to take care of his son, and all she was doing was destroying what was left of his life. But they all needed a fresh start. A second chance. She handed Carlo the match. "I'll let you. When you're ready."

He looked at her sadly, then struck the match against the rough surface of the workbench and dropped the flame into a smear of oil. Rory helped him out the window by the light of the flickering blaze. Once they were on the street, she turned to see flames leaping into the sky, orange and gold swirling up to meet green and pink.

They couldn't stay. The fire would draw not only neighborhood residents with a vested interest in putting it out before it spread to their own homes, but Cohort authorities as well. Rory put her arm around Carlo's shoulders and the two of them walked away from the past going up in flames.

22 Months Later

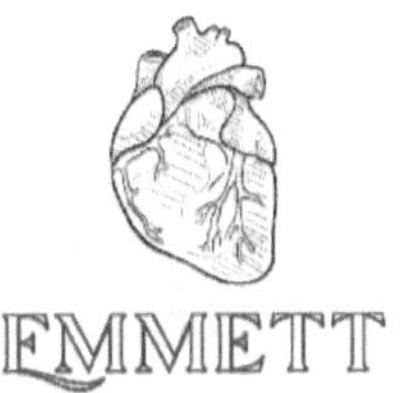

11 BELLS

Emmett plunged one hand into the pail of water on the floor of his cell, breaking the thin skim of ice already forming on top. Even if the water had been warm when a guard hauled it out of the tank on the first floor, the trip five stories up the Bastion's tower had been enough to freeze it.

His teeth ached from the chill as he swallowed several mouthfuls, but it was better than his head spinning because he hadn't drunk enough. He'd learned the hard way that outside the height of thaw season, his water pail always froze solid by midday, and the guards refused to bring more.

Emmett cupped a small handful of water in his hands and splashed it onto his face. Icy trails made their way down his chest, and he shivered. He rubbed one damp hand over the back of his neck, then wiped the water from his face and beard with the edge of his shirt. It was the cleanest he'd manage to get without freezing. Usually, he didn't bother at all, saving the water for his stomach, but it was visiting day, and he didn't want any more of Rory's pity than was absolutely necessary.

Emmett hadn't felt clean or warm in the whole two years he'd been in the Bastion, but he still preferred the prison to the false comfort of the Star Syndicate's mansion. At least here, he wasn't being asked to kill anyone. Yet.

He tried to ignore the empty cell across the hallway, the last tally mark on its wall only halfway carved into the stones. The guards had taken another prisoner last night.

Emmett hadn't known her real name, but he pitied the fierce girl with the bear-clawed fingers who claimed she'd done nothing to warrant being locked up with the worst of the worst. She'd deserved better than dying as a Cohort pawn.

If it was nothing more than a collection of holding cells, the Bastion would have been redundant when all of Rime was basically one massive prison. Letting their criminals kill each other off or succumb to disease in the slums would have been much cheaper for the Cohort than constructing and maintaining such a massive building just to drive home a threat. If all they'd intended was to instill fear, executing any criminal they found worthy of their trouble would have been just as effective. The Bastion's true purpose, Emmett had realized over the course of his incarceration, was far more calculated. The Cohort used the prison to wear down gifteds they thought might be useful before turning them into weapons.

It certainly explained why the only gifteds sentenced to death were the ones who'd rebelled against the Cohort themselves. The rest were left to endure a hellish life until they were willing to do whatever it took to escape. The Bastion ought to have been overflowing with prisoners after the amount of time it had existed. Instead, there was a constant reshuffling of the people inside its walls. Some prisoners, often the ones with the most powerful gifts, claimed they'd been locked up unreasonably for petty crimes. Ten other inmates from Emmett's floor vanished after six months or a year, taken by guards with no warning, on days no visitors were permitted. None of those prisoners had been returned to their cells.

Anyone chosen probably had two options. Agree to the Cohort's terms, or die—but less publicly than rebels. The recruitments were an unprovable rumor, but to keep it that way, the Cohort would have had to silence anyone who could corroborate it.

A wave of dizziness washed over Emmett, and he barely managed to sit down on the shelf that passed for a bed instead of tumbling to the cold stone floor. Giving back a heart that had wrapped itself up in his own had taken a higher toll than handing over the ones the locket held. He'd barely managed to walk into the Cohort's justice hall and tell them he was the heart thief the whole city was hunting before he'd collapsed. His first few months in the Bastion had been spent almost entirely on his thin straw mattress. Even now, the lightheadedness that used to last for several hours or at the most a couple days after a theft was a constant feature of his day-to-day life. As was the hunger threatening to rip him apart from the inside out.

He'd told Rory he was turning himself in to keep Carlo safe from the syndicates that might threaten him the same way Marcus had. It had only been half true. He'd needed to protect Carlo from himself, too.

Emmett looked up when someone knocked on his door. "You have a visitor."

The guard who stepped into the cell had his arms gloved to the elbow with the kind of heavy leather gauntlets used by furnace stokers. A protective collar of the same material wrapped around his neck. Everyone who'd ever been sent for Emmett was always dressed that way. No one wanted to let him touch their skin, even for a moment, and risk losing their heart.

It wasn't an unreasonable fear. As soon as Emmett's gift sensed a living, beating heart in reach of his hands, it clawed desperately to be sated, tearing him to shreds inside in the process. He'd learned to relish the isolation in his cell, where his gift settled back into a tight, aching coil in his chest. The one exception was visiting days. Emmett could bear the throbbing headache and searing pressure in his chest for the one hour a month he was allowed to see Rory. Even though she couldn't talk about Carlo outright, she'd found a way to let Emmett know his son was cared for and surviving.

Emmett had first assumed Rory was trying to hide her occupation based on the number of times she'd told him useless details about fish she claimed she'd caught. Only when she'd surreptitiously pulled the carved dolphin from her pocket near the end of the third visit, pointing to it while continuing to tell her strange story, did Emmett realize that by salmon or trout, she meant Carlo. Rory's attempts to use the limited terms of the fishing industry to pass along information about Carlo's growth, health, and skills were the only news Emmett had gotten about his son for the past two years.

Emmett stood up and let the guard chain his hands and haul him out of the cell.

Halfway down the stairs, his bad leg nearly gave out under him. He barely managed to catch himself against the rough stone wall. He had no doubt the guard would rather let him tumble the rest of the way down the steps than put out a hand to stop him. The chain holding his wrists was yanked sharply, and Emmett stumbled again as he moved away from the wall and continued to limp down the stairs, his old wound aching in the cold.

The guard didn't stop at the usual floor, with its frost-covered bars separating the prisoners from people who could walk away at the end of the hour. Instead, he continued down the staircase, and Emmett could do nothing but follow, trying to keep a little slack in the chain between them. The ground floor was all administration, tucked into the warmer spaces where heat from the massive furnaces actually managed to seep into the walls. Emmett's visitor must have been someone powerful.

His throat tightened. If someone from the Cohort wanted to speak to him, it probably meant they were finally offering him a deal. Or it could mean they'd found his son. Neither of those would end well.

Instead of turning toward the offices, the guard led Emmett to a set of heavy doors. Emmett tensed, steps slowing until the chain between him and the guard pulled tight, and he was yanked forward unceremoniously.

No convicted prisoner was allowed out of the Bastion under any circumstances. Once their sentence began, the only way they'd ever leave the tower was in a death cart, or if the rumors were true, under the employment of the Altrenean empire.

And since he hadn't agreed to one of the Cohort's twisted deals, Emmett knew which fate was waiting for him.

The guard shoved open the doors, and Emmett stumbled out into a small, dimly lit courtyard. A pair of lanterns near the door cast wavering shadows, distorted by thick bloodbriar vines winding their way over the walls, thorns as long as Emmett's fingers tipped with frozen droplets of black poison.

He stared down at the stained cobblestones. No one had bothered to sluice down the courtyard after last night's execution. Sprouting red brambles had already begun twining in thready tangles across the ground, ready to tear into the ankles of anyone passing by.

Emmett looked around for a shrouded executioner. Instead, he caught a glimpse of blonde hair in the shadows above a coat a few shades lighter than the burgundy vines behind its wearer. The guard fumbled with the chain on his wrists, and Emmett jumped when the cold metal fell away.

"Go on then, before someone changes their mind," the man snapped, turning back toward the building. Chain links jingled as he slammed the door behind Emmett.

Emmett decided not to wonder how Rory managed to bribe a Cohort guard, and instead walked toward her, hoping this wasn't some bizarre dream. It seemed all too likely she'd vanish into nothing the moment he got close. He couldn't quite believe Rory was real until he reached for her and his fingers brushed the worn fabric of her coat.

"This isn't a visit," Rory said, digging into her messenger bag and producing a familiar brown coat. The last time Emmett had seen it, that jacket had been hanging on a peg in Katya's bathhouse. He had no idea how Rory had gotten it back. "We're leaving Rime. All three of us." Rory tossed him the coat. "You're going to need this."

Emmett hadn't realized until he'd already slipped his arms through the jacket sleeves just how cold he'd been. The thin shirt he'd been given as a prisoner was useless against the cutting wind. He dug into his pockets for the gloves that used to be inside. They were still there, and he slipped them on gratefully. His gift settled, a persistent hiss in his thoughts instead of a demanding howl.

Its claws digging deep into his own heart were the only reason he was hesitant to take Rory's offer of escape. Inside the prison, Emmett couldn't hurt anyone else. If he went with Rory and Carlo, he risked taking the lives of the two people he cared about most in the world.

The wind whistled through the courtyard, whispering in a voice that sounded a lot like Theresa.

Go. All that waits for you here is death. Outside, you have a chance.

Emmett had no idea what could fix his heart-hunger, but the voice was right. There was no solution in Rime. And if anyone could find a cure for Emmett, Rory would.

"The guard who will let us through leaves his shift at twelve bells," Rory said, tugging on Emmett's sleeve. "We need to go now."

Emmett knew better than to argue with her, even though there were a thousand reasons this would never work. He fell into step behind her.

The closer Emmett got to the gate, the slower his steps became. If the guard decided to slam the gates and turn both of them in for Emmett's escape, everything he and Rory had done to protect Carlo for the past two years would have been for nothing. Emmett swallowed hard. Rory thought through every contingency when she planned. She wouldn't have taken a risk this big and left Carlo without someone to look after him.

The guard at the gate barely managed more than a nod as they walked past, puffing away on a pipe. The distinctive scent of poppy petals drifted on a gust of wind that followed Emmett and Rory out of the courtyard.

Rory led them nearly three blocks from the Bastion before she stopped outside an alley piled high with crates. She repeated a low whistle three times, and Emmett heard an answering coo.

A figure much taller than Emmett remembered emerged from behind the crates, Blizzard perched on his shoulder. A knit cap covered most of his curls, but the few escaping over his forehead whipped sideways in the wind, and the tip of his nose was bright red. Carlo's face had become sharper, limbs ganglier, eyes fiercer than the last time Emmett had seen him. Rory's parenting skills had been enough to keep him alive, but she'd also handed Carlo a ten-inch knife within minutes of meeting him. Now, he looked a lot like that carefully honed blade himself.

"Dad?" The confusion in Carlo's voice hurt. Two years was a long time. Maybe Carlo had started to forget him. "You look different."

Emmett choked back a bitter laugh. He hadn't seen his reflection in anything more than the surface of a water pail or been allowed to hold anything sharper than a shard of ice. He had no idea what he looked like after two years of hunger and cold and isolation. Rory had watched the slow changes over her visits every month. Carlo hadn't.

Emmett was taken completely by surprise when Carlo nearly knocked him to the ground with the force of his hug. Emmett put his hands on Carlo's arms, ignoring the agony in his chest, his gift demanding that he remove his gloves and let his fingers find the pulse in Carlo's throat. He wasn't sure he trusted himself to wrap his arms around his son and hold him close.

Rory cleared her throat. "We need to be going."

Emmett couldn't manage another word until they'd walked halfway through the Smoke Quarter, heading toward the shoreline. He was afraid he'd wake up any moment on his hard bunk in his frigid cell, staring at a stone ceiling. But the ground under his feet was real and solid. So was Carlo's grip.

Only when Rory turned down a street wide enough for all three of them to walk side by side did Emmett finally ask what he'd been dying to since he'd seen her. He took a few breaths before he spoke, trying to calm his still-racing heart and the panting gasps that accompanied more physical activity than he'd experienced in years. "How did you arrange this?"

"Same way I got these." Rory fanned out a set of three papers, as small as the cards street magicians used for their tricks. Each carried the official seal of the Altrenean Empire. The starsilver mixed with the wax, validating the marks, shimmered in the green light bursting overhead.

One false identity document cost a small fortune. Three would have taken more money than anyone but a High Quarter resident could afford. "How…?"

"Saved up some favors." Rory's hands looked thinner than they used to, as did her face. A fresh patch of lichen scabs had appeared over her right temple, adding a new stripe of gray threading through her braid. Emmett wasn't the only one the past two years had changed. "The Quill Syndicate were suitably shocked when I started taking their payment in kind." She handed Emmett his paper, and he committed the false name and employment as a ship's carpenter to memory before sliding it into a pocket.

Rory led the way to a rambling warehouse near the docks. The air smelled strongly of salt and fish, and the dampness cut through Emmett's thin clothes. He tugged his coat tighter around him. His legs, especially the left with its old injury, were trembling from a bone-deep ache. He slumped against the wall, barely stopping himself from sliding down to sit in the snow that had drifted against the boards. He didn't want to make Rory or Carlo have to help him up, and he knew he'd regret letting his clothes get wet once they had to move on.

Rory leaned against the warehouse wall, out of the worst of the wind. She took a small tin from her pocket, pulled out a pinch of something, and tucked it into her mouth the way sailors chewed tobacco. She looked from the tin to him, then held it out. Emmett accepted it gingerly, opening the rust-speckled metal to find chunks of damp, clumped salt. He took one of the smaller pieces and handed back the tin.

"We need to wait for Ricky," Rory said, tucking the salt box back into her coat and looking out to sea. "He's a wrecker. Got us spots on a boat heading out."

Emmett nodded. Wreckers salvaged ships that went down in storms inside the wards. They gave a cut of their profits to the Cohort's port guards, but still usually ended up with plenty to line their own pockets and pass around for favors. Several of the most successful had mansions in the High Quarter, their scarred hands and weatherbeaten skin at odds with the luxury of their homes.

Rory dug into her satchel and produced an oilcloth bag. The pastries inside were cold and chunks of the crust had broken off, but they looked better than any food Emmett had seen since the Bastion doors slammed behind him. Rory handed one each to Carlo and Emmett, taking the smallest for herself. Emmett broke the meat pie in half, forcing himself to swallow the savory filling in small bites. Painful experience had taught him eating quickly after days or weeks of barely enough food to survive never ended well.

Carlo curled in against Emmett while they ate, and he put an arm around the boy's shoulder. Emmett had imagined their reunion often, even though he'd assumed it could never happen. Dreamed of it more times than he could count. Now that Carlo was actually right there next to him, Emmett had no idea what to say or do.

Waves beat steadily on the rocks below, and eventually a small rowboat appeared, low in the water but moving swiftly. It crunched through the floating ice, bumping against the dock next to the warehouse. A wiry young man with salt-crusted skin, short-shaven hair, and a scar running along his cheek climbed out of the boat and tied it off to a cleat.

Rory met him at the end of the dock. She unstrapped the knife sheath from her belt, gripped it by the leather, and held out the handle to the wrecker. He pulled out the blade and examined it with the practiced eye of someone who knew the value of plenty of things. Finally, he slid the knife back into the sheath.

"Just like we agreed, Ricky," Rory said.

"I'm going to miss you, you know that?" Ricky took the sheath and slid it onto his own belt. "You were one of the few halfway honest people left in this town."

"You're just saying that because you got the knife you've been drooling over since we met." Rory cuffed his shoulder playfully. "Now, you've got a captain with a few berths for us?"

Ricky motioned to them to follow him, and Emmett reluctantly pushed himself off the wall, grimacing when his stiff, aching legs protested. Ricky led the way through a maze of upended hulls, tattered nets, shattered masts, and warehouses leaning at crazy angles from the sea winds. He stopped at a pier where a steam-driven crabbing smack was docked, harbor ice piled in bluish heaps in front of its metal-shielded bow. Chipped, rust-streaked white letters painted on the red hull spelled out the name *Arctic Gale*. The traps piled on her deck, lashed down with heavy rope, rose almost as high as her pilothouse. Emmett couldn't imagine taking a top-heavy thing like that out into the stormy West Seas for weeks at a time, in gale-force winds and waves that, according to sailors' tales, rivaled the Iron Peaks. Then again, a captain with enough guts to do that over and over to earn a living was also probably one of the only people bold enough to smuggle three fugitives past the wards.

"Next stop, Ternshaven Port," Ricky said. "You think Rime is cold, it's got nothing on that place." He shuddered.

Rory didn't look in any way deterred. "It'll be perfect."

The guard in a shack at the end of the pier waved them on with only a cursory glance at their paperwork, scrawling their false names on a manifest hanging from a nail in the wall. Emmett's coat hid the most obvious portions of his prison uniform, although if the guard had bothered to lean over his counter, he'd have seen the laceless shoes. Ricky didn't have Cohort papers, but the guard let him pass after the wrecker slid a box wrapped in oilcloth across the counter and promised he'd be off the pier before the docked boat departed.

As soon as Emmett stepped off the gangplank onto the boat, the faint rocking motion hit him with a wave of nausea. He ducked as a pair of Rime seagulls crashed onto the deck, fighting over a fish head grasped in their talons. The birds screeched raucously, slashing at each other with their claw-tipped wings and toothed beaks. Blood smeared crimson against sooty-gray and snowy-white feathers. The birds would tear each other apart rather than give up their prize.

Emmett swallowed down the bile in his throat and clenched his hands into fists. Between his gift shrieking for a heart like the gulls after their offal and the sea swells dropping the deck out from under his feet, he'd be lucky not to throw up before they left port.

A man with a nose as rusty-red and sharp as the prow of his boat emerged from the pilothouse when Ricky knocked on its door. "Emmett, Rory, Carlo, this is Captain Coveland," Ricky said, walking down the ladder with the man behind him. He looked from them to the sea-gnarled captain. "These are personal friends of mine, so treat them right."

The captain's hooded eyes, as blue and chilly as the ice surrounding his boat, raked over the small group. After a long moment he held out his left hand to Rory and Emmett in turn. His right, clenched stiffly by his waist, was a mangled mess that even a glove couldn't fully conceal.

Carlo gaped in undisguised curiosity. Rory and Emmett each shook the boy's arm at approximately the same time.

"Carlo. It's not polite to stare," Emmett whispered.

"Oh, he's perfectly fine," Captain Coveland replied. He whipped off his glove, revealing a twisted mass of scar tissue that might once have been five fingers. "I show this to all the landlubbers. Right here is why you don't lean over the rail at night." He pulled a strange, wavy knife that appeared to be made of bone from a sheath at his waist. "Swordfish are mighty aggressive beasts, and they're worse when they're star-touched. This fella took my hand, but I got his sword. Made me a fine knife." The blade's edges glimmered a faint orange-gold. The captain leaned in closer to Carlo and then chuckled. "Little secret between us, small fry. That ain't what really happened. I smashed this thing in a trap when I was no older'n you." He slid his knife back into its sheath and smiled when Carlo grinned. "Now don't go tellin' my crew and ruinin' my reputation."

Rory smiled as Carlo moved to look over the rail, keeping his hands well away from the edge. "Thanks for humoring him. Teaching him to pay attention to everything he sees has its downsides."

"His secrets shouldn't have to be the only ones he's keepin'," the captain said with a wry smile. He shouted up the ladder to the pilothouse. "Myah! Come give our guests the tour before we cast off."

A slender girl with twin black braids bouncing against her shoulders rattled down the ladder. She looked younger than Carlo, but her brown hands were already scarred with rope burns. "It's almost turn of tide," she said. "We need to get you new clothes before the Cohort guards check us for departure."

Ricky turned and began to walk down the gangplank.

"Take care of yourself now," Rory called after him.

"Don't you worry none about me," Ricky replied, then stepped off the boards.

"Carlo!" Emmett called. The boy hurried to join them, sliding on the icy, faintly rocking deck. Rory grabbed his hand as they made their way to a hatch that led down into the boat. Emmett swallowed a lump in his throat at the sight of their fingers laced together. Carlo had been in good hands for the past two years. Better ones than Emmett's. He tugged at his gloves and followed the others down the ladder.

Below decks, the smell of fish and tar and smoke hung heavy in the air, but it was the first place Emmett had been able to breathe easily in a long time. The three of them followed Myah into a small, cramped living space hung with several rope hammocks. New clothes were folded up in three of the berths, rough bibbed trousers and coarse gray sweaters. The knitting was a different pattern than the Seachosen designs Emmett knew, but still obviously the work of net weavers.

"You'll look like any other crew members," Myah said. "Cohort patrols don't like spending too long looking around our boat. The smell is too much for them." She grinned, showing a missing front tooth. "Just stay busy and let them see your papers when they come through, and you'll be fine. You look the part," she said, gesturing to Emmett. He probably did resemble the grizzled sailors, with his unkempt beard and messy hair.

Once they were dressed in the heavy, worn clothes, Myah handed over several lengths of rope and pointed out broken spots in the hammocks to repair, probably a safe job to give inexperienced people pretending they were the sort to sign on with a crab crew. She didn't seem the least concerned they'd be found out, and everything about her actions was the practiced nature of someone who'd done the same thing a thousand times. As soon as they started tying knots, she vanished up the ladder to the deck.

A few other crew members stepped into the cabin, laying out their own gear and checking their hammocks. A broad-shouldered man with dark blue tattoos covering the backs of his hands cursed out a huge tear in the bottom of his own berth.

Carlo picked up an unused section of repair rope and waved it in the air. Emmett cleared his throat. "We have some extra rope."

The man turned around, his face shifting from frustration to what Emmett assumed must be the extreme chagrin he'd felt the times he'd hit his thumb with a hammer and didn't remember Carlo was in the room. "Didn't realize there was a young lubber here," the fisherman said, taking the rope. He looked from Carlo's knot-tying efforts to Emmett, then Rory. "You folks mind if I show your son a couple tricks so that hammock doesn't fall apart under him tonight?"

Emmett didn't dare look at Rory, even as he heard her sharp breath at being mistakenly identified as Carlo's parent. "That would be fine," he mumbled around the choked feeling that had sprung up in his throat.

Myah had been right about the Cohort patrols. The officers barely came below long enough to make a cursory identification check. Emmett heard one retching over the side after he got back to the deck.

Finally, a voice from above shouted "Cleared for departure". Boots clattered overhead, ropes slapped wood as the moorings were freed, and the soft rocking motion turned into a rhythmic swaying. The engines shifted from a soft idle roar to thrumming like a pulsing heartbeat. Ice crunched and creaked as the bow plowed through it.

Several minutes later, after the boat had reached open water, there was another, louder thud of impact. Emmett flinched as the boat came to a halt. For a terrifying moment he wondered if they'd hit one of the mountainous icebergs sailors claimed floated aimlessly around the ocean. Then he realized they'd come up against the wards. The engines stalled for a moment, and a heavy whine reverberated through the hull.

"What's happening?" Carlo whispered.

"I don't know." Emmett had seen the gates in the city towers that permitted passage through the wards on land, but there couldn't be anything like that in the harbor. He had no idea how the Cohort allowed ships to exit Rime's magical barrier.

A bell pealed nearby, its sound a dissonant echo of the ones that marked time in the city. If Rime's starsilver bells were rung to reinforce the wards, maybe one hanging in the channel watchtower had the opposite effect.

"All ahead full!" someone shouted, and a strange rending noise, like tearing cloth, filled the boat as it moved forward. Magic thrummed around them, a low-pitched hum that echoed below decks as they sailed through.

Carlo pressed himself against Emmett, hands clenched in Emmett's sweater. A crackling sound, like lightning and thunder blended together, rang out behind them as the boat picked up speed and they sailed away from Rime.

Emmett glanced at Rory, who released the hammock rope she'd been holding in a white-knuckled grip. She let out a shaky breath, gave him a nod, then went back to tying knots. Emmett squeezed Carlo's arm in gentle reassurance.

"We're safe?" Carlo whispered.

Emmett nodded. "We made it."

The hands on deck broke into a chanting song Emmett could hear over the thrumming engine. The red-haired fisherman who'd taught Carlo proper knots dug around in his canvas bag, pulling out a couple tattered sweaters and tossing them aside before taking out a battered leather case. He removed a fiddle and began tuning up, the lilting rhythm matching the motion of the deck underfoot. Once the notes were correct, he tucked the instrument back into its case and climbed up the ladder. A few minutes later, a cheerful, rapid melody broke out on deck, echoing through the whole vessel. The footsteps of the crew at work matched it beat for beat.

The waves were larger outside the wards, rolling the boat from side to side. Carlo's face turned an ashy color, and he choked a few times, hands pressed against his stomach. Emmett wasn't fond of the feeling either. He thought he'd gotten used to constant nausea after the past two years, but a pitching, rocking ship was different than the hunger sitting in his chest.

Carlo curled up in his hammock, and Emmett sat down next to him. Blizzard perched on the ropes by his shoulder, and Carlo reached up to scratch the bird under its chin. Emmett didn't think he'd seen Blizzard go more than a few feet from Carlo this entire time.

"I'm sorry," he finally said, to break the silence with something other than waves slapping the hull. "I'm sorry for everything."

"I'm not mad." Carlo sat up a little. "I just don't know what to do now. We've been waiting so long to get you back. We never talked about what happened after that."

That sounded like Rory. Detailed plan to solve a highly specific and theoretically impossible-to-beat problem, and not a single clue what to do if she actually pulled it off. Emmett probably ought to warn her that her plans had a better success rate than she expected, and she needed plans for *after* them. Not that Emmett was the person who should be giving anyone advice.

"I missed you," Carlo said quietly.

"I missed you too." Emmett dug his gloves back out of his pockets and slipped them on, then reached for Carlo's hand. He twisted his fingers into the ones that were so much longer than he remembered. Holding his son's hand again was worth the ache springing up behind his eyes and the feeling of his heart eating itself up from the inside out. "Every single day." He didn't know what else to say. But they had plenty of time to figure that out.

"Where's Rory?" Carlo asked, pushing himself up on one elbow, grimacing when the hammock swayed under him but still glancing around the cabin as much as he could. "She sings to me every night before I go to sleep."

Emmett swallowed. Rory had raised Carlo for nearly two years. Being replaced stung, but Emmett had only himself to blame. He'd left his son in someone else's hands. Emmett looked behind him. He'd assumed Rory was there somewhere, still working on the ropes on her own hammock, but she'd vanished. "I'll go find her, okay?"

"Can you tell the story about the dolphins for us tonight?" Carlo asked. "I tried to tell her but I'm not as good at remembering it as you, and she's never heard it before."

Emmett smiled softly and ran a hand over Carlo's messy hair. "I sure will."

Emmett didn't have Rory's innate sense for someone's whereabouts. Somehow, he still knew she was on deck. He forced himself to climb the ladder, his old wound searing painfully with each step.

When he finally stepped out of the hatch, it was into a night brighter than anything he'd ever known. The sky outside the wards was speckled with a million tiny stars like candle flames in faraway houses. The moon, familiar only from his parents' stories, glowed in a pale silver circle. The gray marks patched across its surface didn't look as much like a dolphin as the legend had led Emmett to believe. He ought to bring Carlo up here when they told the story so he could see it for himself.

Emmett looked up at the thousands of tiny sparks overhead and hoped everything his family said about spirits and stars was true. "If you can hear me," he whispered, "Carlo's safe. So am I." He left out the bit about his chest squeezing with an insatiable hunger. It was a small price to pay for everything he'd done.

He offered up a quiet prayer of gratitude as well, the same one his parents used to say over a good meal. *"For what has been given, what has been spared, and what has been returned, we offer thanks. We see your hands and hear your voice in these gifts."*

Nothing about the past two years had been anything short of a miracle. Rory's survival, his, and a successful escape were all things Emmett assumed he had no right to ask for. Since he'd gotten them, it seemed only fitting to thank whoever might be responsible.

Usually, his family addressed their prayers to the specific god who'd come to their aid, but Emmett wasn't sure to whom exactly he owed his gratitude.

The Seachosen gods required sacrifices before bestowing such favor, and even if Emmett had offered the entire wealth of the Star, he could never have convinced one of them to rescue a murderer. Their sense of justice, unlike a Cohort official's, couldn't be swayed with gifts.

The Frostfolk's impersonal Fate might not have cared if Emmett had killed, but it also would have had no interest in saving his life. It gave its followers exactly what it demanded of them: nothing.

Emmett had never heard of a god both powerful enough to reach through the wards and kind enough not to give up on lost causes. Maybe, like a solution to his gift's insatiable hunger, the answer lay somewhere outside Rime. Someone had to know which deity had intervened on Emmett's behalf.

Someday, Emmett hoped he could thank them by name.

He owed his thanks to someone else as well; someone a lot closer and more tangible than whatever deity had decided Emmett wasn't beyond help. Rory was looking out across the water, one hand grasping the rope holding a stack of traps, the other bracing herself on the rail.

She'd probably scoff at the whole notion, but Emmett firmly believed the moment Rory tracked him down in that alley had been some kind of response to his earlier prayer. He'd been prepared to accept that divine intervention had come after him with a knife. What he hadn't expected was for it to put the knife down and hold out a hand instead. He braced himself against another, milder wave of dizziness, letting his head clear before limping across the deck to join her.

"It's nothing like I imagined," Rory said as he joined her at the rail. A few gulls circled the boat, but their screeching clamor had calmed. They seemed content to glide past on gusts of wind or perch in the rigging, waiting for fishing to begin. "The way my dad talked about the stars, they were so close you could touch them." She looked up. "Somehow, it's even more amazing that they're this far above us. There's so much sky." She pointed to a small figure at the bow, a bright metal triangle in her hand. "Myah can feel them. I wonder what that's like."

Apparently, their guide to the inside of the boat was also their navigator. Emmett had met very few people with sky-focused gifts in their blood. They didn't survive long under the false horizon of the wards.

When Rory looked up at the stars again, the moonlight caught on the silvery lichen scabs crusting her cheek, and Emmett remembered their conversation after he'd stolen Trey's heart. "Why did you do this?" he asked. "You told me you'd never risk leaving Rime."

Rory shook her head. "I wouldn't leave the city for myself." She took a shuddering breath. "But it's no place to grow up. Carlo shouldn't live his whole life there. And there was no way we could have stayed once we got you back."

"You spent two years saving up every favor anyone owed you to break me out. Thank you."

"Oh, I didn't do it for you. I did it for Carlo."

Something bright slid under the boat. Emmett leaned over the rail for a better view. The massive golden glow moved slowly, water parting around a wide tail fin as it breached the surface and slapped down again. Emmett had never seen a living starwhale before. Only the remains brought in on the oil ships.

Rory stared down as well, hands clenched tight around the railing. The whale glided away toward the horizon, then turned. A moment later, it flung itself out of the water, gleaming with speckles and stripes of glowing gold. Emmett could see exactly how the creatures got their name. It wasn't just because they were affected by one of the stars that fell into the ocean. The whale's skin sparkled like the night sky.

A sky that, behind the whale's arching back, burst into a blaze of color ten times brighter than Rime's lights. A vibrant green curtain rippled down, reflecting off the water. Emmett heard a faint gasp from beside him and turned. Rory was looking up at the sky with pure wonder on her face, the vivid glow reflected in her eyes.

"They're here too." Rory smiled faintly. "I thought I'd left them behind. Turns out, the lights of Rime were nothing compared to what's out here."

"Nothing this beautiful is meant to be trapped in a place like that."

The boat swayed, and Rory gasped. She was nowhere close to falling over the rail, but Emmett grabbed her arm regardless. She jumped, hand sliding to her hip even though her knife was no longer there. Emmett let go as the ramifications of what he'd done hit him with as much force as the waves smashing the bow of the boat. He hadn't touched her skin, but that didn't mean he hadn't reminded her all over again of the threat he posed to anyone and everyone he came near.

"I still get dizzy sometimes," Rory choked out as another wave rolled by.

Emmett had never heard of anyone whose heart had been missing as long as Rory's and survived. There were bound to be lasting effects. He'd never properly apologized for ruining her life.

"Rory—"

She stopped him with a single word, turning around to face him. "Aurora."

AURORA

The pitching waves sent Rory's fragile heart skipping. Being out on the water felt like walking on river ice, only ten times worse. Her gift had no solid ground to latch onto. No glowing path appeared in front of her telling her she was moving in the right direction.

She reached for her side on instinct, but even the reassuring solidity of her knife was gone.

Emmett's hand pressed down on her arm for a moment. She tried to lean into the steadying touch, but it vanished before she could truly appreciate it. Probably for the best. She shouldn't get used to him grounding her, not when she'd have to let him go too. She wasn't sure she'd have been willing to sacrifice everything she'd known if she'd truly understood what starting over felt like. Her tethers to the city lost in the warded fog behind them were fading. If she let herself replace that security with Emmett, she'd never have the courage to walk away from him.

Rory had spent the past two years with one goal in mind: reunite Emmett and Carlo. She'd worked, bargained, saved, scraped, and stolen to make it happen. It got her through days when she couldn't leave her bed because her heart fluttered and threatened to stop altogether the moment she sat up. It kept her feet moving when there wasn't enough money in her pockets to feed two people. Made her smile through it all, just to see an answering look on Carlo's face.

She'd never let Carlo believe it would be easy, or safe, but she'd also never wavered in an absolute confidence that he would see his father again. If she'd let that belief falter, even for a moment, they both would have given in to the odds stacked against them. Hope was dangerous, but it had kept them alive.

But the same truth that gave them strength had also kept a distance between them. All that time, Rory had been doing what Emmett had asked. Keeping Carlo safe until Emmett came back. Rory was the stopgap. And now, she was a stopgap with no purpose, burned bridges, and no clear path into the future.

For the first time in her life, Rory Blake was completely, utterly lost.

She was more terrified than she'd been that morning, standing outside the Bastion's guardhouse, hoping her red coat would keep the wrong people from asking any questions about why she was hanging around the prison.

Emmett's voice broke through the thoughts threatening to overwhelm her. "Rory—"

"Aurora."

He looked at her with a small frown. "I know what the lights are."

"That's not what I meant. It's my name." Rime had taken plenty from Rory, but she refused to let it keep her real name. She wouldn't let her mother be the only person in the world who knew it. "My father always said he named me for the lights. He told me I was the brightest thing in his world." Rory looked down at the water, then up again as a flare of green painted the sky. "I gave up that name when I watched a gate guard stab a knife through his chest, just to ensure a man who'd been sliced nearly in half wasn't faking his death. He came to Rime because he thought it would be a safe place for me to grow up, where I wouldn't have to hide my gift." She shook her head, feeling the bitter half-smile on her face. "If it hadn't been for me, he might have lived."

"It wasn't your fault. You were just a child."

"I know that now." Rory took a shaky breath before looking up at Emmett. "I had to convince Carlo that you weren't in prison because of anything he did. Before I could make him believe that, I had to accept that I wasn't responsible for what happened to my dad either." It was the only reason she'd been able to set foot on this boat and leave Rime behind her. She was done paying the price for her father's death. When she'd handed that knife off to Ricky, it felt like letting go of the guilt she'd been carrying for seventeen years.

The fact remained, she'd left the only life she'd ever known. Which made what she had to say next feel like tearing her heart out all over again. "I don't have to stay."

"What do you mean?" Emmett asked.

"When we get off this boat, I can disappear." She couldn't meet Emmett's gaze. It was impossible to look Carlo in the eyes and tell him things were okay when they were out of money or her heart was struggling. His father was just as perceptive. Rory couldn't hide the sadness that would be at odds with her careless tone. "You and Carlo can get your lives back."

"Why would I want you to leave?"

"He's your son. Not mine." The words were hollow in her mouth. "We both knew this was temporary."

"You protected him. You put food on the table and a roof over his head."

A flicker of a memory surged up like a wave slamming into the hull. Gnarled hands pressing a leather bag into Rory's fingers, a raspy voice warning her about pickpockets and wild dogs and cheating vendors. The first of many times Rory had been sent out alone to the market because Old Sue's aching legs were too painful.

Rory had repeated that scene with Carlo more often than she cared to remember. She was supposed to look after him, but without his help on the days her heart felt like a moose had kicked her in the chest, she doubted she'd have survived the first winter. "So did Old Sue, for me. But that didn't mean either of us were fit to take care of a child."

"What do you think makes someone a good mother, Rory?"

"I don't know." Rory hadn't thought about that in a long time. She only knew what a good mother wasn't. "It doesn't matter anyway. Every time my heart gave me trouble, every day I couldn't get out of bed, Carlo was terrified I was going to die. He didn't say anything, but I could see it in his eyes. No one knows what happens to people whose hearts were gone as long as mine. If this gets worse, he shouldn't have to watch me die."

Emmett swallowed, wincing. "Don't you think it might hurt Carlo more if you disappeared after he spent two years with you?"

"He'll have you. He won't miss me."

"That's not true. I came up here to find you because he asked where you were. He wanted you to sing before he goes to sleep."

Rory froze, hands clenched around the rail.

"He wants you to stay. He needs you to." Emmett coughed quietly. "Maybe we both do. I made a mess of raising him alone. You did better than me."

"Not really. I sold my soul too." That last job would haunt her for the rest of her life. "There was no other way to get you back."

Emmett frowned, tilting his head. "None of the syndicates have enough pull to have gotten me out of there."

Rory looked down at her boots. "I went to my mother." It had been the option of last resort, but Emmett was right. No one aside from the Cohort could have put her in a position to break a prisoner out of the Bastion. "She put me in touch with her husband's connections. I did one tracking job for them, in exchange for this."

He didn't press her for the details. He had to know any bounty worth enough to get him outside the Bastion was a job no one could have done with a clean conscience. Rory had needed to offer the Cohort someone they wanted under their thumb even more than a heart thief.

The wanted poster Rory had ripped from the entryway on her last visit to the Bastion had been the only one with a high enough price. The tattered paper was still tucked into her pocket, folded small to hide the accusing pair of catlike eyes. It had been Jax or Emmett. Her father's oldest friend, or the father of the boy she'd sworn to protect. She didn't expect Jax to forgive her for turning the gift he'd given her all those years ago into the weapon she used against him in the end. She'd never forgive herself.

She saw no point in passing that guilt on to Emmett. He was living with enough ghosts of his own. So Rory smiled. "I promised her that if I could get you out of the Bastion, I'd disappear from the city forever. She would never need to wonder if someday I'd turn up and tell everyone in the Cohort who my mother was." She swallowed hard. "And that's why I have to leave you when we get to port." She picked a fragment of rust off the rail and flicked it into the sea. "Because when my mother answered the door, I hated her worse than I hated Marcus when I realized he'd killed my father. Marcus was like a sick wolf that you need to put an arrow in to stop its mindless slaughter. Not something you ever trust. What my mother did was like…like if one morning Blizzard woke up and pecked my eyes out. I was supposed to depend on her, and she betrayed me. I know what it's like to have someone try to replace the parent you loved with a second choice." She shook her head, loose strands of her hair whipping across her face in the sea breeze. "It makes you resent them both."

"Just because you were angry about your stepfather doesn't mean Carlo would hate you. You're nothing like Colin Howe." Emmett leaned on the railing and looked down at the water. "Carlo hasn't just been tolerating you while he was waiting to get me back." He shrugged. "Or were you just tolerating him?"

"I thought that's all I'd feel." Rory laughed, but even to her own ears it sounded more like choked-back tears. "I was going to find someone else to take him. But the longer I waited, the less I wanted to give him up. All I could think was that if Old Sue had handed me off to somebody else, I would have hated her too."

"I'm sorry if this is my fault." Emmett chewed on his lip for a moment. "When I stole your heart back, it got tangled up with mine for a little while. I might have made you care about Carlo when you wouldn't have otherwise."

"I don't think you did. My heart had a lot longer to get mixed up with Marcus's shriveled excuse for one, and I don't feel any uncontrollable urges to murder anyone or take over the world."

Emmett managed a short bark of a laugh at that.

Rory looked up as a shimmering ribbon of green burst into view overhead. "I just don't want Carlo to feel like I'm taking care of him because I owe you something after you got my heart back. I didn't tell him the details, but I think he knows most of what happened."

Emmett's sharp breath sounded choked.

Rory blinked up at the swirling glow. "I'm afraid that when we do tell him everything, he'll feel like I'm only here because I'm paying back a debt. He deserves better than that."

Emmett cleared his throat, and Rory glanced at him. "It doesn't surprise me that you can't recognize what love looks like. You didn't have much of a chance to see it in your own family once your dad was gone. But I can see how much you care about Carlo. You won't hurt him like you were hurt, I know that much." He took a shuddering breath. "But I can understand if you don't want to spend any more time than you have to around the person who almost killed you. Who still could." His voice was choked and shaky, tears sliding down his cheeks and reflecting the lights that had shifted from green to brilliant maroon. "You need to know. My gift…It's changed. I can barely control it anymore. Right now, all my fingers want to do is find your pulse and take your heart again." Emmett sniffed and wiped the back of his hand across his nose. "If you want to leave—"

"I don't."

Maybe Emmett had been right about their hearts getting tangled up. Not enough for Rory to share his feelings and memories, but enough to understand him. Rory's heart would know if Emmett was someone she should run away from. Instead, it was telling her to stay.

Rory slipped off one of her own gloves. Her fingers, in the shifting light, were tipped in purple, and Emmett winced at the sight. Rory slid her hand across the rail and over his, tugging his glove off and resting her palm over the back of his hand. Emmett flinched as if she was the one whose touch could kill, but he didn't pull away.

She slowly twisted her fingers into his.

"If you're willing to trust the guy I heard it from, who was three pints deep at Charlie's, there's a Seachosen band somewhere south of the Iron Peaks that knows quite a bit about gifts like yours." Rory struggled past the weight in her chest to draw another shaky breath. The words she forced out next were barely a whisper. "You might be able to find them."

Emmett looked down at their intertwined hands. "Why are you so afraid to stay with us?"

"Because I think I want to stay for all the wrong reasons." Rory sighed, looking out over the water. "I'm not sure who I am outside of Rime, and if I let you go, I have to face that alone."

"It's not wrong to want to hold onto something familiar."

Rory shook her head. "My mother only ever thought about what would benefit her. Never about what I might want or need." She blinked away the tears that threatened to slide down her cheeks and wiped her dripping nose on her scarf. "Whether I stay or leave can't be a choice about what's best for me."

"I meant it when I said you were a good mother," Emmett said quietly. "You already learned from her mistakes. You proved that today when you traded everything you knew to give Carlo a chance at a better future."

Neither of them had any right to be raising a child. But they were the only family Carlo had. "I'm willing to give it a chance if you are." Rory shrugged. "Carlo's a good kid. He deserves that. Even if he's the only thing you and I have in common, that should be enough."

"So it's me you're just going to be tolerating." Emmett scuffed a shoe over the ice-and-salt crusted deck.

Rory shook her head. Anyone who'd managed to raise Carlo and keep him reasonably safe in the River Quarter and Marcus's house was someone Rory could trust with her own life. Besides, she and Emmett had managed to take down the most notorious syndicate boss in Rime in the first day and a half of their acquaintance. She'd like to find out what they were capable of when they actually knew and trusted each other. "The first time I met you, you stole my heart. Let's see if you can win it this time."

Emmett's fingers tightened in her own.

There was no way Rory could be sure he wouldn't let her go someday, like everyone else had. But she'd never find out if she pulled away first.

"You found her!" Footsteps skittered on the slick deck, and Carlo's uncontrolled slide nearly bowled Rory over. She and Emmett both grabbed his arms before he crashed to the deck. "I was scared you fell over the side. Or that a swordfish got you!"

"No. I'm okay. We were just talking about where we're going next." Rory smiled. "I hear someone wanted a good night song?"

"You have to let Dad tell you the dolphin story first! Because after the song I'll fall asleep, and I want to hear the whole thing." Carlo leaned on Emmett's side.

Emmett slipped his glove back on before putting his arm around Carlo's shoulder and turning him a little. "Yeah, we're gonna tell the dolphin story up here. And you know why?" He pointed up. "That's the moon."

"*That's* it?" Carlo asked. "Where's the dolphin?"

Emmett looked from Carlo to Rory. "He's not up there anymore," he said. "His family finally found him and brought him home."

ACKNOWLEDGEMENTS

I will be forever grateful to Mika Stanard, wearer of many hats when it comes to this book. Thank you for the multiple rereads, the advice to include the much-needed epilogue, the past-tense (and passive voice removal) editing, the Emmett-thought-process input, the medical accuracy advice, the consistent cheerleading, the impromptu literary analysis, and the prayers. Thief of Hearts wouldn't exist without you.

A special thank you to Nadezhda Miloshevska, who reminded me this idea existed, tried to convince me (upon my own request) *not* to write the book because I had too many ongoing projects, and who, when I did write it, backed me all the way. Thank you for being the other voice who insisted this book needed a happy ending. You were right.

I can't thank the White Lake Township Fire Department enough for teaching me how to use an AED correctly and, in the process, sparking the concept of energy transfer heart theft.

I owe another massive debt of gratitude to my incomparable editors, Addison Horner and Jules Dyrud. You saw the potential in this story and gave me the encouragement and the tools to make it better. Thanks for putting up with the creative chaos and for believing in Emmett and Rory…and in me.

And a *very* special thank you to my family, who listen to me ramble about imaginary people and complain about said characters going off script. Thank you for your constant encouragement even if my stories are a little intense for you!

To the Author who put all of them in my path, You knew where this story was going long before I did, and it's a much better journey than any I could have planned.

ABOUT THE AUTHOR

Heather Clark lives in Michigan on a family farm where she developed a love of both storytelling and adventure. She is most fond of stories combining hurt and hope, acknowledging the simultaneous brutality and beauty to be found in the world around her (winter in her home state is a favorite example). When she's not immersed in fictional worlds or exploring the real one, you can find her online at thethistlegirlwrites.wordpress.com or on Instagram @thethistlegirlwrites. Her monthly newsletter—AKA her "messenger pigeon"—is available at substack.com/@thethistlegirlwrites.